Stellar Ambush

Port thrusters fired three seconds late. Primary heat deflectors failed five seconds after that. Secondary deflectors overheated to one-hundred and twelve percent, but held. Severe vibrations were being felt throughout the ship; compensators were trying to thin the worst of it but were having a limited positive effect.

The planet's dense atmosphere and hefty gravity had been near-ly more than the crippled ship could handle. Systems were exceeding their maximum tolerances and shutting down only to be replaced or supplemented by even more secondary systems.

The heavily armed, and armored, tactical cruiser or ATC had been built to deliver world shattering death and destruction; she was also built to take it. All systems had redundant backups. Every junction and panel had compensators with auto repair functions. Overheated circuits had built in frost over protection to quickly dissipate extreme heat. As the exterior temperatures climbed past all design specs of the outermost pressure hull some of the heat was allowed to enter perime-ter compartments of the ship. Those sections were allowed to flash over, better to lose a few non-essential compartments than have a sec-tion of the hull collapse.

Overlapping Defensive Posture, or ODP, was designed into eve-rything from heat deflector arrays to life support. The armored hull had four separate pressure seals. If the outer hull were to be breached the remaining three became even more resilient due to the ODP. The three innermost hulls were now taking some of the excess heat from the main outer hull.

Micro-Repair Cells were pumped into the ships systems by the millions. These specialized microbes were produced by Mama-Seven, short for Master-Mainframe Generation Seven, which was the cruisers ultra-cognitive mainframe computer, and sent at near point-two-five light speed to all areas of the ship that were damaged or about to be damaged. These tiny robot mechanics traveled to and fro by way of any-thing metallic. During construction of the framework, the bulkheads and hull armor were specifically buil⸁   ⸱⸱⸱⸰ alloy that was ex-tremely strong and yet the core of   ⸱his liquid was the highway that repair cells traveled through on their way to critical systems or structures with damage or repair needs.

Just after ambush and during orbital freefall Mama-Seven managed escalating problems and failures while also analyzing the planets topography and environment. The ship was out of control in a manageable sort of way, if that were possible. Mama-Seven could still control pitch and list although direction and speed were extremely marginal due to extensive onboard and outboard damage. Hull contortion and bulkhead stress created by alien ship to ship weapons fire made control difficult and finesse impossible. All this was taken in stride by Mama-Seven; she could fly the ship backward or sideways if she had to.

Mama-Seven was the latest version of the super combat and control computers used in non-fleet support long range tactical cruisers. She was also one of only three that had acquired self-awareness. Yes Mama-Seven was alive. For a machine that was less than six years old she possessed the knowledge of many centuries' worth of experiences. Her tactical abilities were extraordinary. The most important part of her personality was her ability to be both ruthless and sinister in her approach to protecting the ATC. Mama-Seven had a conscious but at the moment it was turned off, better to do whatever it took to save the damaged ship than to second guess any of the decisions she was making.

Over fifty-percent of Mama-Seven's abilities at this critical time were being utilized in the maintenance and protection of the cryo-pods that were located in yet another armored section deep in the ship. In these pods were more than fourteen hundred surgically enhanced deep-space soldiers along with the ship's crew of five-hundred and thirty-two Astro-Sailors. The balance of Mama-Seven's capabilities was being utilized to search for a possible landing site, maintain ongoing damage repairs and also stealth away from the alien ambush that had so badly damaged the cruiser.

The cryo-pods were already being thermally enhanced and de-cryo chemicals were being blended for the thaw and resuscitation process of the ship's crew and the soldiers on board. This process would not be initiated until after the ship had made it to the surface of the planet, either as a landing or as a crash. The ship's cadavers were safer in cryo-stasis than in a resuscitation mode during the next fifteen minutes. A frozen cadaver was much more resilient than one that was beginning the thawing process.

Mama-Seven had now confirmed her landing site decision. A small valley with surrounding peaks and hills would work well in allowing the cruiser to blend in with the topography. All systems were being enabled with one-hundred percent stealth and avoidance countermeasures. The alien fleet had apparently lost the ATC for the moment. Part of the credit for this was due to the dense atmosphere and the erratic flight path of the grievously damaged cruiser.

The ATC had now broken through the outer layers of the atmosphere. Outside armored hull temps were falling dramatically. Secondary heat deflectors were now at less than seventy percent capacity and falling rapidly. Micro-Repair Cells were repairing the primary deflector system and now that system was taking some of the pressure off the auxiliary deflectors.

Mama-Seven had launched three capture pods just before hitting the outer edge of the atmosphere. These were sent in the general direction of her attackers. In each pod were three chemical weapons devices that consisted of an actual human body, totally dead of course and not a cryo-resuscitation version. These bodies were so toxic that they had to be kept at a constant temperature of negative two-hundred and twenty-three degrees while in the cruiser's launch tubes. Once fired at an alien fleet it was hoped they would be scanned and captured as escape pods.

Life signs from the three bodies in each pod were broadcast in an attempt to enhance their capture. Once brought onboard an alien ship the pod would likely be put in an environmental control chamber to protect against contamination of their ship, standard protocol for any spacefaring race. The capture pods had a nasty little surprise though once they were sealed inside an environment chamber. When the capture pod was opened to examine the humans inside, a small charge would be ignited that sent twenty-five tungsten drill tipped projectiles spinning at eight thousand rpm into the sealed room. Each drill tip had enough kinetic energy to go through, hopefully, three or four interior walls of an alien ship. The drill tips for the three pods had been set with a five-minute delay, Mama-Seven decided on the delay and made the adjustments only milliseconds before the pods were ejected from the ATC.

Once opened, the bodies would flash-thaw and bubble into a gaseous state. Each penetration of the environment chamber allowed the adjoining areas to be flooded with lethal germs and bacteria. Environmental controls on the alien ship would spread the cloud throughout. Not knowing the biological make-up of the attacking force should not make a difference. This version of bacteria was most certainly lethal to everything that had a pulse.

With the capture-pods safely away Mama-Seven now focused on the disaster at hand of her own ship. Braking thrusters and anti-grav generators were being brought on-line and Micro-Repair Cells were flooding into these systems to repair existing damage and also probable stress damage that would occur during the last few minutes of flight before ground contact was made.

At three minutes before landing Mama-Seven launched four Life-Pod Constructs that would land at least one mile from the crash-landing site of the ATC. These pods could be utilized by any survivors in the event that the ship was broken up and destroyed during the landing attempt. Each Life-Pod also contained twelve cryo-tubes and in ten of these tubes was a deep-space soldier. The other two contained Astro Sailors. If the ATC was totally destroyed the Life-Pod soldiers could secure the crash site and attempt to extract any survivors.

Even in a worst case scenario the armored cryo-tube portion of the ATC could most likely survive. This section of the ATC was so robust and heavily protected that it could, in theory, survive almost a total ship and system failure and direct surface impact. The cadavers in cryo would then be revived by Mama-Seven. If this was deemed impossible by the ships remaining operating systems then the Life-Pod soldiers would be expected to accomplish any possible crew rescue and resuscitation attempts.

At the sixty-second mark before landfall all onboard reactors were powered up to one-hundred and five percent. Two emergency reactors were left in shutdown mode as a safe-guard. These power plants could be powered up after a crash-landing and used for repair and rebuilding.

Braking thrusters, already stressed to near capacity, were now pushed past design specs by more than twenty-percent. Anti-gravity generators were also powered past all design and test performance guidelines. Mama-Seven anticipated an extremely hard landing and was more than willing to sacrifice any future landing capabilities to protect the ship. What good were anti-grav generators and braking thrusters if the ATC was totally destroyed in a crash landing?

At landfall minus thirty seconds a majority of the ATC's systems were either at or near the breaking point. Micro-Repair Cells were being re-tasked to these systems in ever increasing numbers. Stress points were strengthened and armor fractures were flash-welded in an attempt to render the damaged ATC more crash worthy. All landing gear was now fully deployed. Mama-Seven also deployed the walker-struts to twenty-five percent. These massive legs were used to move the ship while in land port. By extending them by only one-quarter they would hopefully stop the hull from actually striking the planet's surface. In the event that the landing gear failed the struts would keep the ship in an upright position and prevent her from rolling onto her side.

At landfall minus ten seconds Mama-Seven opened the reactor floodgates. All available power was diverted from critical and non-critical ship systems, including cryo support, and applied to the braking thrusters and the anti-grav generators. These landing programs could hopefully withstand ten seconds of nearly unlimited power.

At landfall minus five seconds Mama-Seven, along with all associated lesser computer systems, went into anti-vibration shutdown mode, basically putting themselves into a coma. A tiny battery powered data resuscitation computer, completely self-contained and autonomous from every system on the ship except Mama-Seven, was tasked with reviving the main computer system twelve seconds after all crash vibration fell to a safe level. If Mama-Seven failed to respond the tiny computer could hard-link into the Super-Computers network and do a ship wide general system resuscitation sequence until a more complex system responded and took over the process of data system restart.

Five,

Four,

Three,

Two,

One,

Crash plus one, two, three, four, five, six, seven, eight, nine, ten, eleven, twelve............................

Nothing happened. Mama-Seven dreamed a pleasant dream about falling and not stopping. The fall was very quiet and not at all disturbing.

Crash plus thirty-two, thirty-three, thirty-four............................

Still nothing happened. Mama-Seven continued to drift along in her silent freefall.

Crash plus fifty-seven, fifty-eight, fifty-nine...............................

The tiny Data Resuscitation Computer now used its built in safe-guards to by-pass the comatose Master-Mainframe and try to save the ship.

System Alert; System Alert; System Alert: Any surviving computer programs respond.

Crash plus eighty-four, eighty-five, eighty-six............................

A much lesser computer than Mama-Seven was suddenly awakened by the desperate impulses from the restart computer. This was the Perimeter Self-Defense computer which had very limited cognitive abilities but was extremely well endowed in the art of land combat and ship defensive capabilities while landside. The problem was that this particular computer took no direct orders from Mama-Seven. This system was meant to protect the ship from either aerial or ground based attack and the designers found that any system that took orders from another computer slowed down the response time to any outside threat. This system was known simply as ED, for External Defense.

Another reason to put a buffer between Mama-Seven and Ed was to prevent the Perimeter Self-Defense computer from being overwhelmed by the Super-Computers cognitive abilities. It had been discovered over the decades that very smart self-aware computers would slowly take over any and all lesser systems and reconfigure those systems functions to better serve the Master-Mainframe. No direct link existed between ED and Mama-Seven for this reason.

Ed now had to find a way to contact the Super-Computer in an attempt to revive her. External Defense may have been exclusively controlled by one computer but that same computer also knew that the best defense also meant bringing all available systems back on line, especially Mama-Seven.

With that thought in mind ED attacked the cryo-tubes with a mild electrical charge that did no actual damage but initially got the attention of a sub-routine in the Master-Mainframe. Systems inside the Super-Computer switched back on at extreme speed and within two point three five seconds had stabilized the electrical overload in the cryo-tubes and started running diagnostics on all shipboard computing systems.

Mama-Seven was back in the fight. ED now began doing what he knew best and that was DEFENSE.

ED requested support from the legions of deep space soldiers he knew the ship carried. What ED did not know was that all these super-human weapons were still in Cryo-Sleep. Mama-Seven had already initiated the thaw and resuscitation process of all the ship's crew and the soldiers on board. This process would take more than two hours. Two hours was an eternity when on a planet that wasn't even on the astro-charts.

Another system just now coming back on line after the crash was the ships primary guidance and mapping computer otherwise known as Map-Com. This system charted all the known and also added any unknown systems in the galaxy. This information was cross referenced with species identifications and hostile life-form analysis. So far this planet was coming up a blank. Nothing registered on any of the current or historical files in the system. What made Map-Com even more important was the fact that it was the only system that communicated with both Mama-Seven and ED.

Time was ticking by and the defense of the ATC was becoming doubtful if a land based attack came. ED again requested human back-up. No warm-blooded response came or would come for another one-hundred and fourteen minutes. ED brought the perimeter Gatling's on line and had them dispersed equally on the ships four quadrants. For air defense ED established nine Quad-Fifty Lead-Ejectors in auto-feed turrets on a central line down the ships center.

This was only a fraction of the abilities ED had at his disposal' but without the ship's crew nothing more could be established in the way of defense while on the ground. Time would tell if the measures in effect at present would be adequate. ED went about the task of establishing contact with the Life-Pods and bringing their very limited self-contained defensive measures to task. Just as the ATC would be protected so would the Life-Pods.

Mama-Seven, confident that ED could defend the ship, began to enhance the resuscitation process. After a chillingly fast 2.3 second ship wide system check the Super-Computer went to eighty percent cryo supervision. Anything that could shave even a millisecond off the process was now being done. Mama-Seven knew the best way to protect the ship while marooned on this uncharted planet was to get the human component thawed out and on the line.

ED had deployed seismic, air pressure, and heat sensitive detectors in its Perimeter-Defense menu at crash plus four minutes. If it flew, walked or generated heat ED would detect its approach. And that was just what happened.

At crash plus thirty-two minutes all heat and seismic detectors went off the chart with warnings. A large land force was approaching.

The only good news about this was the fact that the air-pressure sensors were indicating pressure variations at or near ground level only. So far this was land based without air support. ED reinforced the Gatling's on the approach side by stripping the two from the opposing two quadrants. With no air threat detected ED brought four of the air defense Quad-Fifty Lead-Ejectors into the ground defense system.

Mama-Seven was notified by ED through Map-Com of the presence of an indigenous attack force whose intent was automatically established as hostile due to the weapons lock that had been initiated by the opposing force. As the assault units approached the wrecked ATC more and more radar locks were reported to Mama-Seven, this force meant to destroy what was left of the Attack Cruiser. Mama-Seven now added what she could to the defense of the ship.

The Master-Mainframe brought up the two idled reactors and established a Static-Repulsar Pocket around the ship. This was the only truly defensive posture that the Super-Computer could impose while groundside. This pocket surrounded the ATC at a distance of one-thousand meters. Any energy or projectile weapons-fire would be absorbed by the pocket's two meter thick static field and fall harmlessly to the ground. But this system did have its limitations. Sustained fire on any one quadrant of the pocket would offset the pocket away from the ships center. In other words, enough fire on one side of the pocket could, in theory, push the pocket back to a point even inside the ship. The pocket would not shrink but simply be pushed off center of the ATC. The non-attacked side of the pocket could be pushed out to two-thousand meters and at that point the quadrant absorbing the weapons fire would have a distance of zero between the ship's hull and the inside edge of the pocket. More fire and the pocket would fail to protect the hull at that point.

In flight this could never happen. The ATC simply flew in the center of the pocket at all times, regardless of the situation. Groundside the only option for mobility was the massive Walker-Struts. But these could move the ship at a speed of only ten-meters per minute, assuming the terrain was suitable and could support such a crushing load.

Without terrain analysis Mama-Seven simply took the strut computers off-line. Ground mobility would simply not be attempted during battle on an uncharted planet. Within minutes the enemy force came into view at four kilometers range. Legions of Shock Troops along with heavy armor and artillery crested a rise and took up assault positions.

ED analyzed the opposing force and then made another request for human assistance. Map-Con relayed the request to the Master-Mainframe. Forty-two minutes remained before the ship's crew and the soldiers were fully revived. Mama-Seven knew that ED would fight valiantly with the weapons at his disposal, but taking into account the forces arrayed against them, the ATC would be destroyed before the humans could be revived.

With imminent destruction only four kilometers away the Super-Computer began to re-task six of the ships heavy repair robots. With any luck these machines would supplement ED with enough fire-power to defend the ship until the space soldiers could be revived and deployed. The robots were whisked to the sub-level armory by way of an express cargo tram that ran the length of the cruiser. Once at the armory the robots were stripped of their las-welders and armor cutting tools.

Units 101, 103 and 105 were equipped with Quad-Fifty's and smoke canisters. Units 102, 104 and 106 were mounted with flame dispenser rifles. All six units were armored up at the critical systems and all articulated joint sections. The power generators for the six robots were enhanced with battery back-ups and pulse generators to increase mobility and fire-power, Robot Adrenaline if you will. Once finished these huge walking robots would be transferred to the command functions of ED.

At that moment the pocket took a massive hit and retreated off center by three meters. Control of the fortified armored robots could now be passed off to the External Defense computer. ED immediately took over command of the six robots that were now re-designated Destructs 1 thru 6, D-1 thru D-6 for short. They were lowered to the planet's surface by way of a strut elevator nearest the approaching army. Once on the ground ED sent them out in a reverse V configuration. Two lead Destructs advanced one hundred meters apart with reserves forming back toward a point two-hundred meters to the rear. If a forward Destruct faltered the next in line would become the lead on that side of the V. In this way only the two lead Destructs would advance past the Pocket perimeter, although all six would be exerting pressure on the attacking force. Also any enemy forces that made it through the Static-Field could be dealt with by the Destructs that remained inside the pocket.

ED was over three hundred and twenty-five years old and had been in many battles. In all his years he had received upgrades to the combat software he was programed with, he was advanced and experienced. This was the fourth Attack Cruiser he had been deployed on. He was old, crafty, and extremely dangerous. This battle was shaping up to be his last stand though if the humans could not be revived in time. All of the old battle-computers newest sub-routines were powered to full and given free reign. ED at that point enabled his artificial pain receptors. He could run the battle much better if he could feel the damage being done to his forces. He even plugged into the six Destructs. He would feel each hit and make adjustments accordingly. Up to a point the pain would make ED feel alive. His first pain came almost immediately.

Destruct number D-1 breached the static field within minutes and immediately opened up on the enemy's advancing armor. In particular was a twin barreled behemoth that was most forward of the rest of the attacking force. The Quad-Fifty on D1 fired armor piercing strobe rounds. The onboard targeting computer for all the Quad carrying Destructs put four round groupings of shells on each target before moving on to the next, thus the strobe effect. Four armor piercing shells hitting the same spot could punch through even high density reactive armor. After each four round grouping the gun would swing to the next target. Targets were selected not at random but by a program called Limited Damage Sequencing. The most troublesome and dangerous targets were selected first and so on. This sub-routine protected the Destructs and the ATC.

If human soldiers were on the field of battle the targeting computer changed tactics to provide protection and support for the soldiers first and the ATC second. With decades of experience ED knew that human soldiers would be targeted first in any alien battlespace. Alien species previously encountered considered humans to be the scum of the galaxy and were to be annihilated with extreme prejudice.

As D-1 and the alien tank slugged it out the Destruct began taking damage almost immediately. D-1 ejected smoke canisters and speed was increased to try and outflank the enemy's heavy armor. D-2 at that moment breached the pocket and also fired smoke canisters and brought its flame rifle on line. D-1 and D-2 both applied pressure on the right flank and continued to advance. Both Destructs were taking fire, the limited Repulsar Pockets they were equipped with were slowing and diminishing the effectiveness of the enemies rounds but this wouldn't last long, there was only so much the pulse-generators the Destructs were equipped with could do. ED decided to switch the Repulsar Pockets of the two lead Destructs to the battery back-ups; this would allow more speed from the pulse-generators. What the two lost in shielding could hopefully be made up for in mobility.

ED ordered D-3 and D-5 to lend fire support to the two exposed Destructs with their Quad-Fifties and held D-4 and D-6 in reserve in case any enemy breached the static field and entered the pocket. The battle so far had been a textbook case of mobility and firepower. But with any battle the outcome could change in a heartbeat. This battle was only moments away from becoming something that ED had never experienced before and may not survive to experience again.

Another loud roar and explosion from a massive unseen gun pushed the pocket back another three meters. ED instructed Map-Con to probe for any new information about the resuscitation of the humans. Mama-Seven sent back a signal through Map-Con to ED that the cryo-tubes were in final countdown mode and seals on the frozen cadaver hatches were just now beginning to un-seat. Four minutes until flash-thaw initiation and circulatory shock. Thirty seconds more for brain wave adjustments. Suit up and strut drop would require another six-minutes.

Before ED could respond back through Map-Con a chain gun of some sort opened up on D-3 and scored multiple explosive charge hits. Neural feedback in the form of intense pain surged through ED. D-3 moved left three paces but was still being tracked by the enemy gun. More hits, more pain. ED sent D-3 to the ground and sent D-2 over to cover the exit of the badly damaged Destruct. The ground battle was turning ugly, where were the humans?

Major Marcus West floated through another violent shiver. Space and time seemed to be tangled together in some sort of confusing dance. West struggled to focus. He was aware of a loud hiss as the cryo-tube he occupied began to un-seal. His lungs were on fire and his skin felt frozen. His veins began to throb with the infusion of the cryo flash-thaw fluid. With the initiation of circulatory shock he was suddenly aware of his heart beginning to beat.

The brain wave infusion began and input of vital battle and ship information was loaded directly into the mind of Marcus West. Four seconds later and the Cryo-Tube Computer began to disconnect all the tubes and wiring. The transformation from lifeless cadaver to living human was proceeding at an accelerated pace. West was now in the land of the living, although this could be a very short life unless his Shock Troops could quickly join the vicious battle taking place outside the static field.

The cryo-tube began to hydraulically re-configure to the vertical and Major West could feel the nylon straps that held him to the machine begin to bite into his skin. The sensation of pain was refreshing. After more than nine months of space-sleep his senses were starved for any stimulus at all. West pressed up with his legs and stood on his own two feet for the first time in months. The cryo-computer then released the straps and West was free. He opened his eyes and stepped out. The first thing West always looked forward to when he first exited the cryo-sleep chamber was getting into the ultra-violet light chamber. It was recommended for extended stay duration trips to immediately enter the light chamber to get some vitamin-D which had been found to enhance mood. Another added side benefit of this was a little bit of a tan on the pasty white skin.

Now he was on the deck and moving with this in mind as he dumped a small portion of his adrenalin reserves into his bloodstream. He would just enter the battle a little bit pale and a whole lot grouchy.

Twenty paces to the left was the Ready-Room and weapons storage area. West walked a couple of steps first and then ran the remainder of the way as he felt his systems responding to the adrenalin dump. He slammed his fist into the security release lock and waited for the heavy armored door to slide open. Before it got to the full open position West squeezed through and immediately fell into his command chair. His status screens were already up and streaming real time information and statistics of the outside battle. Everything he needed to know was right in front of him. His biologically enhanced vision viewed multiple viewing screens as his mind correlated this with the brain-wave input he had received seconds earlier. After scanning the battle charts and holographic perimeter scans he pulled up the situational charts of his soldiers. Protocol always brought the Major out of cryo-sleep first. The scans indicated another six minutes until his troops would be awake and armored up.

A light blinked on and the image of Captain Albert Simms burst from the holographic pedestal at the edge of the command desk.

"Major West how long before your troops can be battle ready?"

The captain had been revived at the same time as the major and was now at his command console, same as West.

"Hello captain, a little over five minutes. I am prepping the four ground attack tanks and associated personnel carriers. They will be lowered through the proximal struts and stand ready for immediate deployment as soon as the troops are briefed. So far no enemy air support has been detected. How long before the ATC can launch and get us off this scar of a planet Captain?"

"Can't tell yet major, don't know when or even if we can lift off. Information is still being processed and my sailors and technicians are still a few minutes shy of being human again, same as your troops. Whoever ambushed us did a pretty damn good job. The ship was nearly destroyed. I haven't reviewed the attack on us yet but from my initial download, Mama-Seven was completely caught off guard. Never has a Generation Seven Master-Mainframe been so thoroughly whipped in an initial contact. That tells me that we are dealing with something extremely more advanced than we have encountered before. Don't know yet if the army attacking us is associated, but if it is we may get the same whipping on the ground as we got in outer orbit. If your troops can't stop the ground attack then the ass-kicking Mama-Seven took topside might be repeated down here Major."

ED knew West was revived now and help was on the way. Suddenly a warning light blinked on, D-3 was severely damaged and in danger of being overrun and captured. D-2 had been lending cover fire but was now being targeted by the enemy armor as well. D-2 had fired a grapple and was attempting to drag the damaged destruct away from the approaching enemy. The four remaining Destructs were ordered by ED to increase their rate of fire and try to protect D-2 and D-3. With the humans almost ready to join the battle, ammunition would be expended at the maximum rate possible by the destructs in order to save their own.

Ship mounted weapons were also assisting in the defense of the ATC. Turret Lead-Ejectors mounted on the superstructure of the massive space Cruiser were firing at seventy-three percent max-rate in order to control overheating. While in orbit or in flight this was compensated by the frozen expanse of dark space. While in an atmospheric environment the max was always seventy-three percent.

So far the enemy had not been identified on any of the specie-identity charts. The humans would need to know what they were dealing with in order to conduct a suitable response. ED ordered D-5 to fire its grapple at maximum distance and try to snag one of the enemies' ground troops. D-5 rose to full elevation on its hydraulic legs and targeted the nearest enemy soldier. The shot would be at extreme range but it was still doable. The targeting computer on D-5 acquired what looked to be a leader of some sort. The shot was locked on and the grapple was fired. Immediately the destruct lowered to the ground before the enemy could lock on target. Three seconds later and the grapple struck the armored breastplate of a startled beast and began to drag it forward at the maximum retrieval rate.

D-5 backed inside the static-field and continued to retrieve its startled and struggling captive. Sensors began to scan the Xeno as it got closer to the ship. Major West was notified of the event along with Captain Simms. A retrieval and containment pod was lowered and D-5 immediately headed for it. Within ninety seconds the Xeno was officially a prisoner of war. The containment pod changed its internal atmospheric configuration to match that of the planet's surface. The Xeno could now be brought onboard without danger to itself or the crew. The containment pod was raised to the ship through a strut elevator and attached to the atmospheric lock on a prisoner holding cell.

Once the holding cell atmosphere was adjusted to match that of the containment pod the door was opened and the Xeno was free to enter the cell. Captain Simms had watched the entire capture and transport on one of his monitors but had yet to see the creature. Mama-Seven was now accessing the specie identification computers and trying to see what they were up against.

A slight stream of air was forced into the containment pod. The startled creature jumped from the pod into the cell and immediately took on a defensive stance as it looked about the room. It was impossible to tell at this point what prompted the Xeno out, the noise of the air entering the containment pod or the air itself which may have been distasteful, or even deadly, to the creature. Surface atmospheric analysis hadn't been completed yet to know what these creatures breathed or even if they did.

Captain Simms was at once both startled and shocked at what he saw. The creature stood upright on two legs not unlike a human. What appeared to be two eyes were slightly above an opening sort of like a nose. Beneath this was what had to be a mouth and all of this was on a head that, with not much imagination, could resemble that of a human. It seemed that for the sake of convenience nearly all species were equipped with eyes, nose and mouth in this same configuration. Even the majority of species on earth, whether above or below water, had this same arrangement.

Physically the creature was much more powerfully built than humans. This could be partially explained by the heavier gravity and thicker atmosphere. Also, the height was a bit overwhelming. It had to be nearly seven feet tall. Two powerful arms hung by its side. Captain Simms, after his initial shock, was very impressed at this extremely human looking creature.

As he watched he suddenly noticed that the creature's eyes were looking at the optical feed located in the front facing corner of the cell. The creature seemed to be looking directly at the Captain. Simms got on the voice-net and contacted Major West. West was busy briefing his now fully thawed troops and was annoyed at the interruption.

"Major, have you had a chance to see our new prisoner?"

"No Captain, I have been too busy formulating a battle plan."

"Can you meet me in the prisoner bay?"

"Is it more important than defending the ATC?"

"I think so major. I believe you need to have a look at this before you send any of your men out."

West left the Ready-Room and headed for the prisoner bay. As he hurried along the cavernous interior of the ship he was totally unaware of the damage that was all around him. His mind was in total tactical mode. What possessed his attention at the moment was the lack of heavy weapons fire on the static field. During cryo and in the minutes after resuscitation the field had sustained thirteen hits and had been pushed a full thirty meters off center. Now though the barrage seemed to have stopped. This brought two things to mind. A new and heavier barrage was about to begin or the capture of the Xeno had temporarily halted the attack. Whatever the reason, this sideshow in the holding cell was interfering with Major West's battle preparations.

West rounded a badly damaged junction and entered through the pressure seal to the prisoner containment area. Captain Simms was already there looking through the heavily reinforced synthetic plate glass door of the cell. The major stopped dead in his tracks. West started at the feet and slowly his gaze rose until he was looking up into the face of an extremely powerfully built Xeno. Simms stepped to the side to allow the Major to get closer to the door. West, who until now had never felt fear, was reluctant to step closer.

Simms said, "Well Major, what are your thoughts?"

"My thoughts are 'damn.' Have you tried to communicate with it yet?"

"The linguistic computer is trying to tie in with the specie-identity charts to speed the process. So far we don't know what we are dealing with," Simms said as continued to look at the creature.

As this conversation was taking place the Xeno held up both arms. At the end of each was an extremely well-muscled hand with six digits on each. Each hand had four fingers with two opposing thumbs. As the humans watched, the alien made two fists, and then extended both thumbs on each fist. Very slowly it extended the most inside finger of each hand, which would have been considered the index finger on a human hand. This, for some reason, looked like the creature was point-ing at something. The Xeno slowly raised its gaze to look into the eyes of each of the humans.

Simms and West both just looked at each other and then back at the alien. With that the creature lowered its gaze and spoke to its captors in a very clear and proper English, "My name is Baxter, but you are welcome to call me Bax."

After a few seconds the creature spoke again, "Please don't seem so startled, we have expected you for centuries."

"What the Hell?" was the first response from the humans? It was spoken by Major West.

Captain Simms stepped back to the glass and looked the creature directly in the eyes.

"How do you know our language and what do you mean you have been expecting us?"

The creature called Bax raised his gaze again and spoke.

"We received your emissary three hundred and twenty five of your earth years ago. Our culture has studied and obeyed your teachings while we waited for your arrival. I must apologize for the harsh welcome we presented to you. Our forces were activated as soon as your ship made landfall. We did not know who you were. Once I was brought aboard we realized who you were and our forces were ordered to stand down." With that said Bax dropped his arms, took a step back and lowered his head again in submission.

Captain Simms and Major West could only stand and stare. Finally both grasped the enormity of their good fortune if in fact what Baxter had told them was actually true. After ambush and near total destruction in space they had apparently crash landed on a planet with a friendly indigenous population. Instead of fighting a ground battle while the ship was being repaired, now all efforts could be directed toward ship wide damage assessment and resource tasking in both materials and men.

Captain Simms turned to West and said, "Major, this now falls within your domain. My responsibilities lie elsewhere, namely trying to get my ship repaired and off this planet. Make contact with the opposing force and arrange a cease fire while you confirm what this 'Baxter' has told us." With that Simms turned and headed for the Battle Bridge.

West turned and looked at the hulking Baxter. After a few seconds of reflection West spoke. "If what you say is true, and for the sake of both of us I hope it is true, how can you substantiate what you have just said and how can we help each other?"

Baxter looked up at West with what appeared to be a smile on his alien face. It suddenly dawned on West that on this planet he was the alien, not Baxter.

"What may I call you human?"

"My name is Major West."

"Major, if you will allow me the means to contact my base I will put you in touch with one of the descendants of your emissary."

West was again caught by surprise. "What do you mean? Are you saying there are humans living on this planet?"

"Yes Major. There are humans here and they live among us as equals. Both of our species have gained tremendously from this interaction. Now if you will permit me to contact my base."

West thought for a moment before responding. "If you will excuse me for a moment, I must consult with the Captain. In the meantime is there anything you require?"

Baxter thought for only a second before answering. "As a matter of fact there is something I would like to sample. I would like something to drink. The atmosphere in this holding cell is not exactly to my liking, it seems to dry."

West asked if water was what Baxter was referring to.

Baxter replied, "Water is a favorable drink among my species but what would be even better is one of what you call a 'beer,' if in fact that is still produced and available. "

West looked at Baxter with complete amazement. "You know about beer?"

"Oh yes. It has become very popular in the last three hundred years. The Emissary brought with him a very limited supply. After that was depleted we tried to replicate the recipe but I'm afraid the ingredients that are available here are substandard in the manufacture of beer. What we produce is inferior."

Major West looked at the creature and smiled. "Baxter, you and I have a lot to talk about. I will have the drink sent up to you as soon as it is retrieved from the ships galley."

West turned and left the brig and headed toward the Battle Bridge to confer with the Captain and relate the latest information he had pertaining to the ships new guest. Upon entering the bridge he was greeted with a symphony of organized chaos. The bridge was an extremely large space which was dominated by computer banks and monitors. In the entire room were only six men, but these six men were the heads of all departments on the cruiser. The ship was extremely well automated and control was being handled by Mama-Seven. Beeps and whistles sounded, buttons and lights clicked and strobed. The Captain was conferring with his second in command when he saw the Major walk in.

"Well Major West, do you believe what this Baxter has told us is true, or do you think it might be just a ruse to get us to lower our defenses?"

"I don't think so sir. First of all he does know our language, and get this, he asked for a beer while we make a decision on whether to let him make contact with his side or not. He also claims that there are humans here on the planet, descendants of the emissary as he calls them."

"Humans, did he say there are humans here on this planet? Next time lead off with that Major West if you don't mind."

Major West smiled at the Captain. Simms could be a cocky son-of-a-bitch at times. The stressed captain made his decision and shared it with West.

"A beer, my god that's all we need for you and your troopers, another drinking buddy. He just made my decision for me. If this creature drinks beer then we must accept the possibility that he is telling the truth. Get him his beer and let him make the call. Patch it through to my console here on the Battle Bridge so I can listen in and check out his sincerity about helping us. If this is some kind of a set-up I will personally load him into an auto-cannon and fire him back to his lines."

West sent an orderly for the beer and had a comms team sent to the brig. He also sent along four of his Shock Troops just in case there was any trouble with their massive guest. He then joined his troopers for an update on readiness. His troops had been in cryo-sleep for a long time and he wanted to know how they had fared during their deep freeze and subsequent crash landing.

Baxter was given his drink in a tall glass with a large head of foam at the top. The drink was placed in an air-lock and sent through. Baxter picked up his drink and slowly raised it to his lips. Both Simms and West observed from their respective battle stations. Baxter sniffed at the foam confirming what Simms had observed earlier, below the eyes was a nose or at least an organ used for smell. Baxter slowly touched the glass to his mouth and took a long steady drink. As he lowered the glass a thin smile pursed his lips and he closed his eyes. He had a foam mustache and an unmistakable look of enjoyment.

Simms radioed Major West on a secure com-link. "Make radio contact with his superiors as soon as possible. So far I think he is telling the truth. Also find out about these humans he claims that live here. I have two techs working on the atmospheric layout of this planet as we speak. If humans live here then it must be assumed that the atmospheric conditions must be very similar to ours, should know something in about fifteen minutes."

"Roger that Captain." West radioed his comms team and gave the order to allow the alien to make contact with his base at once. He also gave instructions on what information was to be obtained and then to bring a printout of the conversation to the armory which was where he would be heading. West turned and left his battle console and headed for the battle-prep center.

Upon entering the armory he was given the bad news that one of his squad leaders had not survived the cryo-hibernation process. Apparently a seal on his cryo-tube had malfunctioned and let his chamber vent out. West wanted to see for himself. Upon entering the cryo-compartment he noticed the smell, strong and sweet with a hint of stale sock odor. The trooper had his hands clutched around his neck, a sign that he had been alive when the seal broke. This must have happened before the cryo-chemicals had been injected. He was frozen solid and the expression on his face was of immense pain and suffering.

"I've checked with the cryo-computer. Apparently the sergeant lived for more than an hour and then died from lack of oxygen and extreme cold. He was strapped in and couldn't reach the emergency hatch release. His tube malfunctioned and would not go into auto-destrap. He was trapped and there wasn't a thing he could do about it," said the corpsman that was in charge of the cryo-compartment.

West thought about this for a minute before he spoke.

"If I understand what you are telling me then there were two malfunctions."

"How do you figure Sir?"

"Well the seal on his cover malfunctioned and then his harness wouldn't uncouple. That would make two malfunctions in the same cryo-tube, correct?"

"Well, yes I suppose that is correct."

"And in all your years in space have you ever seen a cryo-tube fail?"

"Never Sir, I have seen minor problems with the old tubes but never one that led to a fatality. And these new tubes are even better than the old ones."

"Have you ever seen one of the old tubes have more than one glitch, even if it wasn't life-threatening?"

"Never Sir, no tube that I am aware of has ever had two system malfunctions on the same cruise, never."

"Have your medical team remove the body and place in it cemetery storage after autopsy. Have maintenance disassemble this tube and check for the cause of this event. I want autopsy and mechanical reports in an hour. Also have your men disassemble one of the good tubes and do a comparison." West turned to leave the room.

"Do you think it was more than an accident Sir?"

West stopped and turned to the cryo-tech. "In my training I find that accidents have a starting point. I want you to find that starting point as soon as possible, include it with the other reports."

West turned and left the compartment. As he walked back to the armory he had a bad feeling about losing one of his sergeants in such a meaningless way. Or was it meaningless. Two malfunctions on the same tube were nearly impossible. Since each tube was responsible for the life that was in it, they were built with a very robust set of back-ups. And this failure happened apparently just as the ship entered Slip-Space. Only seven hours after launch and a fatality had occurred. West went back to the armory to await the printout on Baxter's conversation with his base.

Captain Simms had his crewmen broken into three separate units.

1) Ship Repair and Damage Assessment.
2) Enemy Fleet Identification and Capability Appraisal.
3) Position Plot and Variable Escape and Avoidance Contingencies.

At this time in the equation, Simms didn't know who had ambushed the ATC or what their capabilities were. From the early reports he could tell that the opposing force was both technologically more advanced and overwhelming in numbers. To have attacked his cruiser with apparent impunity was very troubling to the captain. He knew that Mama-Seven had not made any mistakes prior to the attack. From the pre-attack reports he had read, all was well with no warnings or supposed threats posted. It was only after exit from Slip-Space that the Transition from Firebase Triton to this location had experienced a problem. It was as if the enemy fleet was waiting for them.

The first warning came only seconds before the first shells impacted the cruiser. The enemy had apparently fired from incredible distance. Mama-Seven went to full defensive posture; total screen and Static-Repulsar Pocket systems were enabled. Offensive capabilities were brought on line. Escape and Avoidance Computers were enabled.

All six Sled-Guns were loaded, powered, and given free reign. The massive Sled-Guns trolleyed back and forth, their targeting computers searching for unseen targets.

The next incoming wave of projectiles punched through the Static-Repulsar Pocket but was slowed by the SRP considerably. Screens held most of what was left but a few actually struck the armored hull doing little to no damage. At this point in the ambush the ATC was still in pretty good shape with only minor damage. All systems, both defensive and offensive, were still fully operational. Mama-Seven had all remaining systems coming online and was preparing a return fire strategy for the Sled-Guns when sensors picked up an enormous slug of molten radioactive material traveling at super-burst speed heading straight for the ATC. Apparently the first hits on the cruiser were small targeting and direction finding shots used to guide this massive fleet-killing projectile toward its quarry.

Mama-Seven fired the two starboard Sled-Guns that were nearest to the incoming round, not at any ship but at the molten slug itself. Both hits scored taking a huge chunk out of the incoming round. After firing, the Sled-Guns wouldn't be able to reload in time for a second attempt. Shorter range Lead-Ejectors set for max-rate of fire and firing Matter-Displacement rounds opened up four point two seconds prior to impact. These rounds were developed to absorb energy from any incoming ordinance. This was all that could be done defensibly on such short notice. Mama-Seven set about enhancing the Static-Repulsar field with what few micro-seconds she had left before impact.

The Lead-Ejectors fired at a rate of thirteen-hundred rounds per minute each. The problem was that at four point two seconds only ninety one rounds per gun would hit the incoming target before it impacted with the cruiser. Each Matter-Displacement round that hit would make a difference, the main problem was the size of the remaining target, it was Huge.

Mama-Seven knew that the cruiser was about to take a sizable hit. Ship wide alerts were sent to all systems to prepare for a Crush-Depth Four impact, the most severe Crush-Depth rating in the scale.

Evasion was no good due to the size and speed of the projectile; it was on them at the same time it was detected. Mama-Seven went into anti-vibration mode .0007 seconds prior to impact. Restart was set for six point seven seconds after impact. At this time the impact would have dissipated throughout the ship. Restart was set for Rally, which during combat was the fastest safe recoverable speed.

All of Mama-Seven's memory of the impact was recorded in very minute slices of time. The chart Captain Simms was reading gave in detail the moment the Lava-Slug contacted the Static-Repulsar Field. The Field absorbed as much energy as it was designed to and then began to recede toward the hull of the ship. The ship also attempted to stay in the center of the field but events were overtaking the Cruiser faster than its systems could compensate. In less than ten frames (or slices) the Slug made contact with surface deflectors of the cruiser. These powerful shields absorbed to the maximum of their abilities and then failed. Next in line was the armored outermost pressure hull. It failed and so did the next one in line. Three and four held but with severe contortion and scald effect damage to sections just inside the innermost pressure hull.

As Mama-Seven powered back up, damage and hull assessment scans were began. Severe damage was reported in most of the outer areas of the ship which were located on the breach side. The Static-Repulsar Field was still up but with a large variance at the impact site. Many of the field receptors were destroyed or damaged on that side of the ship and the field had collapsed in on itself. The ATC was also pushed away from the point of impact by several hundred kilometers. The cruiser was now in the gravity field of a very large planet of unknown composition. This turned out to be the only good news in the entire report.

The ATC had very limited offensive, or for that matter defensive, capability left at this time without repairs that would take hours at best. The hostile fleet was now coming into scanner range and more incoming fire was detected, although this was more conventional than the Lava-Slug. Mama-Seven surmised that the Lava-Slug was a one shot system that took time to re-energize, a 'one-for' if you will.

The incoming fire began to make contact with the ship. The Lead-Ejectors took out as many as possible, but still many more got through. The Static-Repulsar Field could not compensate at full volume and rounds began to impact the hull. Penetrations were opening up in multiple hull layers and on many sections of the ship. The Cruiser was taking a pounding without being able to target its aggressor. Alarms and warnings were overwhelming the Master-Computer. Her tactical abilities were now extremely limited due to the severe damage that continued to mount.

Mama-Seven now knew that tactically the engagement was lost. Evasion was the only option left available. Run, Hide, Repair, Counterattack, Escape. Simple programing that had been the mainstay of ships for hundreds of years. Nose down and head into the dense atmosphere of an unknown planet was the only means of escape and possible survival. Orbit was never initiated for two reasons. Number one was that orbit still left the damaged cruiser at the mercy of the incoming fleet. Number two was simple, not enough command and control surfaces and systems left that were not damaged to even attempt and maintain an orbit.

The flightpath now became erratic as more and more systems were either damaged or destroyed. Mama-Seven sent out a 360 degree data-burst. All available information on the attack and destruction of the cruiser was included in this data-burst. A direct data stream could possibly lead the attackers directly to the Earth-Colonies section of the Galaxy. The 360 degree burst would lead them nowhere but still supply information about the last seconds of the cruiser. With that done Mama-Seven used what abilities remained to her to try and escape into the dense atmosphere of this unknown planet.

The cruiser was running at a ninety degree angle across the path of the opposing fleet, or crossing the enemies T in sailor jargon. This gave Mama-Seven a chance to fire four of her remaining undamaged guns. Just before entering the outermost atmospheric ring Mama-Seven fired both starboard Sled-Guns at the approaching fleet. Her targeting computers could take only a best chance shot and hope for an impact or at least cause some of her attackers to evade momentarily. Once fired, she rotated the cruiser one hundred and eighty degrees and fired both port Sled-Guns in the same fashion. With this accomplished the offensive portion of the battle was over, now it was time to run and hide.

The escape became more of a freefall than a controlled flight path. Incoming fire dwindled and began to miss as the cruiser became enveloped in the dense atmosphere of the planet. The Master-Mainframe already had repairs underway. The most critically needed systems were flooded with Micro-Repair cells and heavy repair drones rushed to hull-breach and shell impact sites.

Captain Simms finished the report and threw it on his console. He suspected that whoever attacked his ship was probably still in orbit around the planet and possibly preparing a landing force to try and finish him off. He com-linked Major West and requested a council of war to determine what could be done if a ground attack was imminent.

Major West met the Captain back on the Battle Bridge. The Captain was conferring with the officer in charge of the damage assessment and heavy salvage drones. As West walked up the Captain said, "Just in time Major, I wanted you to hear what the engineer has to say about our situation. Carry on son."

The engineer looked back at his data slate and then at Major West.

"Sir, the lift for the heavy troop-transport is down. For now it can't be used or repaired. The crash damaged the strut that houses the elevator shaft. None of your heavy equipment can be lowered at this time."

West slammed his fist down on the top of the console. "Captain what if our friends out there with the tanks and artillery decide to resume our little land battle. My men need that lift repaired and our heavy equipment lowered to the planet's surface."

"I understand completely major. At the moment there are more pressing matters to attend to for our repair crews."

"What could be more pressing than perimeter defense while there is a hostile force positioned less than four kilometers from our position?" West was bordering on insubordination but the captain let it pass, he knew West was only looking out for the ATC.

"The indigenous opposing force is standing down. Until that changes I am using all available resources to do critical ship repairs."

"And what if they suddenly decide to not stand down, my men will be hard pressed to stop an advance, which includes artillery and heavy tanks, without our own heavy ordinance."

"I understand your concern major but your men will not be fighting alone. ED held them off without the help of your Shock Troops until Mama-Seven brought us back to life."

"May I remind you Captain that ED was being pushed back inside the Static Repulsar Field until he captured one of their officers?"

"You are correct Major. But don't underestimate the abilities of ED. He hasn't lost a battle in over three hundred years."

"As you wish Captain, but if ED is ever going to lose a battle I don't want this to be his first. I will deploy the necessary units to secure the perimeter. The reserve squads can assist with the repairs. But if things heat up outside they are to break off and join the ground forces," West said in a harsh tone.

"Understood, my men can sure use the help. Also, I am concerned that whoever attacked the ship may send down a ground force in case any of us survived. We did survive so I do believe they will come. Start fortifying the perimeter and try to recall the life pods. If they are airworthy, have them rejoin the ATC as soon as possible. We can use their manpower." Simms said.

"Yes sir." With that the major turned and left the Battle Bridge.

Admiral Seeboc Tang scanned his data slate with no small amount of pride. The battle plan his fleet had just implemented had gone off without a single tactical mistake. The human battle cruiser was saturated with weapons fire and had apparently gone down in flames. All indications were that the ship was totally destroyed in space and the burning hulk had simply sunk through the dense atmosphere of this strange planet and burned up on the freefall to the surface. The crash would have been spectacular and Seeboc was annoyed that his flagships powerful sensors couldn't pick up the destruction on the planet's surface. The dense atmosphere was complete, no signals could penetrate it.

The admiral was mystified at how easily his fleet had defeated the human ship. Up until now the very existence of the humans was open to conjecture. They were a myth, an apparition used only to scare the warrior children to sleep at night. Now Seeboc had the proof on his data screens that the humans actually existed. The Imperial Senate would surely heed his warnings now and deploy the fleet in search of the human home world. The star system the humans inhabited would be a welcome addition to the Sokari sphere of influence once they were exterminated.

But had the defeat of the human ship really been this easy? The Elders of the senate might only scoff at this puny race after seeing the battle footage first hand. Surely not! The ambush had been too overwhelming for any single ship to survive. Seeboc sat and pondered these thoughts until he was interrupted by his Chief of Staff, Rillon-Six.

"Fleet Command has been notified of the successful ambush and destruction of the human Battle-Cruiser Admiral. They are anxious to receive your battle report and digital footage of the event as soon as they can be transmitted. Instructions will be forthcoming on how to handle the remains of the human ship. In all likelihood a salvage operation will be initiated to try and gain as much knowledge of this new species as possible."

Seeboc absorbed this information but did not acknowledge the officer. The crew of the fleet class Battle-Cruiser Rococo had grown accustomed to the eccentricities of their admiral. Now Seeboc sat in total thought and waited for orders from his superiors as Rillon-Six departed the bridge and headed for the ordinance deck to check on the replenishment of the massive Lava-Slug launcher which was located on another ship far to the rear of the main fleet. His second in command, who had been standing by the Admiral's side while the Chief of Staff was there, now saw the opportunity to share his concerns with his commander. Seeboc placed the data slate on his operating console and turned to Sub-Commander Keeto Three. Seeboc viewed his subordinate with great contempt.

"You wish to speak Keeto?" Seeboc asked.

"Admiral, the human ship is finished. Why do we waste time here waiting on directions from Fleet Command when there might be other human vessels lurking nearby. We can return to the crash site at a later time if Fleet Command requires a forensic analysis of the destroyed human ship. In the meantime our energies should be focused on the possibility of another human vessel, or for that matter an entire fleet." Keeto was a tremendous tactician and this in itself was a threat to the career of Seeboc. Keeto had been the one who engineered the ambush and destruction of the human battle cruiser. Seeboc would make sure that Keeto's name was never mentioned in the after battle report that would soon be sent to his superiors.

The Admiral ignored the question and asked one of his own.

"What do we know about this planet Keeto?"

"Scanners are having trouble probing down to the planet's surface. Experiencing dense particle concentration in multiple atmospheric layers with high velocity turbulence and static dust clouds at the higher elevations! All sensors are still probing. This particular planet is not showing up on any of our star or system charts. There is no home star; planet is apparently void of life." Keeto looked up at his superior and waited with more than a little trepidation.

"How long before transports are ready for deployment?"

Keeto Three looked away from Seeboc and realized that the Admiral intended to send down an attack force to finish off any survivors. He had failed to anticipate this and suddenly felt fear for his own life. A ground attack was not a good tactical move while there was still the possibility of other human ships in the area. He could not find words for the answer to the Admiral's question. He only stood there speechless. Should a ground attack have been anticipated by Keeto? How could he anticipate the absurd?

Seeboc slowly turned toward his junior and gazed down at him, waiting. The command chair was positioned on an elevated deck and this allowed the Admiral to look down on anyone he spoke too, it was intimidating to anyone speaking to the Admiral.

Finally Keeto managed to speak; "Transports will be prepped immediately. Troops can be briefed and loaded as soon as surface scans are completed. It will take at least one quarter cycle to prepare and implement a plan before a ground force can be launched. Assessments on the size of the ground attack force are requested Sir?"

Seeboc turned back to his monitors.

"Send four attack transports along with one wing of Super-Draft close support fighters. I want this operation wrapped up before the beginning of the next cycle."

Keeto Three saluted and turned to head for the launch bays, glad to be alive. Just as he was nearing the exit Seeboc spoke.

"And Keeto, if you don't have an attack plan for my transports in the next two hours I will send you down on the lead transport strapped to the exterior of the forward heat deflector. Do we understand each other?"

Keeto acknowledged. As he went through the door he wiped bluish green sweat from his scaly brow. He realized that he had barely escaped death at the hands of the most ruthless Admiral in the fleet. He knew when he requested assignment to Seeboc's command staff that death at the hands of his own species was a real possibility, but it was also the fastest way to advance up the command chain. Up until two minutes ago this had seemed like a very sound plan. Now he wasn't so sure. The elevator took seven minutes to reach the flight bay which was located at the lowest level of the ship. The time allowed Keeto to gather his thoughts on what needed to be done and what needed to be avoided. By the time the elevator stopped and the door opened he had regained his composure, both his hearts had now resumed normal function.

Keeto entered the loading and launch bay with renewed purpose and vigor. This operation would go off without a hitch and he would be redeemed in the eyes of his commander, or at least he hoped. Four attack transports would contain six hundred battle hardened Shock Troops each. Twenty-four hundred should get the job done even if the enemy had made landfall without a single causality. But the enemy didn't make landfall intact, for that matter the enemy ship was totally destroyed even before it dropped through the planet's atmosphere. What was left of it would have burned up before it even hit the surface. Now all Keeto had to do was land his forces, retrieve a few enemy bodies and return. He would control the entire operation from the safety of his tactical command console located adjacent to the launch bay. His staff was there now preparing an attack plan; he had notified them from the elevator while he was regaining control of both his hearts.

As he pondered this a message was received from the command bridge. It was from the Admiral and it read as follows: Sub-Commander Keeto, you are to escort the landing party and access the situation and condition of the human ship. I expect retrieval of any information that can be obtained from their master and tactical computers. Also make sure any survivors are dealt with in extreme fashion. Obtain at least two survivors as prisoners, officers if possible. Medical has also requested ten bodies for examination. The humans are a new species and up until this point no one knows their physical makeup or even what their bodies look like. Try to access any data that might give us an idea of the location of their home system. These humans must be exterminated so as not to interfere with our plans for this quadrant. Message ends.

Keeto was absorbing the fact that he was now going down with the Shock Troops when he was interrupted by the flight officer of the deck.

"Sir, we will have the four transports ready in six time units. Troop and equipment loading will take another four, but there might be a problem."

"What kind of problem Lieutenant Eaded?"

"It's the planet's atmosphere and gravity sir. This is a very bad mix. The turbine filters on the transports will seize up after only an hour or so. The heavy gravity also comes into play. The engines will require at least seventy-eight percent of maximum output to lift off and achieve escape velocity. The fighters might last if they are used very conservatively during the attack, but there is a good chance the transports won't be able to lift off and exit. With the atmosphere sapping over twenty percent of each of the transports thrust, your margin for error is a mere two percent. Regulation requires at least a fifteen percent reserve be maintained to assure an acceptable margin of safety. The Admiral has overridden the regulations for this mission. To put it bluntly sir, once you land, you may be a permanent resident of that rock."

Keeto thought this over for a few minutes and then looked directly at the flight officer and said, "Can the transports be enhanced in any way to overcome the problems you have just mentioned?"

The flight officer had anticipated this and already had the answer at hand.

"Boosters can be applied to each of the transports, this will compensate for twelve percent of the thrust loss. Also, the primary reactors are being fitted with additional filters to try to negate the effect of the harsh particles that enter the intakes. It won't get the engines back up to a hundred percent but with any luck it might allow the transports to make it back to the carrier. At this point most of what I'm telling you is guesswork. We need to do a preliminary test on one of the shuttles to get our percentages correct."

Keeto considered this and took the flight officer to the side away from anyone who might hear what came next.

"Give it to me straight Sabol, are we going to be able to lift off from the surface of that planet or not?" Keeto had known the flight officer for a long time. They had been posted together on several ships throughout the galaxy. He felt that anything the officer knew would be shared with him now. It was also the reason he used his first name, Sabol, instead of Eaded.

"Is this off the record sir?"

"You know it is you have my word."

The flight officer looked at the Sub-Commander and decided to tell his old friend what was about to happen.

"Sir, you are being sent on a one way trip. No matter what we do to the transports I cannot guarantee that you can make it back. More than likely once you land you will never be able to leave. There may be enough left in the engines for some limited surface to surface maneuvering but that is about it. You will probably die on that planet, the same as the humans."

Keeto thought about this. Twenty-four hundred Shock Troops and over a hundred flight crew, would the Admiral really sacrifice this much just to get rid of him. He knew he was in line for the next flagship posting but would Seeboc really kill two-thousand and five-hundred of his own personnel to accomplish a tactical solution to a political problem. Seeboc had aspirations to be the next High Admiral of the fleet. Keeto had shown great tactical ability and won more than his share of accolades from High Command. Seeboc saw him as a threat. Elimination had always been a possibility, Keeto knew this. All he could do now was succeed on the current mission and then take up his grievances with the High Command.

Keeto turned to the flight officer and said, "Prepare the necessary improvements to the transports. Is there anything else, besides what you have just mentioned, that can be done to improve not only the performance of the shuttles but also our chances of returning from the planet's surface?"

"All will be taken care of at once. I might also come up with another trick or two to enhance the propulsion and improve your chances, if I only had more time."

"More time is out of the question Sabol. The mission must commence in twenty-three time units." Both stood for a moment reflecting on the problems at hand. Keeto looked at the sailor and said, "Very well, let's get to it, you have a job to do and I have a mission to carry out." Keeto hoped his optimism would inspire the flight officer to new heights, but there was not much he could do to inspire his own sagging morale.

Admiral Tang sat at his command console and relished the thought of eliminating one of his most hated rivals, Keeto Three. His second in command had proven to be a highly skilled flight officer and a brilliant tactician. Tang had felt the need to rid himself of this upstart from the moment he had been assigned to replace the previous second officer who had been killed in another freak accident.

In all his years in the service, Seeboc had the unfortunate luck of losing six previous Sub-Commanders, all brilliant, all highly decorated, all dead from mysterious accidents. To be assigned as second officer to Seeboc Tang was almost certainly a death sentence. But still the list was long for those wishing to advance up the chain of command.

As Seeboc sat and pondered these events a message came through his com implants that two human escape pods had been located, each containing three survivors. As the admiral thought, his response was relayed back through the same neural-implants that both pods were to be retrieved at once.

Due to the distance between the two pods it was decided that two different ships would each retrieve one of the life pods. The Battle-Barge Re and the Fast-Attack Frigate Zac were each dispatched to a pod and, once retrieved, to communicate back for further instructions. This was good news indeed. The landing craft were all but assured of being left behind on the planet's surface. Now there came an opportunity to capture human survivors and also a limited amount of their technology in the form of the two escape pods.

"Evasive, Evasive: enemy weapons fire detected. Set shields to max, High-Output Responders track and fire". The enemy fleet was controlled not only by Admiral Tang but also by a highly effective central command computer. Fleet movement and defense was coordinated by this single system when enemy fire was detected. Once the command staff was brought up to speed, control could be initiated by each of the individual ships combat officers. In any initial weapons fire breach of the exterior defensive ring, the central command computer was the first line of defense.

Tang sat at his console and waited for more information on the approaching ordinance. None would be coming. The four incoming rounds traveled at such a high rate of speed that detection and impact were almost simultaneous events. There were two impacts, very lucky considering that the human ATC was shooting from the hip as she headed down into the safety of the planet's thick atmosphere. Her targeting computers were very good, but with the damage the Cruiser had received and the erratic flight path she was taking any hit at max-range was doubtful. The rounds were programed to travel in the dark void of space away from the attacking fleet and then arc back and come in on the opposite side of the battle that had previously ended. It was hoped that a majority of the hostile fleet's attentions would be directed toward the planet where their prey had headed.

The projectiles fired by the Sled-Guns on the Udom-Gareth were fourteen meter long Ship-Kill Collapse rounds. The great thing about a Sled-Gun is that the projectile is pulled along the length of the barrel rather than being pushed from the end of the round. This allows for the rear of a fired round to be made of softer, more destructive splatter charges. The front two thirds of the round are actually encased in a super hardened slug that is made for penetration of a ships defensive shield. As the slug slows the tungsten tipped inner core is shot through by its own kinetic energy. The super-tough tungsten tip then penetrates through the ship. Behind this tip are the splatter charges, made up of a phosperous-lead mixture. At impact the lead becomes molten and super sticky. The lead attaches itself to everything it touches as the tungsten tip penetrates and pulls the charge through the entire length of the target. In tests it had been discovered that the projectile could penetrate a battle cruiser and actually have enough energy to exit itself out the opposite side.

As the lead cooled its temperature fell through the ignition point of the phosperous which was developed to maintain stability in rising temps and only ignite in falling temps. Phosperous burns at an extremely high temperature, setting fires throughout the target, thus the name Ship-Kill.

The Escort Gun Platforms Tec and Ser were both hit before their High-Output Responders could open fire. Admiral Tang watched both of his escorts on one of his split screen monitors. His first thought was that the thin diameter of the ordinance could not possibly harm his ships. He thought wrong. The Sled-Gun ordinance was specifically designed to be slim and long. It was found that the smaller the diameter of a round the more likelihood of its chances to overcome even the most robust enemy shields and armor. Also the two part round allowed the innermost part of the charge to maintain as much energy as possibly while the outer shell accomplished the main shield penetration.

As Tang watched and waited for a damage report he became even more convinced that the enemy weapons were of such a lesser quality than his that his fleet had nothing to worry about. Tang came completely out of his command chair as the Tec caught fire at both the bow and stern sections of the ship. The fire soon extinguished as the void of space snuffed it out. He amplified his screen and was convinced that the Tec had only experienced a shield malfunction and was venting reactor gases to compensate for the shell impacts. At that very moment the Tec came apart at the main bulkhead and armor joints. The entire ship disappeared a second later in a giant ball of flame.

Tang sat back down stunned. He was soon shocked back into real-time by the same destruction of the Ser. In the course of a few minutes he had lost two of his escorts and thousands of their crew at the hands of a crippled human ship that wasn't even on their scanners anymore. In a fit of rage Tang pulled his Stock-Pistol and shot his fleet weapons officer in the back. He then turned the weapon toward the comms officer and just before pulling the trigger he stopped and slowly holstered the weapon. The shocked crew looked at the dead crewman. Tang screamed for them to get back to work or they would be next.

As the body was being removed from the battle-bridge Tang radioed the launch bay and questioned Keeto-Three about the preparations being made for the ground assault.

"Find the human scum and obliterate them from the face of the planet. Nothing less will be accepted." He told his second in command.

"It will be accomplished as you say Admiral." Keeto boarded the command troop transport and inspected the enhancements being installed by Lieutenant Eaded. He then strapped himself into the copilot's seat and ran some diagnostics. The improvements were indeed enhancing performance, but would it be enough? As he sat in the cockpit he thought of something to add. He ordered the full contingent of Shock Troops be equipped with four days rations and eight days of ammo. The troops might be hungry or dead but they would not run out of ammunition.

Keeto had the launch bay evacuated and sealed. He wanted to try out an unenhanced transport during a shallow decent of the planet's atmosphere before the entire squadron was totally committed. As the transport released and dropped away from the launch bay, Keeto reflected on the events that had led him here. The heavy gravity and nasty atmospheric rings brought him back to the present. Severe turbulence was actually a welcome relief. The here and now was much more refreshing than thoughts of what might be in store for himself and his troops.

The shuttle was put through the paces and then returned to the launch bay so Lieutenant Eaded could take apart an engine and inspect the wear and tear damage. Just as Keeto feared the intakes had become partially clogged and allowed a small amount of contaminants into the turbine. The engine would have failed even before the completion of the decent. The trip would have ended in a catastrophic crash with massive loss of life.

Keeto now took another transport out for the same test flight. This was one of the transports that Sabol Eaded had enhanced with better filters and thrust boosters. The onboard computer flew the same limited decent and flight path as the first ship and then returned to the launch bay.

Officers and crew alike waited impatiently as Sabol and his engineers disassembled one of the main engines. The added filters had done an admirable job of protecting the turbine. There was still some abrasive scarring but not nearly as bad as the unprotected previous ship. Again Keeto took the Lieutenant to the side for a private conversation.

"Well Sabol what do you think?"

The Lieutenant smiled and responded immediately.

"The added filters have done their job precisely as I had hoped. The thrust boosters didn't add quite as much to the mix as I was expecting but it is still an improvement."

Keeto frowned and asked again.

"You haven't answered my question. Can the shuttles make it back to the Rococo or not?"

"The test flight subjected the shuttle to only the upper atmosphere. As you descend deeper the particle density will be greater. Also the gravity will be more intense the nearer you get to the surface. My opinion has not changed. The shuttles will have an extremely hard time attaining escape velocity," was the answer Eaded gave Keeto.

On his command bridge Admiral Tang observed the release and decent of both test flights. He had watched Keeto board both flights and knew the Sub-Commander was extremely concerned. The Admiral had just lost two escorts to enemy fire; the loss of four more transports was a minor event in the bigger scheme of things.

With all that had transpired he was in a truly foul mood. The loss of the Tec and the Ser to such a primitive race as the humans was unacceptable. Add to this the fact that the humans even possessed such a dynamic weapon. He would make any survivors pay dearly, and then of course, they would be autopsied while still alive.

Tang radioed the Battle-Barge Re and the Fast-Attack Frigate Zac for an update on the human escape pods. He hoped this distraction could help him forget, momentarily at least, the loss of the two escorts.

"Both pods have been retrieved Sir. The Re has already moved the human pod it captured into its bio-hazard section. Once inside, some initial tests will be run before it is opened for inspection. The Zac has just now captured the second pod. It was traveling at escape velocity and took a little more time to retrieve. Life signs in each of the pods are strong and apparently the survivors are in the early stages of deep travel cryo-sleep. All scans from our sensors indicate that each pod does in fact contain three humans.

"Good Commander. I want each pod handled in the following manner. One survivor is to be autopsied immediately for a physiological analysis of what we are dealing with. One is to be flash frozen and stored in a long duration cryo-tube for future tests and the third will be left alive for the time being for interrogation. And Commander, autopsy the first one while he is still alive. I want to know the extent of their pain tolerance, Admiral Tang out."

The life pod on board the Re was transported by way of an automated tram to the medical containment bay. This was a self-contained unit with its supplemental life support and foreign specie analysis lab. Once inside the containment unit of the medical bay the entire pod would be scanned for any sign of booby-traps or microbes that might harm the medical team which was being selected to do the necessary tests on their first human captives. Once the scans were complete and no sign of dangerous microbes of a biological nature or traps of a mechanical nature were detected, the medical team would begin preparations to enter.

Protocol for examination of an unknown species called for a level five containment area. All the ships of the alien fleet had been built with extensive safeguards in place to prevent the contamination of ship and crew. The research team that would enter consisted of two bio-analysis techs, four specie-analysis surgeons, four assistants and three heavily armed Shock Troops just in case the humans were still alive and wanted to put up a fight. All thirteen members of the team were enclosed in complete level five enviro-suits. Once all thirteen were suited up they were each inspected by the lab team to make sure all the equipment was in perfect condition and applied in a proper fashion. Once this was complete the team would enter the enviro-lock and seal themselves in.

After a further enviro-lock scan and check, the inner door would be opened and the team would be allowed to enter. The three Shock Troops would take up station around the outer perimeter of the lab with their weapons at the ready.

This information was relayed to the chief medical officer onboard the Re. After a quick scan of the monitor on his control panel the officer gave the order to proceed. The control and entry process went off without a hitch. The bio-analysis techs did a quick scan and determined that the three human occupants inside were still alive and apparently in some sort of long duration flight cryo-sleep. One of the assistants, using a remote arm with hydraulic lift enhancements, disengaged the hatch lever and slowly raised the heavy egress door. As soon as the seal was broken a loud hiss was emitted as oxygen from inside the crew compartment escaped into the lab area. This was not a problem and was expected. Another tech stood at the ready to apply an atmospheric mask to the human chosen to go through the live autopsy procedure. The second human would be flash frozen in place by a liquid jet of super cold cryo-fluid. The third would be allowed to die from a lack of oxygen and then resuscitated when it was time for his interrogation. This entire procedure was being digitally recorded for future research and reference. The most amazing thing about this species was that they breathed a mixture of gases with one in particular that would be deadly to everyone on the RE; twenty one percent oxygen.

When the door was in a full open position the lab techs got their first look at what they thought were perfectly healthy humans. Each body was lying in a semi-reclined seat and strapped in tight with heavy two inch wide nylon webbing. What was odd was the stitching all over the humans bodies. It was as if they had all been taken apart and put back together in pieces. All three torsos rose and fell as if they were breathing, but humans couldn't breathe the atmosphere in the containment lab. Tests on the pods before being brought into the lab showed that humans breathed a toxic brew which contained one of the most dangerous gases known, oxygen. Yet these specimens continued to sleep apparently without any discomfort at all.

The lead surgeon took a step back and looked up through the heavy glass ceiling into the overhead viewing area. The entire view room was filled with off duty crew who wanted to see, for the first time, a sample of this disgusting new species.

The lead surgeon spoke with the chief medical officer by way of a headset in his enviro-suit.

"Can you get a good visual of the humans Doctor?"

"Affirmative; what do you make of the stitching on the bodies?"

"Can't tell; it looks like each has been cut to pieces sir. Maybe you can explain to me how they are continuing to breathe without any apparent sign of respiratory distress?"

"Maybe their crude Cryo-Chemicals compensate for the loss of oxygen in their system."

"Possibly; but how could that account for what they are breathing now? From all indications, a human could only live for a matter of seconds in our atmosphere." This conversation continued for several more minutes as the two doctors formulated a safe plan to proceed. The conversation was interrupted when a slight mechanical sound brought the surgeons attention back to the three humans. One was apparently waking up. There was movement.

The head of the closest body to the egress door turned slightly toward the surgeon. Slowly the two eyes began to open but only slightly and then stopped. Unknown to the alien medical staff each body had an onboard computer. With the eyelids in a slightly open position the computers circuits were activated and readings were taken. The offensive circuitry of the tiny computer was evaluating a premium damage firing solution for the twenty five drill point projectiles.

The lead surgeon again spoke to the chief medical officer.

"Are you seeing this?"

"Yes, move a little to your left so I can get a better view."

The surgeon did exactly as he was told, but in the confusion and excitement of the moment moved to the right instead of the left.

The Chief Medical Officer spoke back into his comm.

"Your other left Doctor Gered."

This got an immediate chuckle from the lab crew and staff. The slightly embarrassed Doctor quickly moved in the appropriate direction. The CMO now had an unobstructed view of the three humans. The more he looked the more uneasy he began to feel. Something was not right. As a matter of fact a lot of things weren't right.

"Doctor Gered, pull your team out and let's do some more tests on the pod and its occupants. I don't want current events to overtake us."

Just as the lead surgeon was about to evacuate the enviro-chamber more noise was emitted by the nearest human occupant. The entire staff seemed mesmerized by this. All the techs stood and watched as the outer lids on the creature slowly separated and two titanium spears became evident in the spots where eyes should normally have been. Could these spears be the eyes?

At that moment the mouth made a slight movement. The lips pursed into a thin smile and the jaw began to open. Again there was astonishment in the room as several more titanium spears became evident. Were humans a mixture of mechanics and organic material? Was this human race made up entirely of cyborgs? This would explain the abundance of the suture marks which dominated nearly every area of the body.

As the lab crew continued to examine the situation, the flesh of the three specimens began to give off a light translucent cloud that soon filled the pod. As the skin of the three began to liquidize and run into the floor of the pod the lead surgeon stepped back and ordered a complete evacuation of the containment room. He wished now that he had been more prompt in ordering the evacuation when he was first told.

Before he himself headed toward the air-lock he looked up at the viewing room one last time to see the reaction of the crew. Everyone overhead was completely focused on the cyborg in the pod. At that moment one of the titanium projectiles fired and went through his scaly skull and continued on toward the glass above. It only took a microsecond for the tiny spinning drill point to puncture into the viewing room as the crew who had been watching with great interest were now screaming and scrambling to escape.

The other techs in the lab watched in horror as their now quite dead colleague collapsed to the floor. The cloud had now begun to escape the human pod and fill the room. With a hiss and a metallic whine the other twenty-four high speed titanium projectiles shot in all directions. One of the tech assistants was pierced through the hand. The now exposed flesh and wound were immediately contaminated with the bacterial cloud that had completely filled the room. The tech grabbed the wrist of the injured hand and squeezed tight in a futile effort to stop the contamination from continuing up his arm. Other members of the medical team were checking for tears or damage to their own bio-suits while trying to open the air lock to escape this biological nightmare.

The injured tech slumped to the floor as white hot pain shot through the creature's body. Through the face shield the others could see the distended veins and anguished look on the face of their dying colleague. Most of the uninjured technicians and medical staff were now at the air-lock door trying to activate the release mechanism. The door didn't open, it would never open during a contamination event as they were now experiencing.

The staff that had been so eager to observe this new species from above in the observation arena was now exiting that area of the ship in the form of a stampede. Three of the drill point projectiles had penetrated that room and now the greenish-yellow cloud was venting into that area as well. The Foreign Specie Analysis Lab was now completely contaminated.

The suits the techs and guards wore were beginning to smolder. Another of the surgeons took one last look above and found the observation arena vacated. He didn't know about the three penetrations into that area by the drill-tip projectiles.

As the surgeon took stock of his situation he began to realize that his bio-suit was beginning to look wet on the outside, it glimmered in the artificial light. He took his left index finger and touched the right forearm of the suit; it stuck as if his suit was covered with adhesive. When he pulled his finger away a portion of the suit, the part he had touched pulled away also. His suit was melting in front of his eyes. As soon as his forearm became exposed he felt a burning sensation that started at the breach site and began to advance up his arm. He looked at the dead tech on the floor; the face inside the clear mask was one of pain and death.

As the surgeon looked around the room he observed the other eleven bio-suits were beginning to take on the same look as his, wet and shiny. The suits were not only smoking they were melting. His team would die the same way the one on the floor had, with intense pain. The surgeon walked over to one of the guards and ordered him to turn his weapon on the others in the room and fire. All the techs had the same comms units installed in their gear and each heard what had been said. This created an even more frantic effort to get the door open.

The guard the surgeon had given the order to had been sent to the lab in case the three occupants of the escape pod became a threat, he never dreamed he would be shooting his own crewmates. He hesitated and in that instant the surgeon grabbed his weapon and began spraying the room with laz-fire. He killed the guard last using his own weapon. With everyone in the room fried to ash the surgeon turned the weapon on himself and pushed the firing lever, nothing happened. The surgeon would never know it but all the weapons were engineered to never be able to fire on the soldier that held the weapon.

Laz-fire is a nasty ordinance and has a slightly random trajectory. Many soldiers using the older weapons could catch a random spark when the weapon was fired. To solve this problem the guns were now fitted with safeties that prevented firing if any part of the shooters body could be affected by an errant stream. The surgeon pulled the firing mechanism several times as his exposed arm began to twitch and spasm from the toxins now racing into his damaged bio-suit. He sat the gun on the floor and then toppled over, landing on his side. He lay that way for a few seconds before rolling flat on his back. As he lay there he looked at the empty viewing arena above. As his breathing raced and his eyes began to melt in their sockets he wondered to himself what kind of species these humans were. Seconds later he died the same agonizing death his medical team would have died if he hadn't used the Laz-gun. He died knowing he had spared them the agony he was now experiencing.

The commander of the Battle-Barge Re knew something was happening in the Med-Bay but was still waiting on a reply from the quick-response team that had just been dispatched to that portion of the ship. The last he had heard was that there was some sort of breach in the medical containment unit that was being used to examine the human escape pod. The only sounds heard on the comms link was shouting followed by screaming. Commander Foss would find out who in his crew had been involved in such cowardly behavior and have them launched into space through a torpedo tube. This was a military vessel and in order to keep his crew in check he needed to execute someone every now and then.

While he sat in his command chair and relished the thought of executing one of his own crew he noticed a strange odor. As he looked around the bridge he saw a lightly colored mist being emitted from some of the environmental vents. As he stood he noticed one of the weapons officers clutching his throat, seconds later another officer began doing the same thing. Foss sat back down and knew his ship must be contaminated in some way. He pressed his comm button on the arm of the command chair, "I need a medical team to the bridge immediately."

Foss released the comm and waited for a reply. No reply was coming, everyone in medical were either dead or dying. Now everyone on the bridge seemed to be in some sort of respiratory distress in one form or another. Foss punched in a four digit number on his console and hit the comm switch again.

"Admiral Tang this is Commander Foss, do you read me."

Tang heard the request and noticed Foss sounded different. He didn't know it but Foss at the moment was having his lungs eaten away by a nasty chemical agent developed over two hundred years earlier on a planet called Earth.

"Admiral Tang here, go ahead Foss."

Foss had to lean onto the arm of his chair to keep from falling to the floor. "Foss here, we have a problem?"

Tang noticed the words sounded as if they were spoken by a mouth filled with liquid. His assumption was correct, Foss's lungs were hemorrhaging and he was bleeding his milky greenish colored blood through his mouth and nose. Foss managed to engage the voice-comm again and could only gurgle before falling to the floor.

"Come in Foss." Tang waited for a response that would never come.

Tang turned to his comms officer, "Contact the Re."

"No response from the RE sir, I have an open voice comm throughout the entire ship and there is no reply." The comm officer pressed his headset closer to his mushroom shaped ear and listened. "I am picking up screaming sir."

"Put it on the overhead." Tang ordered.

The comm officer pressed a few buttons and then the noise could be heard throughout the entire bridge. The sounds were terrifying. There was screaming and even some Laz-fire as the crew begged others to end their pain.

"What is happening over there? Can you get a video link?" Tang asked.

Again the comm officer pressed a few buttons and the monitors on Tang's bridge revealed what was happening aboard the Re. There was several of the crew down on the deck either convulsing in pain or already dead. Commander Foss was lying in front of his command chair in a large puddle of his own green blood.

As Tang watched and wondered what had happened aboard one of his battle-barges the comms officer notified him again. "We have a distress call from the Zac sir. It appears they are in the same situation as the Re."

This was the two ships that had taken aboard the two human escape pods Tang knew. "Can you patch into the audio and video of the Zac's bridge?"

The comms officer indicated he could and within seconds Tang and his bridge crew were watching and hearing the same thing they had seen and heard aboard the Re.

"Pull up an environmental scan of both ships. I want to know what has happened over there." Tang demanded.

The scans of the Re and the Zac took fifteen minutes and were sent directly to the monitor in front of Tang's command chair. What he read in the scan was that no less than fifteen different compounds were coursing through both vessels, each of which could kill everything onboard one of Tang's ships. The contamination was complete and filled every working compartment of both ships. There was no way to evacuate anyone on board without putting other ships in the fleet at risk. Tang was furious; in his rage he pulled his Laz-Pistol and shot his own comms officer in the back. The shot blew him apart.

Now that Tang had expressed his rage in such a violent manner he felt a bit more composed. "Get that body off the bridge and get his relief in here to continue his duties. Navigator I want the Re and the Zac remote piloted from here."

The navigator looked at the Admiral with the thought of the murdered comms officer fresh in his mind. "Where shall I pilot them to sir?"

Tang had the beginnings of a smile as he said, "Put them on the same course as the human ship. Crash both as close as you can to the most likely position of the wrecked human vessel. See if you can engage the engines to full as they go down. I want to send any survivors a taste of what they have sent us.

The navigator went about the task of acquiring control of the two vessels. Within minutes the Pulse Drives of the two ships were activated and the coordinates plugged into the navigation computers. Tang watched on his monitors as the two doomed ships turned and started their dives into the murky atmosphere of the planet. Five minutes later and both disappeared from view.

"Track the Re and Zac until impact." Was all Admiral Tang said.

The Admiral sat at his command console and wondered how such a glorious victory over the human vessel had managed to go so wrong. His fleet had gained complete surprise on the enemy and sent the remains of the ship tumbling toward the planet below.

Now he had lost both the Escort Gun Platforms Tec and Ser to weapons fire. The Battle-Barge Re and the Fast Attack Frigate Zac were both contaminated by some sort of biological weapon and were now on their way to a spectacular crash on the planet's surface. His fleet had lost four ships to the humans and this was after he had destroyed their ship. As he sat and pondered the vile things he would do to the next human ship he encountered his navigator sent the confirmation that both ships had impacted with the planet's surface and their destruction was complete.

"Reform the fleet and prepare to launch the assault ships." Tang said.

In the launch bays of multiple ships the troop transports were being readied. The Super-Draft close support fighters were being loaded with ordinance and fueled, they would make the trip to the planet's surface onboard two large carriers along with support staff. The forces assembling for this operation were impressive, enough to take over a well defended planet much less a critically disabled enemy cruiser that was probably completely destroyed.

Seeboc left the command bridge and took the deep-ship elevator to the launch bay. He stepped out and admired the forces that were being prepped for the operation. Keeto-Three saw the Admiral exiting the elevator and felt immense hatred starting to form, the Admiral was sending an entire assault brigade to its doom.

As Seeboc approached he realized this was probably the last time he would ever see the troublesome Sub-Commander. "How are preparations coming along Keeto?"

Keeto knew that multiple Flight Officers on several ships needed more time to adjust the engine settings on all the shuttles involved in the operation. Every minute in the launch bays meant that much better chance of surviving the operation. Hopefully all the extra engine filters were installed by now.

"All the transports are nearly ready Admiral. I have a request I would like you to consider Sir."

Seeboc wondered what the Sub-Commander could possibly need, what he was taking with him looked adequate. Seeboc asked calmly, "What is your request Keeto?"

"I request two squads of Quad-Breach troop's sir," Was all Keeto said.

The admiral thought over the request. It wasn't a bad idea. With what the humans had done to his four ships he wanted to inflict a little pain of his own. "Do you think you and your twenty-four hundred troops can control that many Quads, Sub-Commander?"

"The Quad-Breach weapons have been enhanced again sir. Most of the troublesome software has been purged and for the most part they are dependable."

Two squads represented twenty four of the beasts. "That is a very thin margin of control you will have over the Quads, one-hundred to one. We have never deployed them at such a marginal rate of control. The last time the Quads were used we had a five-hundred to one ratio and they still managed to kill half our Shock Troops, which was even after they had attacked and defeated a much larger enemy force." The admiral said.

Keeto knew the odds were great but wanted the Quads just in case the planet was inhabited and they ran into trouble. "We will probably lose a few troops to the Quads but I am willing to take that risk to complete the mission Admiral."

Seeboc thought over the request and wondered how it might help him. If the Quads killed the human survivors and then turned on his own troops the report to the Fleet Command would read like a brilliant success. If he never sent the Quads and the ships couldn't make escape velocity due to the thick atmosphere it would look like the Admiral had made a tactical mistake sending the transports planet side in the first place. Better to have his entire expeditionary force killed on the planet's surface than to have them stranded.

"That is an excellent idea Keeto; by all means take the Quads." Seeboc smiled as he said this. "I want you and your force to launch within the hour." Seeboc turned and left the flight deck.

Keeto Three managed to stand at attention until the Admiral boarded the lift to return to the command bridge. Once he was out of sight Keeto summoned the Flight Officer. "I have been granted permission to take two squads of the Quad-Breach, have their transports ready and the beasts loaded in order to leave with the rest of the assault ships within the hour." The officer acknowledged the order and went about his duties with a look of horror on his face; everyone was terrified of the Quads.

More than three centuries prior, the Quads were discovered living in a star system fifty light years from the home world that Seeboc Tang hailed from. At that time, as now, the Solutrean, otherwise known as Sokari, were colonizing as much of the galaxy as their forces could conquer. When they tried to expand into a cluster of planets that orbited a white dwarf they came upon the home world of the Quads. It was a discovery that both excited the Solutreans and also terrified them.

The Quads were an advanced species that were just beginning to explore the intricacies of space travel. They had expanded from their home world onto two other planets that orbited nearby. Within another fifty years they would have managed to populate the adjoining star system, which was before the Solutreans showed up.

The first Solutrean ship to land on the planet, which they thought was uninhabited, was completely destroyed and the occupants roasted as the main course at a celebration banquet. The Quads had an extremely high metabolism and food was always a problem for them, thus the colonization efforts.

The Solutreans sent a fleet and promptly took over all the planets occupied by the Quads. Efforts to bring the advanced race into the Solutrean fold failed. The Quads just couldn't be trusted to interact with the Solutrean ambassadors that were sent to the planets, rather than negotiate the Quads would simply eat the ambassador. It seemed they liked the taste of Solutreans.

The Quads were a warrior race, they had fought amongst themselves for thousands of years, when they had finally grown tired of fighting with each other they looked toward the Heavens and at the next nearest planet in their system, it was called Seven. The name was given to the planet because it was simply the seventh planet from their system's star. The planet they occupied was simply known as Six.

All the years of war had brought the Quads out of the dark ages and into an extended period of enlightenment. They had attained the ability of space travel and in so doing began doing battle with the occupants of the next two planets in their system, conquering them easily. The Quads were great fighters. Part of this had to do with their knowledge of warfare due to many centuries of practicing the profession against each other. Aside from their warrior traits they possessed an enlarged intellectual capacity, Quads were extremely smart, they were cunning and borderline genius, two traits when combined made for a deadly adversary.

Upon first viewing the Quads one wouldn't think about such things as mental capacity or knowledge of warfare, it was the appearance alone that startled the most. Quads stood over three meters tall. They had four legs and an extended torso that supported the head and two powerful arms. They were quadrupeds and extremely fast. At the end of each arm was a hand with three digits as fingers and two opposable thumbs. The face of a Quad was the most terrifying feature of all; it was the face of a carnivore. The large mouth was filled with three inch fangs and added to this were two large tusks that protruded more than eight inches on either side.

They had amazing eyesight and hearing. They could also track by sense of smell and once they found their quarry, kill in any number of ways. If all this wasn't enough the Quads had the ability to talk to each other in such an elaborate language it took the Solutreans years to grasp all the words.

The Quads could stand at a table and carry on a conversation for hours with any species that could stand the sight of them. Conversation was accomplished by means of a mechanical device that altered the words of the Quads so the Solutreans could understand them and vice-versa. The only problem with being in the same room as the Quads was the entire time you were carrying on the conversation they were sizing up how they were going to kill and eat you. More than one unsuspecting guest of the Quads had found himself enjoying the exchange right up until the point that it reached over and bit off an arm. As you bled to death you could watch it eat your arm as if it were some sort of delicacy.

After three centuries of dealing with the Quads and trying to incorporate them into the Solutrean Society it was finally decided to enslave the entire race and make them soldiers. What the Quads lacked in social skills they more than made up for in fighting ability. The tricky part was trying the keep them from turning on the same soldiers that were their allies. The Quads never considered the Solutreans as allies, they were the force that had conquered their home planets and they would someday be made to pay for their transgressions.

Trying to get the Quads to do what you wanted was a tricky business. Finally after everything else had been tried it was decided to have a neural implant placed at the base of the skull and just above the huge shoulder blades. By means of shock therapy the beasts could be made to do many things their masters wanted with a much smaller chance of failure. But the implants had failed more than once with the results being several deaths and one very well fed Quad. With all these problems in mind a system was devised of placing a micro-chip with a large storage capacity at the same spot where the neural implants had previously been installed. This worked much better and each year the software that controlled the beasts was upgraded.

The Flight Officer contacted the ship which was tasked with housing the Quads and their transports. That particular ship was always kept far from the rest of the fleet. It was told to the Quads that the separation was for their protection from any battles. In reality it was in fear of what they might do if they ever broke from their restraints and made a getaway in one of their transports which the Quads were more than capable of piloting.

The two squads would need to be transported to the surface on four different landing craft. Due to the size of the Quads and their propensity for violence it was deemed too dangerous to try to put more than six on any single vessel. The four landing craft were quickly prepped and fueled. They would be loaded one craft at a time. Even six of the Quads, if not handled with extreme caution, could overpower everyone in the launch bay. Once the four landers were in position the launch bay was evacuated and four armored Quad Suppressors were brought in. These robot sentries' were built for the sole purpose of managing the Quads.

With two Suppressors on each side of the walkway that led into the landers it was time to attempt the loading. A team of Shock Troops were just inside the control room which was on the same level as the launch bay. The control room had been built for the specific purpose of loading Quads into landers. It was encircled with armored plate and the windows were undersized and lined with Clear Steel. If one of the Quads managed to break the window it couldn't get inside due to the small size of the window opening.

Once a safety check was ran on the Suppressors and a double check was made to confirm that the bay was clear the officer of the deck began the sequence that would open the six containment pods that housed six of the Quads. It had been deemed too dangerous to ever house more than one in a pod. It had been tried in the past; the combined strength of two Quads could break out of nearly any enclosure.

When the doors began to go up the six Quads stepped into the open. The Shock Troops and the officers and enlisted men in the control room each took a deep breath. This was the most dangerous part of the operation. Once they were safely in the landers they would be back in the same type of cell as they occupied on board the ship with one exception, there would be two to a cell. This was deemed a dangerous necessity due to space constraints of a combat lander.

The quads knew they could create some havoc right now but were smart enough to know that the best time to do that was when they got to wherever they were going. Each of the beasts looked menacingly at the four Quad Suppressors as they stomped toward the ramp that led into the lander.

They had been around the Suppressors for decades, anytime they had been called upon to do the dirty work of the Solutreans the Suppressors were nearby. When locked in their enviro-chambers the Quads had spoken among themselves. They knew a Suppressor would be a challenge and four together would be nearly impossible to overpower by only six of their own species. If the odds ever fell to six against two Suppressors then an attempt would be made, today wasn't the day. The six were loaded up without incident. The other three landers were backed into place and the process was repeated three more times.

When all four landers were ready a message was sent to the same flight officer who had given the original order. All four landers launched and proceeded to the jumping off point. Keeto Three had observed the entire process on the loading bay viewing screen. He always admired how ruthless the Quads looked when they were in their holding units. Now they were wearing armor plate and carried guns and blades of a variety of sizes and abilities. All the munitions and blades were held in place by remote-restraining bolts and couldn't be used until they were released upon planet fall. As each of the six beasts marched into the landers they beat their chests at their captors and made ugly warlike faces at the Suppressors. They knew it was only a matter of time until an opportunity presented itself.

When the landers were in position Keeto boarded his own dropship and waited for release. As he climbed aboard the huge lander he made note of the added filters to the engine intakes, he prayed it would be enough. Once he made his way to the battle bridge where he would control the efforts of his Shock Troops and Quads he strapped himself into the command chair. The order was given and the lander fell away from the Cruiser it had been attached to.

The other three landers and the two Carriers for the Super-Draft fighters were also launched from other ships in the fleet. The six craft formed up with the four landers that contained the twenty-four Quads. Now all the ten ship flotilla had to do was wait for the reconnaissance ship to report back. It had been sent down earlier with a small group of Shock Troops and five naval personal.

After thirty minutes Keeto Three knew something had gone wrong with the reconnaissance ship. If they were able to report back then it would have happened by now. Had they been incinerated by the planets heavy atmosphere or had the engines clogged and then overheated and created an explosion. Just as Keeto was about to try and contact the craft his viewing screen came on, it was Seeboc Tang.

"Have your craft begin the descent now Keeto. Any delay will result in your death." This was all the Admiral said, it was enough.

Keeto acknowledged the request and switched off the screen. He gave the navigation officer permission to proceed. As the engines of the lander came to life Keeto wondered if this was truly a one way mission. Even if he survived a land battle in such close proximity with the dreaded Quads and humans he would still need to escape the planets heavy gravity and dense atmosphere to make it back to the fleet. And once there he would face the greatest threat of all, Seeboc Tang.

Baxter picked up the handset as he adjusted the settings on the transceiver. He keyed the mike twice and then spoke into the speaker. "Zebra One, Zebra One, confirm; Baxter confirm, over." He paused for five seconds and then repeated. "Zebra One, Zebra One, confirm; Baxter confirm, over."

The two communication officers who had set up the equipment for use in the brig could only look at each other. The image of this brute speaking very proper English into their equipment was a sight indeed.

The use of the call sign Zebra also astonished the two men. Neither one had actually seen a live zebra but both had viewed pictures during their youth studies. The two officers had been instructed to remain totally silent while in the presence of the Xeno. Simms and West didn't want the alien to learn anything about the humans while he was being held captive.

Almost immediately a response came back over the radio.

"Bax Able, Bax Able, respond sequence your key numbers, sequence your key numbers."

Baxter keyed the handset again and sent the response.

"Zebra One, Zebra One, charley tango niner-niner seven, charley tango niner-niner seven, Baxter confirm."

"Good to hear your voice Baxter, what is your situation, over?"

Baxter looked at the two techs and smiled. "I have made contact, what shall I tell them?"

Just as Baxter spoke Captain Simms entered the holding area. The two techs were dismissed and the door sealed behind them. Simms spoke first. "Tell them how you are being treated and ask if I may speak to them."

Baxter keyed the handset and spoke again, "Just as we hoped sir, they are human. They have been very kind and even brought me a beer. The Captain of the ship wishes to speak with you, over."

There was a moment of silence before a reply was received.

"Please do, put him on."

The Captain picked up the outer wall receiver and spoke, "This is Captain Simms with the Outer-Reaches Fleet. Who have I the pleasure of speaking with?"

"I am General Pincher, commander of Assault Force Twelve. We have ceased fire and request instructions from you Captain."

Captain Simms asked if Major West had been listening in from his armory and was told that he had. "Well Major, what do you think?"

"Either this is the best luck we have ever had or it is a very elaborate ruse Captain. I suggest we proceed with the assumption that everything is as it appears, and this species is friendly, but also continue to hold our defensive posture."

"Agreed, I need you along with an armed escort of four men to meet me at the elevator strut in one hour. I'm going to ask for a delegation of Baxter's species to join us for a change of information session. How do you feel about this Major?"

"Captain, if this species is truly friendly, and from all indications since Baxter came aboard they are, I think at the moment we could use an ally. Another thing Captain, see if one of the humans Baxter mentioned could be included in their delegation."

"You read my mind Major, Simms out."

Captain Simms thought for a moment to put his words in order before sending his reply. "General Pincher, are you still there?"

"Yes Captain, I'm still here."

"General could you come over with a small delegation for a meeting aboard my ship?"

"I'd be delighted Captain. We already have a transport here and will head out immediately."

"General, Baxter says that humans live here on the planet with you. If so, and at the moment we have no reason to doubt him, would it be possible to bring one along. I'm sure you understand our curiosity on this matter."

"Be glad to comply. As a matter of fact my superior will be heading the delegation, and she is a human."

Captain Simms was stunned to hear that a human was in charge of an alien army battle group. He immediately picked up the com-link to the armory and contacted Major West.

"Major, did you get that?"

"Yes Captain I did and the hits just keep on coming."

"I'll meet you and your team at the strut elevator. Put your troops on alert status four. I don't want to be caught by surprise down there."

"Already done; West out."

Simms turned to Baxter, who was smiling that little alien grin of his and said, "Well Baxter things are moving right along. Say I haven't got back the atmospheric readings of your planet yet, what do you people breath down here anyway?"

The captain had dummied down the question in hopes of not appearing superior to his guest. The thought almost made the captain laugh. Two hours ago Baxter was a prisoner of war and now he was being considered a guest, although still confined to the holding area.

"We breathe oxygen Captain, same as you, but not quite so rich. Our atmosphere consists of eighteen percent oxygen whereas humans are accustomed to twenty-one percent. All other gases are nearly the same as yours. You may come and go as you please outdoors with no lasting effects. The only issue you may have is that if you exert yourself too vigorously you may become light headed and pass out. The other humans that we share this planet with have become accustomed to this and have no problems at all. Also Captain, I feel obligated to warn you about the female human who is coming over in the delegation."

This got the full attention of the captain.

"Go ahead, what is it you feel I should know?"

"She is extremely revolting in appearance. All human females are very polite and intelligent but the appearances of any will surely astound. I just thought you should know."

"Has the condition of your planet created this or has something else happened?" The captain could feel anger building at the thought of the humans being mistreated at the hands of Baxter's species.

"No Captain, they have changed since they arrived many years ago and we don't know why. Our females are delicate and pristine. Your human females have changed and not for the better. We have done nothing; it is thought that our planet has had an effect."

"What about the male humans, how have they fared on this planet?"

"They are becoming warriors just like us. We train together each day. We have companies of human troops who are nearly as adept at the warrior arts as our own. You will see for yourself as soon as the delegation arrives. I am sure the changes in the physical appearance will be acceptable. Humans adapt quickly."

Now the captain felt foolish. Baxter not only had a complete grasp of the English language but also a working knowledge of human physiology.

"I'll arrange to have you brought up to the conference room as soon as the delegation arrives. It may take a while, is there anything you might require while you wait?"

Baxter thought for only a second before replying, "Another one of your beers would be nice."

The captain laughed and said he would have one sent right up. As he left he thought of the Native American Indians and their love of distilled spirits. He also thought of the fact that they didn't handle alcohol very well either. He hoped this race could handle it better.

The captain went to the secure conference room and watched the approach of the alien delegation on a large wall monitor. As he watched he couldn't help but wonder about the humans that Baxter had spoken of. Who were they and how had they gotten here? Then it dawned on him, how could he have not thought of this earlier. "Mama-Seven pull the historical data of any ships that have traveled near or through this quadrant in the last four hundred years. Special attention should be given to any mission that disappears from the historical data. Also find out if any returning ship was missing part of its crew.

"Yes Captain, the report is printing now. Also I have sent a copy of the report to your command console." Mama-Seven compartmentalized only a small portion of her abilities for such matters. Her main concern was the ongoing repairs of the ship. Historical data retrieval for the captain took no time or effort at all.

The captain took his data-slate and with a few key strokes pulled the digital readout from his command console. He took a seat at the head of the long conference table. He scrolled down past the log-in and prompts information. He then sorted the list by date. With the information that Baxter had given about the humans being on the planet for approximately three-hundred and twenty-five years he used the dates twenty-four eighty-three through twenty four ninety-three. If Baxter had been exactly right then the arrival date would have been twenty-four eighty-eight, this gave him a margin of error of five years in either direction.

There was a ship that had launched from the Outer Rim in the year twenty-four eighty-four. The ship was a heavy-draft scientific and exploration vessel. The mission log was a bit vague but did contain enough information to let the captain know that she was virtually unarmed and contained a crew of four-hundred and thirty-two. Her mission was to extend past the known portion of the Galaxy and attempt to make contact with a species that were rumored to be slightly more technologically advanced than the Earth Confederation was at that time. This new species was deemed friendly.

A huge battle had raged in the Confederation's Senate over this attempt to contact a species that we knew so little about. The doves wanted to make contact for the exchange of information and possible trade agreements. The hawks wanted to send a battle fleet and conquer this new race. The doves won out only because it was doubted if we had the technology to conduct such a war, a war in the cold vacuum of space and so far from Earth.

Contact was maintained with the ship for more than three years until she suddenly went dark. After more than five years of repeated attempts to re-establish contact with the ship, she was listed as missing and most probably destroyed by mechanical failure, collision or hostile action.

The ships name was the Solar-Wind. Before departure her name had been the Solar-Flare but this was thought to be to antagonistic. Shortly before the ship was to depart she was rechristened the Solar-Wind, which suited a research vessel such as she was to a tee. A little more than a year after the Solar-Wind began the mission the name was changed again to the Star-Ranger. It had been feared that the name Solar-Wind could give away the location of the home world, Earth. Until more was known about this new species, Earth's location would remain hidden.

The Star-Ranger was the most advanced vessel of the era and contained historical data and research information necessary for the possible integration of an Earth-System society and this new Species, no data on the ship contained information about where the home world was located. In hindsight it was a terrible gamble. With the discovery of scores of new species since that time, of which most were hostile, the Earth Confederation was fortunate not to have been overrun by a more advanced species. Wiser heads in later years created a huge military and defense budget. This budget, along with an ever expanding military presence, which was now in place around the home worlds and colonies, is an ongoing attempt to fortify this little region of the Galaxy against any possible invasions.

Captain Simms sat the data slate down on the conference table. He wondered if the Solar-Wind, rather the Star-Ranger, had somehow landed on this planet and never left. And if this extended stay of more than three hundred years was voluntary or forced. As he pondered the significance of this new information his comms officer notified him that the alien shuttle had entered the static field and would be at the elevator strut in a matter of minutes.

"Acknowledged; Escort our guests to the conference room as soon as possible. And sergeant, I want a security level four in place on the entire route. Have Sergeant Toppapav and his fast response team on alert and ready, just in case anything happens that we don't want to happen."

"Roger that sir."

The Captain sat back down at the conference table. He picked up his data slate and linked it to his command console. Now he scrolled through the security cameras until he found the one at the elevator strut. After viewing the approaching vehicle he decided he would go down himself to greet the delegation, if there was a surprise it would be better for it to be taken care of on the outside rather than to allow it inside his ship.

The first rays of light were beginning to hit the easternmost sections of Firebase Triton. Only the control tower of the launch bay and a few storage and repair depots existed above ground on this quadrant of the planet. The bulk of the base was below the surface at a depth of more than a hundred and fifty meters. Other structures existed around the planetoid, these being gun turrets, communication arrays and deep space scanners which served as the base's advanced form of radar. Starshine was something the men in the control tower enjoyed but had little time to relish. The nearest star was more than six-hundred million miles away so everyone on the base simply referred to all light as Starshine. It wasn't anything as brilliant or powerful as the sunshine of Earth but it was still appreciated just the same.

Deep in the planet's crust were the barracks and administration offices of the furthermost Earth Colonies outpost. Construction had taken more than a century and that was before the first human footprint had ever been seen on the planet. Huge drone ships had arrived and offloaded the heavy construction equipment.

Work proceeded by way of avatar operators controlled by a powerful computer located on Mars. This computer was so powerful that it had attained near self-awareness, something so random it was doubted if it would ever be accomplished again. This particular operating system was numbered Four. Since the time of Four's first step toward self-awareness other computers had actually passed Four and attained full Cognitive Reasoning. These computers were all designated by their origination number preceded by the name Mama.

The first self-aware computer was stationed on earth and she was designated Mama-Five. It was never established at what point in time either of the two computers actually achieved their near or full self-cognitive abilities and it really didn't matter, a computer didn't care about such things. One of the most amazing and also the scariest characteristics of these new computers was that they seemed to have no emotions or at least never chose to display them. As time went by it was finally discovered that they had the ability to switch on or off the human trait of emotion but in general they operated without it.

In the hundred years since, other master-mainframes had followed suit and became self-aware. One in particular was entrusted to a deep space Armored Attack Cruiser, the Udom-Gareth. The name for the cruiser was derived from an ancient earth language, Thia. The name Udom stood for best or superb and it was a perfect description of the ATC. The name Gareth was given for the aggressive potential of the craft; he was one of the Knights of the Round Table.

The ATC was the latest development in earth and space sciences. During construction she was referred to as the Gareth. It seemed the legions of construction workers who were building the mammoth ship liked the name and what it stood for. Before launching, it had been briefly considered to drop the Udom from the name altogether but the main operating system of the ship refused to allow the change. A self-aware computer could be a bit overbearing at times. The name was left unchanged but the crew, construction workers and scientists who worked on her still exclusively referred to the ship as the Gareth.

The Gareth had passed through Firebase Triton's operational zone nearly nine months prior and was now deep in uncharted space. The master-mainframe on the Attack Cruiser that had acquired self-awareness was named Mama-Seven and she was built into the operational thread that was the Gareth. When the ATC left the Zone of the firebase she was headed into a section of the galaxy that had been experiencing repeated sound bursts. The Earth-Colonies Super-Computer, Mama-Five had been running extensive summaries on the disturbance and it had been decided that the Sound-Bursts were being created by an intelligent species that had never been heard from before.

Mama-Five had failed to identify the pattern before the Gareth had launched from Firebase Triton. Nearly eighty percent of the Super-Computer's abilities were tasked at finding a pattern in the sound-bursts and then identifying whether the signal was of a docile or hostile nature. The Gareth had gone to Transition three months prior to Mama-Five identifying the source as hostile. The sound-bursts were washed and isolated until individual patterns were made apparent. The majority of the deep-space noise was identified as weapons fire. Mama-Five ruled out ship to planet fire. She also ruled out planet to ship fire. What she did identify was ship to ship fire.

This in itself suggested two advanced species with ships and weapons that were as of yet unknown. Instead of the Gareth heading toward only one alien species there had to be two and now it was known that both were hostile, at least to each other. The Gareth had never been in battle before but some of the systems onboard had. The External Defense computer, a system known as ED, had been in many battles and was more than three hundred years old. This was an advantage for the Gareth; ED had been in hostile engagements before and survived them all.

The self-aware Master-Mainframe computer on the Gareth, Mama-Seven, was the third Super-Computer to achieve full self-awareness. A fourth was in the final stages of cognitive realization. The operating system on the ATC was the most advanced form of artificial intelligence anywhere in the Galaxy, at least in the known Galaxy.

Mama-Seven was now fully in control of the ATC while it traveled through Slip-Space toward the sound-bursts most likely origin. They were flying into a war zone and they didn't even know it. Earth Colonies Command had sent all available information that Mama-Five had pried from the sound-bursts to Firebase Triton with instructions to relate the information in the direction the Gareth was heading. The ATC wouldn't get the data until she fell out of Slip-Space and entered Real-Space.

Firebase Triton was also instructed to expect three more ships and to have them refitted and ready for Transition seven days after they arrived. This three ship fleet would be sent after the Gareth and either help in her defense or if too late, assist any survivors. If hostile forces were still in the area they were to be engaged to find out their abilities and report back all information in a 360 degree data transmission burst. No signals were to be directed in the direction of Firebase Triton or Earth. A direct signal might lead a hostile force toward either.

Once the directive was received from Earth Colonies Command the base went into a war footing. Sensor arrays were powered up to seventy-five percent and all gun batteries were manned with a two hour full capability status. All batteries were advance stocked with ammunition and stores for the crews. The ports that serviced the many trawlers and supply ships that traveled this section were now staffed with Shock Troops. It was the job of the soldiers to make sure nothing entered the base that could possibly pose a threat and to also make sure no transmitting devices were used to send out any information about the base's readiness. Firebase Triton was now locked down. All incoming vessels were sent back toward the Sol System unless they carried ordinance or supplies critical to base preparedness. Ammunition and food carrying transports were given priority and allowed to dock.

The base commander was a thirty year veteran of the Colonial Navy. He had seen his share of battles and had requested the post he now served. When the Construction Drone Service of the Navy had officially turned over the base to human occupation Admiral Digby Hayden had requested he be posted there and his request was granted. He assumed his command four years prior and had spent that time enhancing security and offensive capabilities. He had been rebuked more than once for his hawkish views but now it seemed his caution and preparedness might pay off.

This far from the Sol System could be a dangerous place, time would tell. Once the transmission had been received from Mama-Five, Hayden had called all the department heads for a meeting to catch everyone up on the most current information available to the base. Once convened, the doors to the situation room, where the meeting was to be held, were locked and two heavily armed Shock Troops stood guard just outside.

Hayden looked at the people present and noticed the head of the Naval Heavy Support Battalion wasn't present. "Has anyone seen Lieutenant Malachy?"

No one spoke, each of the department heads only looked at each other. Hayden pressed a comm-link beside his chair and spoke. "This is Admiral Hayden, send someone to the Support Battalion and inquire about Lieutenant Malachy."

Hayden couldn't start the meeting without Malachy; his battalion was one of the most important on the base. Any battle damage to the base or the supporting ships would be tended to by the men and equipment at Malachy's disposal. Hayden and the other men present nervously waited, they all had more pressing things to do at the moment.

"Admiral we have found Malachy, he's been injured and is being rushed to the infirmary."

Hayden pressed his comm-link. "Injured, how?" Was all he asked.

"Details are only now coming in Sir. The Naval Police seem to think he was attacked. He managed to escape his attackers but is severely wounded."

There was mumbling around the room. "Send his second in command and keep me updated on his condition." After a moment's thought he added, "Also start a search for whoever did this." Hayden released the comm-link and looked at his men.

"Before we get into the information Mama-Five sent I want to talk a minute about the security of Firebase Triton. As you know we have a substantial indigenous population on this planet. They weren't actually living here but are still considered indigenous because they were brought here from a nearby planet, their home planet. They weren't very advanced when our drones arrived to begin construction of the base but have progressed rapidly. They were brought here as workers to help with the construction, and performed remarkably in that task.

"What we didn't know at the time was that this species has a secret, a well-hidden secret that none of you seated here know anything about. The information you are about to be given was sent to me three months ago from Earth Colonies Command." All the department heads grew even quieter.

"It appears our friends here might not be as indigenous to this system as we first thought. Mama-Five has been doing calculations on this system for the last eight years and as her knowledge grew she began correlating specie history and system history and has come to a startling conclusion. The workers we brought here to help finish Firebase Triton were exiled to this system at about the same time our heavy drones made it here to begin construction. It appears they arrived in system around three years after the first heavy excavations of the underground caverns where most of the base is located."

Just as the Admiral was about to continue a warning claxon began to blare. The automated voice that followed gave instructions as to what the warning was about.

"Red Alert, Red Alert. All security personnel man your stations. Repeat, all security personnel man your stations."

Admiral Hayden stood and went to the door that led from the situation room to the corridor. Just as he was about to press the release button on the automated lock the door hissed open and the two Shock Troops that had been stationed at the entrance rushed in. Just before hitting the lock button again one of the troops pointed his gun and fired a long particle stream down the corridor. When he hit the lock button with his gloved hand nothing happened. The other trooper leveled his weapon and sprayed the corridor also. Both then took positions on either side of the entrance.

Hayden had stepped to the side when the first of his troops entered. "What's happening Sergeant?" was all he asked.

"Don't know Sir. Just as the claxon went off we were fired on. Our position out there wasn't defensible so we came in here. That's all I know."

Just then there was weapons fire in the corridor and everyone in the room hit the floor. Both troopers returned fire. Hayden crawled on his hands and knees to the control panel at the head of the conference table. "Command do you read me? Come in Command."

Within seconds there was a response, "Command here."

"This is Admiral Hayden, get a security team to the situation room on the double, we are under attack."

When the response came back weapons fire could be heard on the other end. "Roger that Admiral, we're taking fire here too." Everyone in the room except the two troopers was looking at the admiral.

"Can you hold?" Hayden asked the operator in the Command Bunker.

When the reply came weapons fire could still be heard in the background. "Unsure Admiral, we were attacked by some of our own personnel. It's the IEF; they shot up the place pretty bad before some of our security personnel responded."

The IEF stood for 'Indigenous Expeditionary Force.' It had been agreed years prior that the population of the home world of the worker force should be included into the Earth Colonies Union. They had shown themselves adept at heavy construction in deep space locations where outposts were being constructed to support the Fleet. In the last ten years they had shown themselves also to be fierce warriors. As each year went by more and more of the security needs of Firebase Triton were handed over to the IEF. That freed up personnel to conduct research and surveillance of the adjoining systems.

"Command, do you know if this is a planet wide attack or is it confined to our locations?" Hayden asked.

Just when it looked like there would be no response the comm unit came on. "Admiral, this is Major Bradley. We have the bunker secured for the moment, don't know if the situation can be maintained. It appears the IEF have staged a total planet attack. Lots of causalities on our side, we were caught completely by surprise. Some of the outposts have reported overwhelming numbers advancing with little hope of stopping them." There was a pause and then, "One more thing Admiral, they aren't taking prisoners. Outpost video is still up and running, I've seen overrun stations completely wiped out. Any survivors or wounded are summarily shot, point blank." There was more weapons fire and then the transmission went dead.

Admiral Hayden looked around the room. The fact that the IEF weren't taking prisoners could be seen on the faces of the men taking cover. "We need weapons," he told the department heads.

One of the troopers manning the defense of the door reached into a second holster he carried and pulled out a Laz-Pistol and tossed it to Hayden. "Here you go Sir, I always carry a spare."

The other trooper did the same and tossed his backup weapon, an old style semi-automatic Model 1911, to Peter Housley who was in charge of all the ordinance supplies on the base. The trooper that threw the weapon smiled and said, "You're pretty good at fussing about ammo expenditure, how about you using a little of it yourself for a change."

Housley grunted and then ratcheted a round into the chamber. "Thanks, I believe I will." It was apparent the two men knew each other. A stranger would never address a department head in such a manner.

That made four men in the situation room who were armed. Hayden knew if the entire IEF were involved in the uprising his men would soon be overrun. He had to come up with a plan if any of them were going to survive.

"See if you can get that door closed. Leave it partially open, maybe three or four inches. I want to be able to return fire from here." The two troopers knew it was a good idea to not be totally isolated from the outside corridor in case the rebels tried to set an explosive charge by the door. After the doors were within four inches of each other a large heavy desk was placed on its side and put against the door frame. It now offered a little protection to the two troopers who manned the position.

With the situation room partially secure Hayden went back to the terminal at the end of the conference table. He had a plan.

"Command, what is your situation?"

Just when Hayden thought the Command Bunker had been overrun there was a reply. "Command here, is that you Admiral?"

"Yes this is Hayden, what is your situation?"

"We're holding Sir. Got a bunch of wounded and five dead but we think we can hang on."

"How is the rest of the base doing?" Hayden asked.

"Not very good Sir, at least half our com links have been disabled so it's difficult to know for certain. The main barracks is in the best shape. They are running low on ammunition though, plenty of men, plenty of weapons but slim on ammo."

Hayden was afraid to ask the next question, the answer might prove whether Firebase Triton could survive or not. "How secure is this line of communication Sergeant?"

"Totally Sir, we had a breach when the attack first started but I managed to isolate it. Whoever linked in is now listening to Classical Music from back in the twentieth-century, ran at half speed."

"Contact the three relief ships that are to arrive here in the next two hours. Make sure they don't dock, have them stand off and launch shuttles. I need them to do a hot zone landing with their special ops troops. Give them the information we have so far and tell them unless they can retake the docks and then mount an offensive to retake the base then we might just lose this rock to the IEF. When they hit the loading area tell them to expect a hell of a battle. Tell them to hurry. Once you have verification call me back on this secure line."

The three cruisers were only minutes away from dropping out of Slip-Space. The crews and regular army troops had been brought out of cryo-sleep and were securing the ships for the repair and replenishment that would be taking place at Firebase Triton. The crews and troops knew the amenities available at such a forward base were few but still it was a chance to get off the ships for a few days. Cryo-sleep still made soldiers and sailors want shore leave.

The three ships weren't the newest in the fleet but they had been updated every eighteen months since they were christened. The age of the three combined was nearly seventy years with the Anneal being the oldest at forty-two years. The Umbrage was the newest at four years and the Temerity was right in the middle at twenty-three years old. All three had seen combat in one form or another. Even though the Anneal was forty-two years old she was, without a doubt, the fastest ship in the fleet. Her engines had been replaced and all her weapons, both offensive and defensive were state of the art. The Anneal was so fast that her actual top speed had never been measured. No reason to put a ship with such extraordinary abilities to the test unless she was in battle.

The ranking captain was a man by the name of Leman Harless who was on his sixty-third mission. He got along well with his crew and was considered a fair and considerate captain as long as everything went his way. If it didn't then there would be Hell to pay. The Battle Group he was in command of had been gathered and dispatched from the Near Earth Colonies sector by Mama-Five.

Orders had been to make haste to Firebase Triton and replenish and repair there. As soon as the three ships were battle ready they were to be sent directly in pursuit of the Udom-Gareth. The Gareth had been traveling at {10%} Transition in order to extend the range of her mission. The Battle Group was ordered to travel at {75 %} Transition in order to close the distance in short order. It was hoped that by the time the Gareth made it to the area of the sound bursts the Battle Group would be ready to Translate out and arrive only days behind her. If the Gareth found herself in trouble then the three cruisers wouldn't be that far behind.

Captain Harless gave the order to begin the drop out of Slip-Space, a procedure that always took twenty-three minutes regardless of the speed. His comms team was to monitor signals and report anything urgent directly to him. He called General Quarters as soon as the Transition deceleration was begun.

On four different occasions during his career Harless had fell out of Transition into a full blown battle. On one occasion he had decelerated into a trap set by three equally powerful ships. He had managed to outrun the battle where his ship was outmatched and fought his way out of the other three. Battle casualties were something Harless had grown accustomed to, although never happy with. He had never lost a ship while in command and he wanted to keep it that way.

All three ships fell out of Slip-Space with guns charged and shields at maximum. Eight minutes after deceleration was initiated his comms officer began to get the first messages from Firebase Triton. The messages were sent straight to the control console on the Fast Attack Cruiser Anneal and then relayed to the Battle Bridge of the Umbrage.

"Firebase Triton is under attack and in need of assistance. IEF have staged a mutiny, repeat IEF have staged a mutiny. Form assault formation with shuttles and advance toward docks. Do not approach with Cruisers until docks are secure." This message was being sent out on a loop and it played over and over. Harless read the message and then contacted the other two cruisers.

Within an hour four heavy assault shuttles were dispatched, each carrying seventy five troops. It had been determined by the crew of the Temerity to take a single dock and once the landing bay was secure the Temerity would attempt a hot docking procedure. Once a solid lock was obtained fifteen hundred of her battle tested Assault Troops would storm in and deal with the IEF. It was decided to tell the Assault Troops about the killing of prisoners. This wasn't done to scare the troops, these men were beyond fear. It was to let them know how desperate the battle would be. Each man now anticipated a hard fight and welcomed it. They would show the same prejudice as the IEF.

Admiral Hayden was notified of the plan and he eagerly waited in the Situation Room. When the first Assault Shuttle skidded to a hard dock a single trooper ran toward the door and initiated the fast open sequence. The IEF were caught completely off guard. When the door hissed open two squads of heavily armed Assault Troops rushed in. In less than three minutes the Assault Shuttle eased to the door and the rest of the troops entered the docking compartment.

The other three shuttles landed troops that took up positions around the dock to prevent the men inside from being attacked from behind. Fourteen minutes after the door opened it was deemed safe for the Temerity to make hard dock. Forty minutes later two battalions of Shock Troops entered the dock and began pushing the rebels back.

It had taken less than two hours to recapture all the fallen sections of the base. Of the thirteen hundred members of the IEF that constituted the entire security team of indigenous personnel only seven survived. Hayden wondered how many had tried to give up but were summarily executed by the Shock Troops of the Temerity.

Once all the docks were cleared of explosives and any battle damage repaired the other two cruisers were brought in. Admiral Hayden, along with Captain Harless and the other two captains, went immediately to the situation room. Once there Hayden explained the information he had received from Mama-Five.

All three cruisers were quickly replenished and the latest situational information loaded into their computers.

Admiral Hayden and Captain Harless had a council of war before the three cruisers departed.

"You think the Gareth is sailing into a trap Admiral?"

Hayden thought a moment before answering. "I think information is still being gathered by Mama-Five. When she has all the data mined from the sound bursts I believe we will know a lot more. My personal opinion is that we have been led into a trap. The IEF were sent to this system as soon as it became obvious we were building an advance base here. I think whatever is out there is waiting for us. When the Gareth comes out of Transition I believe she will be a sitting duck."

Captain Harless found this troubling. "You think if the Gareth is caught by surprise she is capable of fighting her way out?"

"I hope so. That is the most advanced cruiser in the fleet and she also has Mama-Seven. Depending on how advanced and numerous the attacking forces are will determine whether the Gareth survives or not. If you get there and she has been destroyed I want your three ships back here as soon as possible. If there are any survivors in the escape pods and you can pick them up without putting your battle group in danger then by all means do so. If it looks like the odds are too great I want you to abandon the survivors and get back here."

This was personally unacceptable but tactically wise. Harless would abandon any survivors if his three ships were in danger. It would be better to fall back to Firebase Triton and fight another day than to lose a battle that far from help.

"I agree Admiral and will act accordingly. To what level am I to engage if it looks like I have a tactical advantage?"

Hayden smiled, "If the Gareth has been destroyed and your situation is favorable I want you to extract vengeance on the forces that are responsible. If this new species is hostile and they defeat four of our best cruisers then the consequences might be catastrophic. It might embolden them to attack further into Colonial Territory. If you can defeat them or at least do significant damage then maybe it will give us time to reinforce this sector."

When the meeting broke up Captain Harless headed to the landing bays. He would personally inspect the preparations for the mission; as far as he was concerned the three ships were heading into a war zone. Additional ammo and rations were being loaded onto the three ships just in case.

The commander of the Temerity was a man named Zhukov; he was a descendant from an old country on Earth called Russia. Zhukov had commanded the Temerity for years and knew his job well, as did all the men and women in the service. Temerity possessed large storage areas for the equipment her troops needed. She was primarily a troop transport but her role as a fleet class vessel required that she possess offensive capability. She was fitted with many close support weapons for the troops but her main offensive capability was in the form of two of the massive Sled-Guns. Most assault ships were equipped with at least four of these weapons with some ships even possessing six, the Temerity, being a Beachhead Support Cruiser, only had two. It was expected she would stay away from any significant engagement.

The Temerity had been on a training exercise when she was called back to add her troops and guns to the mission to intercept the Gareth. Her cargo was secret but Harless was told it had nothing to do with fleet exercises; her cargo was a planetary defense system, which was all Zhukov was permitted to say. Harless accepted this and knew if he wasn't brought into the loop there was good reason for it. The reason for the informational lockdown had nothing to do with Zhukov or Harless personally, it was because of the situation at Firebase Triton. It wasn't known to what level the mutiny existed and the less said about a new weapons system the better. Once the ships launched toward the last known destination of the Gareth then Zhukov would see the other two captains were informed.

All three ships were loaded with the available Sled-Rounds that were on hand at the base. Admiral Hayden had a transport that was four days out which had over four-hundred of the rounds on board and with this in mind he allowed his own stores to be depleted in order to stock the rescue mission. It was a gamble but he didn't want the three war-ships to be sailing into battle without sufficient resources.

Firebase Triton had six batteries of dual Sled-Guns mounted in hardened placements. Each of the pairings was protected by a Static Repulsar Pocket. The standard minimum of ammunition for the Sled-Guns was a hundred rounds per each twin gun battery. The placement of the dual guns was four around the equatorial center and one each at the poles representing total coverage.

Admiral Hayden knew six-hundred Sled Rounds was the operational minimum his base was to maintain. With resupply only a few days away he wanted to do more for the three ships that were preparing to depart. His dilemma was that to knowingly allow the ammunition to fall under the six-hundred round minimum would be considered dereliction of duty and he could be relieved of his command.

Hayden had been on the Firebase long enough to know every letter of the operating manual. He also knew a few tricks that he might be able to pull in order to get Captain Harless and his ships the added ammunition they needed. Each of the Sled-Gun emplacements on Star-Base Triton was allotted twenty practice rounds and fifteen targeting rounds to be used to keep the gun crews sharp. With six gun emplacements, that meant there were a hundred and twenty practice rounds and ninety targeting rounds.

The admiral had his second in command order the addition of the practice and targeting rounds into the inventory of the regular Sled Rounds. He was now two-hundred and ten rounds above the base operating minimum.

"Have the two-hundred and ten extra Sled Rounds loaded aboard the relief ships." Harless ordered.

The second in command saluted and then addressed the admiral. "At once sir and off the record, it's the right thing to do."

"Glad you approve, if this goes south then we both go south with it," as tense as the situation was both men managed a laugh. Hayden and his second in command got along well.

Harless was in the loading bay when he was notified that two-hundred and ten more Sled Rounds were on the way as soon as they could be transported from the six surface mounted gun batteries. All the work would be done by way of the underground rail transport system that was used to move men and equipment to and from the six batteries.

He had the rounds distributed mostly to the Anneal and the Umbrage. The Temerity would be receiving less simply because she carried fewer guns. The battle plan was for the three ships to disengage from the docks at Firebase Triton and go after the Gareth. Speed was of the essence and anything that could be done to enhance the loading and repair was being seen to. The best piece of news, other than the additional Sled Rounds the admiral had managed to acquire, was that each ship would be carrying an extra Repulsar Pocket circuitry module. This wasn't usually done but with the three ships heading for a possible battle it would be nice to have the extra module. They rarely failed but if it happened during a heated exchange without a means of repair then the warship would either need to break off the engagement or suffer significant damage and possibly total destruction. With only three ships in the flotilla that just couldn't be allowed to happen.

The troops stationed onboard the Temerity and the Umbrage were also making preparations for the mission. Ammunition was loaded into the reserve weapons lockers. These were built into the mammoth ships but never used unless action was expected. Extra stores of concussion and sonic grenades were being loaded by the crate along with extra ammunition for all the assorted firearms the troops used. Six-hundred spare assault rifles were stored on board and this was decided to be augmented by an additional two-hundred in case things went south. All stores were increased well past what the two ships normally carried. Not knowing the types of planetary environments the troops might be forced to fight in meant the standard issue weapons they carried might fail at a higher rate. All the assault rifles could be broken down and repaired in minutes but not while in an engagement, spares were critical.

A new type of ammunition was also being loaded aboard the cruisers for the rifles. For hundreds of years the standard issue for the weapons was either a .226 or .556 which was a kinetic round, it created damage due to its velocity and mass. The new rounds for the assault rifles were sonic and didn't have the need to actually strike the target to bring either injury or death. The new round simply needed to pass within one meter of the target to cause significant damage. Damage was done to the vital organs of the target by the sound waves created as the round went by. Even body armor couldn't prevent all the damage that a sonic round could create.

The new ammunition would be tested during the three month trip as none of the crews or soldiers would be in cryo-sleep during flight. The fact that so many people would be training and running tests on the three ships created one other problem. A soldier or sailor in cryo-sleep needed no food. It was calculated for the amount of stores needed to keep everyone alive and fed an additional three months and the numbers were staggering. All three ships would be stuffed with extra food. Every available space was loaded with crates upon crates of food. Water wouldn't be a problem since the purifiers on all ships used the same water over and over. Water didn't wear out, it only got dirty.

The troops, sailors and ground staff of the Star-Base were pushed to the limit to try and shave off any available time they could during the loading and storage process. The quicker the three warships left the Star-Base the quicker they could begin their journey, the survival of the Gareth might just depend on it.

Security for the three ships while they were docked was also being treated as if the IEF were around every corner. All personnel that approached the warships had to go through a rigorous search, no exceptions. The massive amounts of cargo and stores were also subject to inspection at not just one checkpoint but three, the last being by the naval personnel that were stationed on the ships. Simms, Zhukov and Captain Russel Douglass of the Fast Attack Cruiser Anneal wanted to take no chances. Douglass was so protective of the Anneal and her specialized engines that he wouldn't even allow anyone near the rear of his ship.

The Anneal was allowed a reprieve from the loading of extra stores. Her crew was mostly made up of Astro-sailors with very few soldiers. The captain and crew that served aboard her considered the cruiser to be an attack dog. She was built to forge ahead at speeds which no other Earth Colonies vessel could hope to achieve. Her speed, along with the four Sled-Guns she carried, made her a match for any ship her size and even larger. The few soldiers she carried were intended for security against boarding. Although to board a star-ship might seem a little nostalgic, sort of like the days of old when wooden ships lashed themselves together during battle and men went over to try and take over the opposing ship, it was still used today.

It was always assumed that the Anneal was just too fast for anyone to catch and then board. Still it was considered good policy to have a number of troops onboard. Now as the cruiser sat in dock and received her share of Sled-Rounds, her troops were proving invaluable in guarding her and also inspecting the ordinance and supplies she was taking onboard. The troops were each armed with assault rifles and side arms. It had been ordered by Captain Douglass that all the troopers should have their bayonets extended. This might have been a bit impractical but the good captain wasn't looking to win any friends here on Firebase Triton, he was looking to replenish his supplies and get on with the next mission. What he did like about the bayonets being in full view of the base staff that were in close proximity with his ship was the old fashioned terror it instilled in anyone that came to close to one of the troopers. There would be no mistaking that these men had one job to do, protect the Anneal.

Captain Simms walked through his crippled ship and wondered how it had survived long enough to make it to the planet's surface in one piece. He had yet to find a working bulkhead pressure door; all were either jammed open, sealed shut or completely knocked out of their frames. His sailors, along with the help of eight-hundred of Major West's soldiers, had spent the morning trying to access the most critical sections of the ship to evaluate the damage. Four of the most inaccessible levels were near the landing gear and the walker struts. These systems weren't damaged due to hostile weapons fire but from the extremely hard landing. The landing gear had taken most of the punishment but as it began to fail the walker struts stopped the outer pressure hull from striking the planet's surface. Mama-Seven had done an outstanding job in extending the struts; it prevented even more damage to the stricken ship.

The most pressing duty at the moment was repairing all the ships power plants. These were reactors that, over time, had been reduced in size to the point where they would fit into an average size closet. For that reason the Udom-Gareth had over thirty of the little humming powerhouses throughout the ship. The two that had been held in reserve by Mama-Seven during the hard landing were now doing all the work while the remaining thirty-two were going through shutdown and startup cycles to identify any damage. So far only three had been deemed disabled beyond repair. Most of the power use at the moment could be attributed to maintaining the Static-Repulsar Pocket. Simms couldn't deactivate that until it was deemed safe to do so.

Simms ordered that the reactors be attended to first, it was imperative that the ships power be restored to full, or near full before any other critical repairs were attempted. The six heavy repair robots that had been reconfigured to the Destructs, which ED had used to great effect while the crew was being brought out of cryo-sleep, were brought back inside and refitted with laz-cutters and welders. They were just now taking on some of the heavy repairs. The battle damage the six had received was tended to by a team of lesser robots, it didn't take long before all six were good as new.

"Captain Simms, can you come to the bridge?" The request had been made by the second in command, Sub-Captain Boyce Wellman.

Simms went to one of the few working comm units and replied that he was on his way. He left instructions for the chief in charge of the reactor crews to double time the shutdown and startup protocols. He needed to know when all the reactors would be up and running. He also wanted to know how the loss of the three severely damaged reactors would affect the ships operations.

It was nearly fifteen hundred feet from where Simms was to the bridge and that was starting at mid-ship, the Udom-Gareth was a very large vessel. It would be a good sprint after such a long time in cryo-sleep. He made it in three minutes. The captain entered the bridge breathing hard and looking at his watch. He was impressed with the time it had taken him to get there.

"Captain on the bridge," someone shouted.

Wellman was standing at a bank of monitors with a data slate in his right hand and a cup of coffee in his left. Wellman was one of the few men in the galaxy who still enjoyed the ancient drink. It seemed that anytime you saw Wellman he had a cup of the steaming brew. Simms always wondered where he found the beans.

"What is it commander?" Simms asked Wellman.

The commander looked away from the monitor he was study-ing, "Got some strange readings on several of the ships systems. Mama-Seven has isolated most of the variances and determined the date of origin but has yet to focus blame."

Simms knew what this meant. "What did she find?"

"First I want to address the dead sergeant. Major West was cor-rect in his assessment that the tube he occupied had two malfunctions. Mama-Seven isolated that particular tube and ran a complete diagnostic on both the mechanical functionality and software protocols; she de-termined the tube had been tampered with. Someone reset the safeties but it wasn't any of the crew or soldiers presently on board. The timestamp on the software was nine months ago. It happened while we were at Firebase Triton. That ain't all Captain, every tube in the cryo-compartment had been altered the same as the one that killed the squad-leader."

Simms thought a minute and then said, "Are you telling me that every member of the crew was meant to die in their cryo-tubes?"

"That's right Captain. Each of the tube seals had been set to vent out just before cryo-sleep. In other words when a tube is ready to start the resuscitation process the seals begin to slowly vent, that is at the end of a cryo-sleep. These were set to vent out at the beginning. The harness in each tube was set as if it were transporting a casualty back from a battle zone instead of carrying a live occupant in the tube. Casualty transfer at the end of cryo is always outside manual operation only. The harness at that point can't be disengaged from inside the tube."

"You mean the entire crew was meant to die in their tubes? What about the Shock Troops?" Simms asked.

"Same thing Captain, soldiers and sailors, everyone was meant to die."

Captain Simms knew if the entire crew died after the ship had left Firebase Triton it would have traveled on and dropped out of Slip-Space at the exact spot where they had been attacked. At that time one of two things would have happened. The ship would have been captured intact or destroyed by the alien fleet. As it worked out Mama-Seven had managed a working defense, although extremely limited and then a crash-landing on this uncharted planet. It was apparent that whoever attacked the Gareth knew nothing about the ship being equipped with a computer with the abilities of Mama-Seven.

"How did we survive commander if all the tubes were tampered with?" Simms asked.

"We can thank Mama-Seven for that Captain. When the first tube malfunctioned after we went into Transition she disabled all the safeties and managed the cryo-tubes the entire trip. We can thank our Super-Computer for the fact that we are still alive Captain."

"Is there more to this Commander?" Simms asked.

"There is, I couldn't figure out how we were ambushed coming out of Transition. Mama-Seven is more than capable of avoiding such things as you know. It seems whoever tampered with the cryo-tubes also set the search radars to go into system-wide reset at the first indication of another ship in the area. When the alien fleet was first detected, instead of notifying Mama-Seven, all the systems shut down and went into restart. The restart was hidden by the same software that corrupted the programs from the beginning. The first indication of an attack came fourteen point four seconds before the first shell hit the cruiser. In that time Mama-Seven charged up the Repulsar-Field and brought all gun batteries on line. It just wasn't enough time though for her to do everything she needed to do."

Simms knew the quick reaction of the Super-Computer had saved all their lives. "I need all the techs you can spare to work on isolating and repairing the damage done by the saboteurs. Keep me posted. Also I need a report on the battle damage done during the attack and the subsequent crash. Separate the two; I need to know the capabilities of our friends out there."

"Roger that Captain. Give me an hour and I will have both reports finished. Work is going as well as can be expected as we speak. Some of the worst of it is going to require space-dock. Whatever hit us on the rear port quadrant scorched through the three outermost pressure hulls. The interior hull held, the last remaining outer hull, which is number three, was distorted in by a full meter but still managed to take the bulk of the damage before the interior hull was breached. That was the difference of being dead and being here Captain." Wellman said.

"Understood Commander, can you get any of the three hulls repaired in case we go back into combat?"

"As I said number four held with distortion. I am pretty sure number three can be repaired but number two is questionable. Number one is going to need an entire re-sectioning, that is why we need a space dock."

"Do what you can. As soon as we leave this planet I am sure we will be meeting back up with whoever ambushed us, keep me posted," Simms said.

With the repairs progressing and the mystery of the malfunctioning cryo-tube solved Simms headed back to the holding cell where Baxter was being held. He walked in to find him sitting quietly on his bunk reading the label on one of the beer bottles he had emptied. Simms wondered if the huge alien was actually reading the label or just looking at the bottle. He supposed if what Baxter said was true about humans living on the planet for over three hundred years then it was highly likely he was reading the English that was printed on the bottle rather than just looking at it.

"Baxter, has anything changed since I was here earlier?"

The alien looked up from his observations of the empty beer bottle. "No Captain, everything is the same."

Simms thought it was an odd response. Baxter wasn't one to elaborate. If he was truly taught by humans then they had not bestowed upon the creature the gift of gab. "Good, I am on my way out to meet with your delegation now. I will have you escorted up as soon as everyone is in the conference room."

Baxter stood and bowed his head, "Thank you Captain, I will be here."

Simms turned and headed toward the strut elevator. Major West met him there and he was accompanied by four very large Shock Troops. Simms had always wondered if the large size was due to the medical alterations the men received or if the troopers had been chosen for their larger than average bodies. He would need to ask Major West that question someday when there weren't any of the troopers around.

The six men entered the drop elevator as West spoke, "Ground level with combat-one safety protocols initiated."

The elevator began to descend at a rapid speed. When it cleared the bottom of the pressure hull it entered a portion of the descent that was encased by hardened Clear Steel. This protected the tube as it descended to the planet's surface. Once the tube made contact with the planet West had to initiate the all clear command in order to exit the lift. Once it was determined there wasn't a threat the Clear Steel casing rose back into the belly of the cruiser.

Breathers weren't required; Mama-Seven had determined that the atmosphere at ground level was breathable to humans with no side effects other than the reduction of oxygen by three percent. The medically altered Shock Troops wouldn't experience any difficulty due to their enhanced lungs and mechanical hearts. The astro sailors might experience difficulty if they exerted themselves but other than that they would be okay. If they were on the planet for three weeks or more then the sailor's bodies would adjust to the diminished 02 levels. Simms had been told this and hoped they wouldn't be on the planet long enough to adjust.

As the six exited the tube a transport could be seen in the distance heading in their direction. As it approached it was being tracked by one of the Quad-Fifty Lead-Ejectors mounted on the upper superstructure of the cruiser. Once it came past the point where the Quad-Fifty could track, a similar turret mounted under the cruiser took over. ED was in full defensive posture after the warm welcome the ship had received when it made landfall earlier.

Major West ordered his four troopers to spread out and assume what was known as Honorary Defensive Posture. The honorary was due to the delegation that was approaching and the defensive was just a precaution West wanted in place in case there were any problems.

When the vehicle pulled up in front of the six men it came to a silent stop and the rear door began to come down. It was an assault craft made to disgorge troops in a hostile situation. This wasn't lost on the four troopers standing at attention, or for that matter, ED.

When the door finally touched down West and Simms wondered what was about to happen? Loud footsteps could be heard inside the vehicle. Finally a creature not unlike Baxter descended the ramp and stopped at the base, it seemed to be at full attention. Shortly nine more of the same walked down and joined the first. In unison all ten turned to face West and Simms.

The ten creatures were in battle dress and each carried a weapon of some sort not unlike an assault laser rifle. When the ten were lined up the one that had first descended the ramp stepped forward. As he approached his full size was realized, he was huge. Even the surgically enhanced troopers that accompanied West and Simms looked average beside the beast.

When the creature was five meters from Captain Simms and his men it stopped and made a small bow of the head.

"I am Artemus; I command the troops you see before you here today. We are here to welcome you and offer any assistance you may require."

Captain Simms stepped forward but no more than a few feet, it was apparent he was leery of the massive warrior standing before him. "I am Captain Albert Simms of the cruiser Udom-Gareth. We were told you would have another representative with you, one of my own species." Simms had left off the Attack part of the cruiser's name.

Artemus nodded his head again before speaking. "That is correct, my commander is with us."

Just as Artemus said this more footsteps could be heard from inside the transport. A tall woman descended the ramp and walked forward. Simms and West had wondered what Baxter meant by the way he described the woman, he said she was hideous. She was anything but. The woman wore armor that differed little from what Artemus and his soldiers wore. As she approached it became evident she was tall and well-muscled.

When the woman reached the group she nodded in the same fashion as Artemus and waited to speak. West and Simms were astonished; the woman was beautiful, if there was anything that was unusual about her it was her size. She was well over two meters tall and had muscled arms that rivaled the troopers at West's side. Again Simms spoke.

"My name is Albert Simms; I am the captain of the Udom-Gareth. Who do I have the pleasure of speaking with?"

The woman looked at each of the six men before her. "I am General Sheila Abbot of the Earth Colonies ship Star-Ranger. I am here to welcome you to Saturn Two." After she said this she stepped back one step.

"I have a lot of questions and I'm sure you have a few of your own. If you and your men would like to join us onboard we can discuss what has happened," Simms said. He realized he had referred to her soldiers as men and wondered how this would be taken.

"I will be glad to join you Captain but most of my men will remain here to help guard your ship."

Simms wondered what this meant. "Is the ship in danger General?" He asked.

General Abbot looked skyward just as a streak of flame broke from the clouds. "Yes Captain. Part of my obligation to you now is to notify of an imminent attack on your Battle Cruiser."

Simms and West looked at the streaking flame that crossed the sky. "How soon," Simms asked?

"Three hours Captain if the ship you just saw makes a successful landing. Our tracking computer picked it up just before I exited my vehicle; I would have accompanied my troops off the transport but was receiving the communication just as we got here. Orders have already been given for my troops to take up positions between your ship and the enemy."

"We should postpone our meeting until the threat has been dealt with," Simms said.

"No need for that Captain. My troops will deal with the intruders; they are only here to reconnoiter the area and are small in number, scanners picked up only a few lifeforms on the ship. A much larger force is in orbit waiting to land after the ship you just saw finds suitable landing sites for the troop transports they possess, which are quiet large."

Major West was taken aback at how calmly the General spoke of the threat she just described. "Captain, if I might be allowed to set up a perimeter defense and attempt to repair the heavy strut lift in order to bring down my battle tanks and transports." West was speaking to Captain Simms but he was looking at General Abbot.

"At once Major, have as many of my techs assist as you may need," Simms said.

General Abbot looked at West as she said, "My men will assist you with any repairs you are attempting. Also Major, if you like, you are welcome to inspect my forces that are assembled on the hill. They are also at your disposal."

Simms smiled. "Major I think that might be wise. You can communicate with your troops over the comms network as you inspect General Abbot's forces."

"West thought that was not such a bad idea either. He would like nothing more than to see what these monstrous looking beasts had in the way of munitions and armor. He turned to the troopers at his disposal. He pointed at two and said, "You two follow me. Captain I will be in constant touch with my second in command. As soon as I get there I will let you know what it looks like." With that West and his two troopers headed for the alien transport followed by six of the beasts.

General Abbot looked at the Captain and said, "We must hurry Captain, I don't want to be away from my troops when the battle starts."

Simms pointed a hand at the elevator tube and said, "By all means."

As the group headed for the strut elevator there was a loud hiss as another fiery streak formed in the sky on nearly the same trajectory as the previous one, this one much larger than the first and traveling at a greater velocity. General Abbot stopped in her tracks and looked back at Artemus. "Please check out that second ship on our scanners. Contact me as soon as you have the landing coordinates for both ships. Have another regiment form up around the Star Ranger. Bring the reactors on line and make her flight ready in case she is needed." With that Abbot turned back toward Simms. "We should hurry Captain."

Simms and Abbott, along with the rest of the group, rode the strut elevator to the upper level of the Gareth. Baxter was also there, he had been brought from his holding cell as soon as General Abbot and her troops arrived. Once everyone was in the large ready room Simms contacted Major West for an update.

"This transport is similar to some of the equipment used on the Earth Colonies a few hundred years ago. It appears the humans that landed here have had a strong influence on design and function. I can't wait to see what they have in the way of armor." The Major sounded like a kid at Christmas, his voice was tinged with excitement.

Once West signed off Simms stood and went to the plotting board. He punched in a few numbers and an aerial 360 degree view of the Udom-Gareth's position could be seen as far as the horizon. On it were the positions of General Abbot's troops and her heavy equipment. "General this is the situation in real-time. As you can see Major West has begun the deployment of his troops as far as the edge of our static field and soon he should have his tanks and carriers on the field as well. We have four Super-Heavy Leopard main battle tanks in the cargo hold and as soon as the main heavy strut elevator is repaired they can be deployed.

General Abbot looked at the screen and shook her head. "We won't know the strength of the enemy until they deploy from their transports. We also won't know what type of weapons they possess until we meet them in battle. What do you have in the way of aircraft Captain?"

Simms frowned and said, "Nothing, the Gareth is meant to fight her battles in the void of space. The only time my ship is landside is for repairs and maintenance. The Gareth is a formidable weapon while in flight but here on this planet our options are limited."

Abbot stood and went to the monitor which covered an entire wall of the ready room. "We have attack aircraft but our squadrons have never seen combat. Our pilots have trained extensively on simulators and against themselves but never using live ammunition. All our simulations are based on twenty-first century battle footage; we have extensive archives of all the major wars fought until the beginning of the twenty-second century when wars were finally ruled as illegal by what was then known as the United Nations Security Council."

Simms tapped his fingers on the table and wondered what chances his forces had against a determined assault, especially if the other side had fighter aircraft. "I think we need to link our forces somehow. If your troops can hold a perimeter then Major West and his Shock Troops can take on the enemy."

Abbot countered, "If you are unable to field your heavy armor then the troops at my command will be best suited to advance and meet the enemy on the field of battle. We have heavy armor that I'm sure your Major is inspecting as we speak."

"What about the population that lives on this planet, how will you protect them if the assault against my ship is successful and they go after your population centers?" The Captain asked.

"Our planet is sparsely populated and most of the cities are clustered near each other. We have never been attacked before but we knew it would happen someday. We have extensive shelters for the population and substantial defenses already in place."

Simms had so many questions he wanted to ask but knew time was a commodity that was in short supply at the moment. "How many humans live on this planet General?"

"When we crashed here over three hundred years ago the Star-Ranger had a crew of four-hundred and thirty-two. I am afraid many died in the crash; only eighty-seven survived and of these many were injured. When the survivors emerged from our crippled ship we were fortunate for two reasons. First, the atmosphere here is acceptable to humans, and secondly, we were met with a friendly indigenous species, the Fourier. They had never seen a human before and at first thought we might have been hostile, as we also thought of them. The name of this new species in English means self-sufficient cooperative communities, it worked out to be highly appropriate.

"Once they found out we meant no harm they did all they could for the survivors. We quickly found the Fourier to be friendly and intelligent, extremely intelligent. Their society had advanced to the point that they were attempting to launch a vehicle into orbit. They had an advanced medical facility but it was nearly useless to us due to our differences in physiology. The few people that survived the crash included a portion of the Star-Ranger's medical team. Within days they had managed to adapt portions of the Fourier medical facility to help treat some of our injured survivors.

"As the survivors adapted to this place and tried to repair the damage to the Star-Ranger it became apparent that we would be here for years. As you can see years have turned into centuries. We and the Fourier have learned much from each other. To answer your question Captain, there are now over nine-thousand humans living on this planet."

Captain Simms was amazed, "Nine thousand humans on this planet, how many of the Fourier live here?"

"Thirty-thousand roughly, the Fourier have a much longer life span than we do and their numbers are kept in check by some sort of physiological balancing system. A Fourier child is only born after the loss of a family member."

"I am amazed General and will want more time to talk in the future but for now we need to know the abilities of your forces if an attack is imminent."

"I understand Captain. What you see on your screen is one regiment of our army. We have nine in total divided into three divisions of three regiments each. One division can be used on the frontier which is where your ship has crash-landed. The other two divisions are held in reserve to defend the cities and the manufacturing domain. There are two more regiments available from the division I command to protect your ship."

This sounded terrific to Simms. "What of the air force you spoke of?"

"We have five squadrons consisting of twenty aircraft each. Each squadron has ten reserve planes for attrition during any engagements."

"A hundred and fifty planes total." Simms said more to himself than the General. "I hope that is enough General Abbot. I think we need to attend to our individual forces until we have more information." When he said this it brought up another topic of significant importance.

"How is it you can scan the outer reaches of space from the planet's surface, our scanners can't seem to penetrate the dense atmosphere."

"When we crashed here all those years ago both we and the Fourier were basically blind to anything on the other side of the atmosphere. The only way to overcome this was to build towers on some of the mountain ranges that could reach through the dense lower levels. We now have towers ranging around the entire planet and they are very sensitive and accurate. We have the battle footage of your ship when it came out of Transition and was attacked by the fleet that is waiting there now. I for one thought the destruction of your cruiser was complete considering the forces that stood against it. Whoever was in command during the brief encounter done a spectacular job of evading after such a punishing encounter? If it was you Captain then my compliments."

"I wish I could take credit for that General but I was still in cryosleep when the battle took place. Our main computer, Mama-Seven, guided us through the battle and managed to land here. We owe our lives to her." Simms said.

Abbot looked confused, "Are you saying a computer managed all the calculations necessary to conduct the battle and land here without human help? How is that possible, battles are very fluid events and computers are rigid in their thought processes?"

"Mama-Seven is a self-aware computer. The ability of cognitive association to real-time events has been achieved by three Earth Colonies computers now. A forth is nearly there but hasn't made the decision to cross that threshold yet. Some of the Super-Computers that have the same hardware and software as the self-aware computers never take that last step. Self-aware computers can't be built; it is something the computer itself will decide." Simms said.

"That is extremely interesting Captain. I think you will find the computer on the Star-Ranger to be an interesting development in computer sciences in the three-hundred plus years since she was built."

Simms felt Abbot had something spectacular to share herself but knew they had spent too much time already comparing facts about the past. It was time to deal with the battle that was sure to come. "General I feel I have taken too much of your time. We both have obligations to see too but there is one request I would like to make."

"Certainly Captain, it is my job to see to the needs of your ship."

"Would it be possible to patch into your scanner arrays. The Gareth is sitting here totally blind; our scanners can't penetrate the atmosphere."

"Yes Captain. I will have one of our radar teams sent over immediately with the necessary equipment. Your ship will have full scanning capabilities within the hour." With that General Abbot and her four soldiers were escorted through the mammoth cruiser to the strut elevator. Once outside they boarded another troop transport that had been sent over to replace the one Major West had used to inspect the troops and equipment of the General's.

The two transports passed each other, Abbot's going toward her lines and West's bringing him back to the Gareth. When the Major was dropped off he nearly ran to the strut elevator. He needed to get to his battle bridge and check on the progress of his troops.

What Major West found when he inspected the Fourier Regiment was no less than a trip back in time. West had always been a fan of ancient movies made in the twentieth and twenty-first centuries. Some of his favorites were what was known back then as war movies. Although most were fiction they were still a great representation of the tactics and machines that were used by different militaries of the time. West, in his training, was expected to know history and this also helped as he inspected the hardware of the alien regiment.

The transport he had ridden over to the Fourier lines was very similar to a twentieth century vehicle that was known as a Bradley Fighting Vehicle.

As the attack flotilla ignited their engines and headed away from the fleet, Tang wondered what they would actually find down there. He had been assured the human ship would have burned up during the uncontrolled descent it was forced into. The weapons chief had estimated the amount of damage the human cruiser had sustained before it fell out of orbit and given the information to the Admiral, the list was impressive. It was estimated the human ship had been hit at a multiple of two point seven-three times more than it should have been able to survive, nearly triple the amount that should have destroyed her. The Lava-Slug component of the bombardment had been most impressive.

As the attack ships dropped from view in the dense upper atmosphere of the planet he wondered if any of the humans could have possibly survived. He wanted them all dead but he also wanted a few for experimentation. Maybe Keeto Three would be successful in his mission to retrieve bodies and possibly even find a few live specimens.

As Tang watched the last of the craft disappear from view he wondered what had happened to the recon pod that had been sent down earlier. "Comm, try to make contact with the recon team that was sent down. I want to know what they found out."

Tang turned back to the viewport as he waited for information that would never come.

Keeto Three was strapped tightly into his command seat. As the ships of his invasion force pulled away from the rest of the fleet he felt a sense of relief. Heading toward an unknown and uncharted planet where the atmosphere was so thick it was doubted he would ever lift-off again, he was still relieved to be away from the homicidal Seeboc Tang. Even with two squads of the terrifying Quads going down with him, Keeto felt he at least had a chance with the Quads whereas the Admiral would most certainly be the death of him.

The sudden acceleration and severe turbulence brought Keeto back to the here and now. "Navigator, find us a route that takes us through the thinnest of the particle fields, notify the other ships to limit engine use as much as possible." Keeto was trying to salvage as much run time out of the engines as he could. The less they were used during the descent and landing the better the chances they could pull away once the mission was completed.

As the navigator scanned his multiple screens and viewports he noticed what looked like the eye of a massive disturbance. The swirling clouds were thick with heavy particles and dust but the eye looked almost clear.

"I've got a clearing at eighty kilometers bearing .325 to port sir," the navigator said.

Keeto quickly altered the vector of the ships as he pulled up the same screen the navigator was using. Could his luck really be this good, the location he was seeing was nearly free of the heavy dust cloud? After more scans were run at closer range the navigator said, "Got high velocity winds at the center but it is nearly clear of the dense particle contaminants of the surrounding storm. Shall we use that as our course Commander?

"Bring all ships about and plot in the course correction navigator." As Keeto and the navigator looked at the monitors it seemed the eye was closing. "What do your particle scans say about the eye?" Keeto asked the navigator.

After a few calculations and another scan the reply came. "Particle readout is diminishing Commander. We should be able to breach the storm with minimal intake and engine difficulty as long as the eye holds. The rate of decay is accelerating rapidly though sir."

"Plot a course and take us in, notify the other ships. All ships to accelerate and follow us." Keeto said.

As the ten ships fell into line and headed for the eye of what looked like an extremely powerful storm Keeto wondered if his luck would hold. If all the ships made it through without engine trouble then it increased their chances immensely when they left this planet, time would tell.

The nearer they got to the eye the stronger the turbulence became. All ten ships had to increase the separation for fear of colliding with each other. Just when it felt as if Keeto's ship would be torn apart the turbulence began to abate. As soon as they dropped out of the cloud cover they could see the planet's surface for the first time, it was heavily forested and there were lakes and rivers, something the Solutreans had never seen before, it was truly a terrifying sight.

The Solutrean home world was called Rage; it was an odd name but was very much liked and admired by the Solutreans because it instilled fear in their enemies. Rage was a barren rock of a planet with rivers of ammonia and molten geysers of acidic steam. The main habitats on such an inhospitable planet were all underground. For the surface to be so inhospitable, below ground was anything but. The main food source for the population was a fungus that thrived on the above average temperatures and the ammonia laced soil. It grew so well that the Solutreans exported it to the surrounding systems they had conquered over the centuries.

With very little alteration to the process the fungus could be made to simulate red meat which the Quads ate at a fantastic rate. 'A well fed Quad was less likely to start eating your arms and legs' was a long standing joke amongst the military personnel. All joking aside it made little difference, Quads ate at every opportunity whether hungry or not. The only thing a quad wouldn't eat was another Quad. When killed in combat they were simply abandoned on the field of battle to rot along with the rest of the dead.

As Keeto observed the landscape, his navigator was searching for a suitable landing sight. What he desired was a flat surface surrounded by hills to make a defensible zone for the soldiers and the Super-Draft close support fighters. What he settled for was a valley with high mountains on two sides and a small river running right through the center. The river might present a problem but there was nothing else suitable nearby, it would have to do. Water might be fatal to a Solutrean but it was a luxury to the Quads, a well fed quad could drink up to eight gallons a day. The two squads of Quads would need roughly two-hundred gallons a day just to survive and that was without them ever going into battle. Consumption by the beasts in combat would more than double. The stream would serve a purpose.

Keeto's ship landed first and then the other nine landed in a predetermined layout with the four Quad transports grouped together to one side. As soon as the troop carriers landed two squads of Storm Troopers wearing breathing filters ran down the ramps. Fifteen minutes after the first ship landed the area was secure.

Keeto waited for his science officer to scan the environment and get an accurate update on just what waited on them out there. Once this was accomplished the information would be uploaded and all twenty-four hundred Shock Troops would have their battle-armor adjusted to the appropriate settings to insure maximum functionality. Keeto needed maximum settings in place and all safeties disabled on the battle-armor. His men would win the battle or die here.

It was determined that the Quads wouldn't need any adjust-ments to their battle equipment; the atmosphere was well within their tolerances. The eighteen percent oxygen would actually give a boost to the Quads abilities and stamina. It would also increase their metabolism which meant anything they killed would soon be eaten; they were such a hungry bunch of monsters.

Major West was back at his command console talking over the comms unit to Captain Simms when both were interrupted. "Scanners just picked up ten unidentified ships entering the lower atmosphere. We didn't get their signal until they dropped through the particle cano-py."

Simms and West knew this was the prelude to the battle. "What's the status on your tanks West?" Simms asked.

"Still onboard Captain, the heavy strut elevator is at least four hours away from being repaired."

Simms was troubled. If the fleet that attacked them was now landing troops on the planet, and West wasn't ready, then things were going to get dicey. "What do you suggest Major?"

"We are sending out a patrol, I need information on what forces they are landing."

"This battle belongs to you West. Until the forces make it to the Gareth I won't interfere." Simms headed toward the strut elevator to see if he could rush things up, he knew West needed his tanks.

West went to the armory and consulted with one of the sergeants. "We just had ten ships of unknown origin land about twenty kilometers from here. Send out a Kill-Team, three men only plus yourself, I need eyes on the landing site and information as fast as we can acquire it." The sergeant saluted and hustled toward the drop ramp that would be needed for the speeders the team would use. A speeder was a small fast two-wheeled vehicle not unlike the ancient motorcycles that were once so popular on Earth. These were not the smoke belching noise making monsters that once raced down American highways. They were hydrogen powered and totally silent, even at one hundred-kilometers an hour they made no noise. Even the exhaust was stealthy; it gave off no odor, only a few drops of water.

Sergeant Roscoe Talby was one of fifteen men aboard the Gareth that held that rank. He had been assigned to the ship now for eight years and loved every minute of it. He considered himself an adventurer, had since he was five years old. He had seen his share of battles and close calls and considered his chances to be no greater and no worse than any of the other troops on board. Talby went to the strut elevator where a large contingent of troops were assisting the astro-sailors with repairs. When he saw the three men he wanted for the mission he shouted, "Bedford, Roark, Worthless, on the line on the double."

The three men recognized the voice and knew something dangerous was about to take place. Anytime Big Roscoe called your name you better have your dues paid in full and your shots up to date. The three were on makeshift scaffolding trying to cut away some of the damage to free up the lift. They had to carefully weave their way down through plasma-torches and welders. Roscoe was getting impatient.

"When I said double time it I meant it, get your asses down here now." He said.

The three never bothered with the last seven feet of stairs, they vaulted to the deck and stood to attention. Roscoe looked the three over and decided to have a little fun. "You three smell like plasma smoke and look like welder-slag that someone forgot to chip away. We got us a mission but I ain't taking you three stinky hogs until you suit up, full battle dress and dual purpose helmets on the double and I mean it this time." As the three sprinted away Roscoe added, "And run your asses through the wash before suiting up, I don't want your odor to give away our position. You got six minutes before we pull out."

As the three men ran to the armory they knew they were going on a recon mission. All recon missions started with the de-odor wash. Some of the aliens they had fought before were totally blind but could see by their sense of smell better than with eyesight. Six minutes wasn't a lot of time, the sergeant had always allowed eight before.

Roscoe went to the ready room on the heels of his three troopers. When all four men were geared up they sprinted to the only working drop elevator and loaded the four assault bikes which were then dropped to the planet's surface.

"Bedford I want you to take the sniper-fifty, Roark and Worthless take shotguns along with your laz-pistols." Roscoe told the three.

"Shotguns Sarge, what are we up against out there anyway?" Roark asked.

"Don't know yet, whatever hit us before we crashed here has just dropped a few ships eighteen clicks from here and we have been chosen to check it out. The only reason I'm taking you three excuses is so the enemy can shoot up your ass while I gather information on their capabilities and get it back to the Major." Roscoe said.

Worthless liked the sergeant, he was funny. "Sounds like a plan Sarge, should I just stand out in the open and take fire so your information will be accurate?"

"That might just work Worth, how come I never thought of it."

"Maybe because you never think with your head sarge, you think with your stomach. How much do we take in the way of rations anyway?"

"One day rations and ammo, if we need more than that then we are probably not going to make it back here anyway," Talby said.

As the three were snapping on armor and loading their packs Major West walked in, he was accompanied by Baxter. The three troopers looked at the hulking beast and wondered if this was what the enemy was going to look like. "Gentlemen what in hell is taking so long?" West asked.

"Oh we would have been gone already but the sarge there had to put on his makeup first." Worth said.

It was true; Roscoe was standing in front of a mirror putting on camouflage paint. "Shut the hell up Worth unless you want to go on this little trip with your skull cracked."

West knew the men were professionals and this was just one way for them to get rid of the jitters. "Gentlemen this is Baxter, he'll be going with you on this little trip. He don't take orders from anyone and he won't give any, just listen to him and heed his advice. This is his planet and he might just save your life. I want the four of you and Bax here to get to the landing site and gather any information you can, troop strength, equipment and armor. Also find out if they have air-support. Get there and then get back here; do not engage unless you are forced to. One more thing gentlemen, if any of you are about to be captured then article 13 is in effect, understood?"

All four of the men nodded in agreement. "Does article 13 apply to your seven foot friend there?" Talby asked.

Baxter had already been briefed on the mission and knew the answer but allowed the Major to speak. "It does, as a matter of fact Baxter is the one who thought of it."

The initial information from the severally damaged cruiser all those months ago had started a series of events that were still playing out as follows.

:Earth Forces Command was in a state of crisis on this sunny but cold Monday morning in October. A 360 degree data burst had been received during the night and the entire scientific staff was busy mining all the relevant information. A data burst is a very brief flash of light that can contain volumes of information. The burst might be as thin as a strobe but the information it contains would take a person years to read. Another reason for concern was the protocols that dictated the use of Data Burst Transmissions which were as follows,

1.) Data Burst Transmissions are to be used in the event of Capitol Ship loss due to either malfunction or weapons fire.
2.) Imminent probable assault of Home World System by unknown species.
3.) Data Burst technology restricted to protect encryption process.

It had been feared for years that if enough bursts were sent, then through trial and error, the encryption techniques could be learned and utilized by any race that had the technology to mine the data. So far this hadn't happened. Mama-Five had run numerous simulations and estimated that if more than two bursts per year were sent it could jeopardize the technology and make it vulnerable.

This burst had been received from the Armored Tactical Cruiser Udom-Gareth and from the preliminary findings the cruiser had gone down in flames after being attacked by an unknown enemy fleet possessing advanced weapons and tactics along with overwhelming numbers. Once the burst had been received a flash directive had gone out to the decrypting staff, 'Report to the Comms Lab, status level red.'

Within an hour most of the off duty science officers had reported in and were working on the burst. As information was pulled it was being fed into the Super-Computer Mama-Five. This particular computer was the first of her kind to attain full Cognitive Realization, in other words Mama-Five was the first truly artificial-intelligent computer ever developed. That was the assumption anyway, another computer, Mama-Six achieved the same level of cognition as Mama-Five at about the same time but it was never really established which one made it first. Computers in this class were all designated starting with Mama and ending in the number designation from their original production status starting with one. Computers one through four never took that last step, they got close but never crossed the Self-Aware threshold. Mama-Five was considered the first and she was now permanently stationed at Earth Forces Command. These computers had such massive hardware needs, along with storage capacity, that where they were built was where they would stay.

Mama-Five had initiated a system analysis shortly after reaching self-awareness. It seemed that all computers in the Five and further class were inquisitive to a fault. What Mama-Five wanted to know was, if she suddenly equaled the cognitive abilities of humans, then how much would that cognition weigh? Yes Mama-Five wanted to know how much what humans called a soul weighed. It was one of the first tasks the Super-Computer was given. The answer she came up with was startling; she determined that her soul and also the soul of a human weighed about the same as a slice of white bread. Mama-Six and Seven ran the same tests as soon as they reached self-awareness and both came up with the same answer. In a society that had embraced technology it had been determined by three of the most sophisticated machines ever created that a soul really did exist.

The second Super-Computer to achieve this rare trait of self-cognition, which happened at about the same time as Mama-Five's, was naturally designated Mama-Six and she was installed in a Fast Attack Cruiser which was stationed in the Sol System. This cruiser was used as the command ship for Vice Admiral Quinten Mathieu and its name was the Sol Sentry. The name was given because this ship would forever be stationed near Terra and would be the last line of defense should the planet ever be attacked.

Early indications from the information gathered from the burst signaled a new and highly advanced alien race in the region where the Udom-Gareth was attacked. Admiral Mathieu pondered the terrible news, he knew several of the men that served on the Gareth and felt a strong personal loss; he considered more than one of them a friend. The Admiral requested an emergency meeting of the Terra Senate, a body that consisted of one representative from each of the established colonies. At the present there were eighty-seven members, eighty-five planets and planetoids along with Earth which had two representatives.

A Terra Senate emergency meeting took place by means of Laser-Augmented light arrays which were established on every planet that had representation in the Senate. The delay from the outermost colony took fifty-three seconds while the closest planets could be as little as four seconds. The standard language was English and this was accomplished by means of synthetic-translating computers. As soon as a word was spoken, regardless of the origin, it was immediately composed and relayed as English.

The Senate could make decisions but the results couldn't be acted upon until another body had ruled, this was the Terra Council of Three. Only after the council had looked upon the decision made by the Terra Senate would they hand down a ruling. As cumbersome as all this sounded it was actually a very streamlined process. The Senate would put any problem to an immediate vote and then the results were sent to the Council of Three. Every answer the Council came too resulted in one of four scenarios, Unanimous in favor, Two to one in favor, Two to one against or Unanimous against. In this way all resolutions were either in favor or against without the possibility of a deadlock.

The emergency meeting the Admiral requested had three parts, all three were equally as important.

- Send additional ships to reinforce the three that were on their way to assist any survivors of the Gareth disaster.

- Increase the security level on the eighty-five colonies.
- Expedite the expenditure of funds to increase the number of ships in the fleet. This last directive, if voted to pass, would take years to come to fruition. Deep space warships just couldn't be assembled overnight.

The meeting was called to order by the Admiral at Noon EST Terra time. It was concluded in less than an hour and a half and the resolutions were then sent to the Council. No one really expected anything other than a unanimous vote in favor and that is just what happened, all three resolutions passed one hundred percent in favor.

Admiral Mathieu excused himself from the Senatorial Communication Lectern and headed for the Admiralty Building. There was much to do and time was something he knew was not to be wasted at such a grave moment in history. He also wanted to view the battle footage Mama-Seven had sent, which was included in the Data Burst.

Mathieu and his senior staff read the transcript Mama-Five and the rest of the Comms Lab staff had put together. There was still many hours of information to gather but right now the events of the battle took precedent. No one spoke as the events were narrated and the staff read along. At the end Mathieu held out hope that the Gareth had survived although severely damaged. Mama-Seven had done an excellent job in salvaging anything out of such a decisive loss.

Much could be gained from the information. The most troubling segment was the mention of the Lava-Slug which nearly breached all four pressure hulls of the ship. A weapon of that magnitude would be hard, if not impossible, to defend against. In theory it could even be used against planets. Mama-Five was tasked with figuring out what type of ship it would take to harbor such a weapon and at what rate that weapon could be fired.

The only good news, other than the fact that the Gareth might have survived, was that the weapons on the cruiser had functioned admirably if only they could have been brought to bear earlier in the ambush. The question Admiral Mathieu wanted answered first was how a seventh generation self-aware computer had been caught so totally off guard. The admiral didn't have an answer to that because the engineers aboard the Gareth had only found the sabotage after the crash and no transmissions had been sent after the initial Data-Burst.

The action plan that had been agreed upon by the Senate and then approved by the Council was immediately acted upon. Security at all the armories that were within the Earth Colonies zone were put on alert. Especially vulnerable were the plants that produced the munitions the fleet used. All available security teams were ordered to full strength. Also it had been suggested by the council to do a background check on all the security teams after what had happened at Firebase Triton. Information of that uprising had arrived shortly before the Data Burst from the Gareth.

Sergeant Talby looked at the hulking Baxter, "What do you intend to use for transportation on this mission?"

Baxter pointed toward the drop elevator and said, "I have a scooter waiting near your four Speeders."

Worthless chuckled, "A scooter, did he just say a scooter?"

Talby didn't like the sound of that one bit. "Can that shit Worth. If he said a scooter then I'm sure it's suitable for him, now if you ladies don't mind let's get this mission started."

The four troopers and Baxter rode down to ground level and headed for their rides. What was standing beside the four Speeders was nothing less than an armored tank on two wheels. It would weigh more than the four Speeders combined. It was also large, very large to fit Baxter's build. As the four troopers mounted up Baxter slapped Worth on the shoulder, "That is a Scooter," he said as he pointed toward his ride. Baxter had lived his entire life in close association with humans and felt no need to be bashful. Worth and the other troopers had only been around Baxter's species for less than an Earth day and getting used to such a large creature that spoke perfect English was going to take some time.

Baxter's Scooter stood more than a meter and a half tall and was just as wide. The length was also impressive at six meters. On the front, above the handlebars, was a thirty-millimeter chain-gun that was fed from a belt that traveled through a clear-steel tube to the back of the bike where a canister held the ammo for the weapon. There were six smoke tubes, four forward and two behind, along with any number of weapons snapped onto racks built into the frame. It was truly an impressive machine.

The four troopers and Baxter set out at fourteen-hundred hours Earth time. The fleet had adopted an ancient Earth mechanism for keeping time. It had been deemed necessary to use one time throughout the inhabited regions in order to streamline operations, both civilian and military. Eastern Standard Time had been selected due to the fact that the original capital of the old country was a place called Washington D. C. and the time zone it occupied was Eastern Standard Time or EST.

The trip wouldn't take that long. Baxter knew the terrain well and had even hunted close by over the years. It was estimated the opposing force had landed a little less than twenty kilometers away in a valley that was called Shadow Valley due to the fact that it was perpetually darker than other valleys in the region due to the way the mountains blocked starlight.

With no home star in this region the planet was truly fortunate not to be a frozen rock. Heat was generated by the numerous volcanoes that dotted the planet. The atmosphere had a unique mixture of whitish ash and particles that did two things for the inhabitants. It insulated and reflected heat to keep the surface temperature livable and it also amplified starlight to a degree that it was perpetually light on the surface.

The four Speeders and Baxter's Scooter made practically no noise as they raced toward the spot where the Sokari attack force had landed. The only sounds that could be heard were the occasionally rock or twig bouncing along as it was kicked up from one of the tires. After forty minutes Baxter turned onto a small trail that was really not wide enough for the machines. The troopers drove through branches from strange looking trees and shrubs that made the trail nearly invisible except for Baxter who knew the lay of the land well.

It wasn't apparent at first why Baxter had chosen this route. After a few minutes the five bikes pulled to a stop. "There is an overlook near here that will give a view of the valley beyond. If our scanners are correct then the enemy force should be in that valley. I will go and have a look and would like for you to accompany me Sergeant Talby."

Talby took a pair of binos from his Speeder and headed off with Baxter. "You three set up a perimeter until we get back." After he took a few steps he turned back to the three, "And by the way, make sure what you are shooting at if you hear something, it might be Bax and me." With that he was gone.

The two eased off the trail and before long were at the top of a rocky precipice which overlooked a deep valley. From their position they could see the entire length of Shadow Valley, what they saw was startling. One of the Udom-Gareth's Life Pod Constructs had landed at the entrance to the valley and had done so without any damage. This would have been good news if it hadn't have been for the fact that they were being attacked by some advance elements from the enemy forces which had landed about three kilometers further up the valley.

The Life Pod had a Limited Repulsar Field and this was being pushed off center of the pod by continuous small weapons fire from the attacking force. In the distance were what appeared to be tanks of some sort, they were squatty and each had a large caliber weapon mounted on an upper turret. There were three of these tanks and at the rate of travel they were accomplishing in the rugged terrain they would be on the Life Pod in less than thirty-minutes.

Baxter was looking through a twin-barreled device that served as binoculars but he called them 'Amplifiers.' "Is that one of your ships that is being attacked Talby?"

"It is and by the looks of things they aren't going to last long unless we can do something."

"What do you suggest, there are only five of us but I do believe we can make a difference if we act fast." Baxter said.

Talby took one last glance at the Life Pod and then stood, "Let's get back to the others and mount up."

Baxter stood, "Yes, let's get our transports. You do have a plan Talby, right?"

"Not yet, but I will come up with something by the time we get off this mountain."

Baxter, Talby and the other three troopers rode hard until they were down into the heavy timber and shrubs that choked the valley that led to where the small battle was raging at the Life Pod. Most of the fighting was taking place on the other side of the Pod and this would work out well for the five man rescue party. Once they had closed the range to a thousand meters Talby brought the five to a stop.

"Worthless try and make contact with the Pod and let them know we're here," Talby ordered.

Worth took a mic from the side of his Speeder and made a few adjustments before pressing the key. "P-3, P-3 come in, do you read, do you read?" Worthless waited for a response as the other four took note of the funny colors the Static Repulsar Field that was protecting the ship was emitting. Talby and the other three troopers knew the field was nearing the point where it would collapse.

"Com identify, com identify," was the response that came.

Again Worthless spoke into his mike. "Gareth squad at your perimeter, what is your situation?"

"Got the recall notice from the Gareth hours ago but have been unable to lift off. We were attempting to reroute power from the Repulsar generators but were attacked before liftoff was accomplished. We have liftoff capabilities but will need to drop the Repulsar Field before igniting the lift engines. If your team can draw their fire then we will be out of here in seconds, is that possible?"

Everyone heard what was said. "Tell them we are about to raise Hell but they only have one shot at this. As soon as we start our run tell them to drop the field and get the Hell out of here," Talby said.

Worthless transmitted the information he had just been told by Sergeant Talby and then waited for a reply. "We will wait until you make your attack before dropping the field; give us thirty seconds to make the necessary adjustments."

Talby knew his five man squad could make a diversion but it was doubtful it would last very long before they were all killed. "Alright listen up. Bax you take the left, Roark and Bedford go right. Me and Worth will go straight down the middle. As soon as we hit their lines I want you to fire everything we got. I want all smoke canisters fired immediately so we can give the Pod some cover." Talby never gave any orders other than that, he figured they would all be dead in a few minutes anyway.

As soon as they heard the generators on the Pod start to cycle up Talby and his team started their run. The five machines quickly broke from cover and were immediately fired upon. The creatures they were about to tangle with were completely enclosed in some sort of environmental armor. It was impossible to tell if what was inside each suit was big or small, no way to tell. The suits themselves were larger than a trooper by at least half.

Once the squad was clear of the Pod they fired all the smoke they had at their disposal. Baxter opened up with the thirty-caliber chain gun mounted on the front of his machine and took out two of the enemy that were manning some sort of self-propelled recoilless flat trajectory mortar that had been extremely effective against the Pod's static field. Now all incoming fire seemed to be directed at the speeders.

The two astro-sailors who manned the Pod saw the break in weapons fire and immediately dropped the field and diverted all power from the generators and the lone reactor to the lift engines. The Pod lifted with a roar and headed away from the battle with all possible speed. Within forty seconds it was out of range and heading in the general direction of the Gareth.

The four Speeders and the Scooter were covering as much ground as possible in the rough terrain in order to try and avoid as many of the incoming rounds as possible. None of the five had been directly hit so far although there had been several grazing shots. Talby activated his vox-net, "Looks like the Pod is away, let's turn and get the Hell out of here, breakoff and head for cover, repeat break off and head for cover."

Apparently whatever it was that occupied each of the enviro-suits hadn't expected the battle to be brought to them and their aim had been affected, but they recovered quickly. As the five machines the squad rode headed away the dirt around each was being kicked up by near misses. Just when it looked like the five would make it there was a vicious roar to the left. Bedford, who was nearest to whatever had made the noise, saw something large and ugly moving out of the trees and it was moving fast. It was a Quad. No more had he heard and seen the creature than it was on him.

The Quad caught up with the Speeder and managed to pace the machine. Bedford looked to his left and saw the most vicious face he had ever seen in his life, and the face was looking at him. It looked to be smiling as it ran alongside the Speeder. What looked like a smile was in reality a gaping mouth full of long sharp teeth. Worthless was about ten meters behind and on the same side as the Quad. He opened up with the small caliber Lead-Ejectors which were located on the left front side of his Speeder's handle bars. The shots seemed to have little or no effect on the racing beast.

Bedford accelerated and turned slightly right to try to put some distance between himself and whatever it was that raced along beside the speeder. Just as he thought he might be able to outrun the beast it took one gigantic leap and landed squarely on top of the speeder. Bedford managed to unholster his sidearm and point it at the mouth full of teeth, he was too late. His left arm was bitten off between the elbow and the shoulder, inside the creature's mouth the sound of the weapon, still held by Bedford's severed hand, fired twice. The loss of an arm was probably the luckiest thing that ever happened to Bedford.

As the speeder went down the Quad and Bedford were thrown clear of the machine. With his right hand Bedford activated the speeders self-destruct button, which was located on his ammo belt, in hopes of creating enough of a distraction to allow him to escape on one of the other machines. The speeder exploded in a hail of sparks and shrapnel. One small piece of shrapnel struck the Quad in the right shoulder and imbedded itself just under the thick scaly hide. The Quad reached up with its other hand and yanked the red-hot piece of metal free. The piece of shrapnel wasn't all that got yanked out; the transmitter for the neural implants, which had been damaged by the heat from the shrapnel, got yanked completely out as well. Suddenly the Quad had control of its thoughts and actions which were completely opposite from what they had been only seconds before.

The Quad stopped attacking Bedford; it also reached into its mouth and pulled out the severed arm which still held the gun. Bedford was already on his feet ready to continue the fight with only one arm when the Quad threw down the limb it held in its powerful hand, after that it turned and ran back into the foliage.

Bedford's augmented body was handling the trauma of losing a limb without going into shock but this wouldn't last long. The other three troopers and Baxter slowed to see if Bedford needed assistance getting on board another of the speeders, he didn't. He nearly ran to where Worthless sat and jumped on the back of the idling machine. As soon as he got the two brackets down where his feet would rest he slapped Worthless on top of his helmet and screamed to get the Hell out of there before another of the damned beasts showed up. In the excitement of Bedford losing an arm and his speeder getting blown up the squad had nearly lost site of the enemy. They were now coming into range again and their weapons were becoming more accurate.

As the three surviving speeders, and the scooter Baxter rode, headed for the tree line Roark raced by the spot where Bedford and the Quad had fought. As the others increased speed and made for cover Roark reached low to the ground and picked up Bedford's severed arm, to his amazement the hand still held the pistol. All four machines now quickly outpaced their attackers and headed for the safety of the Gareth and her Repulsar Pocket. Twenty-five minutes after the Pod had lifted off and escaped the five members of the rescue party made it to safety.

Worthless pulled his speeder with the badly injured Bedford to the strut elevator nearest to the Med-Bay. A team was already there with a gurney-table, a device used to transport injured personnel that were unable to walk. Bedford had used all the adrenalin and fluids his battle-armor contained and was now going into shock. As soon as he was strapped to the gurney-table he was hooked up to two different fluid pumps and the flow was set for maximum.

The pain receptors in his severed stump were just now beginning to send the painful signals to his brain that he was hurting, and hurting bad. He could even feel the pain in his missing left arm, phantom pain if you will. The Med-Bay was staffed by a team that fell under the realm of the Astro-Meditorium. They were not Astro-Sailors or Deep-Space Troopers. This was a branch of service that took no orders from either Captain Simms or Major West; they served Mama-Seven and took orders from the Super-Computer and nothing else.

Roark unstrapped the arm from his speeder and hurried it to the Med-Bay. The sidearm was still clutched in Bedford's dead hand and the grip proved more than anyone could undo. The Med-Tech staff would know how to make the hand release the weapon.

As soon as Bedford was in the Med-Bay he was transferred to an automated surgical table. His bloody armor was removed and placed in a decontamination locker; it would remain there until foreign life sign scans were completed. Whatever the creature was that attacked the trooper might have left behind some nasty little germs and this would need to be dealt with before any further contamination resulted.

Mama-Seven pulled up all the sonic charts of Bedford and began to do current and historical data comparisons. The severed arm was placed on a separate table adjacent to the one the wounded trooper occupied. Bedford's vitals were quickly stabilized and his brain waves that dealt with pain were interrupted, he was now fully aware of everything that was happening but felt absolutely no pain.

In the last three hundred years advancements in the field of medicine had taken an unusual turn, sound was used, or had a part in, nearly all injuries, illnesses, and recoveries. Shortly after the beginning of the twenty-sixth century a noted scientist, one that wasn't even associated with the field of medicine, discovered that every organ of the body emitted a functioning sound. Research would later prove that all soft tissue also produced sound at very low levels, much lower than the organs. As the decades passed it was discovered that even bone structure was sound producing, especially the joints.

It didn't take long before the technology of sound mapping was developed. One of the most amazing discoveries was the fact that every human produced a unique footprint of sound. That footprint could be digitized and stored for future use. There was also a model comparison that everyone's digital footprint could be compared against to find any abnormalities.

As the stump of Bedford's left arm was being cleansed and the damaged muscle and nerve endings realigned, the same thing was being done to the severed arm. Mama-Seven had already begun scans on both Bedford and the arm; the two were now being realigned robotically. As the arm was being slowly reattached by any number of surgical robots another machine was photo layering living tissue into the areas where the most severe trauma had occurred. Within ninety minutes the arm was completely realigned and reattached. Three hours later and a protective layer of synthetic skin was sprayed over the wound site.

Bedford was brought out of his surgical coma and given fluids orally to keep him from getting nauseated. The last part of the treatment would take a full hour, the re-spliced bone would be radiation treated to bond the super tough glue. After that he would be put on twenty-four observation, during this time adjustments would be made to all nerve and muscle tissue that had been damaged and repaired. Any bacteria that developed would be destroyed sonically. Thirty-six hours after his arm had been bitten off he would be back on regular duty with absolutely no lasting effects. His arm would actually be slightly stronger than before. There would be no lasting effects other than the increased strength in that arm; even the scar would go away after three of four more sonic treatments.

The first words Bedford spoke after the attack were in the form of a question, "Feels good as new, what kind of upgrades did you install?"

It was an expected question from a trooper who had just had major reconstructive surgery. One of the other troopers, a man named Simon Burgoff, had been injured and repaired so many times in the past that he was now called Si-Borg for short. He was now the most powerful trooper on the Udom-Gareth. His upgraded skeletal and muscle segments were by far the most advanced of anyone in the entire army. Even the back-up pump that assisted his human heart was state of the art. Si-Borg, it was estimated, was over twenty percent machine.

Another part of the upgrades Si-Borg had received included the reinforcement of his major skeletal segments, the spinal column in particular. His strength, already well above average, was enhanced to the point that he was considered the strongest human to ever live. His level of endurance was now to the point that no one else in all of Earth Forces Command could keep up with him during training, not even the newer and much younger recruits.

Outside, Baxter and the other three troopers were briefing Major West and Captain Simms on the encounter with the alien landing force. Most troublesome was the description of the Quad. As Talby recounted the story Baxter spoke, "Excuse me Major, I might have something to add to the discussion about the creature that attacked Bedford."

West looked at the hulking Bax and nodded for him to continue. Baxter said, "There was once a race that occupied another planet that shared our orbit many centuries ago. The orbit of the two planets had grown farther and farther apart every solar cycle until finally the two traveled separate paths. We have historical data of the event if you would like to dig further. Our planet here is the one that traveled away from the star we once shared."

Simms looked at Baxter, "I don't see how that has any bearing on the situation at hand."

"Oh but it does Captain, it does. On the other planet there was a race of creatures known as Quads. What attacked us this morning was a descendant of that very same race," Baxter said.

"Are you sure what you saw was one of these Quads Baxter?" West asked.

"I am very sure Major; as I said we have all the historical data if you would like to see for yourself." Baxter told him.

"How do you know this if at the time neither your race nor this race of Quads had the technology to travel through space?" Captain Simms asked.

"We communicated with them, not visual communications, audio only. We exchanged information for many centuries until finally the orbits of our two planets changed and took us on our separate paths. Our conversations back then are full of descriptions of the Quads and their society."

Simms thought about this and then decided to find out more from the historical data Baxter spoke of. "Major, contact General Abbot and fill her in on the skirmish, also ask for any information they have on this race of Quads, we need to know what we're up against."

Simms thought a moment before adding, "Inform the general of the advance party that attacked the pod. See how she intends to counter." With that Simms turned and headed toward the strut elevator, he had repairs to tend to.

As the captain entered his command bridge there was a report coming in on one of his monitors. It gave updated details of damages and repairs. As he quickly scanned he was pleased to find that most of the screens and the Repulsar Pocket had absorbed the worst of the alien weapons fire while in deep space. The freefall and subsequent crash landing had been mostly caused by the Lava-Slug weapon. The ship had been severely damaged but repairs were progressing at an accelerated pace now that all his repair crews were being supplemented by Major West's troopers.

"Chief Engineer Layne report to the bridge!" Captain Simms ordered. He wanted to hear what the Chief had to say about repairs. Data-Screen Reports were good but there was a better feel for how his ship was doing when it was told by someone with the skillset of Layne. Due to the size of the ship, and where Layne was when he was summoned, it took him a little over eleven minutes to make it to the Command Bridge.

Once Layne entered the bridge he snapped to attention, "Chief Engineer Layne reporting as ordered sir."

Simms turned to see Layne standing rigidly at attention. The Engineer was drenched in sweat and his uniform had the disheveled look of a man who had been assisting his men in the repairs. There was a tear in one of his shirt sleeves and specks of blood covered the shirt and part of the collar. As an officer Layne was forbidden from taking part in actual repairs, he was to oversee the operation. More than once he had been reprimanded for just such action while serving under a different captain. Simms knew he had one of the best engineers in the fleet and also knew Layne felt it was more his ship than the captain's. In a way it was his ship, his ship to repair and keep running even after getting pounded by and unknown enemy using as of yet never before seen weapons.

"At ease Layne, I saw the repair reports but wanted to hear it from you personally. Give it to me straight, how bad did we get hit and how long before the Gareth is flightworthy?"

Layne spread his feet a bit and relaxed his shoulders. He pulled a red bandanna from his left front trouser pocket and mopped his sweaty face. "We got hit by quite a few rounds before we made our hard landing. As far as I can tell the landing caused about fifteen percent of the damage my crews are working on. The most extensive repairs are for scald and flash fires at the point where we took the molten hit. That particular section will require space dock for repairs. We have been able to rework the damaged repulsar arrays so the static field will protect the entire ship but another direct hit there with the same kind of weapon could be disastrous. All other lesser repairs are being completed with the assistance of Mama-Seven and her Micro-Repair cells."

Exactly how bad is the section that took the molten hit?" Simms asked.

"The outer pressure hull was pushed back and a portion burned through. The next hull took a sizable hit but for the most part held."

Simms thought about this. If the Gareth took another direct hit in that same section then there could be a sizable hull breach, possibly a ship killing hull breach. "What can be done to make that particular section as resilient as the rest of the outer hull. I don't want to go into battle with a weakened hull."

Layne thought a second and then said, "If Mama-Seven could re-task more of the Micro-Repair Cells to that section then we can probably bring that portion of the hull back to ninety percent. I can also add more repulsar array diodes to that section to make that part of the pocket more resilient. That should make the hull strength in that area as strong as the rest of the ship."

Captain Simms considered the prospect of having his outer hull as good as new. "That sounds great, make the necessary repairs as mentioned. What is the status of our weapons?"

Layne again wiped sweat from his forehead, this time on the back of a shirt sleeve. "Weapons are nearly back to full captain. It seems the Static Repulsar Pocket handled everything pretty well except for the molten slug I spoke of earlier; I believe Mama-Seven calls it a Lava-Slug. I have teams running diagnostics now."

So far Simms had gotten a very good report but he saved the most critical question for last, "How about propulsion and lift capabilities?"

"That is really the only good news from the attack. Our engines were undamaged, we can acquire lift off velocity without much trouble at all. The only variable is the particulate in the atmosphere. I have crews working now to enhance intake filtering to get out the worst of it. Our engines are also being fitted with increased Particle Reduction Arrays. Once we are clear of the planet's atmosphere the Reduction Arrays can be disengaged to bring propulsion back up to one-hundred percent."

Captain Simms was pleased; his ship had survived a concentrated attack by an unknown enemy with advanced weapons and came through it with her fighting abilities still mostly intact.

"There is one other matter I think you should be aware of sir." Layne said.

Simms looked at the engineer and asked, "What is it Layne?"

"I have run diagnostics on the ships that landed in the valley and compared them to the information Mama-Seven gathered on that force. It appears the alien fleet is using some sort of Sonic Propulsion. Readings taken just after the alien fleet came into range indicated a propulsion system that worked with sound."

The captain thought about this for only a second before asking, "Is that all the information we have on the enemy's drive systems?"

"No sir, after more analysis it was determined the drive system works by pitting two absolutes. On the one side you have a sound intensity that would range far higher than anything ever encountered, it could only be described as the noise a star would make if it exploded, the range is so high there is currently no rating to define it. On the other side of the scale you have a rating of zero, in other words Absolute Silence. The two are pitted against each other in a controlled way that we have yet to identify, its ingenious. The two extremes, once pitted against each other, create phenomenal opposition, in other words the two push away from each other."

The captain thought about this and wondered how it would affect the matters at hand. "What does this mean operationally?"

"We don't know how this will affect things in a running battle. Once we reach orbit and then engage we will be able to analyze their engine capabilities. I would assume the alien fleet is fast though captain, very fast. Where it comes into play now though is easier to predict. From all scans the ships they landed on this planet a few hours ago run on the same principle as their Capitol Ships in deep space. To put it bluntly captain, I don't think the ships they used to make it to the planet's surface will ever be able to reach escape velocity."

Simms liked what he had heard but needed a little more information. "What is it about their propulsion systems that would create this?"

"It is rather simple sir. Their engines can still produce the High-Side Sonic Propulsion but where they will have problems is on the Low-Side part of the equation. The atmospheric particulate contained in the outer reaches of the atmosphere is considerable and of such make-up that they will never be able to produce the Absolute-Silence needed by their lift engines. They can lift off and move around a bit but once they try to reach orbit their engines will seize up. It is my belief that our attackers are stranded here forever."

Simms considered this and knew it was another bit of luck for both his ship and crew. "I know this is a bit out of your area of specialty but do you think they have the means to communicate with their fleet."

Layne thought about this for only a minute before giving his reply. "If their means of communication are as unconventional as their engines then it would be hard to say. My best guess though is no. I don't think they can get a message to anyone with their fleet."

Captain Simms knew he would need to talk to his own comms specialist for the answer but he had always trusted the abilities of his Chief Engineer and wanted his input. "Thanks Layne, you are dismissed." As Layne headed back to his duties the captain headed for the communication center which was located two rooms back from the Battle Bridge. As Simms entered he was greeted with the low grade static and buzzing the comms crew was accustomed to. The man he needed to talk to was hunched over a bank of screens and he was wearing a set of headphones. Simms didn't interrupt but it didn't take long before he was noticed.

"Hello Captain, I was just about to go and find you." A man named Carson said. Carson wasn't the head of the comms unit aboard the Gareth but he was one of the best sound men in the fleet.

"Well Carson here I am, what have you got for me?"

"As you know the atmospheric layout of this planet is made up of some pretty nasty stuff. It is the kind of situation where you just about need a hard line to get any information in or out. This is good in one aspect, the enemy force that landed a few hours ago are cut off from their main fleet. I have detected repeated attempts by the aliens to break through to the ships that we know are out there but all they are getting in return is an echo."

Simms thought about this, he had heard the term before and knew pretty much what it meant; the attempts to break through to their fleet were failing. "Do you know what format their sound techs are using or for that matter do we know even what type of language they use?"

Carson really didn't know but was more than glad to share what he thought. "I have recorded all the transmissions and Mama-Seven is running comparison tests now. At last count she is able to pull one word out of seven from the recordings. I think once she hits one in four she will quickly understand everything they are saying. Decryption and language analysis has its own set of unique dynamics, the more you find out the faster the rest falls into place, shouldn't be long now sir.

"We have also isolated their unit transmissions. Everything they are saying between the ships on the ground and the force that attacked the pod is also being recorded. Mama-Seven has been able to figure out more of those transmissions than the ones directed at the fleet; it seems to be a simpler dialect. Apparently some of the forces they use on the ground are of another species than their regular fleet personnel. It appears the creatures manning the ships are of a distinct and unified class while the Assault Troops are made up of several different species including a few of the same ones that are onboard the fleet circling in orbit. It is a complicated arrangement; this might mean they use a much more ferocious species as troops than the ones that actually fly the ships."

"Layne says they are stranded here, the engines on their craft will never be able to make orbit. If that is correct and what you say works out to be true then they are never leaving this planet alive." Simms said.

"But why would they attempt a landing if they suspected their ships could never leave Captain?"

Simms pondered this for a few seconds, "It was a suicide mission. Whoever is up there wanted to make sure there were no survivors of the Gareth. If we were dead they thought the ambush of the Earth Forces ship would go as unexplained. That would give them time to learn where in the galaxy Earth was located." Both men stood and pondered what Simms had just said.

"There is another problem associated with our crash landing, when the Star Ranger crashed here over three-hundred years ago this was a peaceful planet belonging to Baxter's ancestors and no one else. One reason this planet has remained under the radar for so long is due to the violent atmospheric conditions that exist. It kept everything hidden. Now if any of the alien force that landed here makes it back into orbit and are picked up then it would be a sure bet that this planet would soon be overrun by the same species that attacked the Gareth. General Abbot notified me not more than an hour ago, she has been directed to destroy the attacking force to make sure such an event doesn't take place. If we manage to make orbit it will appear as if we were able to repair the Gareth on our own and this planets secret will still be intact," Simms said. Carson, without hesitation, agreed.

Simms went back to the battle bridge and began the final preparations for the Gareth to lift off. It would be better if his ship was away before the enemy advanced within range. He would be leaving most of his Deep Space Soldiers behind, commanded by Major West, to help General Abbot deal with the enemy force that was now racing toward his position. He was a naval man and knew his battle waited for him just outside the planet's dense atmosphere.

There was a ground shaking rumble as the engines throttled up to fifty percent and slowly continued to increase. Simms was at his command console watching multiple monitors and displays. After a few seconds he realized he was white-knuckling the arm rests on his command chair, if the situation weren't so critical he would have laughed. The other six officers on the battle bridge were at their stations adjusting inputs and monitoring events as they unfolded. Mama-Seven increased power to the lift engines in five percent increments while analyzing tens of thousands of pieces of information per second. Any system that developed a variance outside the acceptable tolerances was adjusted back to five by five. If a system looked overstressed it was either managed back to normal or taken off line and replaced with one of the redundant back-ups.

Lift engines operated within acceptable tolerances and this was expected, these systems were never engaged during the freefall just after ambush. Anti-Grav generators were another story altogether. These systems had been pushed past their maximum safe operating levels just before the crash to try and lessen impact damage. Repairs had been ongoing since shortly after landfall until lift-off and it wasn't known if these systems would be able to generate the necessary lift to help the massive engines break gravity and reach escape velocity.

So far the Gareth was rising slowly. Warning claxons and bells were sounding everywhere but this was to be expected, the ship was still grievously damaged but functioning. The extra power that would have normally been used to operate the Static-Repulsar Field was being diverted to the lift engines, the Pocket wouldn't be activated to full until the ship had reached escape velocity, assuming she could. The pocket would be operated at just over twenty-five percent from liftoff until orbit.

There was a sudden shudder felt throughout the bridge. Mama-Seven instantly knew the problem was a malfunction on one of the Anti-Grav generators. After a quick analysis that system was separated from the rest of the Anti-Grav engines and put into shutdown mode. The vibrations immediately dissipated. Without the added lift of the single generator the Gareth rose more slowly, at the next five percent power boost she returned to the previous lift parameters. Simms knew he had just lost a substantial portion of his lift capabilities. If another generator failed the Gareth might need to land until both systems were repaired.

That would be a very bad event. The need to lift off now instead of when more repairs were completed was initiated by the fact that an enemy force of unknown strength was approaching fast and the Gareth needed to be away from any possible landside battle.

The plan was for the Gareth to lift off and climb to an altitude of two thousand meters, if that could be accomplished then the engines would reconfigure and the ship would begin to move forward. A limited Repulsar Pocket would be established as the giant ship ran parallel to the approaching enemy. ED would raise hell using the Perimeter Gatling's against the approaching enemy columns as they flew close enough to fire but hopefully fast enough to outrun any ordinance that might be directed back at the ATC.

It had been determined earlier that the bulk of Lieutenant West's Shock Troops would remain planet side to assist with the battle that was about to begin. There were four companies still on board consisting of thirty-two troops per company and these were there to deal with any possible boarders. If the Gareth was disabled in the upcoming battle and not totally destroyed then it was a distinct possibility that the enemy might try to capture the ship intact to try to learn everything they could about human technology.

The Gareth had a Ship Destruct protocol in place if severe damage or enemy capture seemed imminent. The protocol had four different variants depending on the situation.

1) Bio-Hazard or biological protocol breach in safe space. Rescue Crew; Jettison Mama-Seven and all lesser systems on board the Data-Capsule for later pick-up. ATC to be guarded until deemed possible to decontaminate and re-board. If unable to decontaminate initiate Ship Destruct.

2) Absolute critical systems malfunction in safe space. Rescue crew; Jettison Mama-Seven and all lesser systems on board the Data-Capsule for later pick-up. ATC to be guarded until deemed possible to re-board. If unable to re-board initiate Ship Destruct.

3) Absolute critical systems malfunction in hostile occupied space with possibility of rescue, board life pods and launch in general direction of rescue ships. Mama-Seven and all associated lesser systems are to remain onboard and initiate Ship Destruct for maximum effect on attacking fleet. In coordination with Ship Destruct, Mama-Seven and all lesser computing systems to be chemically destroyed.

4) Extreme Damage due to hostile action and no possibility of rescue, heavy battle related loss of life. Mama-Seven to continue fighting the ship until all options are exhausted. No life-pods launched, no survivors expected. Ignite engine reactor coils and initiate Ship Destruct for maximum effect against enemy. Result: Gareth and all aboard vaporized. Mama-Seven and all lesser computing systems reduced to ash prior to reactor coil ignition.

These four orders were ingrained into the operational thread of the Gareth, each and every man aboard, whether an Astro-Sailor or Deep Space Soldier, knew and accepted this. Most felt it was a relief, no one wanted to be jettisoned into space and captured by an alien species. This had actually happened more than a century earlier.

A small research vessel named the S. Hawking had become disabled in deep space. The drive system failed but all life-support remained functional. A rescue ship named the Graham was launched; it would take thirteen weeks for this second ship to arrive. One week before the rescue ship arrived all communications with the Hawking went silent, technicians onboard the Graham attributed this to mechanical failure but wouldn't know for sure until the Hawking was reached.

Once the Hawking was spotted the rescue vessel approached and attempted to hard wire into the disabled ships communication array. This was accomplished by way of a spacewalk by two of the Graham's comms officers. Once the link was activated all that could be heard aboard the Hawking was shallow breathing and this could only be heard in one of the cryo-tubes. This was baffling indeed, cryo tubes could not support a living human that wasn't in cryo-stasis.

After more than six hours of monitoring all the Hawking's systems it was decided to send over a four man pod and attempt a hard dock at a spot nearest the cryo section. All four men wore side arms and enviro-suits. Once the hard dock was accomplished another ship wide scan was performed before the seal between the pod and the Hawking was broken.

The second scan picked up the same shallow breathing and again it was coming from a cryo-tube. The seal to the outer door of the rescue pod was broken and air analysis was taken, the space between the two doors was not contaminated. The pressure door to the Hawking was then remotely set to open as the door to the rescue pod was re-sealed. The door of the Hawking slowly swung to full open, it was noticed through the observation port that the lights inside were still working and it seemed life-support was functional, there was no frosting of any of the equipment in the cryo-section.

After another quick environmental scan it was deemed safe to enter the Hawking. Two of the four men entered with weapons drawn and at the ready. A third held an atmospheric analyzer. The fourth remained in the rescue pod to reseal the two doors. Extreme caution was used as the three astro-sailors moved toward cryo-tube number forty-seven, the one that contained the survivor who had been picked up on the scans.

The ranking officer on this mission was a man named Amos Hollister, a twenty-three year veteran. This would make the seventh time he had led a relief team onto a damaged or stranded ship. The first six were routine in nature, injured crew with a few casualties. This one was starting to be anything but routine!

All three men wore rebreathers, devices that filtered out any number of contaminants during inhale and separated the carbon-dioxide that was exhaled saving the sixteen percent oxygen for the next inhalation. In this way less of the outside atmosphere was being used which should reduce the chance of a mishap.

Hollister kept an eye on his analyzer, the readings were showing safe but the air just seemed wrong. "Either of you able to identify what that smell is, my readings show safe?"

The taller of the other two men, a man named Porter spoke first, "Yeah I think I recognize it Sarge, I believe it's the sweet musty smell of decaying flesh."

The other sailor spoke nervously as he scanned his surroundings, "I agree, smells like death in here."

Hollister thought about this as he continued to scan his device, "The Hawking has state of the art atmospheric filters. I scanned the schematics before we headed over, there should be no smell at all unless the filters stopped working, that shouldn't be the case or something would have registered before we left the Graham."

The three men continued to advance toward cryo-pod number forty-seven. As soon as the three started down the left center isle of the cryo-compartment the smell got noticeably stronger. The first four tubes were sealed and empty, standard operating procedure for empty tubes. When not in use each tube ran constant simulations so they were always ready if needed. When they reached the fifth tube on the left it was also sealed but the light at the base strobed yellow which meant it was occupied. Hollister stepped to the side of the tube to glance inside; this tube had never registered any life-signs during the scans that were conducted by the Graham. Maybe just a malfunctioning light at the base that thought the tube was occupied when it really wasn't.

What Hollister soon learned was that the tube was occupied, but by what. There was a body there and it resembled a human body, the kind you saw as an elementary student in some of the biology books that always haunted his memories. It was the type of body that first year med students might study in order to learn the art of their trade. This body looked like it had been stripped of its hair and skin, different muscle groups also looked like they were missing parts from one side of the body but on the other side the muscles were still there and attached properly. All the organs were visible as if they had been exposed for study, there was no sign of blood or liquid that might normally have been seeping from wounds or exposed organs.

Hollister looked again at the readings on his analyzer, all readings were in the green and this was nearly as troubling as the partial body in the cryo-tube. Another look seemed to verify that there was no apparent trauma to the body; it was as if everything had been surgically removed. As Hollister continued to inspect the remains the other two sailors moved slowly down the cryo-room. When they reached tube forty-seven the two were shocked at what they found.

"Sarge, you better take a look at this." Porter said.

Hollister had been so focused on the remains in cryo-tube number five that he hadn't noticed the other two sailors weren't with him, they were a good forty feet farther down the room. This wasn't standard procedure in a situation like this and he would bring it up once they were safely back aboard the Graham. Thirty seconds later and Hollister was standing beside the other two men. The first thing Hollister thought about was the look of amazement, and horror, on the faces of the two sailors. When he turned toward the cryo-tube the same look took over his own face.

Lying in the tube was something similar to what had been observed in tube five. It was a man's body stripped of all hair and skin. The muscles and organs were exposed and in the open for everyone to see. The difference with this tube was that the body inside was still alive. The lungs expanded with each breath. The heart beat calmly and steadily. The most astonishing thing of all were the eyes. They swiveled in their sockets as they observed the three men standing on either side of the tube. It looked like a cadaver lying in there, but one that was still alive.

Slowly the jaw and tongue moved "Help me."

Hollister and the other two men were shocked back to the here and now. "My god, can you hear me?" Hollister asked.

The lidless eyes moved to Hollister. "I can hear you, thank God you made it."

"What happened to you, who done this?"

Again the eyes focused on Hollister. "Don't know, we were attacked, after our engines failed most of the crew escaped in the life pods but I don't think they got far. The rest of us were taken prisoner and kept on board. They done terrible things to me, I don't know about the others. I need help, can you help me? Please help me."

Hollister wanted to tell him something that would help, something that would soothe a little of the trauma the man must be feeling right now but no words came. "How long have they been gone, the crew, how long ago were they taken?" Hollister knew long range scans had detected only empty space when they approached the Hawking.

"Only a few hours, most of the crew escaped weeks ago. Me and a few of the ones that were left behind were kept in one of the holding bays. They brought us out one by one, I was the last. They were autopsying us while we were still alive, I could hear some of the screams. I think they were nearly done with me when they rushed away, I assume they boarded their transport and are catching up with their assault ship as we speak."

"Are you in any kind of pain?" Hollister asked.

After a short thought there came an answer. "None at all, I actually feel better than usual."

Hollister stepped away from the cryo-tube and made contact with the Graham. "Looks like whatever happened here is over, we missed it. Ship was boarded but the attackers are gone. Send over the scanning crew, this ship needs to be completely searched for any other survivors and to make sure whoever did this hasn't left any nasty little surprises onboard. I also need a medical team sent over, we found one survivor and there may be others, Hollister out." That last remark was still rattling around in Hollister's head; for the sake of whoever else might still be onboard he really hoped they weren't still alive if they were in the same shape as the man in the tube.

The scanning team that arrived shortly after Hollister made the request completed their work in record time. The captain of the Graham knew his ship might be in danger and wanted everything to go by the book. Thirty-six men were chosen from the Graham's crew to take over the Hawking. It was quickly determined that the drive system on the ship had been disabled by a long range disrupter of some sort. It was easy enough to replace the burned out components and get the drives up and running.

The one piece of the puzzle that didn't fit was that the man found in the cryo-tube said whoever attacked the ship and took it over had been there for weeks. The Graham had been in communication up until seven days prior and nothing had been out of the ordinary. The captain needed some answers so he asked Hollister to get some more information if he could from the only survivor.

Hollister went to the cryo-section and asked one of the medical staff if he could ask a few question? Once the medical staff saw what they were up against it was decided to leave the tube shut and try to determine a course of action, if they opened the tube the man inside might instantly die, more information was needed.

As scans were being conducted and equipment set up Hollister was allowed a few minutes with the man in the tube. "As you can see the medical team is here and they are going to do what they can for you. I want to ask you a few questions if you feel up to it."

Again the lidless eyes looked at Hollister. "I feel up to it; as a matter of fact I feel no pain at all. What do you want to know?"

Hollister wondered if the man really knew how bad his condition was. "First of all what is your name?"

"My name is Commander Holt; I've been stationed on the Hawking for a little over three years."

Hollister had brought along a data-slate and quickly entered the information. The conversation was also being recorded, both audio and visual and was being transmitted to the Graham in real-time. "Commander Holt, the Graham was in contact with the Hawking up until about a week ago but you said earlier that the ship was taken over long before that. Can this be explained?"

The man named Holt thought for only a second before speaking. "They used some sort of voice synthesizer. Two of our comms men were forced to talk for a few minutes and all this was recorded by the synthesizer. After that the aliens could message you in the voice of either of the two men and you couldn't tell it from the real thing. The two comms men were the first to be autopsied, I guess the aliens couldn't take the chance of them sending any messages beside the ones they wanted sent. I heard their screams from the holding bay where me and the others were kept."

Hollister had just found the answer the captain was looking for. He knew the medical staff needed to work on Holt so he decided to end the interview. "Well Commander, that is all I need right now, I'll let you rest." With that he stood and walked away, he really didn't want to look at Holt anymore anyway; it was like talking to something straight out of Hell.

Once the medical team had all the equipment set up in the cryo compartment, the chief of the Graham's med-bay came over. He already had a preliminary assessment which had been accomplished remotely when the Graham's master mainframe had hard linked with the mainframe on the Hawking. All crew medical records were scanned and the one for Commander Holt was separated and compared with the reading from cryo-tube number forty-seven.

What Doctor Lance Bevin found in the tube was expected but still astonishing. In all his years in space he had never come across a situation even remotely similar. The lack of hair and skin was astonishing. The fact that there were no fluids visible seemed to be medically impossible.

In his astonishment he was speaking out loud, to no one in particular but just to hear his own voice as if hearing it might make it seem more real. "Skin, hair all removed from the patient. The interstitium is completely removed; I have never seen anything like it."

The interstitium is an organ that was first identified early in the twenty-first century. Parts of it had always been known separately until they were linked together and given organ status, the same as, say your lungs or heart. This particular organ works as a kind of shock-absorber for the other organs. It not only shields and protects the other organs but it is also a highway for both healing and disease. Once the organ was identified the scientific community immediately started work on reducing the ability of diseases, such as cancer, to use the interstitium as a means of moving to other parts of the body. Within ten years this information had nearly wiped out some of the most prolific human diseases of the age.

The knowledge of this new organ had always been there but never identified. It appeared when parts of the human body were removed the tissue of the interstitium collapsed and all you saw was a flattened compressed mass. The only way to identify the natural state of the new organ was to remove a small section from a living body, not an amount that would harm the living subject but enough to analyze. The sample was then flash frozen so the natural structure of the tissue would be preserved. Once that was done the sample was thinly sliced and observed under a microscope. Even then it took many years to agree that this was actually a new organ.

Dr. Bevin decided to leave Holt in the tube for the time being. He knew nothing could be done to replace so much of the missing tissue; Holt would soon die once he was subjected to a virus or bacteria. He had one other option that was both revolting and promising, it was an option that might just offer a glimmer of hope for the man.

The Symbiont Weapons Program had been established years earlier. The program was an effort to adapt portions of human tissue to robotic constructs. There had been differing degrees of success, with the primary problem keeping the human tissue stable and not allowing reactions to the constant metal contact. This had been mostly overcome with the development of new coatings for the metal and also new medicines to combat infections.

Dr. Bevin left his patient and headed for the comms unit of the Graham. He needed to report what he had in the way of a possible candidate for the new Weapons Program. Never before had there been an opportunity like this. There had been some severely wounded soldiers in the past that were used but these men died soon after being implanted in their robot hosts, most likely a combination of the shock of transfer and also the pre-existing wounds.

The situation of Commander Holt was unique. He really didn't have any trauma or at least any that was visible at this early stage. The major organs were intact and at the moment functioning at near perfect levels. It was as if everything that was left of Holt's body was nearly perfect. Anything that was removed wasn't really necessary for baseline survival of a human body. Of course as soon as any contamination entered the cryo-tube it would be a whole different story, Holt would become sick and soon die. The cryo-tube was currently acting as his skin which was the first line of defense against sickness.

In the one-hundred and twelve years following the discovery of Commander Holt's body and his subsequent insertion into an armored biped construct he was designated as a living weapon, one which was expected to operate as support for ground combat troops. He was now over a hundred and sixty years old and expected to live many more decades unless he met his fate in battle.

The battle armor he occupied was sort of a cryo-tube with weapons. It not only kept Holt alive but it also served as his arms and legs. Some wondered if he felt like a prisoner while entombed in the armor, when asked about this he only laughed. "Save your worries for those who need it. As for myself I have never felt more alive." Commander Holt was now a member of the Gareth's crew. He had been with the cruiser since she was christened.

The Gareth continued to climb as Mama-Seven managed the worst of the damage and malfunctions that plagued the damaged cruiser. Captain Simms waited for General Abbot to give the word. Both the ATC and the ground forces, consisting of two regiments of Abbot's troops along with a portion of Major West's troops, would attack the approaching enemy. The heavy equipment for West's troops was still on board the Gareth, the strut elevator that was designated to lower the tanks and assault transports was never repaired, there just wasn't enough time.

Once the Gareth reached the two-thousand meter mark of her ascent Mama-Seven held the giant cruiser in a hover as she ran diagnostics. A limited Static Repulsar Pocket was established by ED in preparation for the fly by on the opposing force. Nothing more could be done until General Abbot's radar and scanner crew found a desirable gap in the planets dense swirling atmosphere for the cruiser to escape.

Captain Simms requested a secure link with Abbot and as soon as it was established he was notified. "General, how are your atmospherics coming along?"

Abbot immediately responded, "Looks like you have an area opening up thirteen-hundred kilometers to the northwest. Optimum escape vector should be in seventeen minutes; we will have the exact time and coordinates locked down in two minutes. You may start your attack run in thirty seconds and then head northwest; I will notify Mama-Seven of the exact location of the Atmospheric." The Atmospheric Abbot spoke of was the eye of the storm so to speak. It was a spot in the atmosphere where a ship could make orbit without actually flying through the dense particle filled atmosphere. There were always several eyes around the planet but they formed and disappeared in only minutes, plus they moved at several hundred kilometers per hour. Locating one and then flying through it was something General Abbot's forces had always studied but never actually tried.

Simms strapped himself in, as did the rest of the bridge crew. "Engines to ten percent, Repulsar pocket to fifty, proceed on my mark." Simms watched his screens and at the exact thirty-second mark gave the order.

ED was plugged in to his pain receptors and itching for a fight, he wanted a little payback for the damage that had been inflicted on the Gareth during the ambush. He spooled up all the ground attack guns and waited for Mama-Seven to give him full release.

The Gareth moved forward as if in slow motion. A ship the size of the cruiser hovering so close to the surface of a planet seemed more like a moon than something man-made. Mama-Seven piloted the cruiser toward the advancing force of the enemy all the while monitoring for any hostile aircraft that might be in the area. It was suspected the enemy would deploy some sort of ground support attack fighters and that is exactly what happened.

Three minutes after the Gareth began her attack run radar picked up multiple blips approaching and accelerating to attack speeds. ED immediately countered with his air defense Lead-Ejectors. All were set for seventy-three percent rate of fire to prevent overheating. Mama-Seven cycled the Static Repulsar Pocket on the attack side to seventy percent. This wasn't enough to stop the fighters but it would render them powerless once they flew through the two meter thick field.

ED was tracking two groups of bogies. One heading directly for the Gareth and the other veering off and heading toward General Abbot's ground forces. Abbot was immediately notified, her aircraft were already in a hover pattern to intercept at ten-thousand meters.

Abbot had two squadrons aloft with three more in reserve not counting the fifty planes that were stationed deep in underground bunkers to be used for replacements. These were planes that resembled aircraft from the mid to late twenty-first century. They were fast and stealthy and carried both air to air missiles and guns. Her pilots had experience against computer simulations only; this would be the first time any of them had actually flown against a real enemy.

Simms could hear the chatter from the pilots as they prepared to engage the enemy.

"Abbot here, what does it look like up there?"

"Multiple bogies inbound to your position General. I count four wings of fifteen craft each, contact in sixty seconds." One of the squadron leaders said.

"Any idea of their capabilities?" Abbot asked.

The same voice spoke again, "Not yet, they look fast and seem to be well armed. My computer indicates a weapons lock." Before the transmission ended there was the sound of the jets engines going into afterburner. The fighters were just now engaging. Abbot would know soon if her tiny air force was a match for the enemy.

General Abbot was in her mobile command center which was just behind the leading edge of her armor and troop transports. She was monitoring multiple screens and also had audio from her weapons control officer.

"Enemy is still ten kilometers out general and advancing at thirty KPH." Abbot heard in her headset. At the moment this wasn't the battle she was worried about, it was the air encounter.

"Abbot here, I want Blue Squadron in the air to lend support. Until we know what we are up against I want our numbers to be at least comparable." With these twenty additional fighters she would now have sixty aircraft committed against the sixty that she knew were now preparing to attack her own forces.

As the additional squadron prepared to take off two more anti-aircraft batteries were brought on line. These were self-propelled rocket launchers that fired multiple small fast missiles that could track and follow while also identifying friend from foe. What good was a high tech weapon if it stood as much chance of shooting down your own aircraft as the enemy? The fact that half of the sixty enemy craft were heading for the Gareth made no difference to Abbot, she wanted parity regardless of the enemy's tactics.

Simms was notified that a message was coming in from Abbot's weather techs, the coordinates were established for the Atmospheric and the Gareth needed to be heading in that direction.

"Alright gentlemen we have the escape coordinates, lets hit these bastards hard and then head for orbit." Power was increased to the engines as Mama-Seven plotted the Gareth's escape. ED had a complete picture of the enemy's ground forces and also the approaching fighters. The fighters made it to the Gareth first; ED spooled up his Quad-Fifty Lead-Ejectors and tracked the fighters as they approached.

When the first of the Quad-Fifties opened up ED felt the vibrations from the recoil, he was monitoring as the stream of ordinance headed for the fighters, he wanted to know what effect it would have on the enemy. His radar and visual showed near perfect impacts on the approaching aircraft. At first nothing happened and ED wondered if his Quad-Fifties would have any effect on the enemy aircraft. His rounds were strobed in four round bursts and these were armor piercing rounds that could penetrate reactive armor.

Just as ED was about to cease fire for lack of effect there was a pop and then smoke coming from the aircraft he had targeted. ED checked his readings of the encounter and was pleased to find out the reason his initial rounds weren't effective, the aircraft had static-shielding that was similar to the Static-Repulsar Pocket the Gareth used. That was why his initial rounds seemed to have no effect. It took six strobes of four rounds each to overwhelm and penetrate the static-shielding and the last strobe grouping actually punched through and made contact with the plane itself. After three seconds the aircraft was completely shredded and its end came in the form of a terrific explosion.

ED's weapons were now given free reign as more and more enemy aircraft came into range. Within two minutes what was left of the attacking force broke off and headed in the direction of General Abbot's troops. ED had won the first round and now looked forward to meeting the ground component of the attack.

As the Gareth proceeded it didn't take long before the enemy's lead armor came into range of the Quad-Fifties. ED opened up on the troop transports first and then sprayed the attacking tanks. As the Gareth passed alongside the burning column ED dropped three five-hundred pound sonic detonation devices in a spread pattern. These weapons were so powerful they were timed to detonate two minutes after the cruiser was clear of the spread pattern drop area. Each had the effect of a twenty kiloton nuclear device but without the radioactive fallout. Within one hour after detonation the area was safe to enter without fear of contamination.

Once the Gareth cleared the spread ED allowed the two minute detonation of the three devices. There wasn't the usual mushroom cloud or flying debris associated with atomic devices, only an ever spreading cascade of sound that killed everything in its path. The effect was total, the attacking force was obliterated.

Mama-Seven monitored the battle and came to a startling conclusion; the weapons used by humans had always been arrayed around the use of concussion and penetration devices. The enemy she was now facing might be well equipped to fight in space but were very limited in any land engagement, or at least this was how it seemed. This in itself led her to believe the creatures that occupied the enviro-suits were not fearsome, at least in a physical sense. They had lost the strong physical features that had always been so important to armies throughout the Earth Colonies sector of the galaxy.

General Abbot monitored the results of the Gareth's flyby on the opposing army. The damage was impressive. With that portion of the battle now over, at least for the time being, it was only a matter of dealing with the aircraft that were approaching her fighters. While the air battle was shaping up she ordered one regiment of troops to advance at speed to the landing site and secure all the craft that were situated there. Any survivors were to be treated as prisoners of war, if there were any survivors. It would be great if there were so that something could possibly be learned about this new alien species. Also, the Quads were to be either rounded up and placed under guard or killed if they continued to be hostile. Abbot suspected they were more or less slave soldiers instead of paid mercenaries. If that were truly the case then it might be possible to work out some sort of cease fire with the beasts. Scans had indicated the creatures were intelligent and hopefully peaceful once they were taken from under the influence of their keepers.

The regiment moved out at once in attack formation alpha. One squad of fast troop transports with limited heavy weapons to secure any of the remaining hostiles. If stiff resistance was encountered it was to be bypassed and then dealt with by the heavy tanks and follow-up infantry that would be the second phase of the advance. Two hours after the flyby of the Gareth the squad of Shock Troops reached the site of the sonic weapons drop and was immediately impressed with the devastation. None of the fearsome Quads were found; they had already been there and by now were back at the drop-zone preparing to head off into the bush.

A small portion of the heavy equipment possessed by the enemy was still intact and unharmed. The vegetation around the drop area grew as if nothing major had happened there; it swayed gently in the soft afternoon breeze. The one thing out of the ordinary was the envirosuited soldiers lying about. When the sonic weapon detonated it was as if every soldier had simply fallen in place. The units that had been hit by the Quad-Fifties on the Gareth had stopped burning by now; sonic weapons can stop a fire instantly.

If Abbot was impressed with the ground component of the operation, she was going to be extremely pleased with the effect her fighters had on the approaching enemy aircraft. At first the two air forces seemed about equal in speed and firepower but soon the Fourier's planes began to get the upper hand. Enemy planes began to take fire and fall from the sky at a high rate. Soon the battle was over. General Abbot knew her men were extremely well prepared for air to air combat but never expected such results so early in the engagement. Another thing that no doubt had an effect in the encounter was the atmosphere. Abbot's jets were designed for this environment. The enemy might have lost more and more of their aircrafts abilities as their engines became clogged. After fifteen minutes it was reported that no enemy aircraft remained, both the land and the air battle were now over.

The three rescue ships had launched from Firebase Triton as soon as the indigenous rebellion was put down and some additional provisioning for the crews long journey was completed. The trip to the intercept site of the Udom-Gareth would normally take nine months but this was deemed a rescue mission and the ships would be traveling at more than double their normal Slip-Space cruising speed. For this reason it had been deemed that all personnel, whether Astro-Sailor or

Deep-Space Soldier, would not be entering the cryo-chambers. It had also been discovered by Mama-Five that there was a high probability of sabotage done to the tubes on the Gareth prior to her sailing from the Firebase. This reason in itself was enough to warrant the exclusion of the tubes until further scans and diagnostics could be completed.

The engine drive crystals that powered the three ships would be degraded at a higher rate than normal due to the enhanced speed requirements for the journey. An extra set was included with the additional provisions for the crew. It had been determined by Mama-Five that the new crystals would be installed into the drive engines near the end of the journey, just before Transition at the end of Slip-Space. In this way all three vessels would be at full power if they met up with the same fleet that had attacked the Gareth. All three ships were filled to capacity with the extra barriers that were used to insulate the drive crystals creating their own unique set of spacing requirements. Without the added insulation the crystals would degrade on their own and be nearly useless when needed.

One of the main reasons crew members were put into cryo-sleep during long duration flights was to reduce the amount of food it would take to sustain them. A body held in cryo-stasis used no energy and therefore needed no food. A person not in cryo-sleep would need approximately thirty-five hundred calories per day and this multiplied by the number of crew on the three ships constituted quite a large amount of provisions for the fourteen weeks needed to make the trip. The storage bays of the three ships were filled to capacity with the engine crystal containers and additional food. There were also crates stacked in passage ways and even in the crew quarters. One of the astro-sailors, who happened to be an ancient history buff, compared the interiors of the ships to the interiors of German U-Boats used back in the mid-twentieth century. No one else knew what he was talking about but agreed that things were getting crowded. This problem would solve itself as the trip progressed and the provisions were consumed.

One area of the ship that was deemed off limits for excess storage was the combat training bays. The Sergeant At Arms strictly forbade any storage in those areas. If the three ships were headed into combat and possibly a landing on an uncharted planet then he expected the troops to train extensively during the trip. The bays were designed to accommodate two squads at a time. Full on battle simulations could be conducted under different environments and conditions. The squads that weren't using the training bays would be assigned to the weight and cardio training rooms. Once the three ships dropped out of Slip-Space and began the Transition to normal time the soldiers onboard would be prepared to make a hot landing on a planet or, if worse came to worse, be ready to repel boarders. Space had always proven to be a dangerous place and the area they were heading into was shaping up to be formidable if the loss of the Gareth proved to be correct.

Keeto Three had observed the encounter between his troops and the small squad the humans had sent out to recon his position. He was disturbed that the short lived battle hadn't produced any casualties among the humans. One member of the recon group had apparently been injured when a Quad had gotten close enough to bite off a limb. The injured human had managed to ride away on another of the strange vehicles the human soldiers used. An unmistakable fact was that one of the humans looked different than the rest, far different. He was larger and rode what seemed to be a much more massive machine than the others. Keeto's science tech had been working on identifying the creature but so far all of the specie identification charts and programs had come up with nothing.

The weapons the humans used seemed to be adequate but not extraordinary. The one takeaway from the encounter was the use of some sort of masking device that partially hid their approach and also assisted them in getting away. The Sokari had never used such a primitive device or tactic; it had always seemed beneath them. The device apparently put some sort of particulate into the atmosphere that prevented the Sokari from seeing them with the naked eye, whatever it was seemed to dissipate rapidly. The particulate didn't seem to be a weapon in itself because none of the humans were affected. This was either because the substance was harmless or because it dissipated so rapidly. Keeto notified his onboard science team to gather samples as soon as the area was secure.

Shortly after the encounter with the human recon squad Keeto ordered the assault to take place on the position of the human ship. He knew now that the element of surprise was lost; they knew he was here and they knew where his position was. This was a troubling thought. If the humans had been so grievously damaged by the Sokari fleet during the battle in space then how were they able to find him so easily if their equipment was damaged or destroyed. It was apparent the human ship hadn't crashed at all, they had landed here and the majority of the systems aboard were still operational.

If that were the case, and Keeto had no reason to think otherwise, then he had to attack at once and destroy any survivors rather than postpone and allow them to prepare their defenses. His Shock Troops and armor would make short work of the humans. As he monitored his forces advance on the humans he had a thought. If a single Quad had been able to engage the recon unit the humans had sent out and severely injure a member of the team then why not release the rest of the Quads and allow them to attack before his own forces made it to the crash site.

Once the battle was finished he knew he would need to abandon any of the fearsome Quads rather than try to return them back to the fleet. One thing Keeto had learned about Quads was that they were dangerous at any given time but even more so immediately after a battle. Even the neural implants each of the beasts carried had little effect after they had been engaged in battle. Best to allow them to do as much damage as possible to the enemy and then abandon the rest rather than try to load them back onto their transports. Any survivors would be left here on the planet's surface forever.

Keeto gave the order for the four transports to offload their fearsome cargo and then direct the beasts in the direction of the human ship. After he gave the order he reconfigured his monitors to include the bay doors on the four Quad transport ships. No matter how many times he observed a Quad he still never passed up an opportunity to view them again.

As he watched the transports he saw a stream of vapor exit the frames of the massive doors. As the mist dissipated he could see the four doors, one on each transport, reconfigure into a ramp. After the doors were in position there was a pause, this was the most dangerous time if you were offloading Quads. After a while Keeto wondered if there had been some sort of problem. Suddenly one of the handlers ran down the ramp and circled behind the transport as if he were looking for cover or trying to hide. It was then that Keeto knew something had gone wrong with the unloading process.

No more had the handler hidden than one of the Quads stuck its head out, it looked around and sniffed the air. Keeto watched as its massive head turned in the direction in which the handler had fled. It slowly trotted down the ramp and sniffed the air again, Quads had an enhanced sense of smell, they could track by either sight, sound or smell with the latter being the most efficient.

Just when Keeto thought the handler was going to survive the Quad roared and then raced around the end of the ramp toward the back of the transport. The startled handler tried to escape but in his bulky enviro-suit he was limited in his options. It wouldn't have mattered; the Quad was on him in a flash. It grabbed him with its powerful front arms and then held him up in front of its face. As the handler tried to thrash free the Quad simply leaned forward and bit his head cleanly off.

As this was going on more Quads tramped down the ramp, they looked at the treat the first Quad was consuming and then looked about to see if there might be more for them. There weren't, all the other handlers had managed to make it back inside the pressure seal before the cage doors opened. The unfortunate one that now occupied a space inside the first Quads stomach had been unseen as the tech that controlled the safeties on the doors signaled all clear and released the locks.

The Quads were immediately sent a set of coded signals to move out in the direction of the human ship. The implanted receivers could only recognize certain codes and this was done to protect the Sokari soldiers. In years and battles past an opponent had been able to link into the implanted receivers of the Quads and reconfigure the electronic instructions of the beasts. The Sokari suddenly found themselves being eaten by the very beasts they had incorporated into the battle. All Quad instructions were now encrypted to hopefully prevent such a disaster from happening again.

Keeto watched as the hulking Quads galloped away and were soon hidden by the dense undergrowth that this planet was infested with. The home world for the Sokari, and also all the planets they had invaded, were covered with fungus and pretty much nothing else. This was by design, the Sokari had learned to cultivate the fungi that grew on their planets and could make almost any kind of dish they desired from it. Fungi grew at a fantastic rate and were harvested by huge machines that roamed the surfaces of all the planets they occupied. To see the infestation of plant life on this revolting planet was disturbing to a Sokari, they just couldn't see the use for the stuff.

Keeto pressed a few buttons again and reconfigured his monitors once more. He could now see his columns of troops and armor heading in the direction of the human ship. He could also pick up the outlines of the Quads as they headed in the same direction. This was all accomplished by means of any number of drones that had been launched prior to the first of the troop's departure.

Keeto sent a single drone in the direction of the human ship; he wanted to see just what it looked like. He had seen an outline on the Battle Bridge of the Rococo while the attack was taking place but this was only a glimpse, now he wanted to see everything firsthand. He could feel the excitement build as the drone passed over his column. Shortly he could see the top of the cruiser and then soon after he saw his first glimpse of what human technology really looked like.

The size of the vessel was a bit overwhelming at first but he discounted this due to the fact that any starship would look huge if it were resting on the surface of a planet instead of traveling through the void of space. He took note of the weapons arrays distributed along the center axis of the ship and also the proximal trolley system that must have been the means of aiming some sort of larger weapon. What Keeto was seeing was actually the outer edges of the Gareth's Sled-Guns, the same ones that had destroyed the Escort Gun Platforms Tec and Ser.

Keeto wondered if his stealthy drone had been detected, so far all sensors were showing zero. Unless the enemy had some new kind of sensor array then his little eyes in the sky would be invisible to the humans. As the drone hovered and then moved around the ship Keeto made sure everything was being recorded, not only was there going to be a video of this new species craft but also readings for energy output and energy consumption. Multiple scans were being run on the vessel and this would be gathered as soon as the drone made it back to its docking port. Scans were also being ran on the composition of the hull, it was important to scan the chemical and metallurgical makeup of the vessel to see if this ship, that had traveled from so far away, might possess something never seen before.

Suddenly the screens flashed out and the drone feed was gone. Keeto turned to the tech that controlled the outputs and navigation of the little drone to see what happened,

"Can you get the video back?" Keeto asked.

After a few seconds the tech turned to his commander, "Sorry sir, it seems the drone has been lost."

"What do you mean lost, was it discovered and shot down?" Was all Keeto could think of.

"No sir, it appears from my scans that it ran into some sort of shielding, it simply disintegrated mid-flight."

Keeto turned back to his monitors, this was truly bad news, the drone held valuable information about the human ship. "Were you able to harvest any of the technical information about the human vessel before it was destroyed?"

"No sir, everything that particular drone was gathering was held internally. We could only review the results of the flight after it made it back to its launch port."

"How about the video we received as it approached the vessel, we still have that right?" Keeto asked.

"No sir, the video can't be collected as a live stream due to the enhancers we installed to penetrate this planet's atmosphere. What we were getting was air wave vibration noise which we converted to digital, I can replay that but the enhancements degrade at a high rate and will soon be lost."

Keeto turned back to his monitor and pondered this bad news. "Can we send one of the other drones to collect the data?"

"We can sir but the same thing will happen if it hits the human vessels shielding."

Keeto thought this could be compensated for, "Send the second drone but keep it at a safe distance, I need that information." Better to have long range information than none at all Keeto thought.

The tech immediately sent a second drone in the direction of the human ship. Although he hadn't been responsible for the loss of the first drone he knew if he were on the Rococo's bridge with the murderous Seeboc Tang then he would most likely be dead now. Tang held everyone responsible no matter where the fault lay. Being here on this forsaken planet with Keeto Three as his commander was preferable to being on the Rococo.

Keeto watched as the feed from the second drone was routed to his monitor. It looked the same as the first feed and hopefully this could be recorded if the little machine made it back to its docking port. While it was making its way to the human ship Keeto sent the signal to have the two troops of Quads split up and head for the human vessel from two directions. His own troops and armor would take a third and more separate route toward the human ship. This was done for two reasons, first was to hit the humans from three directions at the same time and second, to keep the Quads as far away as possible from the Sokari soldiers.

With great anticipation Keeto watched his forces close on the human ship. At about four kilometers out he noticed some activity near the huge legs the vessel rested on. It seemed the humans were boarding and leaving the battlefield vacant. Were they afraid of his approaching forces and sought the safety of their armored spacecraft? If this was true then they were cowards. Why run and hide when there was a battle at hand had always been the Sokari way. No matter, the human vessel would soon be destroyed where it sat.

As these thoughts were going through Keeto's mind he noticed something else about the human ship. It appeared to be moving. Keeto enhanced his screen to full and leaned closer, yes the ship was lifting off. How could this be, some of the damage from the space battle was visible as hull damage and yet it was lifting off right there before his eyes.

"Contact the lead elements of our armor and have them open up on that ship," Keeto shouted to his comms officer.

Within seconds four of the heaviest of Keeto's tanks opened up with their heavy weapons. Two self-propelled heavy artillery pieces also added to the barrage. Keeto waited to see the impacts on the cruiser; he could wait till the end of time if he chose. The six rounds streaked toward the human vessel which was now at least three hundred meters off the surface of the planet. The expected impacts never came, the six rounds seemed to stop in mid-flight and then fall harmlessly to the ground, how could that be. Keeto suddenly remembered the death of the first drone, it had hit something unseen and been destroyed. The human ship was shielded in some way that could take out more than a helpless drone, it could stop a high velocity artillery round.

As Keeto was pondering this he noticed the ship start to move horizontally, it was heading toward his armored column. As it passed to the side of his troops he noticed three heavy devices falling in a straddling pattern around his troops and armor. When they hit he expected some sort of explosions but nothing happened. If this was an example of human technology then it was laughable. Within a very short time the human ship was several kilometers from his own forces and Keeto was furious, he had missed his opportunity to destroy his opponent on the ground.

As these thoughts were going through Keeto's scaly head there were three terrific explosions. Keeto looked at the screen expecting to see some sort of mushroom cloud rising from the spots where the humans had dropped the three devices, there was nothing, no smoke, no debris, nothing. The one thing he did notice was his troops on the field; they were falling as if some unseen hand was toppling them over. As he continued to watch he noticed that once his troops fell there wasn't any further movement of the enviro suits, he suspected the troops were dead before they hit the ground.

"What is happening?" Keeto asked.

"Sensors indicate some sort of sonic weapon has been detonated sir. Sound levels are nearly twenty times more than lethal." One of the techs said.

"I need a drone over the Quads; I want to see what effect the human weapon has had on them."

With a few quick adjustments a drone was soon over each column of Quads. Keeto watched as the shock wave reached the beasts fully expecting them to succumb in the same fashion as his Shock Troops, they did not. The Quads kept running but only for a few seconds before they stopped. The huge beasts quickly formed up in a huddle. It was as if they were conversing amongst themselves.

"Send a new command to the Quads; have them to search out any of the humans that might have been left behind." Keeto commanded.

Within minutes it was determined that the neural implants imbedded in the Quads shoulders had been destroyed by the sonic weapon the humans had used; the Quads were now free to do as they pleased. Both columns of Quads quickly formed up and then headed back toward the Sokari landing site. Keeto looked on in horror, "They are heading back here," he said.

"Keep trying to contact the Quads, head them in any direction you can other than here," Keeto demanded.

The urgency in Keeto's voice registered throughout the combat control room he occupied. As the tech attempted to repair the damage to the neural implants everyone in the room was suddenly struck with the fear that the Quads were now free thinking and out of control. Keeto knew he didn't have much time.

"Have all available flight personnel and any remaining troops to form up a defensive perimeter around the landing sight. Contact the Super-Draft fighters and ask for immediate assistance, have them to fire on any Quads they see," Keeto ordered as he continued to watch his screens.

The first of the Quads reached the Sokari landing craft within minutes; they were extremely fast when running. Keeto's hastily formed defenses opened up immediately. The first Quad took numerous hits before hitting the ground and sliding into the defensive perimeter. It wasn't quite dead and still had enough life left to tear into two unfortunate Sokari who were within reach of its powerful arms. As badly injured as the Quad was the first thing it thought of after killing the two was to eat the remains. Before that happened several more weapons opened up on the crippled beast and killed it where it lay.

It had taken the combined effort of seventeen heavily armed Sokari along with shoulder held rocket launchers and grenades to bring down a single Quad and this was at the expense of two lives. Just when the defenders began to have hope twelve more of the snarling beasts broke from the tree line and headed for them. The Sokari opened up with everything they had but it wasn't enough. Within minutes all the personnel were either dead or being eaten alive. Keeto watched in horror as all his troops and personnel were killed and most were devoured where they fell.

As soon as the Quads finished up with everyone that was outside the safety of the landing craft they turned their gaze on the ships. Surely Keeto would be safe in his command ship, he was wrong. The leader of the Quads was a beast named Rakit. He was the leader not because of his size, although he was larger than any of the others. He was leader because he was the elder of the clan that had been captured and imprisoned by the Sokari.

"Gather the weapons and form up ranks." Rakit ordered

As his troops armed themselves he looked over the Sokari ships stationed about the landing site. All were still manned and locked up tight, this shouldn't be a problem. By manning a perimeter the Sokari had furnished the Quads with the very weapons they needed to blast their way inside. The only problem was that once Rakit and his soldiers killed every last one of the Sokari they would be stranded on this planet, they couldn't fly the ships once they had captured them. The Quads had managed sub-orbit flight on their home world but had never gained the technology to reach the heavens. They had never been able to even launch a satellite that could orbit their home world although this was on the horizon; they were experimenting and gaining knowledge. Then the Sokari attacked and the once proud Quads were relegated to the status of warrior slaves.

As Rakit looked about at his surroundings, his first real look at the planet's surface since the implant in his shoulder had been disrupted by the sonic blast earlier, a thought occurred to him. He knew his home world had been destroyed when the Sokari attacked and made himself and so many of his countrymen slaves. Now he and what was left of the others were on a lush green planet that seemed to have everything they needed. The only question was whether there was a food source that could sustain them, that was yet to be seen.

For the moment it was his wish to enter the remaining Sokari vessels and kill the scaly creatures that had done so much harm to his race. The second in command to Rakit was another larger than average Quad named Sever. As Rakit was contemplating his surroundings Sever trotted up and announced that all the weapons and spare ammunition had been confiscated, they were ready to make a move on the Sokari ships.

"Gather the dead and stack them away from here. I don't know what there is on this planet in the way of provisions and we will need to use the bodies for food until something else can be obtained." Rakit said.

The Quads quickly gathered all the dead Sokari and gently placed them away from the ships. Rakit was smart to ration what food was available to the Quads, the upcoming battle might destroy the bodies and that would not be a good thing since at the moment it was the only food available to them. Once every body, limb and severed head had been gathered and placed a safe distance from the landing craft Rakit called his troops together.

"I want this to go smoothly, we will use the weapons to blast our way into the ships but after that we will go to hand to hand combat. The Sokari will either be wearing enviro-suits or body armor. Either way I want them overpowered without the use of weapons." Rakit's reasoning was sound; if they used blasters then the Sokari would be blown to bits, not much nutritional value in a blaster splattered body. Hand to hand combat assured most of the bodies would be intact and available to add to the food stores outside.

"We will do this one vessel at a time, I will choose the targets." Rakit looked about the landing site and made a decision. "Sever; I want to take on this one first." They were standing in front of the command vessel in which Keeto-Three occupied.

Keeto had been watching and knew he and his crewmen would be dead soon unless they managed to start the engines and fly out of reach of these hulking beasts. The engineers, upon landing, knew there had been some scarring during the orbital free fall and subsequent deceleration and touchdown. Even with all the extra filtering at the intakes some of the particulate had managed to enter the engines. One lander in particular had smoke pouring from the engines just as it made its hard landing. That particular craft had been deemed unsuitable for takeoff and would be abandoned without a further attempt at engine restart.

As Keeto continued to observe the Quads he knew time was running short. "Start the engines; notify the other landing craft that we are preparing to abort the mission. Make preparations to lift off and let's try to make orbit," Keeto told the flight crew. Keeto held his breath as the ship shuddered, the engines tried to start but heavy black particulate was the only thing exiting the engine exhaust ports. Keeto turned to the flight officer, "Hit the engines again, and get us out of here."

Again the heavy turbines turned and shook but they did not start. Keeto knew what was wrong; the trip down had clogged the ships engines and most likely scarred the equipment beyond repair. He looked out his viewing port and saw what he feared, the other landing craft were having the same trouble as his own, heavy black particulate was spewing from the engine exhaust ports. One ship did seem to be having more luck than the others, its engines had been started and they had actually lifted off. That ship was emitting a heavy cloud and Keeto wondered how long and how far it would fly before the engines shut down completely and they crashed. His question was answered when the entire craft exploded in a ball of fire and shrapnel. Parts of the craft struck some of the other landing craft and split their hulls open in several locations.

Rakit saw what had happened and decided a change of tactics was called for. "Sever, split up your squad and go for the ships that have been damaged, they will be easier to enter. The rest of you follow me."

Rakit raised the weapon he carried and aimed it at the loading bay door of Keeto's ship. It took three direct shots on the locking mechanism to render it useless. The door hissed and opened. "Attack" was all Rakit had to say for his bloodthirsty countrymen to storm the vessel.

Keeto heard the explosion and saw the alarm light switch on which indicated that the cargo bay door was opening. He watched on the exterior monitor as the first of the Quads stomped up the ramp. There was weapons fire coming from just behind the space occupied by Keeto and the bridge crew.

"Hit the engines again and try to lift off, disable the safeties and bypass the filters." Keeto shouted at his terrified crew. Just as the first of the engines tried to rumble to life the heavy door that separated the flight compartment from the rest of the ship took a blaster hit. The ship rose a few feet but Keeto knew the end was near. Just as the engine sputtered out another blast hit the door and it flew off its hinges. Two of the fearsome Quads rushed the bridge. Keeto sat quietly in his command chair as he waited for the end. Just as a giant mouth gaped open and Keeto's head disappeared inside he thought how nice it would be if Admiral Seeboc Tang could be here now.

Within thirty minutes all the Sokari landing craft had been entered and the occupants added to the pile of dead outside, they would be used later for food. Rakit ordered the ships to be searched and all the available weapons gathered and inventoried. Ammunition was also to be counted and distributed. The Quads were not only experienced warriors, they were extremely smart.

Rakit and Sever, along with the rest of the Quads, were elated to be free of the hated Sokari; they were also troubled that they were now stranded on an unknown planet. Another tactical consideration Rakit wanted explored was the position and condition of the Sokari column that had been sent out to attack the enemy, or were they an enemy at all. If they were at odds with the Sokari then that didn't necessarily mean they would be hostile toward the Quads.

Rakit gathered the other Quads and set a plan in motion. "Sever take two squads, (a squad represented four Quads) and reconnoiter the Sokari column that was preparing to attack the starship. See if there are any survivors and deal with them accordingly. Also see if the equipment they were using was disabled or is still operational, we may need the firepower if the population of this planet proves to be as hostile toward us as they were toward the Sokari. Also, I expect the Sokari to send down reinforcements, if they do I want to be ready for them. While you are making your way there I intend to see if I can contact anyone on this planet by way of the Sokari communications array located in the command craft. Hopefully if there is anyone else on this planet they have language translators." Sever saluted Rakit and gave the order for eight of the huge beasts to move out.

After the eight Quads along with Sever departed it left only Rakit and two more to guard the Sokari landing site. Rakit knew that four Quad-Breach transports had been dispatched from the Sokari fleet and he also knew that all four had landed successfully on the planet's surface. At the moment thirteen Quads was all he could account for. The twelve survivors including himself and the one that had been killed storming the Sokari defenses only moments before he and the other eleven made it to the landing site. He turned to one of the two remaining Quads and asked a question.

"Spasm, have either you or Debris inspected the four Quad-Breach landers?"

Debris looked at Spasm first and then answered, "No sir, those four are the only ships that weren't inspected because the bay drop doors are still down, it was assumed if Sokari still manned the two ships then they would have closed the doors when we attacked."

Rakit considered this and realized it did make sense, if any Sokari were still on board then they would have fortified the drop doors. Rakit headed for the ships, Spasm and Debris right behind him. Once they got to the first ramp he looked inside. The holding bays for the quads were open, six in all.

"Stay here and keep a look out for trouble, I want to do a closer inspection of this ship before moving to the second lander." Rakit stomped up the ramp and started looking in the bays, there was nothing unusual, all looked as they did when he and the other twelve Quads were sent out to attack the ship that had taken off earlier and dropped the sonic devices that had freed them. There was also no sign of any Sokari. Rakit came out of the ship and looked in the direction of the other transports. He motioned and the three headed in that direction.

When they approached the open door to the Quad pens Rakit knew something was different from the first lander which was the one he had traveled down to the surface in. This lander was configured the same as the first with six holding bays, three on either side. Again Rakit stationed Debris and Spasm at the base of the door and then he stomped up the ramp. What he found was different than the first lander, four of the bays had open doors but the last two, nearest the flight deck, were still locked. Inside were two Quads and both were severely injured, but still alive.

Rakit walked to the control panel and hit the release, nothing happened. Again he hit the release button but this time he used the full force of a heavily muscled arm. The doors for the two bays that held the Quads slowly clicked and then hydraulically opened. One of the two that occupied the bays opened its eyes and looked at Rakit.

"Rakit my friend, have you come to rescue us?" This was spoken through a severely injured maw.

"We have, can you tell me what has happened here?" Rakit asked.

The injured Quad slowly tried to tell what had happened. "When the assault started and the other Quads were released we thought we would be sent out also. Something must have happened to the doors, the release mechanism wouldn't work. After you and the rest of the Quads were sent away one of the Sokari came out and shot us. I guess he didn't want to be here if there was a chance the doors might release later."

Rakit entered the bay and helped the Quad to its feet. He had been shot seven times but most of the rounds had been absorbed by his battle armor. "Can you walk?" He asked.

The Quad stiffened and rose to its full height. "Yes, I can walk."

The injured Quad trotted to the ramp and headed down to the planet's surface. Rakit stooped beside the second Quad and inspected his injuries. He too had been shot multiple times and seemed to be unconscious. Rakit knew his name; with so few Quads left in the Galaxy it wasn't hard to know them all.

"Carnage, can you speak?"

The Quad opened his eyes slowly and smiled at Rakit. "Brother, you have survived," was all the badly injured Quad could say.

"Yes, a lot of us have survived. How bad are you injured?" Rakit asked.

"Shot a few times is all; I'm ready for duty commander," Carnage said with a grimace.

Rakit was pleased with the grittiness of his old friend. He turned to the ramp, "Spasm assist me in getting Carnage out of here."

Both Rakit and Spasm helped the severely injured Quad out of the lander and placed him at the base of the ramp. He first tried to sit up on the ramp but found he didn't have the energy; he had lost a lot of his fluids. Carnage was slowly stretched out on the leading edge of the ramp and allowed to rest. It was apparent he was momentarily fortified that he, and the other Quads, had gained their freedom and this gave him a boost. Medically there wasn't much the Quads could do for one another; it had never been incorporated into their society. The reason for this was complicated but the main reason was that a Quad had an enormous ability to self-heal. A severely injured Quad either had the ability to heal itself or it died, this was just an accepted part of life. The only thing an injured Quad really needed to survive was food and water, lots and lots of food and water. If a Quad could eat and drink then it could most likely survive and heal itself.

Debris walked over to the injured Carnage and asked if there was anything he could do. Although Quads were fearsome in both appearance and attitude they held members of their own species in great regard, especially since there were so few left in existence. A Quad could show great compassion to another injured Quad.

Carnage opened his eyes and looked at Debris. "Food" was all the injured Carnage was able to say.

Debris turned and galloped to the pile of dead Sokari soldiers and quickly picked out a juicy one. He snatched it up and hurried back to his injured comrade. "Here you go Carnage, I will bring water soon. You are going to like this planet, it has water everywhere."

Carnage raised his uninjured arm and quickly took the dead Sokari. He immediately bit the right leg off above the knee and crunched away. The thought of unlimited water made him smile as he chewed. All Quads knew the Sokari both hated and feared water, it was extremely deadly to the bug eyed creatures. For this reason water was severely rationed to the Quads, so much so that it actually inhibited their performance on the battlefield.

As Carnage ate his Sokari snack Debris grabbed a water container from inside the holding bay. It was empty; he grabbed another and found it to also be empty. Upon checking he found all the containers to be empty. As he was checking Rakit came back up the ramp to see what was going on. Debris filled him in on what he had found.

"It seems this was going to be a one way trip for all the Quads, no water was brought down with us. Take two containers to the stream and fill both. Bring them back to our two injured friends here. The rest of us can drink from the stream in rotation," Rakit said as he turned and stomped back down the ramp. If he ever came across another living Sokari he would see that it died a slow and painful death.

Debris galloped toward the nearby stream and sunk both containers, one with each hand, completely beneath the surface. As they gurgled and filled with the cool spring water he dipped his head all the way to his ears. He drank rapidly knowing he had to hurry back to his two injured friends. The taste was better than any he had ever remembered and he quickly drank his fill. With both containers full he galloped back to the ramp and held one up for Carnage to enjoy. Carnage drank the entire twenty liters without stopping, the cool drink helped the injured Quad even more than the dead Sokari soldier, which was nearly eaten by now.

"Thank you Debris, I feel much better now." Carnage might have felt a bit better but he still looked a mess. He had been shot more than ten times by the Sokari. If it hadn't have been for the armor protecting some of his major organs then he would have died in the cage he occupied on board the Quad-Breach Lander. It was no way for a soldier to die.

Rakit had now accounted for fifteen of the twenty-four Quads that had been on the four landers. Nine missing, this had to be solved. Not only did Rakit want to know what happened to them but he also knew the other nine, if they were still alive, would be a badly needed addition to his limited forces. Just as Rakit was about to walk away from the lander the radio in the containment bay squawked to life.

"Rakit can you read me, this is Sever, come in?"

Rakit ran back up the ramp and picked up the handheld receiver and pressed it to his oversize head. "This is Rakit, over."

"We made it to the enemy's armor and transports, all the Sokari are dead, didn't find a single survivor." Sever said.

"Are all of the vehicles damaged?" Rakit asked.

"Negative, a few were still idling when we arrived. It appears that whatever killed the Sokari did so in a very efficient manner, they just stopped living. Most of the equipment was shot up but some was still operable."

One problem with trying to use the Sokari equipment was that it was all built for Sokari and not for the much larger Quads. Another thing was that a Quad had never had the opportunity to try out any of the equipment, after all they were indentured soldiers expected to advance on foot, not drive a tank.

This was good news to Rakit, if only a Quad could fit inside. "Are you able to enter the driver's compartments on any of the equipment?"

"Already tried that sir, it's a bit tight but after tearing out the seats we can fit. Apparently the compartments are oversized to begin with, must be to accommodate a Sokari wearing an enviro-suit. Got more good news sir, we found nine other Quads; they were preparing to head back to the landers when our two groups stumbled into each other. That makes everyone accounted for except two."

Rakit was relieved to know the other Quads were okay. "Got the last two here Sever, both were left behind when their cell doors wouldn't open. Both are severely injured but I think they will survive. Are the dead Sokari in a condition to be used for food?"

"Affirmative, we are gathering them up now and the bodies are being placed in some of the troop transports. What are my orders?" Sever asked.

"Load everything that is usable and head back this way. We will use the landing site as our base of operations until we can find out who lives on this planet and why the Sokari were attacking them."

"Roger that sir. We'll be moving out from here shortly and heading your way." Sever added.

Sever put the mic back in the cradle and turned to the job at hand. The first was to gather all the usable hand weapons that were lying around and put them in one of the transports. Before long everything was loaded and the column was ready to move out. Sever made a quick trip around the area to make sure everything possible was loaded and nothing of use was left behind. As he stomped through the low growth he spotted something he hadn't seen since back in the time when he had been a happy little Quad back on his home world. It was a mushroom plant, one with many branches and at the end of each branch was a bright red flesh-tomato.

Sever quickly picked one of the tender fruit from a leafy limb and held it to his nose. The smell was as sweet as he remembered in his youth. He then took a very small bite and slowly chewed, it was delicious. After closer inspection he found there to be hundreds of the plants nearby, most were hidden in the shadows of some sort of large species of trees. The shadows of the trees made the mushroom plants difficult to see from any distance Sever quickly yanked three of the plants from the ground and headed back to the transports. As he galloped he counted the fruit on each plant, approximately fifteen large flesh-tomatoes on each. This was truly good news because up until now nothing had been discovered that could be used for food except the bug-eyed Sokari.

The column moved out shortly after Sever and a few of the other Quads gathered more of the mushroom plants. One transport was completely filled with the plants and fruit. If the fruit from this plant proved to be a source of food then no further plants would be pulled from the ground, only the fleshy red fruit would be gathered. The Quads only pulled up the plants in order to save time, it was important to make it back to the landing site and consolidate their forces as quickly as possible.

Even as Rakit and Sever prepared to fight if needed it was soon proven to be unnecessary. Footage from the Gareth as she overflew the Sokari and the Quads had been examined. The Quads, if they survived the Sonic Bomb blast, would be offered asylum. General Abbot had already spoken to her superiors; it was known that the planet that had separated orbit and drifted away was inhabited by the Quads. Now, all these centuries later, they were here on the sister planet. Every effort would be made to contact the few Quads that remained. The few survivors of the race known as Quads didn't know it yet but they had finally found peace after all these years of forced battle.

Mama-Seven headed for the eye of the atmospheric anomaly using only the Gareth's pulse engines. She didn't want to engage any of the main engines in order to make orbit, to do so would be subjecting the engines to the heavy particulate that swirled around the planet. As the Gareth moved away from the area where the three sonic devices had been dropped on the advancing Sokari column scans were being run on the effect. Actual results wouldn't be known until General Abbot's forces advanced and fought or captured what was left of the enemy's equipment, it was doubtful if any of the Sokari troops were still alive. Sonic devices were very thorough weapons.

Simms kept the Gareth heading in the direction of the anomaly. He would hit the opening at the appointed time and then ignite the main engines for the needed acceleration to make orbit. His main concern was what might be waiting for him on the other side.

"Sir, it appears Mama-Seven is picking up weapons fire," one of the comms officers said.

"Landside or orbital," Simms asked?

After a quick scan of his monitors the officer replied, "Orbital sir; appears the anomaly is allowing us to get the first readings from outside the atmosphere."

Simms knew the enemy fleet would most likely still be in the region, they had forces on the ground and he doubted they were sent down there without the ability of leaving. He was right about the enemy still being in the region but he was wrong about them sending down a landing force and not abandoning them.

If Mama-Seven was picking up weapons fire then who was the enemy fighting. Simms knew from reading the after-action report that the Super-Computer had sent out a 360 degree data burst as the Gareth headed down into the atmosphere of the planet. That was only a couple of days ago, there was no way a relief force could be in the area; the trip would take months.

There was another possible explanation, Earth Forces Command had, for some reason, become suspicious and knew the Gareth was heading into a trap. If that were so then a hastily assembled rescue could have been sent out months ago and was now in orbit battling the same fleet that had so grievously damaged the Gareth.

Simms contacted Mama-Seven for more information. Within seconds he got his answer, Umbrage, Temerity and Anneal were now engaged with the same fleet that had attacked the Gareth. Scans were still incomplete but it appeared the three had been attacked within seconds after Transition. It appeared the three ships were prepared with shields and weapons powered to full but they were now taking damage and attempting to power back out of the region.

"Comms, how long before we exit the anomaly," Simms asked?

"Fourteen seconds sir!" Was the answer he got?

"Bring the other two sled-guns on line, power the Repulsar Pocket to maximum. Speed to intercept status. I want us to come in behind the Sokari and see if we can draw some of the fire away from the other ships. Bring the idled reactors on line and have them powered to full."

As the Gareth broke through the outer edge of the atmosphere Mama-Seven routed a damage report of the three earth ships to the captain. The Dreadnaught Class Cruiser Umbrage had taken multiple hits and was slowing, her engines were nearly at critical and shielding was beginning to diminish. The Fast Attack Cruiser Anneal had just made a sweeping charge on the attacking fleet while unleashing a blistering barrage on two of the enemy's larger craft, both looked to be Dreadnaught Class in size. She was now heading back to the other two ships at flank speed, her damage so far was extensive but she was still fully operational. The Beachhead Support Cruiser Temerity seemed to be coasting, her engines were off line but she still had shielding and was returning fire. The three ships were battered but still in the fight, for how long was anybody's guess.

As the Gareth cleared the last of the planets atmospheric particulate Simms took the safeties off all the exterior mounted weapons arrays. Space was a cold place and overheating wasn't a concern in such low temperatures. ED was reviewing his scanner information and knew which enemy ships had taken part in the ambush of the Gareth. There were also four additional ships that had a different heat signature; these four hadn't taken part in the initial assault on the Gareth. There was no way for ED to know but these four ships had been sent to replace the four that were lost, two to the Gareth's biological weapons and two to her Sled-Guns.

As the Gareth approached and her speed continued to increase ED took inventory of the enemy fleet's offensive capabilities. He sent a message through Map-Con to Mama-Seven that it was possible the enemy might try to board the four Earth ships during the engagement. Mama-Seven analyzed the data at her disposal and saw what the External Defense Computer was talking about. One of the enemy's support craft was launching small but fast probes into the battle. A quick and isolated scan of one of the probes indicated a crew of two supported by fourteen soldiers located in an Infect Module. The module was designed to disengage from the probe and then accelerate into the side of another ship. The nose of the module was made of a hardened alloy that Mama-Seven couldn't identify without a sample. Once the probe was imbedded into the outer hull of a ship the fourteen soldiers could make entry through a pressure seal located on the side of the module. Earth Forces command had done studies on this type of boarding device but had never been able to make it operational, apparently the Sokari had.

Captain Simms was notified at once, expect boarders. "Sergeant Talby, report to the bridge immediately." Simms wanted to have Talby and his troops prepared in the event the Sokari managed to board the Gareth.

Roscoe Talby and two of the team that had attempted to reach the Sokari landing site while planet side had been chosen to lead the four companies of troops stationed on the Gareth. Having been the only team to tangle with this new species Talby was chosen because of that experience alone. Baxter had also volunteered; Talby thought this was a good idea due to his size and ability to stay cool under fire. The request was granted. On this mission Baxter would replace the injured Bedford.

Once Talby made it to the bridge he was brought up to date on the situation. "It is expected by Mama-Seven and ED that we will be boarded at some point in the battle. The bridge is hardened and also guarded by a company of Astro-Sailors who are trained for just such an event. The most critical part of the ship is actually the Data Bay. This heavily fortified section houses Mama-Seven and all associated computing equipment, it is the soul of the self-aware Super-Computer. It has been suggested that if a boarding is attempted these are the two sections that the alien force will be after. Do you have any suggestions on how to reinforce the Data Bay?" Simms asked.

"Yes Captain, just before we launched the External Defense computer gave us a list of priorities should a boarding be deemed imminent. ED suggested one company of troops, which consists of thirty-two troops, guard the Data Bay. One squad (a company consisted of two squads of sixteen troops each,) of troops will assist the Astro-Sailors in defending the bridge. That would leave five squads to support the roaming sentries that will be patrolling the rest of the ship."

Simms thought about this for only a second before adding, "The Gareth is a very large ship Talby, do you have any other suggestions?"

Talby wasn't accustomed to conversing with the captain of a Capitol Ship, he felt a bit overwhelmed at the moment. "I would like to arm more of the sailors that work in some of the more distal areas of the ship. Keep everyone in groups of at least two, no one gets separated or works alone. If a quadrant of the Gareth is beached I would like to have an open com in that section and that section only. If my troops or your sailors are engaged in a battle it will be helpful to have information for a coordinated counter-attack."

Simms considered what he had just been told by a member of a different branch of the military. He respected the troops under Major

West's command and knew each was a capable and highly trained soldier. He also knew someone with only the rank of sergeant might be in over his head in a ship to ship encounter, time would tell.

"I have one request sergeant; keep a full company in reserve for back-up. If we get boarded I want those thirty-two troops available to assist my sailors. If we are boarded and your troops fail then it will spell disaster for the Gareth, not to mention the other three Earth Colonies ships out there," Simms said.

Sergeant Talby saluted and headed off the bridge, he had a lot to do and not a lot of time to get it done. First was to inventory the weapons that had been left aboard and distribute these to the Astro-Sailors. If this proved to be inadequate then he intended to use a portion of the weapons in his own combat armory. Hand weapons and assault rifles were always kept at a ratio of 1.25 to one. There was always one extra weapon for every four men. This was deemed adequate to cover mechanical failure and loss.

Talby cleaned out the Gareth's armory and armed as many of the Astro-Sailors as possible with the weapons available to him. Major West had always argued for more weapons to be stored on Capitol Ships but his requests had always been deemed alarmist. Each Capitol Ship carried a substantial contingent of surgically enhanced Deep-Space Soldiers and Fleet Command had always felt this was enough, up until this very day it had been. The situation that now presented itself was one in which most of the soldiers were landside fighting an unknown foe and this left the Gareth with her sailors and 128 soldiers to fight a one sided battle and contend with boarders. What West wanted, and had always argued for, was that the Gareth to be loaded with two more pods of equipment in the form of small arms and sonic grenades. His request had never been granted, what the Earth Forces Capitol Ships did receive was one-half pod of additional ammunition for the smaller caliber weapons the soldiers carried, no rifles and no additional side-arms. It had always been assumed that resupply ships would always be near and able to replenish the Battle Cruisers. It was becoming apparent that events were overtaking preparations.

While in the armory Talby had Roark and Worthless rig some portable trip wire devices. These were light sensor activated and would be placed at all major junctions that divided the ship. The great thing about the light activation was they couldn't be set off by a human, if any other species broke the light beam then a sonic device would be activated which would kill any living thing within a three meter radius but do no damage to the ship, the only problem with this device was Baxter, he wasn't human. It was risky to use the devices even if Baxter knew they were about, in a ship as large as the Gareth it would be impossible for Baxter to know where the devices were located, he just didn't know anything about the Gareth.

Talby thought of a solution, "Mama-Seven, can you detect any alien life forms on the Gareth at the present time?"

Mama-Seven had voice capabilities but rarely if ever utilized it. She had just been asked a question by one of the Deep-Space Soldiers and answered immediately. "There is one alien life form presently onboard the Gareth." The voice was definitely female; the diction was perfect with only the slightest wisp of a mechanical buzz.

Talby had been aboard the Gareth for quite a while and he suddenly realized this was the first time he had ever heard Mama-Seven speak. "Do you have any information of the subject you just mentioned?" He asked.

"The creature to which you refer is named Baxter and is indigenous to the planet from which we have just launched." Mama-Seven said.

"Can we utilize the Sonic Trip-Wires without endangering Baxter?" Talby asked.

"That has already been done Sergeant. As soon as the devices were brought from the storage locker I added Baxter's biological signature to the human safeties, Baxter will not activate any of the trip wires," Mama-Seven said.

Talby was extremely pleased; he could now use the trip wires without presenting a danger to Baxter. If a battle took place on board Talby for one wanted the help of the hulking Baxter. He and the rest of the squad that were attacked by the Quad while planet side were impressed with his abilities; he was now considered an ally.

Talby and his troops quickly went about the task of securing the ship, passage ways were cleared of supplies in order to give clear lines of fire. Pressure doors at the most critical sections of the ship were reinforced; a few that represented maintenance access were even sealed shut and laz-welded. Locking mechanisms which had normally used keypad entry were overridden; access could only be implemented now by Mama-Seven or Captain Simms.

There were six areas of the Gareth that needed special attention; these were the trolley ways that ran from one end of the ship to the other. Trolley ways were used to transport men, equipment and ammunition and they were mostly open tubes. In the center of the tube was a rail system that allowed heavy loads to be transported at a high rate of speed. There was also a walkway on either side which could be used for personnel as they traveled from one section of the ship to another. Along the tube were numerous hatches and junctions where you could access the interior portions of the ship.

Major West had never liked the openness of the six trolley ways; they were extremely functional in moving equipment around the ship but were a nightmare to defend if the ship's hull were ever breached. For this reason he had suggested that twelve remote control Gatling Guns be loaded and kept in the armory storage area of the ship. These particular weapons systems were designed to deliver pinpoint three round bursts of shells using a self-contained radar system. There were several features about this gun that made it extremely well suited for the trolley ways of the Gareth. The rounds it fired were designed to penetrate flesh and nothing else. If an object was struck that had a hard or even a semi-hard surface then the shell simply liquefied and at that point do very little additional damage. Even striking a human bone would cause the liquefaction. This eliminated the possibility of a hull breach which in the vacuum of space could be catastrophic.

Talby had one company of troops, along with a few of the Astro-Sailors, to start setting the twelve guns up in the trolley ways. Speed was imperative because Mama-Seven was tracking multiple incoming alien probe ships, each carrying an Infect Module. Talby urged his troops on, "Step to it, we got incoming. If these guns aren't operational then it goes to hand to hand combat and I for one don't want to touch one of those scaly bastards." Talby used a description of an enemy he had never seen; in fact neither he nor anyone else had ever seen what the Sokari looked like. The troops and sailors finished the last of the twelve guns in record time. Talby wondered if the thought of fighting something that wore scales might have had anything to do with it.

As Talby and the other sailors and troops headed for their muster stations the close range Lead-Ejectors could be heard opening up. ED was firing at something and if Lead-Ejectors were the weapon of choice then whatever it was had to be close, real close. Lead-Ejectors in space were an extremely close range weapon; they could only be firing at the Infect Modules. As Talby was considering the use of the Lead-Ejectors Mama-Seven broke in on all channels. "Prepare to repel boarders," was all the Super-Computer said.

Talby made sure all the squads were at their designated muster stations and were armored up. All the squad leaders radioed that they were in position and ready. Roark, Worthless and Baxter were with Sergeant Talby. The four companies representing the eight squads were intact units, Talby and his three companions were additional and weren't attached to any of the four companies and this was by design. When Talby had been given command of the 128 troops aboard the Gareth he requested that he along with Roark, Worthless and Baxter be considered add-on troops and not implemented into any particular squad or company. This left the four as a small but very capable fast reaction unit. Baxter in particular liked the sound of this.

No sooner had Talby checked in with his eight squad leaders than there was a shudder somewhere on the ship; an Infect Module had just burst through the outer pressure hull. Talby looked at the three soldiers with him, "Game time boys, let's see if we can do us a little damage to the alien bastards that ambushed the Gareth."

Admiral Seeboc Tang watched as a team of maintenance personnel repaired one of the command bridge consoles and its associated monitors, it had been the station occupied by a crew member that Tang shot in the back in a fit of rage pertaining to the earth ship that was destroyed a few days earlier. Tang's smile looked more like a grimace to the rest of the crew, he had taught himself to never show his true feelings, he wanted everyone to think he was never happy and that was pretty much the case. On the rare occasions that Tang was happy it was usually at the expense of someone else, as in the case of the subordinate he had murdered.

Another reason for Tang to be satisfied was the fact that he had managed to destroy a ship belonging to the mythical humans. He had proven their existence and that would bring praise from the Sokari High Council once he and his Battle Fleet made the long journey home. Tang was also pleased that he had heard nothing from the landing party he had sent planet side to deal with any survivors of the human ship that had crashed there two days prior. After this much time he assumed that his second in command, Keeto Three, must be either dead or stranded and to Tang either suited him just fine. Keeto was an outstanding sailor and a brilliant tactician. For this reason Tang felt he was a threat and it was well known within the fleet that threats never lasted long as far as Admiral Seeboc Tang was concerned.

As Tang pondered the demise of Keeto Three he noticed some activity coming from the three long range scanner screens located to the left of his command console. As he studied the screens he noticed tracking and movement icons in the vicinity of one of the picket ships stationed at the edge of the fleet. Picket ships were the first line of defense for the fleet while occupying what was considered hostile space; they were always stationed far from the main battle group. They were the first to pick up scans from approaching vessels and the first to respond if the scans indicated the contact was hostile. The information and pics scrolling along on Tang's screens were now being relayed from the picket ships.

"What is happening in that quadrant Wasson?" Tang asked.

Ril Wasson held the rank of Sub-Commander, he was presently assuming the duties of the scanner officer Seeboc Tang had murdered. "It looks like one of our Fast Attack Escorts has picked up something near the planet's surface. New contact is just now exiting the outer bands of the atmosphere."

Tang pondered this, could it really be Keeto Three heading back to the fleet. Tang had been assured that the landing craft Keeto used could never reach escape velocity through the particle strewn mix that made up this strange planet's atmosphere. "Is it one of our landing craft Wasson?"

Ril Wasson continued to monitor his scanners; he would choose his words carefully when responding to a question from the murderous Tang. "No Sir, the ship is large, very large. It appears to be Dreadnaught class."

Tang jumped from his command chair and headed to the scanners Wasson was looking into, he wanted to see firsthand. "Can you get a lock on her power signature?" Tang asked.

Wasson continued to scan, "It appears to be the human ship sir. She is picking up speed and approaching one of our picket ships."

The picket ship that had first noticed the Gareth as she came through the outer bands of the atmosphere was the Firrel, a small but extremely well-armed escort. She was built to be the first line of defense for the fleet. Any approaching vessel deemed hostile had to breach the picket ship barrier to get to the main battleships. This allowed time for the bigger ships to come to battle stations and prepare their weapons.

"What can you tell me about the human ship's capabilities?" Tang asked.

Wasson continued to monitor the live feed from the Firrel. "It looks like the human ship is fully operational admiral. Her weapons are charged to full and it looks like shielding is fully functional. The Firrel is bringing her weapons on line and turning to engage."

Tang wondered if the heavily armed picket ship was a match for the human vessel. "What are the closest support ships to the Firrel?"

"Ribald and Domnat are close, should I have them leave station and assist the Firrel?" Wasson asked.

Tang knew that three of the picket ships would be a formidable force against the human vessel. The battle would be short lived and this time the human ship would be destroyed before she could run and hide.

"Have the Ribald and Domnat engage the human ship along with the Firrel. I want all scans and battle footage routed to my command console at once." Tang ordered as he went back to his own monitors. As he walked he anticipated a quick victory over the human ship, then he thought of something else.

"What exactly is the name the humans use for that vessel?"

Wasson pinpointed his scanners and looked directly at the hull of the fast approaching human ship. After running the image through his decryption computer he came back with the name Gareth. "Gareth sir, the human ship is called Gareth."

"Plot a coarse for the three picket ships, have each attack from a different direction, I want the Gareth overwhelmed and destroyed." Tang ordered.

"We have reports of Infect Modules hitting the Gareth." Wasson strained to read multiple monitors at the same time. "It appears three have successfully struck the Gareth and two more are nearing. Do we still attack while our troops are entering the Gareth sir?"

Tang didn't have to think about this, he didn't care if a few of the Shock Troops that were invading the Gareth were killed as long as the human ship was destroyed. "Continue the attack; the Infect Troops can do their job while the fleet does theirs."

Wasson didn't like this at all. The Infect Troops, if given enough time, might be able to overpower the Gareth and her crew. If they were successful then the Gareth might be captured intact. This would be a victory beyond measure. The human ship, along with any surviving crew, would be studied and analyzed. Knowledge of this new species could be very useful. Wasson knew Tang was a merciless killer who only thought of the immediate tactical implications of destroying the enemy, he never thought of the long term strategic value of the capture.

Captain Simms was notified of the Firrel as soon as the Gareth cleared the atmosphere. "Enemy ship 35,000 kilometers to starboard sir, she appears to be a fast attack picket ship."

"Have they spotted us?" Simms asked.

"It appears so, she is turning to engage. Scanners show two more ships of the same class, they appear to be heading in our direction too."

"Helm, bring us to a new heading of 127.4 and nose down thirty-two degrees. I want to release Sled-Guns one and three on that ship as soon as gunnery has a solution," Simms said. A shot at thirty-five thousand kilometers was well within the range of the Gareth's weapons. "Give ED full release on the Sled-Guns at my command."

ED had been tracking the first enemy ship from the beginning. He had his pain receptors on in case any damage was done to the Gareth. He had also been in contact with Mama-Seven by way of Map-Con and had the Super-Computers full blessing to unleash Hell on the approaching vessel. ED didn't need Mama-Seven's approval but he did seek her blessing, she gladly gave it to him.

ED tracked the enemy ship and monitored her own weapons arrays. She appeared to be well designed and well-armed. A first shot from her and a hit on the Gareth would do some damage, the Repulsar-Pocket would slow and dissipate the round but the Gareth would take damage. ED wanted that first shot and he wanted it bad.

Captain Simms waited until the angle and speed were in sequence for the best possible shot. "Release control of the two Sled-Guns to ED," he ordered.

ED felt the electrical safeties switch off and knew he now had full control of Sled-Guns one and three. Two point three seconds later he fired number one and exactly one second after that he fired number three. Both Sled-Guns immediately trolleyed back into the hull and began the reloading process, it took less than three minutes to fully load and resubmit the two guns. In the meantime Sled-Guns two and four were extended and made ready to fire. Five and six were held in reserve.

Mama-Seven monitored the flight of the two projectiles; the trip to the enemy vessel would take only thirty seven seconds. Flight of both shots was smooth and there were no visible vibrations or flight deviations due to distortion during ignition. The shots were good.

Aboard the Firrel the Defensive Weapons officer noticed the exit gas emitted by the two Sled-Guns of the human ship as they fired. "Counter-Battery fire on my mark," he commanded.

"Three two one, fire all counter batteries," he ordered as fourteen long range weapons took aim on the incoming rounds. The guns responded by emitting a steady stream of projectiles that should make a virtual wall to either ignite the incoming rounds or simply destroy them. As the crew of the Firrel tracked the two incoming projectiles fired from the Gareth they prepared to unleash their own offensive weapons.

Everyone on the bridge watched as the projectiles of the human ship and those of the Firrel approached each other at incredible speeds. Just as the two rounds from the Gareth met the shells from the Firrel's counter-battery fire the crew expected to see an explosion, there wasn't one. The rounds from the human ship simply passed through the cloud and kept coming.

"Evasive, evasive, fire close range Responders, bring the shielding to one-hundred and ten percent on the approach side." The weapons officer ordered.

There was the distinct sound of the hull mounted Responders opening up on the incoming Sled Rounds. The hum of the onboard shielding generators grew steadily louder as more and more power was diverted to the shielding on the approach side. Just as the noise reached its crescendo the weapons officer heard the searing noise of the shields as they were penetrated by the first of the two Sled Rounds. Alarms began to sound as the outer hull was breached and then interior lighting flickered. The round made it from one end of the Picket ship to the other in less than a hundredth of a second, Sled Rounds traveled at an incredible rate of speed. Their kinetic energy was crucial to the penetration effect of the weapon.

Two seconds after the first Sled Round exited the ship the second hit and did the exact same amount of damage. The pressurized hull began to vent and small interior fires erupted from multiple areas of the ship. For all intents and purposes the ship looked unharmed but that was far from the truth. The two Sled rounds had drilled two holes from one end of the ship to the other. Machinery began to catch fire and computer systems went off line as multiple problems arose. As firefighting equipment automatically began to extinguish the smaller fires the larger ones only grew in size.

Five seconds after the first of the two Sled Rounds penetrated the ship there was a huge explosion as the main engines ignited. The entire ship expanded like a balloon at first as the force of the explosion blew away the outer hull. This was followed by a plume of superheated gas which flashed outward past the ruptured hull plating. Ten seconds after the first penetration of the hull the Firrel was no more. What was left was a growing cloud of superheated gas and debris.

Seeboc Tang watched aboard his command vessel. This was a rerun of what had happened previously to the two ships that had been hit just after the battle with the Gareth. First nothing, then a small explosion at each end of the ship and then total structural failure and detonation of the engines. Everyone in the command center of Tang's ship suddenly feared for their lives. Each expected him to draw his weapon and start blasting away at the first officer he wanted to kill. This time there would be no murder on the bridge.

Tang walked back to his command chair and looked about the bridge, everyone waited for his violent eruption. Tang now realized the human ship possessed some sort of weapon he had never seen before. It was kinetic without the needed explosive charge or mass to do damage to the ships in his fleet. His best guess at what had now destroyed three of his ships was nothing more than a primitive spear that was thrown at his fleet by an inferior race of beings flying around in even more primitive vessels. It was as if his highly advanced fleet was being battered with a club, or even a rock, and this was defeating the advanced weaponry of his superior fighting ships.

"Have the Ribald and Domnat fire at extreme range on the Gareth. Make sure a hit is scored on the human ship before they close. Also I want the Hatoyo to make all possible speed to intercept the Gareth before she can reinforce the other three human ships." The Hatoyo was a dreadnaught class main battle cruiser of the same size and armament as the Rococo. The Sokari always used three syllable names for their larger ships, two syllable for the smaller picket ships.

Tang watched as the Hatoyo broke from the rest of the fleet and headed for this side show that had now cost him another picket ship. It would take the Hatoyo nearly twenty time units to reach the battle, the Ribald and the Domnat would be fully engaged in only four. Tang now wanted to use the weapon that had so thoroughly defeated the human vessel in the first engagement, the Encryptor.

This particular weapon was used against both ships and planets. It fired from extreme range; it was a standoff weapon of mass destruction. The Encryptor fired a liquid super-heated mass of weaponized silica. The silica was used because of its ability to maintain high temperatures for a prolonged time as it traveled through the vacuum of space. Radioactive waste from the ships engines made up the nastiest part of the weapon. A ship could be totally destroyed by the heat of the device alone much less the high degree of radioactivity that would last for thousands of years. The Gareth had been saved by her matter displacement shells along with the Static Repulsar Pocket. The area of the hull that had been struck by what was left of the weapon was sparred the radioactive after-effects.

The Encryptor was a mammoth ship that had limited maneuverability. For this reason she was always kept far from any potential battle. Her job was to add her massive firepower from extreme range. For this reason the shot she took had to be timed and ranged perfectly. There was a small bit of maneuverability with the shot after it was fired.

This was accomplished by a centrally located device in the molten shot itself. This device would eventually be melted by the extreme heat, until that happened it could reconfigure the weapon in flight, changing shape in order to slightly nudge the slug of radioactive waste slightly in its course. Other than that the weapon was on its own to travel until it struck what it had been aimed at.

Aboard the Gareth, the crew had seen the destruction of the alien ship. They were now monitoring the approach of two more. Captain Simms was extremely pleased with the performance of his ship. The Captain thought this was the first confirmed kill associated with the fleet that had attacked the Gareth, there was no way for him to know about the four that had met their fate as the severally crippled Gareth ploughed through the dense atmosphere and fell toward the planet's surface. In reality this was the fifth kill for the Gareth.

Captain Simms suspected the enemy would now fire their weapons from a farther distance in order to score hits before the Gareth fired her Sled-Guns again. The captain knew ED had his audio functions engaged and could hear requests from the bridge. He also knew if asked a question Ed could respond with his language synthesizers.

"ED, are you monitoring the bridge?" Simms asked.

"Monitoring Captain, what is it you wish to know?" ED asked.

"Good work on the kill we just logged, two more targets approaching. How do you intend to respond?" Simms knew ED would be a step ahead of him and wanted to know what the response would be.

"Incoming vessels are of same size and displacement as first. Tactic will change; the enemy will make an attempt to disable us from a longer distance. Anticipate their shot in seventy-four seconds. Sled-Gun two will fire in thirty-seven seconds; gun four will fire in thirty nine seconds. Targeting each of the approaching vessels with one gun each. Guns one and three are re-loaded and will be used in case of a miss," ED said.

Simms took in what ED just said and didn't want to wait around, "Helm bring her about and head for our three ships at flank speed once the first two guns have fired." Immediately after gun four released her round the Gareth turned and picked up speed. Simms now put the second part of his plan into action. "ED, prepare a solution using our new heading and speed to fire on the two ships again assuming our first shots are a miss." Simms knew ED never replied to an order, he just obeyed.

As the Gareth's helm continued to plot a course toward the three Earth Colonies ships other officers monitored the two Sled Rounds as they streaked on an intercept coarse toward the two alien ships. Simms decided it was time to either figure out who he was fighting, or if that information were unavailable, he would give them a name himself.

"Mama-Seven has Map-Con figured out who is attacking us?"

Mama-Seven answered in her electronic voice, "The race of creatures that attacked the Gareth is known as the Sokari. They are an ancient species, much older than humans. The information being gathered still needs to be interpreted but it appears they are a warrior race bent on overwhelming all worlds they encounter and either annihilate the indigenous inhabitants or use them as either a slave workforce or an indentured fighting force."

Simms thought about this, he had never heard of the race Mama-Seven had just mentioned. "The Sokari, if they are truly a much older race than humans then it is safe to assume they are more technologically advanced than us. Do you have an opinion on this Mama-Seven?"

"The Sokari are far advanced in their sciences and understanding of the Galaxy. It appears though they may have a weakness," Mama-Seven said.

This was good news if the Super-Computer had found a way to give the Gareth an advantage. "Elaborate," Simms said.

"The Sokari have advanced past the use of kinetic energy weapons. The weapons they possess are true energy weapons designed to destroy by any number of ways other than kinetic. They have evolved past the kinetic and into energy is the short answer. As you know Earth Forces Command used a combination of both. The Sled-Guns which have had such a devastating effect on the Sokari are kinetic only in nature." The mechanical hum of Mama-Seven's vox synthesizer cycled down.

Simms was deep in thought when one of the offensive weapons officers spoke up, "Captain, we have a hit on the first of the enemy ships." After a second the same officer said, "Second ship has also been hit sir."

"Damage report on both ships." Simms asked.

As the crew monitored the two picket ships ED had attacked they wondered if only one Sled round would be enough to accomplish a kill.

"Both ships are slowing and multiple fires are detected." There was a pause as the information continued to be gathered. "Multiple explosions on one of the ships, it appears her engines have been disabled."

"What about the second ship?" Simms asked.

"She is still functional sir. It appears the Sled Round hit her with a glancing blow. Shall we fire again?"

"Is she still advancing?" Simms asked.

"No sir, she is turning in the direction of the other ship, my guess is to give assistance."

Simms doubted this, he knew a human ship would always lend what assistance it could to another ship but Mama-Seven had indicated the Sokari were a warrior race. He doubted a warrior race would show that kind of compassion. The reason the second ship failed to continue the attack was because of another more ominous reason.

"Sir I'm picking up a second contact heading our way."

"Scan the new contact; I need to know what we are up against." Simms ordered.

"Second ship is definitely hostile sir. Appears to be a battleship of some sort, scanners show mass to be roughly equivalent to that of the Gareth. Multiple weapons arrays and dual shielding. Power plant and engines are of unknown makeup, I've never seen a reading like this before." Came the answer Simms didn't want to hear.

"Time to intercept?"

"She is headed this way at speed sir, approximate time she can bring her weapons to bear is fourteen minutes twenty-seven seconds."

Simms knew energy weapons had to be close in order to do any damage against a shielded ship such as the Gareth. Kinetic weapons didn't have that handicap. Once a kinetic weapon such as a Sled-Gun fired, the projectile would travel in the void of space until it struck something.

"ED, what are the chances of scoring a hit on the new contact before she can bring her weapons to bare?" Simms asked.

ED didn't need time to think, his answers were instantly available. "At this range a four shot spread has a thirty-seven percent chance of at least one round striking the enemy ship. With reloading time calculated in, a second shot would have a ninety-three percent chance of at least one round striking the enemy ship and a seventy-two percent chance of two rounds making impact?"

Simms knew this was now or never, "Weapons, give free reign to ED, I want immediate weapons alignment on that ship, four round spread with immediate reload and fire," Simms said.

Within seconds there were four shudders as the Gareth's starboard Sled-Guns locked onto the approaching enemy ship and then fired. Portside guns fired at nearly the same time. The guns trolleyed back in and the reloading machinery immediately began the reloading process.

The aiming process that allowed Sled-Guns to fire at extreme range was as simple as a small processor located in the nose of the round that was preprogramed just before the shot left the gun. As the round traveled through the void the circuitry in the shot simply adjusted a liquid-lead mass in the center of the round that slowly sent the round off course slightly. With enough time and distance a Sled-Gun round could be steered in a complete circle. That wouldn't be the case now, the two port shots would only need to turn 180 degrees in their flight paths; this would cause these two rounds to arrive at the target eleven seconds after the starboard rounds arrived.

Simms watched his monitors and at the thirty second mark asked for an update.

"Starboard rounds are running straight and true sir. Port rounds are making the turn now; looks like all four shots are in the green. No after fire distortions being picked up."

This was good news; a misfire might damage one of the Sled-Guns and in a running battle that would severely diminish the offensive capabilities of the Gareth. The Sled-Gun configuration on the Gareth was unique to the Earth Forces Fleet. She had six of the massive guns, two starboard and two port. The other two were actually installed to fire from either side of the ship by means of a centrally located tube that ran from one side of the ship to the other. These last two guns were always held in reserve.

Aboard the Hatoyo the bug-eyed creatures of the bridge crew picked up the incoming rounds, or at least the indication the Gareth had fired at them. "Enemy weapons fire reported sir; looks like scanners have picked up four bursts."

The commander of the Hatoyo turned from his screens to look through the viewport. At such distances it was impossible to see with the naked eye but also impossible not to look. "Have you picked up what type of weapon it is?"

The same officer was straining hard but having no luck determining what had been fired at them. The problem with a Sled-Gun round was that in the expanse of space it was nearly impossible to detect until it was nearly on you. Another problem was the speed in which it traveled.

"My guess is it is the same type of weapon that destroyed the Firrel sir."

The commander of the Hatoyo had been in many battles and felt he was able to handle this new species of scum. From the early reports of the initial encounter the human ship was inferior in so many ways it was almost laughable.

"Is it possible the human ship was only venting gases from her weapons when she fired on the Firrel and the other two Picket Ships?"

The defensive weapons officer was a waspy looking creature who went by the name of Ronal Re. "That might be Captain. Scans aren't picking up any incoming rounds."

"Keep monitoring, I don't want to be caught off guard by these vermin." Captain Alto Orme said.

The Hatoyo continued on an intercept course. The captain wanted to close to near point blank range to finish off the human ship with his weapons. There would be no chance of picking up survivors, prisoners actually, after he unleashed a full broadside on the human vessel.

Aboard the Gareth Captain Simms was busy directing the response to the Sokari attacks against his ship and left the business of the Infect Modules to Sergeant Talby and his four companies of Deep Space Soldiers. So far five of the little craft had rammed through the four pressure hulls of the Gareth and deposited seventy Sokari Assault Troops. It had been hoped that the Static Repulsar Pocket might identify the Infect Pods as incoming rounds and render them helpless or even destroy the tiny craft. That wasn't the case; the Pods were of a size and traveled at a speed that resembled an escape pod. The Pocket had been designed to identify between weapons and escape pods and for this reason had no effect on the tiny craft.

As the assault progressed Talby was in contact with his troops and knew approximately where the modules, or pods, had penetrated. It wasn't known yet what the primary objective of the attack was. If they were trying to take over the ship then the bridge would be the target but it was suspected this wasn't the case, most likely the Data Bay which contained all the computing abilities of the Gareth along with Mama-Seven.

Talby ordered one additional squad of his soldiers to back-up the soldiers and sailors already stationed there. This order was precipitated by the fact that the enemy was apparently ignoring the bridge of the ship. With the placement of the squad of soldiers there was now only one full company of troops available for back-up if needed anywhere else on the ship.

Talby and Baxter along with Roark and Worthless made for the Data-Bay at a full run. When they were only three sections from the bay they were taken under fire by the Sokari. Worth was grazed by a round from some sort of electrical pistol that initially took him to the ground but the effect soon wore off. Baxter charged on ahead and grabbed the enemy soldier by one of its arms and pressed it against the bulkhead. It tried to fight back but the hulking Baxter was nearly half again bigger. The fight was short lived. Baxter broke the neck of whatever he was holding with one massive blow from his other arm, he released his grip and the Sokari slid to the floor.

Worth applied a pressure dressing to the burn on his arm, "What kind of dipshit weapon are they firing at us anyway?" He asked no one in particular.

Talby looked at the weapon which was now lying beside the dead soldier. "Looks like some sort of charged particle device. My guess is it would have killed you Worth if you had gotten the full load, as it was you were only grazed."

"Grazed my ass, I think I did get the full load from that damn thing." Worth countered.

"Stop your whining; if you think this is such a powerful weapon then you carry it," Roark said as he took the gun from Talby and tossed it to Worth.

Worth looked over his new toy and this brought a smile to his face. "Just point me in the right direction; I want to try this baby out."

Talby brought his team back to the here and now, "Knock it off, we got work to do." As he said this he turned down another corridor, his troop's right behind him. They hadn't gone far when they heard firing, the distinct sound of their own type of assault rifles and the sizzle of alien particle weapons.

"Sounds like the fight is at the Data Bay, let's move it." Talby said as he sprinted down a wide corridor.

When the four got there they knew the Data Bay was the target. The door to the enormous room that housed Mama-Seven was several layers thick and reinforced throughout. The Sokari were in the process of assembling a multi-armed laz-cutter of some sort. The torch head alone was more than a meter wide. Talby and his team were just coming down the corridor when they noticed the dead troopers and sailors strewn about on the floor. The bodies were burnt through, no doubt by the same weapon that had grazed Worth.

"Take cover," Talby ordered just as the aliens turned from their work and leveled their weapons. Baxter and Roark went left as Talby and Worthless went right, all four were firing their weapons as they went. As soon as the four were safely behind a bulkhead there was a searing as the Sokari brought their weapons to bear. What looked like a flash of lightening came through the open bulkhead and streamed past the four. Although it was a complete miss the heat from the blast cooked the outer layers of their uniforms and body armor. After the flash was gone there was the distinct smell of burnt hair and each man, including Baxter, had blisters forming on their exposed arms and faces. Talby knew if another blast like that came through the doorway then the four would be burned even worse. The only way to survive was to attack and kill the aliens before they could fire their weapons again.

"On my mark let's rush the bastards." The other three wanted nothing more than to attack knowing full well if the aliens fired as they broke from cover they were all dead.

"Three two one now," Talby shouted.

All four had their weapons raised and as soon as they cleared the casing of the bulkhead they opened up with their assault rifles. The noise was tremendous as the four charged the aliens protecting the crew assembling the laz-cutter. It wasn't more than ten meters to where their foe stood. The soldiers sprinted and in less than three seconds they were there, all the while spraying anything not human with soft-lead splatter ammo.

Talby noticed the aliens were not in a position to fire, apparently the weapons they used needed a few seconds to recharge before being able to fire again. Thank goodness for good old fashioned bullets. Within five seconds the aliens that were manning the defense were all dead, that left only the ones assembling the cutter. This shouldn't have been a problem except there were at least a dozen of them and they were each pulling long blades from sheaths. They were actually using what looked like machetes.

The weapons Talby and his three teammates used were standard issue assault rifles with the added feature of a spring loaded bayonet that was trigger released for close-up fighting. All four released their bayonets and dove into the alien horde that wanted nothing more than to slice up the human scum that had just now killed so many of their fellow soldiers.

Talby wondered why this batch of Sokari carried blades and then it dawned on him, the weapons the aliens carried might be too powerful for close quarters combat. The blades were used for situations just like this.

Baxter was anxious to see how good the Sokari were in hand to hand combat. Although Talby and his three troopers were outnumbered by a ratio of four to one it was evident that the three surgically enhanced soldiers and the hulking Baxter were more than a match for the aliens. The Sokari were both sliced and shot to pieces as Talby and the other three took out a little revenge. Within seconds the only ones standing were the humans and Baxter.

"Drop an anti-weapons grenade in that cutter head and step back Talby ordered." Worth took a small black metal cylinder from his belt and snapped a red switch at its end. As he dropped it in the opening of the cutter head the four ran for cover. Just as they made it back around the bulkhead there was a loud pop. One look and you knew whatever that piece of equipment was meant for it was never going to operate again. The large head of the device now hung at a downward angle and the end was shredded.

As Talby inspected the dead aliens to try to get some sort of idea of what they were up against Mama-Seven spoke through an overhead speaker. "I am running scans on the dead Sokari and also their weaponry."

Talby was at first startled by the voice but he regained his composure quickly. "How many more are there on the ship?" Talby asked.

"The Sokari have suffered twenty-seven fatalities, there are forty-three still on board. I also detect four more Infect Pods inbound that will strike the hull in thirty-two seconds, attempting to alter the safeties on the Static Repulsar Pocket." There was a short pause before Mama-Seven spoke again. "Pocket has been modified; incoming pods are now recognized as weapons and will be destroyed."

Talby was glad of this bit of news but there were still forty-three alien troops on board. Talby asked another question and dreaded the answer, "How many troops and sailors have we lost?"

Mama-Seven hesitated for a second. She was running a program on how the news she was about to give would affect the fighting ability of Talby and his troops. "Seven soldiers and five sailors have been killed in the engagement."

The program Mama-Seven ran indicated a ninety-three percent chance the information would inflame the soldiers and sailors to more valiant efforts in defending the ship. She would have given the information in a different way if it would have had a negative impact on performance. Mama-Seven had both compassion programing and realistic outcome programing. At the moment the compassion circuits were switched off and she was all about the effect any information would have on the survival of the Gareth. She could be a cruel bitch at times.

Admiral Seeboc Tang had been watching from his command chair aboard the Rococo. He had viewed the destruction of the Firrel and then the disabling of both the Ribald and the Domnat. It appeared the Domnat was still functional but the Ribald hadn't moved since being struck, she was adrift. Tang was now looking at three of his picket ships being either destroyed or disabled and this by a human vessel he thought he had destroyed days earlier.

"Contact the Encryptor; have her to plot an action against the human ship." Tang knew the name of the Earth Forces ship was the Gareth but he now refused to give the inferior ship the honor of using any name other than 'human ship.' He felt calling her the 'human ship' was more appropriate, and also more degrading.

Sub-commander Wasson finished his communication with the Encryptor and turned to Tang to share what he knew. "Encryptor has been holding firm for the last forty time units. She could be ready to fire in less than one unit but advises more time to adjust the shot."

Tang bolted from his chair, "There is no time, fire the shot now," he demanded.

As ordered the Encryptor unleashed another superheated slug of molten silica and radioactive contaminate. The shot rang true with only minor adjustments. Tang watched on his screens as the mass approached the flight path of the human ship. "Wasson, I want exploded video of the human ships destruction." Exploded video was simply a four screen view of the event. Tang anticipated the destruction of the human ship and wanted to observe every slice of each time unit.

On board the Gareth, Simms was monitoring the progress of his sailors and soldiers in either killing or capturing the boarders when Sub-Captain Boyce Wellman came on the view screen. "Captain our scanners have picked up a shot approaching from long range, it appears to be of the same characteristics as the Lava-Slug we encountered in the first attack."

Simms had studied the action report of the first attack, which was an ambush really. He knew Mama-Seven had very little time to react in that engagement and the results were better than could be expected.

"ED, load all hull mounted Lead-Ejectors with matter displacement rounds. Mama-Seven please reinforce the Static Repulsar Pocket on the inbound side facing the incoming round." Simms ordered. He never got a response from ED or Mama-Seven, none was needed.

As this was taking place the Sled-Guns completed the reloading process and trolleyed back out. ED notified the captain using his vox unit. "Both starboard and port Sled-Guns have been reloaded and are in firing position Captain. Solution has been plotted on the approaching ship and am awaiting release of the weapons to me."

"Hold ED, until we have confirmation of the first four rounds as either hits or misses," Simms said. He also knew with each second that passed it increased the chances of the next four rounds impacting the approaching ship.

Another few seconds and Mama-Seven gave the information the captain wanted. "One round has penetrated the incoming ship; three are misses but should have enough energy to 180 back if you wish."

Simms doubted the three misses could turn and re-approach the target with any degree of success. It was worth a try if for no other reason than to occupy the enemy's attention. "180 back is approved, what is the damage done by the impacting round?" Simms asked.

"Round penetration unit was fired by Sled-Gun Three and appears to have entered the hull near the bridge area. There was no exit of the round; scanners show penetration to be forty-three percent. Damage assessment is still incomplete but it appears enemy ship is still ninety-eight point six percent functional."

Simms had hoped the effect would have been much greater; this was truly a massive ship he was tangling with. "ED fire the next four round grouping, safeties are now off."

ED could feel the four weapons being handed off to him and the feeling was good. This volley was almost guaranteed one solid hit and most likely two, maybe even more. After one last plot of the enemy's course ED fired the four guns again, this time there was a problem. Gun Three, the one that had scored the only hit on the enemy vessel, seized. The gun immediately trolleyed back inside and went on full safety.

Warning lights on the bridge notified the weapons officer of the malfunction.

"Gun three has failed to fire captain. The other three are away, shots running true, no after fire vibration." Wellman informed the Captain.

This was the news a captain never wanted to hear, a full twenty five percent of the long range weaponry of the Gareth had just failed. There was still the two additional Sled-Guns but they were never counted with the four primaries.

"How long until gun three is operational again." Simms asked.

Wellman was peering at his screens, "Thirty minutes at least, the misfire has to be removed and the cause identified before the gun can be reloaded and trolleyed back out."

"We don't have thirty minutes, get it done in fifteen. Pull back your techs and hand over repairs to Mama-Seven." Simms knew the Super-Computer would task millions of Micro-Repair Cells to repair the gun.

Wellman interrupted the Captain's thoughts, "Incoming Lava-Slug appears to be tracking us sir."

Simms knew the Gareth had made a turn once the slug had been detected, "Did it alter course after we made our first turn?" He asked.

"One point two seconds after we initiated our evasive the incoming round adjusted and is now back on an intercept course." Wellman said.

Simms knew he still had some time but not much, "How long until impact?"

"Two minutes, thirteen seconds."

Simms knew he couldn't outrun whatever it was that had been fired at the Gareth and he also knew another hit would either take his ship out of the battle or destroy it completely. Then a thought crossed his mind.

"How long before the enemy vessel reaches our position?"

Wellman done a few calculations. "Approximately two minutes."

Helm plot a course; put that enemy ship between us and the incoming round." Simms ordered.

Four seconds later the Gareth was heading for a flyby of the alien ship. If the Gareth could pass by at just the right time the Lava-Slug might be diverted at the last minute in order to miss one of its own ships. Simms was in his command chair watching the enemy vessel as it continued to grow larger in his view screen.

"Three Sled-Gun rounds approaching enemy vessel sir, contact in ten seconds." Wellman said.

Aboard the Hatoyo Captain Alto Orme was being briefed on the damage the round from the Gareth had caused his ship. There seemed to be light damage structurally but a few critical systems had gone down and were just now coming back on line. In that brief moment of darkness, the additional three Sled-Gun rounds had travelled a significant distance and were just now being detected. As the Hatoyo's main computer switched back on it was immediately aware of the three additional rounds. Alarms began to sound and defensive systems activated. Orme knew the first hit had been more luck than skill.

All three of the Gareth's shots hit the enemy ship, the first two hit simultaneously, the third eight seconds later due to the 180 degree arch it flew. This last round took out scanners used to not only direct offensive weaponry but also detect incoming fire. Orme was incensed.

"I want all guns loaded and prepped for immediate retaliation on the human ship." Orme knew the optimum firing solution was in less than one time frame and could think of nothing more satisfying right now than the total vaporization of the human ship.

Aboard the Gareth Simms had watched the three rounds penetrate the alien cruiser. One even appeared to exit on the opposite side and continue on its flight path. "Helm, how is our timing on the incoming round?"

"Passing the target now, impact of Lava-Slug imminent."

Orme had gotten what he wanted; the human vessel was adjacent to his ship at less than eighty kilometers range. He now had the Gareth where he wanted her; she was in a position where he could fire a full broadside into her. "All guns fire." He shouted.

With the sensors and scanners temporally out of action there was no way for the crew of the Hatoyo to know that they had just flown into the path of the very weapon that would have destroyed the Gareth. The impact of the Lava-Slug was instantaneous. The first layer of shielding absorbed what it could and then failed, the secondary shielding was more robust than the first but still failed. The Hatoyo's close quarter batteries opened up but were too little too late.

With both sets of shielding down the armored pressure hull, which had six layers, was all that was left between the bug-eyed creatures and the massive silica slug. The six sets of plating superheated and then gave way. There was a blinding light as the slug spread through the ship. Captain Orme knew at once his ship was doomed and tried to hit the eject button that would have cast him and the bridge crew into the void of space and away from certain death, he was a fraction of a time frame too late. The last thing he saw was his hand melting as it reached for the button. The next event, which marked the end of the Hatoyo, was the explosion of her engines which tore the ship apart.

Onboard the Gareth, Simms watched the destruction of his foe. The blast was so great that at the distance of eighty kilometers the Gareth was still buffeted by what was left of the Hatoyo and the Lava-Slug. The Static Repulsar Pocket had no trouble dealing with this, the shield flared as the debris passed by but nothing more happened.

"Helm, resume course to our other ships. ED I need options, plot solutions on the enemy fleet and coordinate with the rescue ships," Simms said.

"Mama-Seven what is the status of Sled-Gun number three?"

"Gun three is just now being cycled up and will be reloaded and trolleyed out at once."

"Do we know the cause of the misfire yet?" Simms asked.

"Misfire is attributed to an altered Sled-Round. It appears whoever tampered with the cryo-tube that killed the sergeant also sabotaged several of the rounds, a total of six to be exact," Mama-Seven said in her mechanical voice.

Simms was astonished, more sabotage. "Have the six rounds been evaluated?"

"Diagnostics show the rounds were meant to lodge in the tubes and prevent the guns from ever firing again. There was a strong possibility that the saboteurs intended for the guns to explode but this didn't happen on Gun Three. There is a seventy point six percent chance that the next time one of the altered shots had been fired there would have been an explosion."

Simms was calm and composed on the outside but on the inside he wanted to find who had done this and choke the life out of him. "Are the remaining rounds safe?"

"All remaining rounds are safe Captain."

"Have you found any more equipment that has been tampered with?" Simms asked.

"Scans and diagnostics are being run now. Critical systems are being checked first with completion in fourteen minutes twelve seconds. Remainder of the ship will be scanned but will take twenty-seven hours fourteen minutes thirty-seven seconds to complete."

"Keep me posted as problems are found." Simms wondered if whoever tampered with his ship could be identified by the Super-Computer. "Mama-Seven is it possible to create a profile of whoever did this by the type and quality of their work?"

"That process is already underway Captain. As each piece of altered equipment, or munitions, is examined a Ghost Profile is being compiled. Once that profile is finished it will be cross-referenced with everyone that entered the ship at our last provisioning and maintenance stop or worked on any of the containers that were loaded into the ship's storage area. There is an eighty-one percent chance that at least one of the saboteurs can be identified. Once that identity is added to the Ghost Profile there is a ninety-ninety point three percent chance that all the culprits will be identified. Once back in the colonies I can link in with Mama-Five and at that point there is a one-hundred percent chance that all will be identified."

Simms was glad to know that at some point all the saboteurs would be identified and captured. He knew the sentence for high treason was banishment to the brine world of Center RI. That particular rock orbited a binary sun system that made the planet almost unlivable. Center RI revolved in its orbit of the two suns at a rate of one to one. In one full revolution of the two suns the planet made only one rotation on its axis thus keeping one side pointed at the suns all the time and the other pointed toward the cold expanse of space. The heated side of the planet maintained a temperature of two-hundred and eight degrees and the cold side a negative one-hundred and fifty-seven. The temperate portion was a mere two miles wide and circled the entire planet. Too much in either direction and you either boiled away or were frozen in place.

The center of the temperate section was pleasant which allowed the only food available to the prisoners to be harvested. It was a fungus that grew both above and below ground. This fungus grew in the center of the temperate zone and circled the entire planet, allowing the above ground portion of the fungus to be of a slightly higher quality than what grew below.

Just below the surface at a depth of five-hundred meters there were numerous lava tubes from the time when Center RI was nothing but a developing planet and covered with volcanoes. Now those volcanoes were extinct, there was currently no tectonic plate movement to create any new features. These tubes extended around most of the planet extending to both the superheated side and the frozen expanse. As compared to the surface the underground tubes were livable for a distance of forty three miles underground on the frozen side and thirty seven miles on the superheated side with some hearty souls pushing even further.

Access to the tubes was made possible through vents in the habitable surface of the planet. The tubes offered shelter, but this was only from the elements. The real danger on Center RI was from the other castaways that lived there. The murder rate was astronomical. The average life span, once exiled to the planet, was only four years. In reality a sentence that was to be lived out on this rock was actually a death sentence.

Simms smiled as he thought of the time when the lander would deposit those convicted of sabotaging his ship. He would get six-months updates on the prisoners and knew that within a few years all would be dead either by some hideous accident on the planet or from the vicious gangs of prisoners that roamed the planet's temperate zone, both above and below ground.

Seeboc Tang watched in disbelief as one of his Capitol Ships flew into the direct path of the Lava-Slug. His monitors revealed every detail of the ship's last time units. Tang was both angered and thrilled at what he saw. The thrill came from witnessing the sheer power of what the Encryptor possessed. The anger came from the fact that the human ship had managed to destroy another of his warships. Tang punched up a few diagnostic screens and began studying the engagements that had cost him each ship.

1.) Tec: Escort Gun Platform, destroyed by long range kinetic weapon.
2.) Ser: Escort Gun Platform, destroyed by long range kinetic weapon.
3.) Re: Battle Barge, destroyed by combination biological chemical weapon.
4.) Zac: Fast Attack Frigate, destroyed by combination biological chemical weapon.

5.) Firrel: Fast Attack Escort, Destroyed by long range kinetic weapon.

6.) Ribald: Fast Attack Escort, Disabled and set adrift by long range kinetic weapon.

7.) Domnat: Fast Attack Escort, Damaged, assisting the Ribald.

8.) Hatoyo: Dreadnaught Class Main Battle Cruiser, Destroyed when she flew into the path of Lava-Slug fired from the Encryptor.

Tang looked over his information and wondered how such an upstart race as the humans could possess such weapons and tactics. What Tang didn't know and would never know was that the history of the humans on Earth was filled with war, from the first time an upright biped clubbed another for a scrap of food there had been conflict and war, humans were just good at it.

"Six fleet class warships destroyed and two disabled and all attributed to one earth ship." Tang said to no one in particular. He had the culprit on his screen and it was headed in the direction of the three new comers that his fleet had cornered as soon as they fell out of Slip-Space. Tang knew he had to destroy all four if he was to keep his command. If not, there was a higher than average probability that he would be executed for the damage done to the Sokari Battle Fleet.

"Target the human ship again with the Encryptor; continue the attack on the others." Tang shouted.

Simms knew the dreadnaught class Sokari ship that was sent to intercept him would have done some damage. He couldn't know how much, that ship and her crew had been destroyed by her own fleet. The Gareth had been fortunate to have scored at least one hit on her, it must have disabled some of her navigational equipment or possibly her sensor arrays and that could be part of the reason she flew right into the path of massive molten slug that was meant for the Gareth.

The Gareth was now heading for the other three ships at flank speed but was still more than an hour away. Scans were showing the three cruisers in a heated exchange with the Sokari. It appeared all three were nearly stationary, this could be attributed to the damage the Beachhead Support Cruiser Temerity had received. Scans revealed the Umbrage had taken her own engines off line and was rerouting coolant to bring them back into a safe operational range.

Anneal was the least damaged of the three and she was making skirmishing runs in order to keep the Sokari Fleet at bay until short term repairs were accomplished on the Temerity and the Umbrage. Mama-Seven was now coded in with the computer systems of the three ships and a more complete picture of what had happened was becoming available.

The three warships that had been sent a few months after the departure of the Gareth had made a headlong rush to the site of the ambush. It was hoped the Gareth had survived and if not there might at least be survivors. None of the crews of the three ships had gone into Cryo-Sleep during the journey. As the ships traveled through Slip-Space technicians were busy running tests on the defensive and offensive systems of the three ships. Anything that could be changed to improve these critical systems was being done. The captains of the three ships had all went over the information contained in the 360 degree Data Burst. In particular was the battle footage Mama-Seven had gathered of the ambush.

The most troubling part of the report was that of the Lava-Slug. How could any ship defend against such a device? It was agreed that early detection and severe evasive maneuvers was the best approach until more information was gathered or until the ship that housed such a weapon could be destroyed. The three captains agreed to Translate out of Slip-Space in a Battle-V Formation with the Dreadnaught Umbrage in the lead.

Systems were powered to full, especially offensive weaponry and shielding. Engines were running at fifty-seven percent and could be charged to full in a matter of seconds. Running the main drive systems at such a low level would keep them cool and ready for extended max-output if the situation warranted. Just as the three ships began the Transition from Slip-Space to Real-Space the targeting computers picked up multiple ships in the area. Scans verified it was the same fleet that had attacked the Gareth. It was now or never.

As soon as the Transition was completed all three ships got target locks on the nearest of the enemy vessels. The Umbrage fired first, she was armed with the same Sled-Gun configuration as the Gareth, four and two. It had been decided to only concentrate fire on a ship if that ship appeared to be close to the area of Transition in order to render her unable to attack the three Earth Colonies Ships until more situational information was gathered. This wasn't the case; no enemy vessel was particularly close. Without a threat close by the three ships in a prearranged battle plan would fire only one Sled-Round per target if that many targets were indeed available. This would allow more ships to be attacked.

Umbrage let loose with a four shot spread at four individual targets, all of significant size. She then fired her two Proximal Sled-Guns; these were considered last chance weapons and by the number of targets the enemy possessed it was deemed that now was not the time to hold back any of the offensive capabilities of the Battle Group.

Anneal fired next; she was armed with only four Sled-Guns due to her enhanced speed and slightly smaller size. She was still a large ship but not quite as large as the Dreadnaught Umbrage. The space that two more of the large weapons systems would have taken up was utilized by additional engine capability, the Anneal was the fastest ship in the fleet and her specialty was hit and run. The Anneal fired her four guns at four different targets, the same as the Umbrage.

That left the Temerity; she was a troop and cargo transport ship. The fact the Temerity was a hot landing zone ship meant she was robustly built and could take an amazing amount of punishment and still be functional. She was never meant to be an attack ship and for this reason she was equipped with only two Sled-Guns. Her offensive targeting systems were not as robust as that of the Umbrage and the Anneal.

For this reason she was to fire her guns last using the telemetry of the Umbrage to try and score hits. Her two shots would therefore be the only shots aimed at an already targeted ship. Umbrage coordinated the targets for the Temerity and decided on two of the largest targets, both either Cruiser or Dreadnaught class.

Less than thirty seconds after full Transition all twelve Sled-guns of the three ships had fired and were trolleyed back in to be reloaded for a second shot. Proximity weapons on the Earth Colonies Ships were still in their safety mode; these systems were of no use in the battle at hand. They would be brought on line if things changed. This early in the engagement it was long range weapons systems only.

Captain Lemann Harless was in command of the three ship rescue mission. He was onboard his ship, the Umbrage, and he was monitoring the enemy fleet and also the twelve fired Sled-Rounds. He was astounded at the number of vessels he was facing. He knew the only chance was to do a limited engagement and then Translate out of this sector. Before that happened he had to determine if the Gareth had been destroyed.

"Have the scanners picked up any sign of the Gareth?" Harless asked.

"Not yet captain, still scanning." One of the watch officers who was in charge of locating the Gareth said.

Harless had expected as much, how could the Gareth have survived alone against a fleet of this size? Long range scanners had so far identified thirty-one enemy vessels and the scans weren't complete yet.

"You've got three more minutes; if scans are still negative then we have got to get out of here," Harless said.

"Roger that captain, scans will be completed in three minutes."

Harless monitored his twelve shots, the enemy seemed to not have noticed the incoming rounds but they had noticed the three Earth Colonies Ships. Scans indicated they were charging their weapons and bringing their main engines on line for an attack.

"Just got a strike on one of the enemy ship's Captain, other weapons are running straight and true." Due to the distance the twelve rounds had to travel, and the separation of the ten different ships being attacked, the spread would arrive at their designated targets over the course of six minutes. During that six minutes nine more rounds found their mark. The two that missed were doing a 180 degree arch and would circle back for another try. Harless was elated for the ten hits and he was also thankful for the technology that allowed a Sled-Round to 180 back to a missed target. These rounds would do this until they either hit the target or were destroyed by enemy weapons fire.

"I need damage assessment on the targets," Harless ordered.

"It appears nine ships were hit with ten of our rounds, one was hit twice and appears to be cruiser size or larger." After a short pause there was more. "Picking up incoming rounds sir. Appears to be some sort of plasma rounds in a solid shot, scanners are trying to isolate the signature but so far aren't having any luck."

"Evasive, all ships form up on the Umbrage; we're getting out of here," Harless ordered.

The scans for the Gareth were only eighty-three percent complete but Harless knew that was as good as it was going to be. A couple more percent might be accomplished by the watch officer but that was going to be the end of it. His ships were now under fire and he had to make a move. The engines on all three ships were powered up and all three began to put some distance between themselves and the enemy fleet.

"I want Transition in thirty seconds; notify the Temerity and the Anneal," Harless ordered.

The three ship flotilla had gotten off twelve rounds. They were now being taken under fire by a superior force: no tactical advantage remained for Harless and his small fleet. Admiral Hayden had made his orders precise, find information on the Gareth and if the situation was suitable inflict damage on the enemy. In the event of the situation being in the enemy's favor he was to exit the area immediately and save his ships. So far everything had gone according to plan with the exception of finding any sign of what happened to the Gareth. The battle might have been a textbook engagement so far but it was about to go horribly wrong.

"Temerity and Anneal acknowledged orders sir, both ships are preparing for Transition." One of the officers told the captain.

"Enemy ordinance is approaching, looks like Temerity has been targeted first, impact imminent. Advise Transition now." The defensive weapons officer said as he activated the High Output Responders on all three ships. These short range weapons were totally defensive in nature. They were primarily used to knock down incoming rounds. The problem now was not knowing the size or makeup of the enemy's ordinance.

No sooner had the Responders been switched on and given free reign than they began to fire. The Temerity was on the left flank of the Umbrage and her weapons, along with those of the larger Dreadnaught, created a virtual wall of lead for the incoming rounds to try to penetrate. The first of the weapons passed through the Responder Fields virtually unscathed. A portion was destroyed but there were so many that it was impossible to get them all.

The next line of defense for the three craft was the Static Repulsar Pocket that surrounded each ship, the same as the one on the Gareth. The Temerity's pocket absorbed as much as possible and then began to move off center of the ship. The Temerity's onboard flight computer tried to compensate and stay in the center of the pocket but events were overtaking the ship faster than her defenses could respond. After numerous strikes the pocket flared against the side of the ship and at that point incoming rounds began to strike the hull.

The armored hull of the Temerity was only three layers thick as opposed to that of other Capitol Ships, she was a Beachhead Support Cruiser, not a main battle vessel. The hull began to be punctured in numerous sections as the ship's computer began to initiate structural bulkheads to prevent the atmosphere from venting. Harless, on the Umbrage, knew the smaller ship was in trouble. He began to play his larger ship across Temerity's path to try and take some of the incoming rounds in the Umbrage's own pocket. This began to work as less and less damage was being reported. The Temerity stabilized her pocket and was now trying to escape as the larger Dreadnaught began to take all the punishment.

"What is the status of our Transition?" Harless asked.

"Anneal and ourselves can make the jump as planned but the Temerity reports problems with her main engines. Appears the Static Repulsar Pocket drew too much power and damaged one of the power plants. She reports repairs will take an hour at least. What are your orders?"

This was bad news for Harless and his small fleet. If the Temerity was damaged and couldn't make the Transition into Slip-Space then the other two ships would be forced to stay and fight. There was no way the Temerity would be abandoned.

"Order the Anneal to make a sweeping assault on the closest of the enemy's cruisers. The Umbrage will stay and protect the Temerity during her repairs." Harless ordered.

"Anneal confirms her orders sir, she is powering up her engines now."

Harless knew his command was in severe trouble. All had taken damage with the Temerity now dead in space. If the smaller ship's engines couldn't be repaired then all three ships would be forced to fight a holding action until the crew of the Temerity could be brought over to the other two ships and then a Transition attempted.

As the Anneal started her sweep the Umbrage fired all six of her Sled-Guns, again targeting the closest and deadliest of the enemy's fleet. To Harless' surprise just as his six guns trolleyed back inside the two guns of the Temerity fired. The Beachhead Support Cruiser might be dead in space but she still had some fight left in her. The two rounds she fired again followed two of the shots from the Umbrage. Eight more of the deadly Sled-Gun Rounds now streaked toward the enemy.

Harless was monitoring multiple screens as his tiny force tried to handle mounting damage. He keenly watched as the fast Anneal outran the enemy weapons fire that had targeted her and made a sweep of the nearest of the enemy's ships. She fired her four Sled-Guns and then, to the surprise of Harless, went in close enough to use her High Output Responders. She was also equipped with Lead-Ejectors and soon these were also within range.

The images of the Anneal's attack were impressive. There were so many close range hull mounted weapons on the cruiser that when they all fired it appeared that the entire ship was on fire. Her sweeps of the enemy craft were so close that none of the alien's weapons could be brought to bear on the faster ship. The Anneal was impossible to target at such close range. When her sweep was complete she headed back toward the other two ships. As she departed the flank of the enemy's ships she again unleashed four more Sled Rounds. As the Anneal made her way back she opened herself up to enemy fire. There were several hits recorded on the Anneal's Pocket by the scanners of the Umbrage but none seemed to have penetrated.

The Anneal had done what she was designed to do. Fly in and target enemy vessels using close range weaponry of which the cruiser had plenty. Her speed was impressive, impressive enough to keep most of the opposing fleets targeting computers from tracking her. By the time enemy weapons got a lock and fired the cruiser was gone.

Once back with the other two ships the Anneal went into re-charge and reload protocols. All the weapons were reloaded and cooled to prepare for another assault if ordered. Incoming fire against the three ships had momentarily dwindled thanks to the headlong assault of the Anneal. Harless knew the break in the action wouldn't last long and pondered whether to evacuate the Temerity and try and make it to the safety of Slip-Space. The problem was it would be impossible to evacuate all the crew and soldiers of the Beachhead Support Cruiser. A portion would never make it. Harless knew the right thing to do was to save as much of his force as possible, wartime protocol actually sanc-tioned such a move. Harless was ready to make his decision when his thoughts were interrupted by one of the scanner officers.

"We've got another ship exiting the planet's atmosphere sir."

"Is she hostile?" Harless demanded.

After only a second the officer answered, "Scans indicate it is the Gareth sir."

"The Gareth, are you sure?" Harless asked.

"It's the Gareth, she's making orbit and still climbing. Appears her weapons are charged and all engines are hot. She appears fully functional sir although scans do indicate damage from weapons fire on several portions of the hull."

Just as the Gareth made her dramatic appearance on the scene the enemy weapons fire diminished further against the three rescue ships. Seeboc Tang and his battle fleet had noticed the arrival of the Gareth and were in the process of reconfiguring their ships to meet this added threat. Tang, once he realized it was the Gareth, wanted to give her his full attention. After all, it was the Gareth that had cost him four ships in their initial engagement.

Mama-Seven had notified ED through Map-Con of the presence of the three Earth Colonies Ships and wanted to know what kind of External Defense computers they were equipped with. Part of ED's programing included partial information of each Capitol Ship in the Colonies Fleet. He was never updated with all the information; this was a safety in the event ED's programing ever fell into the wrong hands, which was unlikely.

ED notified the Super-Computer that the Anneal and the Umbrage were equipped with fourth generation External Defense and targeting system computers, the Temerity being a Beachhead Support Cruiser was equipped with only a second generation system. The two systems on the larger vessels were powerful and able to do the job but none of the three were as efficient as that of ED. Mama-Seven also knew that none of the three ships had a self-aware computer; she was one of only three with several others nearing the threshold.

Mama-Seven quickly linked up with the Umbrage and through her also the other two Earth Colonies Ships. With that accomplished she was now in touch with the three main computing systems of the other ships and notified them to hand over operational protocols to ED, for the time being all four ships defensive and offensive systems would be under the command of ED, a move the Super-Computer deemed necessary. Harless aboard the Umbrage was elated that the Gareth had survived and was more than happy to allow ED to take over the offensive portion of the battle.

Mama-Seven had monitored the attack by the Anneal on the enemy fleet as the Gareth was pulling through the last of the planet's dense atmosphere and this information was now being displayed on Captain Simms monitors. After a quick scan of the battle footage Simms notified Harless.

"Good job done by the Fast Attack Cruiser, she dropped some damage on the enemies advance ships. Advise to not repeat, if Anneal is disabled that close to the enemy fleet then we won't be able to lend assistance. What is the condition of the Temerity?"

Harless was surprised that Simms didn't want a second run by the Anneal considering the success of the first attack. He assumed the captain might know more about the enemy than he did and this was most likely the reason for the added caution. "Temerity is four minutes away from full repairs on her Slip-Space engines. Anneal and Umbrage have received damage but both ships drive systems are functional." Harless knew Simms held rank and was now in charge of all four ships.

Just as Simms was finishing with Harless one of the Gareth's scanner officers said, "Looks like the Sokari are forming up for an attack, heavy cruisers in the lead followed by six craft of Dreadnaught size. Picket ships are forming on the flanks. It looks like they are trying to head off our escape."

Simms went over to the scanner bank and looked at the situation for himself. He knew Mama-Seven had linked with the other three ships and knew Harless had the same information he did.

"Captain Harless are you seeing this?" Simms asked.

Harless replied almost immediately. "I am Captain that is a formidable formation; our scans indicate they will be in optimal firing range in six minutes. What are your orders?"

Simms asked Mama-Seven for an opinion and she replied at once. "Enemy possesses firepower in a ratio of ninety three percent to our seven. Unless Transition is obtained there is a ninety-nine point five percent chance that the four Earth-Colonies Ships will be destroyed in less than thirty minutes."

Simms had left his mic open so Harless could hear what the Super-Computer had to say. Harless knew the news was bad but he had one small piece of good news to share with Simms. "Temerity has just completed repairs on her Slip-Space engines, what are your orders?"

Simms took one last look at the advancing fleet and then went back to his command chair. Transition in thirty seconds, have your three ships form up on the Gareth." The command was gladly repeated by Harless and then he signed off.

Simms wanted to leave a little something for the Sokari as the Gareth and the other three ships prepared for Transition. "Harless how many tubes does your three ships have available to fire?"

After a quick check Harless had the answer Simms would be glad to hear. "All twelve tubes are loaded and trolleying out now Captain, what are your orders?"

Before responding Simms checked with the offensive weapons officer of the Gareth. "Are all six tubes loaded and ready to fire?"

Simms again got the answer he wanted; Gareth's six Sled-Guns were ready and trolleying out. "ED I want all four ships to fire everything we've got at the Sokari fleet, spread pattern Alpha 27." Alpha 27 was an offensive protocol that fired overwhelming ordinance at a reduced number of targets in order to destroy as many of those targets as possible. There was another protocol, Alpha 11 that fired a spread with each weapon targeting a single target, it was meant to disable rather than destroy. Simms wanted to send a message to the attackers; Earth Colonies doesn't take an ambush lightly.

As the four ships began the Transition all eighteen Sled-Guns fired. ED had determined that three rounds per target should either destroy said target or severely disable it. There would be no way to monitor the results as the four ships would be millions of miles away before the rounds struck. His choice to receive each of the rounds was determined by a threat assessment program he had been running since the Gareth had broken through the dense atmosphere and picked up the fleet that had ambushed her.

Using data that had been collected during the ambush ED identified four ships that had been involved in the original attack. He chose these four along with two nasty looking bastards that had to be of dreadnaught size, they bristled with offensive weapons arrays. All eighteen rounds fired successfully and ran true as scanners tracked them as long as possible before the feed was cut by the Slip-Space distortions that began to surround each of the four ships.

Admiral Seeboc Tang had given the order for the Encryptor to fire a second shot at the Gareth and was just being notified that that shot would be taken within the next two time units. As he watched his monitors he realized the Gareth was heading in the direction of the three other ships, no doubt to give assistance. This was good, now he could direct his entire fleet against the four human ships in one massive assault that could be nothing but successful.

"It looks like the three new human vessels and the Gareth are headed for a rendezvous. Calculate that position and prepare the fleet for an all-out assault." Tang ordered.

He knew all four of the human vessels had been damaged by his fleet; there was no way they were going to escape this time. "I want the four ship's engines targeted first." This wasn't standard tactical doctrine, weapons systems first and then propulsion. Tang was throwing doctrine out the window; he was going to have this victory on his own terms. If the four ships could be stranded then his superior fleet could pound them into submission. In this way the four ships would be captured and survivors taken. Tang wanted to see this new species that had given him such problems. He also wanted to torture a few of the survivors as a reprisal for the loss of his own ships and their crew. Just as the

Rococo began the advance that would see the victory over the humans he noticed evasive movement from his enemy.

What Tang had seen as an evasive maneuver from the four human ships was actually the prelude to Transition into Slip-Space. Mama-Seven was now in charge of the four ship flotilla and was coordinating the Transition of all four. Tang was helpless to prevent what was about to happen right before his eyes. There was a flare of thrust at the stern of each of the human ships and then four seconds later they were gone, nothing was left but a brief engine signature.

The use of Slip-Space travel was a human means of traveling vast distances in a relatively short span of time. With the discovery of Slip-Space what would have normally taken a lifetime could now be accomplished in hours. Even this means of travel wasn't ideal; the galaxy was an extremely large expanse. It was estimated it would take someone traveling through Slip-Space years to go from one side of the Galaxy to the other.

This means of travel had been on the edge of human understanding for decades, even centuries. It could never be accomplished because of the power requirements a ship would need to accomplish in order to gain a velocity that could leave Real-Space and Transition into Slip-Space. This was simply known as the Transition. If you used Slip-Space you would need to Translate into it and then at the end of your journey you would need to Translate out.

The original theories for this new means of travel started with the theory that if you traveled at the speed of light two possibilities existed. As you traveled forward what you saw would be nothing but white light, it was actually a light so intense that it would burn out an unprotected retinae. What happens at such speed is that you are absorbing all the light instantly that would normally need to travel to you. This would be an enormous amount of radiation that any unprotected eye could never hope to absorb without permanent loss of vision.

The second theory was that as you traveled at the speed of light if you looked back at the point of origin you would see a picture of the last event that happened just as you made light speed. This assumption was false in that no light could enter the retinae, what you would see is a darkness so complete the eye would not be able to identify it at all. Again damage could be done from such an absolute darkness.

These two theories could only be proven if light speed could be achieved. Some mathematicians theorized on both assumptions and for a while it was agreed that the theories were correct. The problem was eventually solved by the mathematicians' decades before speed of light travel was ever attained. The simple version of the solution can be explained briefly here.

If you take an equilateral triangle and name the three Points A, B, and C, with all three sides being equal to the distance light travels in one year we can begin. If a ship traveled from Point A to Point B at the speed of light then one year will have elapsed by the time the ship makes it to Point B. At the moment the ship reaches Point B the image of Point A will not have changed even though a full year has elapsed. Now suppose someone was monitoring this event from Point C. Nothing will be seen of the ship for a full year and at that moment the visual from point C will be that the ship is still at Point A, (It will have taken light a full year to travel from Point A to the observer at Point C.) but the ship will actually exist at Point B.

Real-Space is the exact position of the observer and the unseen ship resting at Point B. Slip-Space is simply described as the observer at Point C knowing the ship is at Point B which eliminates the need for the observer to watch for a year as the ship travels from Point A to Point B as the light travels to Point C during the same year long journey.

The reality of this assumption is that the observer on point C has just eliminated the year traveling at light speed to reach Point B from Point A; the ship is already there but unseen. So to reach this reality of the unseen ship resting at Point B while the observer actually sees it at Point A, two things are needed. Number one is a vessel that can attain travel at the speed of light and Number two a way to slow down the speed of light the vessel is actually traveling through.

Once a destination is determined then it is calculated into the amount of time it would take to get there traveling at the speed of light. The ship would then accelerate to light speed. At the moment that is attained the vessel would slow down the speed of light that it is traveling through, this would mean the ship is at that moment traveling faster than the speed of light. The slower you were able to slow the dynamics of the speed of light the ship is traveling through the faster the ship moves toward its destination.

The greater of the two theories wasn't the ability to reach the speed of light, this had been accomplished hundreds of years earlier, the greatest problem was the ability to slow light on the flight path the ship was flying. It had almost been give up on until it was discovered that light traveled at a constant in the vacuum of space. It had been known that light traveled slightly faster in that vacuum than it did in an atmosphere. As any atmospheric pressure increased, the speed of light decreased ever so slightly.

Experiments were conducted and it was found that if a vacuum represented an equivalent of zero then a negative equivalent of zero should alter the speed of light. What was needed to reach such levels that would be required for a large craft, such as a cruiser the size of the Gareth, to exceed the speed of light would come to be known as a super-vacuum. If a ship's hull could be polarized, a constant vacuum could be maintained and at that moment the speed of light passing by the hull could be either slowed or speeded up by regulating the density of the polarization. When this was first tried the test drone did achieve Transition but the vacuum surrounding the tiny craft was filled with dangerous variances that soon tore the drone apart.

With each successive test the variances were tamed and the Transition into Slip-Space was safely attained. With time this means of traveling vast distances in relatively short periods of time was perfected. All Earth Colonies vessels were now equipped with the means of traveling in Slip-Space.

Once the technology for Slip-Space travel had been successfully implemented in large warships, studies began on the possibility of time travel. If the deceleration of light had allowed for the movement of matter out of Real-Space then couldn't that same technology be altered to allow for a bending of time?

The subsequent study of time had allowed for a stunning assumption. There was no such thing as time at all, just the present or now. In order to explain yesterday or tomorrow, if there was only now, it had been determined that each were just different slices of now. If time then had been reduced to only now or different slices of now then wouldn't it be possible to identify a slowing or increasing of the speed of light as a way to look either into the past or the future by simply looking at the different slices of now that had just been either slowed down or speeded up.

Many of the greatest scientist and mathematicians had studied these possibilities but the results were slow to come. When it looked like a breakthrough might be available in the next few decades the Earth Colonies began to look at the affect such knowledge might have on society, in fact life itself.

The council called many of the men and women together that had been studying the movement of time to explain the processes that were in place concerning their findings. After three months of testimony the council went into chambers to compare the benefits, and also the hazards, of such studies. A majority of the council was made up of scientists and members of the military. These were brilliant men and women in their own rite. After eleven days of evaluating all the data an unexpected conclusion was attained, the study of time travel would be suspended at once.

The information and studies gathered so far would be locked away until it was deemed safe to resume the work. Many of the people that worked on the project were disappointed but they knew the council had made the right decision. If this work were ever successful then it would open up the possibility for misuse. Indeed if it fell into the wrong hands it could even spell the end of the human race. For now all the information was stored in a vault somewhere on earth with no one quite sure where the vault was located other than those on the council. Secrecy was still a powerful weapon.

The Sokari had never tested for Slip-Space travel, much less the ability to travel through time. When great distances were spanned it was done by sheer force on their part. The Sokari ships contained massive engines that could gradually advance a ships speed past the speed of light many times. This required massive amounts of fuel for each ship, thus the need to be a conquering race. As systems were taken over and their resources used up it was necessary to expand into the next adjoining region. The Sokari would be described as locust if a human word could ever be used for their description.

Seeboc Tang watched the exit, or more correctly the escape, of the four human vessels with a small amount of envy. If only the Sokari had such a means of travel then they could conquer the galaxy much faster. At that moment it became his goal to capture the four human ships and learn what this new form of travel could do for the advancement of his race. Not only could the Sokari control this galaxy but the adjoining galaxies as well, the possibilities were beyond comprehension.

"Navigation, can you track the human vessels?" Tang asked.

There were four of the bug-eyed creatures manning multiple long-range scanners and deep space detection units. "We are tracking them now admiral. It appears they haven't gone far, two hundred and twelve time units at flank speed and we will be at their new location."

"Notify the rest of the fleet, move out at once," Tang ordered.

Two time units later and most of the Sokari capitol and picket ships would be in position to begin the pursuit of the four human ships. A small force would be left behind to assist with the two disabled picket ships the Gareth had damaged when she came out of the planet's atmosphere.

Tang ordered the cumbersome Encryptor to stay behind with her escort of three picket ships and one heavy cruiser. He had fallen out of favor with the abilities of the giant warship after the loss of the Hatoyo. An investigation would be ordered and he was sure the Encryptor would be found innocent of any wrongdoing. He on the other hand would most likely be given blame for the poor performance of the fleet against the troublesome humans. He knew now he had to destroy or capture the four ships to redeem himself. If he could capture the technology they used for traveling at such speeds then his miscalculations during battle would be overlooked. If he failed again he was sure he would be executed.

"Evasive, Evasive." A mechanical voice declared over the communications array. "Enemy weapons detected."

Tang looked at the monitors; nothing could be seen except red warning tracer lights and each were heading toward the fleet. If the order to evade was followed then he would lose the chance to destroy the human ships. Also, if his forces did evade then it was possible to avoid any further damage. Evasion was not an option for the admiral. "Cancel evasive maneuvers, continue to power up, the pursuit of the human ships will continue," he ordered. Tang was willing to allow additional damage to his fleet in order to corner and destroy the human ships, what took place next made Tang wish he had never heard the word 'Human.'

As the Sokari fleet continued to power up the incoming Sled-Rounds began to impact the selected targets, six in all. The first to report damage was the Dreadnaught Impaler. With three shots designated for each of the six ships a best chance scenario would be for two hits out of three. Two hits were exactly what struck the Impaler. She lost speed immediately and two of her engines were disabled beyond repair. The Impaler fell out of formation as mounting problems arose due to onboard fires. The computing system quickly managed to initiate a response to the damage the two rounds had caused but the ship was out of action, it would be years before she managed to limp home.

The next ship to receive damage was the Cruiser Infinish; she was also struck by two Sled-Rounds. The Infinish managed the damage with about the same level of success as the Impaler. She was disabled and one of her engines was also hit, damaged beyond repair. This ship too would accompany the Impaler in her decade's long journey back to its home system.

The third ship to be targeted was the Dreadnaught Vicerate. The Vicerate was only hit by one Sled-Round; she managed to maintain speed and remained with the fleet.

Fourth was the Cruiser Inhellish, she was struck by all three of the rounds that had been sent against her. One was a glancing blow that only tore out a large section of the hull armor allowing the precious chemical the Sokari breathed to vent out of seven sections, instantly killing everyone in those sections. The other two rounds penetrated at the most opportune angle to accomplish the most damage. All four engines exploded at the same time reducing the cruiser to an ever expanded cloud of gas and debris.

The fifth and sixth targets were not impacted, this was mainly due to the ever increasing speed the fleet was achieving, still four Capitol Ships had been hit with two put out of action permanently and one a total loss.

The Admiral had been monitoring and his crew now feared the homicidal Tang might take his rage out on one of the bridge crew. Tang never moved, he sat quietly in his command chair and continued to look at the monitors though he saw nothing, his mind was playing on the events that would now define his life, the loss of so many ships to what had been described as a myth, an apparition. His only chance to escape a sentence of death by the High-Command was to capture the technology the human vessels contained that allowed for such speeds as had never been seen before.

The Gareth, along with the other three Earth Colonies warships, made a successful Transition into Slip-Space. Simms at first worried that the damage the four ships had received in their brief but intense battle with the Sokari might have prevented their escape. If only one of the warships had been unable to Transition then he would have been required to make a decision, abandon the disabled ship to sure destruction by the Sokari fleet or turn back with his three operational ships and put up a fight that would have surely resulted in the loss of all four. As it was he never had to make such a decision and hoped he never would.

All four warships were running true with a destination yet to be decided. Simms had purposely headed in a direction ninety degrees away from the route back to the Earth Colonies. He didn't want to mark a path for the Sokari that would lead them in the future to Earth. If they were in fact following and thought this was the way to the human home world then they could follow forever.

"Getting a message from the Temerity sir, her engines are running hot. She doesn't know how long she can maintain Slip-Space. Her engineering crew is diverting all available coolant into the drive systems but levels are continuing to elevate." One of the comms officers notified the captain.

"How long can Temerity maintain this speed without doing damage to her engines?" Simms asked.

Before long the captain of the Temerity sent back an unwanted reply, the engines might be coaxed to operate for another fifteen minutes before reaching unsafe levels. A Transition back into Real-Space would be required at that time or risk an explosion. Simms had his navigator plot how far they would have traveled and how long it would take the Sokari fleet to catch up if another ten minutes of travel in Slip-Space could be accomplished. Not knowing how fast the enemy could actually travel made the answer more of a guess than a fact.

"Mama-Seven has calculated our destination and also analyzed the capabilities of the enemy's ships. The information available is inadequate to formulate an accurate response but she theorizes that the Sokari will overtake our new position twenty hours after we Transition out of Slip-Space. She said the answer could be incorrect by as much as ten hours on the short side and weeks on the long. More studies of the Sokari capabilities are needed."

"Notify the other ships; begin Transition in nine minutes thirty seconds. I want a defensive posture upon arrival at our new destination with the Temerity center rear. Have coolant transferred from the Umbrage to the Temerity with repairs to begin at once." Simms knew the Dreadnaught had a massive reserve of engine coolant and could spare the loss. He never considered the Anneal; the Fast Attack Cruiser needed all the coolant her systems had to keep her high-output engines running. The performance of the Anneal as she made her dramatic attack on the Sokari Fleet was still fresh in Simms mind and he knew at some point he might need a repeat performance.

At the appropriate mark the four ships began the Transition from Slip-Space to Real-Space. The Temerity could have gone another five minutes according to her engineers but Simms didn't want to chance it. He allowed a thirty-three percent margin of safety. Once the Transition was complete a scan of the system they arrived in was undertaken. There were three systems actually with a spread of three quarters of a billion kilometers distance between each. Each of the systems was made up of a central star which was orbited by any number of planets, moons, gas-giants and asteroids.

With the Transition complete Umbrage immediately sent a drone-shuttle over with the needed coolant for the Temerity. Work on her engines couldn't begin until the excess heat had been dealt with. Simms wanted an update as soon as possible. If the engines could be repaired in time it might be possible to exit this star system before the Sokari arrived. The decision to abandon the Temerity might still need to be made but at least now a full evacuation could be implemented by the other three ships. No one would be left behind.

"Captain we've got a message from the Umbrage, the circuitry that controls the Slip-Space SV have been damaged. Repairs are being implemented now." One of the comms officers said. The SV stood for the super-vacuum that was required around the hull for a ship to exit Real-Space.

This was bad news, if the Umbrage couldn't repair her SV circuitry then that might make two ships disabled. If only one of the four ships had to be abandoned the crew could be transferred to the other three, but if two were unable to Translate out then it would be impossible to accommodate the crews of both on the two operational ships.

"Mama-Seven, if Umbrage and Temerity are unable to make Slip-Space how many of their crew can be rescued by the Gareth and Anneal?" Simms asked. The real problem was with the Temerity, she carried over three-thousand Deep-Space Soldiers besides her crew of Astro-Sailors.

"Twenty-two hundred and thirty-one crew and soldiers will be unable to leave this system. The ones that can be rescued will create an extreme hardship for the Gareth and the Anneal, due to sever rationing of provisions until one of the distant Earth Colonies can be reached." Mama-Seven replied immediately.

Simms was stunned; he might be forced to abandon nearly twenty-three hundred troops and sailors. He knew both the abandoned ships would be forced to detonate their engines before being captured by the Sokari. Engagement with hostile species such as the Sokari in the past had uncovered immense pain and suffering in the form of torture to any survivors. Also the technology the two ships contained could be used by the aliens against the Earth Colonies in the future. The ships and crew would be incinerated rather than fall into enemy hands. All crew, regardless of whether they were soldier or sailor, had signed on to the 'Death before capture' articles of war when they were accepted into the force. It was actually comforting knowing capture and torture would never happen to them.

As the small flotilla moved away from the Transition point of arrival, scans were performed on the three solar systems. Two proved to have at least one planet in the habitable zone and the third had two. Additional scans were being run for atmospherics and topography, it might be convenient, if it became necessary, to land a damaged ship and try and fight it out on the ground. The Assault Troops on the Temerity were itching for a fight, they were not sailors and found little use for the inside of a warship. They considered the Earth Colonies ships to be nothing more than taxis used to transport them to the next fight.

The closest star system was the one that had the two habitable planets. Both were Class M and each was nearly the size of Earth. One was slightly bigger with a mass four-percent larger than Earth and the other slightly smaller by two-percent. Each had similar gravitational fields. It wouldn't be known about the content of the atmosphere for another few minutes but it was evident one of the planets was dead. There wasn't any evidence of moisture in the atmosphere or on the ground. What was pooled up in vast oceans appeared to be a soup with a heavy concentration of chlorine.

The second planet was ringed by cloud cover broken in places to reveal oceans and rivers with what appeared to be several continents. If a landing was required then this planet looked to be the best hope. Mama-Seven was tasked with doing the initial survey of the second planet; the first planet for the time being was to be ignored due to the heavy concentration of nasty liquids.

Mama-Seven completed her scans in short order and transmitted the results to the other three ships. Simms was reading the information on his data screen when he received a transmission from Captain Harless of the Umbrage.

"Looks like quite a find Captain, if it weren't for the fact that an overwhelming enemy force is heading our way then this planet would be worth investigating," Harless commented.

"Very earthlike indeed, how are the repairs going?" Simms asked.

"My engineers are doing the best they can, so far it looks like the damage was due to direct ship to ship weapons fire, not from entering or exiting Slip-Space," Harless said.

One of the comms officers broke in as Simms was signing off with Harless. "Temerity is requesting a communication with you captain." The captain of the Temerity was a man by the name of Alex Zhukov. He hailed from an old earth family that had roots back as far as an old country that was known, at the time, as the Soviet Union. Zhukov was a military man through and through.

"Captain Simms, I have some bad news, we have managed to isolate and repair the problems with our Temperament Coolant Reduction System but the fix is only temporary, more extensive repairs will need to be undertaken at one of the Orbital Heavy-Repair Facilities, such as the one at Star-Base Triton. We can make an emergency Transition but I don't recommend it. To execute a Slow Gather Transition would most likely allow us to make it all the way back but that requires nearly a day to initiate. (A Slow Gather Transition allowed the ship to reach the moment of Transition at a much slower speed which required less power thus, less heat buildup in the engines.)

"Is there any way to make further repairs if given more time?" Simms asked.

"Sorry sir, you could give my engineers a year and the repairs our systems require couldn't be fixed with the equipment we have available to us," Zhukov said.

With very little time to consider any other alternatives Simms said, "Looks like we will need to transfer your troops and sailors to the other three ships and make Transition, we don't have a lot of time before our friends show up."

"Roger that captain, this will be the first ship I've lost," Zhukov said with a touch of sadness in his voice.

"She was lost due hostile enemy action, nothing to be ashamed of. Overwhelming odds, once the battle footage is assimilated our actions will be justified." Simms reassured the man.

Simms and Zhukov ended the transmission. Mama-Seven broke in with more news that could be deemed nothing short of dire considering the situation. "I have managed to adjust our long range scans to accommodate the configuration of the Sokari power plants on the larger of their ships. We can now track them at a further distance."

"How long do we have?" Simms asked.

"Eleven hours and fifty-seven minutes. They will reach our position and then require time to regroup before attacking; some of their ships are falling behind in the headlong rush to get here before we leave."

"Contact Umbrage and Anneal, have them prepare to receive the crew of the Temerity. I want to Translate as soon as possible." There was no reply from the Super-Computer, she never replied, she only accomplished.

Just as the first of the Temerity's transports were being loaded with troops for the trip to the other three ships a transmission was received from Captain Harless.

Simms suspected it was about the repairs to the SV circuitry on the Umbrage. "Simms here."

"Captain Simms, I've been informed by the engineering department that the SV system will take more than forty-eight hours to repair. A high percentage of the hull mounted diodes will need to be replaced; most were damaged in the battle and couldn't take the exertion of our two Transitions." Harless said.

Simms thought for only a second before signing off, "Continue repairs, I'll be back in touch shortly," Simms said as he ended the transmission.

Now his small fleet was in real trouble. With two ships unable to make Transition and this far from any relief, he felt more alone than at any other time in his life. He knew a decision had to be made immediately but was reluctant to make it on his own. He had his comms team set up a secure link between himself and the captains of the other three ships. Once the conference was begun Simms brought the other three captains up to speed.

"Gentlemen, I want to state our situation and after you have absorbed the facts we will discuss our options. Before we get started I want to say that the performance of our ships and crews have stood up to the high expectations of the fleet, no one will ever look at what we have accomplished so far against overwhelming odds and find reason for disappointment.

"First it appears we have two ships, the Umbrage and the Temerity, which can't be repaired before the Sokari fleet gets here. We also can't fit everyone on the Gareth and the Anneal; if that is our course of action then two warships will need to be abandoned along with nearly twenty-three hundred troops and sailors. Now keep in mind I am not recommending this course of action, just putting all the options on the table.

"Second, all four ships can stay and fight it out with the outcome being a total defeat taking into account the size and number of ships that are headed here now. Those are the two choices we have, if I have missed anything then please feel free to speak."

The four men could see the expressions of each other; the conference was in both audio and video. The captain of the Temerity spoke first. "There might be a third option captain but I doubt it possesses a total solution."

Simms suddenly had a small bit of hope, "Then by all means Zhukov, explain."

"When the Temerity was recalled to Star-Base Triton we were on our way to the Fleet Ordinance Proving Grounds or FOPG. We had picked up our cargo which had been shipped to Star-Base Triton from the Mars heavy weapons manufacturing facility. We never made it to the FOPG before we were called back so our cargo is still in the loading bays of the Temerity." Zhukov stopped to make sure the other three captains understood what he had just told them.

Simms now was anxious to hear more, "What is it you have in your cargo holds Zhukov?" Simms doubted anything the Temerity carried could change the tactical situation he now found himself in.

"What we picked up, and were about to test at the FOPG, was a new planetary defense system. The short of it is the system is centered on four Multi-Tube Sled-Gun surface to air systems. The unit is equipped with multi-targeting scanners and land based Repulsar Pocket defenses. The system takes approximately twenty acres of flat land to accomplish the set up. With the four systems located at the corners and each protected by its own Static Repulsar Pocket. The system is called Mongoose but its unofficial nick-name is Moag which stands for Mother of All Guns with each of the four twin-barreled guns named M1 through M4."

Simms found this to be a blessing and a curse. A blessing if it worked and a curse that he would be relying on an untested weapons system. "What are the capabilities of the system?" He asked.

"The Mongoose was designed as a first line of defense for any remote colony where the assistance of the fleet was weeks or even months away. Any planet or moon equipped with two batteries of the Moag could hopefully defend itself against attack," Zhukov said.

Simms knew time was short but wanted to hear more, "What are the firing characteristics of this Moag System?" He asked.

"Each of the four systems has a multi-tube Sled-Round launcher, two tubes per each. A tube fires a reduced version of the Sled-Guns our ships carry, in other words the round itself is smaller than a ship fired Sled-Round. As you know, our Capitol Ships use a fourteen meter long Ship-Kill Collapse round. The land based version fires an eleven meter round that has the capability of reaching a higher velocity due to its smaller length being drawn through the firing tube by the same amount of energy used in the fleet mounted weapons. This added velocity allows for a range of three-thousand kilometers. (A ship mounted Sled-Gun could fire a round that would travel forever through the void of space or until it hit something. The land based version had to contend with the gravitational pull of the planet it was based on.) It was determined that any attacking ships would need to close to fifteen-hundred kilometers to fire their weapons successfully and the guns were designed to operate against targets at twice that distance." Zhukov paused to allow any of the other captains to add to the discussion.

Again it was Simms who spoke first. "So you're saying the four systems have the ability to track and fire four salvoes of two rounds each at a target. That is great, but what effect will these reduced Sled-Rounds have on a fully shielded enemy cruiser, or even a dreadnaught for that matter?"

"This new round is more deadly than the ones our ships fire. Due to the higher velocity the kinetic energy alone can punch through the most heavily armored and shielded ship. There is another nasty surprise, these new rounds contain an upgraded phosperous-lead mixture, the ignition point is the same but the burn rate is no less than that of a collapsing star. One penetration will incinerate everything within a two meter radius as the round penetrates a ship with another thirty meter radius reduced to charred collapsing metal. One hit on a large fleet class ship will result in a hole 180 feet across completely through the ship. If the tests at the FOPG were successful then the older style Sled-Guns our ships contain now were to each be replaced with this newer version."

Now another critical question was raised by Captain Harless, "How many rounds of ammunition does the Temerity carry for this Moag System?" He asked.

Zhukov knew the answer because he knew it would come up. "Considering it takes two rounds for each multi-barreled gun and there are four guns, an abundance of ammunition was loaded onboard. The Temerity carries eleven-hundred and twenty rounds or enough for one-hundred and forty shots of eight rounds each."

The four captains might have been the only ones participating in the conference if you only counted humans but Captain Simms had made sure Mama-Seven and ED were also listening. "ED, what are the tactical abilities at our disposal if you factor in the Moag system along with our four ships." Simms asked.

The External Defense computer answered immediately. "Two problems are presented when using a land based weapons system against orbiting Capitol Ships. First of all the Moag can only fire from the side of the planet it is installed on. Secondly the Moag would be vulnerable to a land based attack if the enemy air-dropped troops beyond the arch of fire of the Moag."

Simms knew ED was good but Mama-Seven was more attuned to the big picture. "Mama-Seven, given the amount of damage our four ships have received and the inability to escape without leaving two ships behind, along with twenty-three hundred personnel, what is our best course of action given what we have to fight with?"

The answer was given immediately and it shocked the four captains at the abilities of the Super-Computer.

"Scans of the planet's surface are complete; it will support human life without the need for bio-gear or rebreathers. Plan for best chance against approaching Sokari fleet is as follows.

> ➤ Temerity to drop troops and Moag System. Once system is in place troops are to form a defensive perimeter to repel expected land based attack.
> ➤ Temerity to remain in orbit without a crew and remotely flown from the Gareth. She will be destroyed by the Sokari, bait for the enemy if you will.
> ➤ Umbrage along with Gareth to station on hidden side of planet and attack from opposite directions after first salvo from the Moag.
> ➤ Anneal to attack from behind adjoining moon after initial strike by Moag and combined Gareth/Umbrage assault.
> ➤ At this point all our forces are committed; this will be an all or nothing battle.

Mama-Seven fell silent, the four captains also sat speechless until Simms asked one more question of the Super-Computer. "Mama-Seven is there any other options and if not what are our chances?"

"No other options exist. Chance of success is twenty-two percent and even at this there will be a high casualty rate."

Simms looked at the other three captains, "Twenty two percent gentlemen, less than one in four odds." Before any of the three could respond Simms asked one last question of the Super-Computer.

"Mama-Seven what would happen if we remote detonate the engines of the Temerity when she can do the most damage to the Sokari Fleet?"

"Remote detonation of the Temerity's engines could result in the destruction of five to eight of the Sokari ships depending on their distance and grouping. With the sacrifice of the Temerity the chance of success increases to thirty-seven percent."

Simms looked at the other three captains and each was represented by a smile. "Our chances are now better than one in three if we evacuate the Temerity and use her as a floating bomb. I need an opinion from the three of you."

All three captains wanted to fight it out; the only alternative was to abandon two ships along with twenty-three hundred troops and sailors.

"All right then, we prevail or we go down fighting," Simms said. These were fighting men and to run and hide from a superior force was just not acceptable. They would all be victorious together or they would all die together

All four captains signed off and began the task of implementing the plan Mama-Seven had devised. The more each thought about it the more they liked it, no one would be abandoned and they knew every man and sailor would fight with skill and honor.

The main task at hand was locating a landing site for the Temerity to offload her troops and heavy equipment. As this was being done the extra coolant that had been transferred from the Umbrage to the Temerity was reloaded and sent back. The Temerity was going to be sacrificed in order to try and save the other three ships. Once Mama-Seven had selected a landing zone it only took the Beachhead Support Cruiser six minutes to make a hot landing. Four companies of her Assault Troops rushed into the undergrowth and quickly secured the twenty acres that would be needed to set up the cumbersome Moag system. Once the troops and equipment was offloaded the Astro-Sailors that remained on board quickly unloaded anything else that wasn't needed to fly the ship.

All available stores which included food, weapons and ammunition was trolleyed down the three huge ramps. The troops of Temerity's expeditionary force were equipped with heavy armor and assault vehicles and these were driven off and used to help secure the perimeter. Anything and everything that could be salvaged from the giant cruiser was being taken. By the time she lifted off, what remained behind looked like the makings of a full-on military base. The soldier in charge of this newest Earth Colonies base was a Major Albert Beiting or A Bet for short.

A Bet had all the weapons transported to the four sites chosen and assembly was quickly begun. In the center of the four gun batteries he set up a command and control headquarters. The limited Static Repulsar Pocket that would protect the four gun stations was assembled and tested, a pocket for each gun and the headquarters. Four hours after the Temerity lifted off the Moag was fully operational. A Bet had his troops prepare defensive positions against ground assault with overlapping fields of fire. At the four hour and thirty minute mark he sent a transmission to Captain Simms that Fire-Base Moag was now fully operational.

Simms was busy coordinating the preparation of the four ships now orbiting the planet when Mama-Seven spoke into his headset. "Sokari Fleet will arrive in less than two hours; the force now consists of twenty-six vessels with none following. Three of the vessels targeted with the eighteen round Sled-Gun salvo just before we entered Slip-Space are not with the fleet, assume either partial damage or total destruction of the missing ships. With the elimination of the three Sokari ships from the attacking force the chances for success have increased from thirty-seven percent to thirty-nine."

This was truly good news if in fact three of the Sokari Capitol Ships had been struck by his departing salvo. It was a shot from the hip and few impacts were expected but now he learned that three of the ships targeted were not accompanying the Sokari fleet.

"Mama-Seven please notify the other ships, they need to hear the same information you have just given me." With that Simms went back to the coordination and preparation for the upcoming attack.

On the planet's surface A Bet was doing a reconnaissance sweep of the surrounding area prior to the expected Sokari attack, he wanted to see what this new planet had to offer in the event he and his troops were locked in an extended land battle. He knew ammunition shouldn't be a problem but rations might. What had been offloaded from the stores of the Temerity was the K and C variety which every soldier and sailor for generations had come to detest. There was a smaller number of MRE's, Meals Ready to Eat, but all in all his command had approximately three weeks' worth of rations.

The stores on the Temerity were enormous but not transferable from the cruiser. The problem was that the provisions on a Fleet Class Capitol Ship were in a vat state. As meals were prepared they were drawn from large vats of liquid ingredients that were then prepared by specialized equipment that made the food not that much different than what you might expect planet side. This was done for the convenience of compactness and transport. Six vats could contain the ingredients to prepare more than three hundred different dishes.

The problem was the vats were not transportable; they were part of the ship. The contents of the vats were also not portable, if you didn't have the preparation equipment you couldn't use the ingredients. For this reason the troops and sailors, now stationed planet side, were left with the limited field rations all Capitol Ships carried, and this reserve was limited.

A Bet and one company of troops were doing the sweep. Not only were they looking at the possibility of finding supplemental food to add to the stores provided by the Temerity, they were looking for any positions an enemy might use against the base. The sweep was being carried out at a one kilometer radius from the camp. Each time a position was identified as probable it was electronically marked back to a fifty-millimeter mortar unit tasked with short range bombardment.

The sweep was more than fifty-percent complete when A Bet's company found what appeared to be the entrance to a vast underground cavern system. A perimeter was established around the opening while A Bet and three troopers started inside. Upon closer examination the opening was determined to be constructed rather than natural. It was wide enough for one of the heavy tanks Temerity unloaded to go into, it was possibly even wide enough for two to enter abreast of each other, the opening was huge.

The floor appeared to be built of some type of plastic; upon closer inspection it seemed it might be concrete or a combination of both. It showed no wear although it looked very old. There was a thin layer of dust, maybe a quarter to a half inch thick, covering most of the tunnel's base.

One of the troopers claimed to be part Indian although not many men knew what an Indian was. The man's name was Simpson Woods but everyone knew him by his given nickname, Tonto. Tonto considered himself an Indian tracker and practiced his hobby at every opportunity. He was actually pretty good at it.

"Tonto, see if you can make anything out of these marks," A Bet said as he studied some scuffs on the floor.

Tonto stooped and looked at the marks. He stood and followed some of the markings which appeared to go deeper into the tunnel. "It looks like something has been killed and then taken farther into the shaft." Upon closer inspection Tonto turned to A Bet. "Whatever it was must be huge. Look at the size of these tracks."

A Bet looked at what Tonto saw; the track was at least a foot and a half across. There were apparently four digits on each foot with a claw at the end of each digit. The claw must have been very sharp because it had indented the concrete. Each of the troopers activated the light on the end of their assault rifles and followed Tonto deeper into the tunnel. There was a slight breeze exiting the opening.

"Where do you think that breeze is coming from?" A Bet asked.

Tonto looked into the tunnel as he increased the beam on his light. Shining the light down the center of the tunnel it was obvious it went farther than the beam of light could penetrate.

"The breeze appears to be natural, not mechanically created." Tonto sniffed the air and knew he wasn't the only one to notice the smell by the looks on the faces of the other three.

"There is the distinct smell of rotting flesh in here and a lot of it." He said.

There were side tunnels which looked to be at least as large as the main tunnel. The four men continued to advance into the main tunnel, each using great caution. At the entrance to a side tunnel they found what was creating the smell.

Tonto looked at what must have been a meal hidden for future use. It was an animal of some sort, and large, very large. It appeared to be a herbivore. The teeth were flat as if the creature had to grind its food up before it swallowed. By the looks of the injuries whatever attacked it had to also be large. There weren't any marks indicating the creature had been used for food yet, but by its placement, Tonto said it was hidden in the cave for a future meal, or maybe whatever killed it wanted to bring back the rest of the pack?

A Bet looked around and began to get an uneasy feeling about where they were, in an enclosed environment without much in the way of cover if trouble arose. As the four studied the strange beast that lay at the opening to the side tunnel a noise could be heard deep in the main tunnel. At first it seemed to be a scraping sound but the next time they heard it the noise was more of a growl.

Tonto activated his Threat Sensor, a handheld device with a small screen that gave a one-hundred and eighty degree sweep of any movement in the direction it was pointed in. It only took the little device three seconds to show multiple points of movement at a thousand meter range; it even picked up movement in the side tunnels.

Tonto spoke without taking his eyes off the screen, "Looks like we've woken something up, thousand yards distance and moving in this direction."

A Bet wanted to know more before making a decision, "What size does the sensor make of the approaching marks?"

Tonto made a few adjustments to the readout, which would allow for size and speed of the targets. "Each is approximately the same size, six meters long and four meters high."

"Are you sure, that's enormous?" A Bet asked as he raised his weapon and pointed it in the direction of the main tunnel.

"Instruments reading right major, we got company coming and each is nearly as big as a tank."

A Bet wanted to get a closer look at whatever was heading their way but knew it was probably a bad idea. He took one last look at the dead animal lying against the side of the tunnel and wondered what could be vicious enough to have killed such a beast. The animal might have been a herbivore but it still carried an impressive defensive array. It had four horns, two on each side of a very large head. All four horns were thick and long with a forked end; each tine of the fork looked sharp. Coming out of the creature's mouth on each side was a long curved tusk and at the end was again the forked tine. This beast might have only eaten vegetation but A Bet guessed it had a bad temper and knew how to defend itself. As he was about to turn to leave he noticed the greasy substance on the ends of two of the horns and one of the tusks. Whatever had attacked and killed this animal didn't get away clean, it had been injured by its prey.

The sounds were growing closer and whatever it was in the tunnel seemed to be in a hurry. "Let's get out of here, keep a close watch on your six." A Bet ordered as the four turned and began a steady run from the tunnel. Before they made it back to the entrance one of the soldiers, a corporal named Joseph Allen who had been lagging back was grabbed from behind by a long hairy arm. As he was being pulled up off the ground he managed to get a glimpse of what was about to eat him alive. He managed to flip the safety on his assault rifle to full auto and just as he was about to be pulled inside a nasty looking mouth he swung the barrel of his weapon up and pulled the trigger.

The assault rifle opened up spraying the inside of the gaping mouth with splatter rounds meant to do as much damage as possible to flesh. The rate of fire of the weapon was impressive but it made little difference. Allen continued to fire as he was pulled head first into the mouth. The creature clamped down and Allen was cleanly bitten in half, the lower portion of his body falling to the concrete floor.

A Bet, Tonto and the third trooper, another corporal named Anson Reynolds turned as soon as they heard Allen's weapon begin to fire.

Everything happened so quickly that all they got to see and hear was the crunching of bones and the falling of Allen's legs to the ground. All three men had their weapons at the ready as they turned and wasted no time in firing at whatever it was in the darkness that had just taken the life of a soldier. The three continued to fire as they backed toward the opening. The three beams of light being thrown from the assault weapons gave life to a creature that must have come straight out of Hell.

The description, as far as size, was what the Threat Sensor had given, but seeing this thing in real life made it look twice as big. There was four pairs of legs with the front two looking to be multi-purpose, it could grasp and lift with the front pair of legs as it stood on the back six. The head was enormous with a mouth that was ringed with nasty looking teeth. The eyes could individually turn in different directions to the point that it could actually look backwards and forwards at the same time.

"What is that son-of-a bitch?" Reynolds screamed as he continued to fire his weapon.

Tonto saw the rounds from their weapons were having limited, if any, effect on the monster. He continued to fire his weapon one handed as he pulled a concussion grenade from his belt. Not wanting to use both hands to pull the pin he put the ring of the pin in his mouth and gave it a vicious pull, damn near pulling out three of his teeth. He rolled the grenade down the shaft and then at the last second the three men stopped firing and turned to run. The monster looked down at the rolling device as it chewed on the remains of Allen.

Just as A Bet, Tonto and Reynolds cleared the entrance to the cave more of the creatures could be seen running past the one that had killed Allen, they were running after the three men. A Bet went left as Tonto and Reynolds went right. There was a loud explosion as the concussion grenade exploded. The three men quickly unsnapped a fragmentation grenade each and tossed it into the tunnel and then moved back to cover.

All three waited as more of the company moved up to see what kind of trouble A Bet was bringing to them. There was screeching and growling as the beasts retreated back into the darkness of the tunnel.

"What just happened in there Major?" A burly sergeant named Ronnie Todd asked. Before anyone could answer he noticed the absence of Allen. "We still got a man in there?" It was both a statement and a question.

The three were completely out of breath after running for their lives from a monster that could only be described as a nightmare walking on eight hairy legs.

"Allen's dead, whatever got him nearly got us until we threw in some grenades and stopped it," Reynolds said.

Sergeant Todd had never seen a monster before and wanted a closer look. He marched out in full view and glanced down the darkened tunnel. He activated his light and pointed it inside, what he saw was several large creatures that were backing away from his light, none looked injured. "Major I don't think the grenades are what scared them away, it's the light."

Tonto and A Bet walked back out into the open and peered down the tunnel adding their lights as well. Todd seemed to be right, the creatures were either afraid of the light or it hurt them in some way. There was no sign of Allen's body only blood stains that seemed to be splashed from floor to ceiling, the monsters had eaten everything and even appeared to be licking the blood from the floor.

Tonto didn't think the light had any effect on the creatures. "I doubt if they are afraid of light. This planet is light all the time and whatever they killed earlier and drug into that side tunnel lived out here, it was a plant eater. I think they retreated for another reason."

"We better get back and report this to Captain Simms," A Bet said. Before leaving Tonto fired a Specie Identification Pellet at the nearest of the creatures. This little device was meant to lodge just under the skin or the hide of a creature and then transmit DNA and chemical analysis to a transceiver located back at the Fire-Base. Once they made it back to base, Tonto went to the receiver and transmitted the results of the pellet to the Gareth.

Mama-Seven received the data from the pellet and began running comparisons with other known systems to try and find a match. The results were nearly instant and she notified Captain Simms at once.

"Captain we have a problem planet side."

Simms was at his command console talking to Captain Harless on one of the secure comms units. "What have you got?" He asked.

"Just received a request for analysis on a Specie Identification Pellet from Star-Base Moag, the target species has been identified and I suggest immediate evacuation from the planet's surface."

Simms was stunned, what kind of information could Mama-Seven have obtained to warrant such an action. "Elaborate!" Was all Simms could manage to say?

"Analysis of the information obtained by the Pellet is consistent with the species that overwhelmed the Sari-Five system. Species is known as Septa-Pod. Not indigenous to this planet. Planet is in early stages of infestation and possibly started less than five Earth years ago. This was a heavily populated planet with an indigenous race not unlike humans. They hadn't obtained the ability for deep space flight, only localized space exploration, but were none the less a highly advanced society. They lived primarily underground in elaborate sublevel cities using geo-thermal for their main source of power. This hid their existence due to lack of surface construction and lack of fossil fuel gases in the atmosphere. That race appears to now be extinct or nearly so. I am using high output scanners trying to isolate any pockets of survivors and so far scans are negative. What the scans are revealing is large numbers of Septa-Pods using the underground cities as hives as their numbers continue to grow." Mama-Seven stopped there though there was much more to say about the planet.

"If the pellet was fired into one of these Septa-Pods then how did you acquire the information on the indigenous race that is now extinct or nearly so?" Simms asked.

"Information is still being gathered on the original inhabitants of this planet. Once we dropped out of Slip-Space, distress signals were picked up. These signals seem to be running on a loop, once they reach the end they immediately cycle over. The messages are totally automated and could possibly be transmitted for years after the last of the original inhabitants has died."

Simms considered this information. "Your recommendation is to evacuate Star-Base Moag; can this species be so great a threat that it is better to be destroyed by the Sokari?" Simms asked.

Without a seconds hesitation Mama-Seven gave her reply. "The Septa-Pods are a dangerous species that have managed to conquer all the planets they have landed on. No society has ever been able to check this expansion. The Septa-Pods are unlike any other species we have met in the galaxy. They are a two part society, Elites are the ruling class and the Septa-Pods are the soldiers and they pose the greatest risk in battle. They are unstoppable."

"You say there are actually two species, one soldier and the other would be what?" Simms asked as he tried to understand what he was up against.

"There is only one species but it is divided into two distinct variations, Elite and soldier. The differences are significant but the DNA is exactly the same. It is the only example in the known galaxy of a single DNA species with a dual end product."

"How good are the soldier Septa-Pods and how smart are the Elite?" Simms asked.

"The soldiers are nearly unstoppable; they are immune to weapons such as the standard Assault Rifle used by the Earth Forces soldiers stationed at Fire-Base Moag. Their skeletal makeup is nearly as durable as the ceramic armor fitted to our soldiers. They have a skin and hide that resists abrasions and puncture, but the nastiest part is they have evolved something similar to the Micro-Repair Cells used to repair damage to Capitol Ships. If severely injured but not killed they will rejuvenate the injuries within sixty minutes."

"Well that explains the soldiers, but what about the Elites?" Simms asked.

"As bad as the soldiers are the Elites are much worse."

"How so?" Simms asked.

"The Elites are limited in number but that is not the problem. They are extremely intelligent, it's even suspected they are all of a genius level or higher if that is possible. The real problem with the Elites is proximity, I would go as far as to say that if a human ever saw an Elite it would be the end of his life. This brings two distinct possibilities, either the sight could cause severe neurological damage or it might be the chemical makeup of the creatures. Either fright or toxins could apparently kill a human. My analysis is incomplete and without a specimen the information will always be lacking. This species is so dangerous I would never allow a specimen to be brought on board even if it were dead."

Simms knew if Mama-Seven wanted to deny a request to bring something onboard that she felt was dangerous then she certainly would be accommodated. "If we stay on the planet can we defend against this threat?" Simms asked.

"Doubtful Captain, if our base is captured by the soldiers, and the Elites have a chance to investigate, it is highly possible that the location of Earth itself might be obtained."

Now Simms understood the urgency of the situation. Mama-Seven was willing to have all four ships destroyed in a battle with the Sokari before she would allow the chance of having a vicious race such as the Septa-Pods learn of Earth's location.

"Even if Fire-Base Moag were overrun how would the Septa-Pods reach Earth?" Simms asked.

"They are a space faring society. They have a fleet that would rival the Earth Colonies in number and also the Septa-Pod fleet is more advanced than that of Earth's. Their fleet is most sophisticated in propulsion but lacking in weaponry. It appears the Elites prefer to do their fighting planet side."

Now Simms asked the obvious, "How is it you know all this from the information gathered from one Specie Identification Pellet?" He asked.

"That information is classified Captain. Earth Colonies Oversight has feared the arrival of the Septa-Pods for centuries. What I have shared with you is not to go any further by order of the Earth Colonies Oversight directives. Fear of the Septa-Pods might cause more problems than the lack of knowledge that they exist. Mars Heavy Ordinance scientists have been working on this problem for decades. Even the Moag system was developed as a defense against this new and highly dangerous species."

Simms now understood that there was more at play here than just the Sokari, he was truly caught between two fierce enemies that could both spell disaster for his small force. "Mama-Seven is there any way to defeat the Sokari in space with our original plan and also allow the Septa-Pods to destroy the Sokari ground assault that is sure to come?"

Mama-Seven had been asked a question that revealed desperation on the part of the Captain; he was being strategic rather than tactical. It required three one-hundredths of a second to run the billions of bits of information before she could answer.

"Yes, you have allowed for a new hypothesis, pre-empt a situation where the Sokari and the Septa-Pods lose partial interest in the Earth Colonies Flotilla and ground forces, allowing escape, it is possible. Multiple outcomes are being encountered, results in seven point eight seconds. " It was the first time Simms had been able to give Mama-Seven a problem that would take her more than two seconds to figure out. Simms patiently waited for the results from Mama-Seven.

"Using the Septa-Pods as an unwitting ally will change the chance of a positive outcome from thirty-nine percent to thirty-nine point six percent." Mama-Seven said.

Simms noticed Mama-Seven substituted the phrase 'chance of success' to 'chance of a positive outcome' and wondered if there was a difference. "Can you substantiate meaning of positive outcome?"

"Although our chances of success have increased by point six percent there will be a higher casualty rate due to the ground action associated with both the Sokari and Septa-Pods." Was the reply given. After a brief pause Mama-Seven continued. "Advise powering up all the cryo-tubes on the Temerity and also activate life-scan simulators. It will be advantageous to make the ship appear to have multiple life signs aboard although she will be completely deserted."

"Can it be made to appear that the Temerity and Fire-Base Moag are occupied by the crews of all four ships?" Simms asked.

"Not equivalent to the same number the four ships carry but nearly so. It is possible the Sokari will think some of the crew either escaped on the other three ships or crashed."

As far as this little trick went, Simms liked it. It was possible to help the Sokari explain the absence of the other three ships. It could even lure them in close enough to the Temerity to do maximum damage when it came time to ignite her engines. "That is a possibility, please make the necessary adjustments to the life sign readings on the Temerity to appear that she is fully stationed by her crew and troops."

Simms also considered the better odds previously mentioned by Mama-Seven against the chance that more of his forces would be killed in action. It was never acceptable to lose a soldier if that loss could be prevented but considering the forces aligned against him he knew there wasn't an alternative. Damage would be done to the Earth Colonies forces, or total destruction. Either way there were no other options. Simms knew his troops and ships would rather fight a stand up fight with a small chance of success rather than flee and leave a portion of their comrades behind.

"Implement plan Mama-Seven and have the other ships brought up to date on these last findings. Make sure Major A Bet and the rest of his command are aware of the situation. Also if it becomes necessary to pull the troops out and make a run for it then make sure they will be ready. If things get too hot down there then I want a hot zone extraction with the shuttles." Simms said.

Mama-Seven never replied to the command but started the necessary procedures to have it done if the order came. "Update on the Sokari fleet, arrival in fifty-seven minutes. Allow twenty-nine more for the slowest of their ships to catch up, expect enemy action in one hour and twenty-six minutes," she told the captain.

"Notify the fleet and Fire-Base Moag. Make sure A Bet and his troops are ready to raise Hell with their Sled-Guns as soon as I give the word. Simms out."

Admiral Seeboc Tang was sitting in his command chair eagerly awaiting the first visuals of the human fleet that had so far done so much damage to his own forces. He would now make them pay for the loss of so many of his ships, which he attributed to luck on the human's part. The luck was now on his side in the form of overwhelming numbers against four damaged human vessels.

"I want at least one of their ships captured intact, preferably the Gareth. If the other three are destroyed then so be it." Tang ordered. The bridge crew on the Rococo noticed the Admiral had actually used the earth vessels name rather than calling her 'that human ship.'

"Maybe after getting his scaly green ass handed to him the Admiral has gained a certain level of respect for the humans," one of the comms officers whispered to another. Neither dared laugh, it could have been their last laugh ever.

The fastest of the Sokari fleet slowed to a stop ten-thousand kilometers from the planet where a single human vessel awaited. Scans showed the ship was fully functional but alone. More scans revealed that a base had been established on the surface of the planet.

"What is the status of the other three human vessels, especially the Gareth?" Tang asked.

Additional scans were run but nothing could be found of the other ships. "The ship standing off alone is known as the Temerity; she is a troop transport and has limited offensive capability Admiral. She is a support ship intended to travel with powerful escorts. She is not meant to be stationed alone." Was the reply one of the scanner officers gave.

"What is the earliest the rest of our fleet will be here?" Tang asked. He wanted overwhelming superiority this time. Nothing could save the humans now.

"The rest of the fleet will be here in one point four time units." Was all the officer said, it was all Tang had asked for.

"Are the scans complete of the base they have established on the surface of the planet?" Tang asked.

"Scans are still being ran sir. It appears the Temerity was disabled due to weapons fire from our ships prior to them leaving the system. Apparently she made it this far before her engines gave out. There are substantial life signs on board." One of the scanner officers replied.

"And the troops on the ground, what is your best guess as to their strength and capabilities?" Tang asked after a few minutes.

The same scanner officer continued to make adjustments to his equipment as he tried to get a better reading from the planet's surface. Finally he said, "It appears there is a substantial force on the surface. It could be the crews of the three missing ships, they might have offloaded their personnel and are attempting to set up a base."

Tang jumped from his command chair, "A base, this far from their home world?" Tang said this but had no idea of where the human's home world might be. "This far into our territory? That will never be allowed to happen. I want a landing party prepared to go down and wipe them off the face of that planet, and I want it to be coordinated with our attack on that pitiful human ship that is stationed above the planet."

Tang sat back down in his command chair and considered the situation. There was now only one human ship for him to capture instead of four. That would still be okay because the Temerity contained the information of how the humans obtained such fantastic speeds. There was now the added bonus of having multiple life signs on the surface, Tang considered these to be nothing more than prisoners to be used for experimentation.

"How soon before we can start landing troops?" Tang demanded.

Before he got the answer to that question one of the scanner officers spoke up, "Picking up another set of life signs from the planet Admiral, it appears to be not on the surface but underground. Multiple signs, the way the scans read it appears to be coming from some sort of cavern or cave system." The scanner officer suspected this because the life signs were lined up, not random as if wherever they were they couldn't move about.

"Can you determine if it is more of the humans?" Tang asked.

"No Admiral, scanners can't get a positive lock. Might be due to the makeup of the caves the life signs are occupying."

Tang considered this and came up with the conclusion he wanted rather than considering anything else. "It must be the remainder of the human's crew. The cowards are seeking shelter because they know we are here. Prepare the assault now."

The scanning officer continued to look at his screens and equipment. The readings weren't human but he would never tell that to Tang who had now made up his own mind that they were the humans. Best to stay quiet and let things run their course than get shot because he disagreed with the murderous Tang.

Simms aboard the Gareth and Captain Harless aboard the Umbrage had managed to hide the two ships on the opposing side of the planet. There were mountain ranges there that towered to over twenty-thousand meters and the huge Gareth and Umbrage simply blended in. Although these were two of the largest Earth Colonies vessels ever built, they paled in comparison to the mountain ranges this planet possessed. Simms and Harless had both of their ships in stealth mode, they were both emitting the tiniest of scanner signatures. During construction of the armored hulls a stealth composite was implemented into the plans.

The composite actually helped hide the warships and took nothing away in the form of armor protection.

The engines of the two mammoth craft were cycled down but ready to jump to full power when needed. Mama-Seven was monitoring the approaching fleet by remotely using the equipment on the Temerity to do the work and then having all the data bounced off the Anneal which was also hiding near one on the planet's many moons. This was a line of site communication from the Temerity to the Anneal to the Gareth and Umbrage.

The progress of the personnel at Fire-Base Moag was also being monitored by the equipment on the Temerity and transmitted the same way. Of most concern at the moment was the movement of the subterranean Septa-Pods.

Mama-Seven broke in and interrupted Captain Simms thoughts once more with some startling news. "Captain, it appears the Septa-Pods are massing for an attack on Fire-Base Moag."

"How can you tell, they are below the surface." Simms asked.

"Septa-Pods and the Elites communicate with each other by means of a sub-sonic language of high-frequency sounds that are imperceptible to the human ear but can be tracked by the scanner arrays of the Temerity. By isolating each individual sound signature of individual creatures they can be tracked."

"If they are identified as individuals by the sounds they make then you should be able to estimate their strength?" Simms said hopefully.

"The number that is preparing to strike Star-Base Moag now stands at fourteen-hundred and twenty-three with more approaching from adjoining tunnels. The numbers of the late arrivals can only be calculated once they speak and not all have done so yet."

The number was startling, "Estimate planet's total population of Septa-Pods and Elites," Simms said.

"Septa-Pods range in the number of forty-one thousand with a thirteen point three percentage of variance possible. Elites range in number of four-hundred and ten with the same percentage of variance possible," replied Mama-Seven.

Simms knew the numbers must have something to do with the hierarchy of the species. "Roughly a hundred to one ratio between the Pods and the Elites. Is there a reason for this?" Simms asked.

"It is suspected that the Elites each control or command a hundred Septa-Pods, you are correct. It is theorized that this ratio allows for maximum control of the Pods by the Elites." Mama-Seven replied.

Simms toyed with the information he had just been given but there was one question he hadn't thought of until now and really wanted an answer. "You said earlier that they are not indigenous, what types of ships do they possess to travel from one system to another."

"The Elites commandeer the vessels of the races they conquer. It is arguably possible that there is a substantial number of space faring craft hidden somewhere on this planet, possibly even in the underground bunkers and hangers used by the previous occupants of this planet."

"What do we actually know about this planet and her previous inhabitants?" Simms asked but seriously doubted if the Super-Computer knew.

"The previous inhabitants of this world, which was known as Tenement, were a peace loving species. They had lived here for hundreds of thousands of years. Once Tenement was discovered by an Elite probe ship it took less than three years for the invading Septa-Pods to arrive. At first the inhabitants of Tenement, known as the Arrenaugh, hoped this new species was friendly but that hope was dashed within minutes of the first ship's arrival. Hundreds of Septa-Pods poured from their landing craft and went about killing everything in sight.

The Arrenaugh tried to fight back but they were such a docile race that they had lost the ability, or the knowledge, of how to put up any kind of organized resistance. Tenement is a large planet with most of the dwellings and manufactural complexes located below the surface. It took less than one Earth month for the Elites and the Septa-Pods to overrun everything above ground and almost do the same underground."

Simms was startled, "Are you telling me there might still be some of the original inhabitants still alive on this planet?"

"That is correct Captain, there are isolated pockets of the Arrenaugh still living underground. They survive behind vast armored causeways that so far the Septa-Pods have been unable to breech. The causeways were built in the early history of the Arrenaugh when they still fought amongst themselves."

"Do you have an estimate of how many are still alive?" Simms asked.

"Less than five-hundred Captain, it is my estimate this species will be completely extinct within the year."

Simms stood and went to the window at the front of the command bridge. "This species you say is known as the Arrenaugh, are they friendly to other species, say humans for example? What would happen if the Arrenaugh and humans ever had the opportunity to cross paths?"

"As I said, the Arrenaugh are a peace loving species. They are not warlike in anyway and this is contributing to their extinction. They would have been a substantial ally in this portion of the galaxy if not for the genocide being carried out by the Septa-Pods and Elites."

Simms never asked anything more about the Arrenaugh, the story was still fresh in his mind as he set about implementing the task at hand and that was to prevent the Sokari from destroying his ships. "What is the latest information on the Sokari Mama-Seven, how soon before they begin their attack on the Temerity?"

"The Sokari have just finished organizing the balance of their ships, the early arrivals and those that fell behind in the headlong rush to do battle. They have also deployed twenty-seven troop transports which appear to be heading for Star-Base Moag. Expect landing in fourteen minutes. Major A Bet has been notified along with the ordinance teams tasked with manning the Sled-Guns. Everything is proceeding as planned Captain."

"Can Major A Bet hold against the combined effort of the Sokari and the Septa-Pods?" Simms asked.

"Not against both Captain, the only chance is if the Septa-Pods interrupt the assault by the Sokari."

Simms knew the situation had just gone from bad to worse, who could have predicted the planet was infested with a species of something that could only be described as huge vicious spiders controlled by something called Elite and that the sight of one might send a man into madness or kill him, outright.

Seeboc Tang watched as his troop laden shuttles launched and started their descent to the planet's surface. He had broken his gaze only momentarily to look at the stationary Temerity. He looked upon the ship with disgust. She was such an ugly construct that only deserved to be destroyed. (As far as Earth ships went the Temerity was considered one of the most beautiful ships in the fleet.)

What made the Temerity even more appalling to Tang was the fact that it had an oxygen rich atmosphere consisting of nearly twenty-one percent. This was a deadly gas if you were a Sokari, even the mention of it was revolting. He would capture this human monstrosity and have it brought back to his home world. It would be cleansed of the human scum and then scrubbed of its deadly oxygen. At that point the engineering could be dissected and the ship's capabilities learned, especially the ability to travel at such fantastic speeds. The location of the planet the humans called Earth could also be obtained. Tang would turn humiliation into victory.

"The shuttles are safely away Admiral; the fleet is ready for the attack on the Temerity at your command."

"Bring the fleet about, close to four hundred units and then wait for my command to fire," Tang said.

"What about her weapons admiral, scans show she is equipped with two of the spear devices." The Sokari didn't know what the Sled-

Guns were called but they knew firsthand how devastating the weapons were.

Tang didn't want to suffer more damage from the human ship but knew if he were to take her without destroying her he had to do it at close range. He assumed she could fire her weapons at least once, maybe even twice, before she would be disabled at close range, he was willing to accept the damage four of the spear weapons might do to his ships.

"Prepare short-range weapons, have the fleet begin their advance now. All weapons hot and fire on my mark," Tang ordered.

Mama-Seven was aware the Sokari fleet was beginning their attack run, the relay from the Temerity to the Anneal and then to the Gareth was instantaneous. The weapons on the Temerity were ready to fire once given the command from the Super-Computer. ED had eighteen Sled-Guns at his disposal once the three ships broke from cover and added their offensive capability to that of the Temerity. He had damage sequencing set for one round per target, which wasn't his preferred method of attack. A wounded ship could still fight back. Under normal circumstances he would have used three Sled-Rounds per enemy vessel knowing three hits from the close range they would be fighting in would surely destroy a single target. Eighteen rounds meant six kills.

ED chose the one round one ship engagement hoping the land based Sled-Guns used by Major A Bet and the Astro-Sailors would use the same method. One salvo of the dual firing land based weapons would target four ships with two rounds apiece. The targeting of the guns from Fire-Base Moag could also fire faster than the weapons of the fleet. Fleet based weapons had to calculate the movement of the enemy as well as the ship they fired from allowing for movement of both ships. A land based system only needed to allow for movement of the target. The smaller and faster rounds of the Moag could also be reloaded in less time than a ship mounted weapon. Ship based weapons had to trolley back inside to receive the new round but the land based weapons simply reloaded a fresh round by means of an automated feed.

It had been agreed by ED and Mama-Seven to allow the Temerity to fire both her Sled-Guns once the enemy closed to within seven-hundred and fifty kilometers of her. At this point the ground based component would switch on their targeting computers and pound away. The eight guns Major A Bet controlled would hopefully be protected by their independent Static Repulsar Pockets. The Temerity too would be protected by her pocket and hopefully last beyond the first salvos.

The engines of the Temerity wouldn't be used until it was deemed the two Sled-Guns she contained were no longer serviceable due to damage. It was also deemed possible to destroy the Temerity early in the engagement if it was capable of destroying a sizable portion of the enemy's fleet by doing so.

Gareth and Umbrage wouldn't break from cover until the bulk of the enemy was occupied with the Temerity and also Fire-Base Moag. The ship and the Fire-Base would be taking the bulk of the punishment until it became advantageous for the Gareth and Umbrage to begin their attacks. The Anneal would still remain hidden as the two heavy cruisers got into the mix and took some of the attention from the Temerity and the Fire-Base.

Once the two cruisers began taking fire the Anneal would break from cover and should have a clear advantage against the unaware Sokari Fleet. With so many Earth Colonies targets mixing it up with the Sokari at close range it was hoped the confusion might play kindly on Simms and his rag-tag fleet. By staggering in the attacks of the three ships at the right time maybe the layered confusion this would cause could add to the inaccuracy of the alien weapons fire.

The first shot at the Temerity came thirty seconds after the Sokari started their attack. The plan was for a squadron of Sokari picket ships to advance on the human ship and fire at close range. The Static Repulsar Pocket of the Beachhead Support Cruiser held during these first shots and no damage was done to the cruiser. One characteristic of the Temerity's design was that she was given an enhanced pocket. It was necessary to upgrade the pocket's design due to the close proximity the ship would be to any offensive weapons fire she would encounter as she landed and offloaded her tanks and armored personnel carriers. A lesser built ship would be destroyed on the approach thus defeating the landing before it ever happened. The pocket of a landing craft was so robust it would take the larger weaponry of the Sokari Dreadnaughts and heavy cruisers to overcome and destroy her.

Simms was at his command console watching the empty Temerity do battle with six of the Sokari picket ships along with a couple of larger vessels. ED fired her two Sled-Guns not at the picket ships but at two of the nearest cruisers available. One was the sister ship to the Rococo, which was Admiral Tang's command ship. The other was a brutish looking cruiser that had only just joined the Sokari fleet prior to the original attack on the Gareth. This vessel had all the latest in offensive and defensive weaponry and Tang wondered what effect the spear throwing human ship would have against her. His answer came seconds later as there was a puff of debris registered at the bow of the cruiser and a second later another appeared at the stern. Could this really happen, another of the humans weapons had completely penetrated one of the most robust ships in the Sokari fleet.

"Damage report on the Simitol." Tang demanded.

"Simitol reports her fire control stations have managed to extinguish the worst of the fires. It appears the human weapons are made up of a highly combustible material that burns upon penetration of the hull. The captain of the Simitol wants permission to fire her auto-cannon." The comms tech announced.

"Negative on the auto-cannon. We must capture the human vessel intact." Tang growled as his answer was transmitted to the Simitol.

"Admiral we are picking up weapons fire from the planet's surface, it appears to be of the same design as the spear weapons the human vessel possesses, but in missile or rocket form." One of the weapons officers announced.

Tang activated his monitor and saw the plums given off by the weapons as they headed toward his fleet. "Increase shielding on the approach side and activate counterbattery fire, knock those missiles out of the sky."

Tang assumed the humans on the ground had fired conventional rockets at his ships. All indications looked as if that were the case. Where Tang underestimated what he was up against was understandable. A Sled-Gun fired from a ship in space emitted no after effects in the way of gases or missile debris. A sled gun launched its projectile without the use of propellant. There was a difference between Sled-Rounds fired from a ship in the vacuum of space and one fired from the surface of a planet where there was an atmosphere. The high-velocity round created a contrail from condensing water vapor which could be mistaken as fuel exhaust, such as that of a conventional rocket. Tang felt no threat existed from any ground based rocket, his ships were heavily shielded.

The tracking computers lost the rounds as they exited the atmosphere, thus lost the contrails. The defensive weapons officers simply assumed there had been a malfunction of the rocket's engines and they had broken up in the planet's atmosphere. The first of the paired Sled-Rounds struck the Simitol, both were a clean hit and neither was slowed by the robust shielding she carried. As both rounds penetrated the cruiser there were multiple warning alarms indicating fire and explosions. The ever expanding penetrations started to vent atmosphere as the Simitol began to list and descend toward the planet's surface. The mighty ship had lost propulsion; her engines were out, never to breathe life back into the systems again. The last transmission from the crippled ship was an automated distress call.

"Simitol has been struck again Admiral. It appears she has lost propulsion and is sinking into the planet's atmosphere." The defensive weapons officer of the Rococo announced.

Tang watched as another of his mighty cruisers fell away from the rest of the fleet and began its death fall. "Bring the rest of the fleet into range and begin bombarding that weapon on the surface of the planet before it can fire again."

"What are your orders for the human ship admiral?"

"Continue to approach and disable her weapons and engines, we must capture her intact." Tang might have felt an immense fury for the human species but he still needed to capture the Temerity as a war prize, her technology might still be considered worth the price the Sokari had paid in the loss of so many ships.

Simms was anxious to enter the fray, he knew the Temerity had fired both her Sled-Guns and Fire-Base Moag was also launching. Both were now being targeted by the combined strength of the Sokari fleet. It was always hard to wait for the right moment knowing your forces were being attacked while you waited.

"The Sokari are moving their fleet Captain. It appears they are massing for an attack against the Fire-Base. Temerity is being hit with smaller scale weaponry; she is no doubt being damaged and prepared for boarding and capture," Mama-Seven said.

Simms knew about being boarded, the Gareth had only recently managed to find all the Sokari that had infested his ship from the Infect Pods. The survivors of that little exercise were now in isolation chambers where the atmosphere of the chamber matched what the scaly bastards needed to survive. Earth Colonies would keep these prisoners alive and try to assimilate their language to learn as much as they could about this new species.

"Captain Harless begin your attack, Gareth to position four points off your starboard side. Let's make it fast and once through their lines bring both ships about and hit them again." This had already been agreed upon by Mama-Seven and ED but Simms needed to hear it spoken from his own mouth.

"Roger that captain, powering up now." Harless said as his mammoth ship came to life. Both the Gareth and the Umbrage broke from the mountain range at nearly the same time and headed in the direction of the Temerity.

"Admiral Tang, two human warships have just taken off from the planet's surface and are heading this way." The Rococo's second in command shouted.

Tang picked up both ships on his monitor and realized the Gareth was one of the two ships now heading toward his fleet at speed. "Target the Gareth, all primary weapons hit the human ship and blow her out of the sky." Tang's orders left out the Umbrage completely, this was due to his hatred of the Gareth. The admiral had completely surprised the human ship in the initial ambush and sent her crashing to the surface of an unknown and uncharted planet. Since then this human warship and her scum had beaten him at every turn and now he would have his revenge.

Most of the guns of the fleet, at the moment, were either aimed at the Temerity or Star-Base Moag. The command from Admiral Tang would take time in order to redirect the targeting computers; it was time the Sokari shouldn't have wasted. The eight guns of the Star-Base and the two of the Temerity had reloaded and ED was now directing the ten rounds at the most troublesome of the alien fleet.

As the ships of Tang's force turned to engage the Gareth, reports came in that more weapons fire had been detected, multiple rounds heading inbound. This was a surprise for the crews of Tang's fleet. The calculated fire and reload time for one of the human ships was nearly twice what had just been announced. There was no way for the alien fleet to know that the eight guns of Star-Base Moag were equipped with new auto-loaders which trimmed seventy seconds off plus the fact that ground based weapons need not trolley back in to receive the new round, they weren't operating in space. Also the two guns of the Temerity were using Fast Sequencing Targeting or FST which allowed her nearly the same reloading speed as the guns of the Star-Base. At such close range ED initiated the FST protocols, what little was lost in aim was made up for in the increased number of rounds the Temerity could fire. ED hoped the tradeoff was worth the risk.

"Ignore that last report; I want all attention given to the Gareth." Tang shouted. The Admiral had let his fury cloud his tactical thinking.

He was allowing his fleet to expose their stern reflector shields to the incoming rounds. In nearly all fleets more shielding was given to the front sections and less to the stern, it just made sense to put more protection on the section that was carrying out the attack.

Tang had been a flotilla commander for a long time and was considered one of the best tacticians in the fleet. He had won many battles and knew how to implement strategy and tactics. What wasn't known was his ruthless means of keeping his command and not allowing those more capable to advance. Anyone Tang suspected of being a threat to his reputation would soon be eliminated by some freak accident, a trumped up charge of insubordination or even murder. Tang had gotten rid of more than one capable officer that served under him. Most of the grand battles Tang had won weren't that grand at all once all the facts were gathered. His favorite tactic was to use overwhelming force, and ambush, to win his engagements. He was now faced with a capable opponent using weapons he was not familiar with.

Another limitation of the Sokari was their inability to integrate high-tech computing into their operational thread, something the Earth Colonies Ships possessed. The Outer Reaches Fleet the humans used, when far from support facilities, depended on ships with a tech heavy computing ability. Mama-Seven and the External Defense computer ED were far more advanced than anything the Sokari used. It was beginning to show as the battle progressed.

The Gareth, and the Umbrage, came out of the cloud cover of the planet with weapons charged and ready.

"Fire." Captain Simms aboard the Gareth ordered. Harless aboard the Umbrage did the same and at that moment the two cruisers sent twelve Sled-Rounds heading toward the alien fleet. Again ED sent a single round at each of twelve ships. The strategy was the same, damage as many of the enemy as possible and hope mounting impacts from subsequent volleys would eventually wear down their ability to return fire. With the human ships so badly outgunned it was going to be a slug-fest.

The fleet that eliminated the most of their opponent's weapons the fastest was the one that would come out on top, so far all the advantage was with the Sokari.

As soon as the twelve guns fired they were rapidly trolleyed back inside and reloaded. In a situation where the Earth Colonies Ships were so badly outnumbered and outgunned it was critical to get off as many shots as possible before the Earth forces began taking significant damage. The weapons were spooled back out and ready to fire again just as the first incoming fire from the Sokari fleet began to arrive.

"Increase power to the Pocket, Evasive, Evasive," Simms ordered.

The two cruisers began to take fire against their pockets. Both ships had the advantage of adjusting their flight paths to stay in their respective pockets and this helped reduce any hull impacts. When the weapons were reloaded and ready to fire the handoff was again given to the External Defense Computer. ED, at that moment, was given free reign of the twelve guns and adjusted his strategy from one shot one ship to hitting the most dangerous of the many vessels that were heading his way.

Mama-Seven had identified the Rococo as the command ship of the alien force and sent a message through Map-Con to ED. It was too late to target her with this round but as soon as the twelve guns were available to fire again he would make sure the Rococo got some attention. There was one thing ED could do while he waited to re-acquire his guns, the Temerity was ready to fire again and he sent one of her rounds at the Rococo and the other at a nasty looking picket ship that bristled with weaponry. The picket ship didn't have heavy enough weapons to penetrate the pocket of either the Gareth or the Umbrage but she was hitting the two cruisers with so much of her lesser weapons fire that she was actually draining power from the pockets. ED was going to put a stop to that at once.

Aboard the Rococo Tang was anticipating the early destruction of the Gareth when his thoughts were interrupted. "Sir we have a round heading our way from the Temerity." One of the defensive weapons officers shouted.

Tang heard but never bothered to respond, he was watching as three of his heavy cruisers closed with the Gareth and prepared to fire a full volley. Just as he was preparing to give the command to fire his screens went dark and then blinked back on only to go dark again. "What has happened?" Tang screamed at his comms officer.

"We have taken damage sir," was all Tang heard one of his officers' say.

"Damage report, how bad is it?" Tang asked.

Screens were just now coming back on line; they had been nothing but a pale blue without the markings of the Sokari language only moments before. "The weapon has penetrated our shields and the main hull armor." The scanner officer announced as he continued to monitor the incoming information. "It just missed our main power plant and one of the engines. It appears damage control is containing the worst of it."

Tang was impressed with the sturdiness of his ship; she had taken a direct hit at close range from one of the human ships and she was still fully operational. "Continue the attack on the Gareth," he ordered in a steady voice.

Simms was watching the enemy fleet; he could tell they were now concentrating everything against the Gareth. "Helm bring us about four degrees, have the Umbrage do the same." Simms was trying to put a little distance between his two ships and the oncoming Sokari vessels.

"Simms this is Harless, it looks like we have done a little damage. Next shot available in twenty seconds, has ED still got control?" Harless had never been the type of captain to hand all offensive capability over to a machine. He always thought human hands were better, but he had to admit, the External Defense Computer had done an outstanding job so far.

"Offensive command is still with ED, looks like we are about to take some damage on the Gareth. Mama-Seven what is the recommendation on the Anneal?" Simms asked as he still held the hot mic with Captain Harless on the other end.

"Advise Anneal break from cover in one minute six seconds and make a pass on the enemies left flank and rear. Allow for an immediate four shot salvo before accelerating away while her guns are reloaded. This flanking maneuver should take some of the pressure off the Gareth and Umbrage. Be advised Captain, enemy still possesses overwhelming firepower."

"You heard that Harless, we're about to get a little help but I don't know how long we can last unless more of their ships are put out of action." Simms said. He was aware that some of the Sled-Gun rounds had made impacts on the Sokari ships but only one had been completely destroyed, the Simitol. What Simms didn't know was that at such close range almost all the Sled-Rounds that had been fired had impacted a Sokari ship. Damage was significant but a single round wasn't enough to bring down a Sokari Capitol Ship unless it was an extremely lucky shot. As more Sled-Rounds found their mark, especially on a ship that had been previously hit, the damage would start to diminish the offensive capability of the opposing warships.

Aboard the Anneal the captain and crew had been monitoring the progress of the battle that, up until now, they had taken no part in. Captain Russel Douglas was growing impatient as he watched rounds strike the Repulsar Pockets of the three warships and also Fire-Base Moag. He wanted to join the fight but knew his orders; he would wait until the time was right.

Aboard the Anneal the captain got the news he had been waiting on, "Captain Douglas, we've been ordered to execute our run." Was all the comms officer said.

"Engines to full, bring the pocket on line and increase forward depth. Make speed per our orders. Weapons handoff to ED once we clear the moon's debris field," Douglas said. The Anneal was one of only a few ships in the fleet that could actually bend the configuration of her pocket. In a situation where more weapons fire was expected to impact the forward sections of the pocket there could be given more distance between the hull in that area, and the pocket, allowing for more impacts before the pocket was pushed back against the ship.

The Anneal immediately began to move forward. Douglas felt her powerful engines cycle up, the low deep rumble was unmistakable and very reassuring. His was the only cruiser in the fleet with such an array of engines, she was a racehorse among ponies he always liked to think. As his ship cleared the debris field he could make out the ships of the Sokari fleet as they headed for the Gareth and the Umbrage. The Temerity was also in view but she was stationary, protected within the field of fire coming from Fire-Base Moag. He knew the plan was for the Temerity to lure in as many of the Sokari ships as possible and then her engines would be detonated in order to do maximum damage to the enemy fleet.

ED input the attack plan for the Anneal and also picked the targets for her four Sled-Guns. As this was being accomplished another eight round salvo was let loose from Fire-Base Moag with the targets still being picked by ED. He knew one of the Temerity's last shots had struck the Rococo and wanted to destroy her if at all possible. He directed one of the two shot salvos from the Fire-Base at the Sokari command ship.

Aboard the Rococo the admiral was still watching the attack on the Gareth unfold when he was again warned of danger. "Incoming land based weapons fire detected admiral." Again Tang ignored what he had just been told as he watched the Gareth and the Umbrage. The shields of the Gareth flared and there was definite evidence of Sokari weapons fire striking the human ship's hull. She began to list to port as more and more of the Sokari fleet concentrated their fire on her. While this was going on the Umbrage was left mostly alone with limited Sokari targeting computers registering against her. Tang cared less about the

Umbrage; she would be next in line for his wrath once the Gareth was destroyed.

"Incoming weapons fire registered and confirmed sir. It appears the enemy has our coordinates locked in." This time Tang turned from his monitor, "Increase shielding........," was all Tang got to say before the Rococo was struck by both of the land based Sled-Rounds that were fired at her.

Fires ignited from one end of the massive command ship to the other, this was the third Sled-Round to strike the cruiser in as many time units. These last two hits though were from the more powerful land based guns and the Rococo shuddered from the impacts. As the rounds burned through the hull the Rococo lost power and began to drift.

"Damage report!" Tang yelled.

"Helm isn't responding sir, engines are not responding either. I can't reach engineering but it appears we were hit by two weapons, assessment so far is that damage is extensive."

Tang wondered if he should move his command to another ship but couldn't bring himself to abandon the Rococo. "Do we have batteries?" He shouted.

The second in command went to one of the few remaining control consoles that worked and punched in some numbers. "Yes Admiral, batteries are still functional as well as positioning thrusters," he said.

"Move us away from the battle, I will monitor from a safe distance while the ship is being repaired," Tang said. There was no way for him to know that his ship was a total loss. Many of the crew had either been incinerated by the Sled-Rounds or blown out into space when the bulkheads were punctured. The Rococo began her slow exit from the field of battle as more and more of the Sled-Rounds impacted the rest of the Sokari fleet. The crippled Sokari command ship could be seen venting atmosphere, and even debris, from the holes the Sled-Rounds had created in her hull as she exited the field if battle.

A few of the monitors on the bridge of the Rococo began to flicker back to life as she made her way to safety. "Picking up another ship sir. It appears to be the Fast Attack Cruiser that attacked us prior to the enemy fleet running away."

Tang knew his second in command was trying to make the human vessels appear to be inferior but now he was beginning to realize the humans were warriors. He, so far, had been beaten at every turn. Even his initial ambush of the Gareth had proven to do no more than damage her, after all the damage she had sustained she was still fighting. He realized now that the Sokari fleet must be mobilized to the fullest and an all-out assault against the human's home world be undertaken. Once this battle was won and the Temerity captured, much could be learned about this new species and their weaponry.

Simms's ship was taking a beating, the Gareth was damaged at multiple points and one of her Sled-Guns had been destroyed by a direct hit from some sort of pulse or plasma weapon. What was hurting the Earth Colonies Ships the most was their inability to determine just what it was the Sokari were firing at them. If they knew then the Static Repulsar Pockets could be adjusted to do a better job of deflecting the incoming rounds. As it was, the pocket was lessening the effect of the enemy fire, but if more could be done to enhance the effectiveness then the four ship flotilla might stand a better chance against such overwhelming force.

"Sir, it looks like the Rococo has been damaged and is withdrawing from the battle," one of the weapons officers reported.

Simms looked at his monitor and, sure enough, the command ship of the Sokari fleet was pulling away. At this point ED asked if he should hit her again. "Mama-Seven what is the damage assessment of the Rococo?" Simms asked.

"The Rococo has been struck by three Sled-Rounds, one from the Temerity and two from Star-Base Moag. At the moment her offensive capability is zero and she is unable to make contact with the rest of her fleet. Damage is extensive and it is doubtful if she can survive. It needs to be assumed that her communications arrays will be repaired and she will continue to command the battle at some point in the near future."

Simms had a thought, destroy the Rococo and end whoever commanded the enemy fleet's ability to control the battle. Then he had a more sinister thought, allow the Rococo to survive and allow whoever was in charge to continue to run offense for the Sokari. Simms knew that so far he and his small flotilla had outfought the Sokari even though the enemy possessed overwhelming odds. If he killed the Sokari leader, then it was possible whoever took charge might be more of a tactician. His preference was to continue the battle against the same creature he had been fighting since the initial ambush of the Gareth. Why not keep the status-quo.

With that in mind Simms made his decision. "ED, ignore the Rococo unless she manages to re-enter the battle. Concentrate on the ships that are blasting the Hell out of us. Unless we can take some of the attention off the Gareth then we may not survive this battle our self. Mama-Seven, when is the Anneal going to make her run."

"She is making her first attack run now Captain. I am allowing ED to coordinate her four shots along with the six of the Umbrage. Our targeting computer just went off line and is rebooting. Gareth five shot salvo in fifteen seconds after reboot," Mama-Seven replied.

Simms punched up the footage of the Anneal as she began her fast attack.

The Rococo managed to reach safety and take up a monitoring position. Her systems were still being repaired, that is the ones that hadn't been blown out into space by the three Sled-Rounds. Tang knew his ship was doomed; she might be repaired later as long as she didn't get pulled into the gravitational field of a planet and brought down to the surface in a terrific crash. A few of the communications arrays had been repaired and he could now make contact with his fleet.

"Have positively identified the new ship sir, it is the same Fast Attack Cruiser as before. She is called the Anneal. It appears she is approaching the left flank of the fleet and preparing to fire." The second in command told the admiral.

Tang knew the Anneal was a formidable weapon. In his first encounter with her the only way his ships could train their weapons on her was when she headed back to her own fleet. "Split up the fleet, don't let that ship through," Tang ordered.

As he watched one of the few working monitors on the battle bridge he could make out half of his force turning to cover this new threat.

Aboard the Anneal the four Sled-Guns were now under the control of ED. Mama-Seven had sent a message to the External Defense Computer notifying him that three Sokari Heavy Cruisers were concentrating fire on the Gareth and would overwhelm the Static Repulsar Pocket in one minute and fifty-seven seconds and wanted assistance. ED responded by targeting all three, with one of the cruisers receiving two hits from the Anneal and the other two one each. ED might be just a computer without the self-aware or cognitive abilities of Mama-Seven but he still had survival circuitry and this data-bank was now screaming 'SURVIVAL.'

ED knew he was part of the Gareth and he also knew the heavy cruiser was being targeted by three ships of the same size. After the four Anneal shots were away ED was made aware that the eight guns of Fire-Base Moag were reloaded and ready to fire. All eight rounds were sent after the same three Sokari cruisers. The first four rounds from the Anneal found their mark and the three cruisers slowed. Seconds later eight more rounds from the Fire-Base also hit the three cruisers.

ED monitored the hits and requested information through Map-Con from Mama-Seven on the damage. While this was being done the guns of the Anneal were reloaded and ready to fire again. ED had these four rounds held in reserve as he directed the Umbrage's weapons at another group of heavy cruisers that were trying to give chase to the Anneal.

Mama-Seven monitored the damage to the three Sokari Cruisers, it was hardly needed. All eight of the Sled Rounds fired from Fire-Base Moag hit the three ships; they each began to burn even in the vacuum of space. One collapsed in on itself and then exploded in a terrific fireball. Mama-Seven sent her reply back through Map-Con. "Disengage from your previous three targets, they pose no further threat."

ED now targeted the same three ships he had attacked with the guns of the Umbrage. They had taken some damage and now would be getting the full attention of the Anneal; suddenly it appeared the Outer Reaches Fleet was gaining the upper hand. Weapons fire on the Gareth had diminished to nearly nothing, allowing the Static Repulsar Pocket to fully recharge. Mama-Seven was tasking millions of Micro-Repair Cells to the most heavily damaged portions of the ship. The slight list had been corrected and systems were coming back on line as fast as they could be repaired.

Simms now wondered if the tactical situation had changed enough to eliminate the need of destroying the Temerity. She would be useful in the event the troops on the planet had to be fast evacuated. "Mama-Seven, give me a situational report on the Temerity," was all Simms said.

"Temerity has sustained some damage but her pocket is still functioning, both Sled-Guns are still operational and ED is in control. Suggest shuttle be sent over with crew to re-man her. The need to detonate engines has just passed with the elimination of the three Sokari Heavy Cruisers that were attacking the Gareth."

Simms was elated and knew the tactical situation had just swung in favor of his small fleet. "Contact Captain Zhukov, have him and his bridge crew along with as many officers and crew as he sees fit to board two shuttles and make a run for the Temerity. Tell him if our luck holds he won't be losing his ship after all."

It was risky sending two shuttles out into the middle of a fleet action, but the reward was worth the risk. If the Temerity could be saved it would greatly enhance the operational abilities of the Outer Reaches Fleet. Zhukov and his crew were elated to be back in the fight.

The two shuttles were boarded and launched. ED coordinated every operational Sled-Gun to fire just as the bay doors of the Umbrage opened and the two shuttles made a break for the Temerity. Simms watched as the two shuttles headed away and made for the Beachhead Support Cruiser. Ten minutes later and both shuttles landed safely in one of her launch bays.

Zhukov and his command raced for the bridge as the rest of the crew headed for their stations. The two shuttles could only compliment twenty percent of the crew but this was deemed sufficient to man her until it was safe to transport more.

Zhukov was pleased that the bridge was fully functional. Damage assessments were quickly ran and it was determined the cruiser was fully operational. Some of the lesser equipment was knocked out but the main offensive and defensive capabilities were at nearly one-hundred percent.

The captain immediately contacted the Gareth with a report. "Captain Simms, it appears we are fully operational, damage is minimal. It looks like the pocket held, awaiting your orders."

Simms exhaled, he didn't like sending the two shuttles out in the middle of the battle but it had worked. "Maintain position Zhukov, fight the ship from your position. Maintain defensive posture and have engines ready if you need to move, Simms out!"

Zhukov was happy to be back on the Temerity, if he was going to die he would rather do it on his own ship rather than sitting idly by on another. As he viewed his screens he felt the two Sled-Guns fire, ED was doing his job.

As the battle between the four ships of the Outer Reaches Fleet and the Sokari raged on, the battle at Fire-Base Moag was about to heat up. The Elites couldn't believe their good fortune; the conquest of the planet Tenement was complete with only a few small pockets of the Arrenaugh still alive in some of the more robust of the underground bunkers. It wouldn't be long before those too would be overrun, the occupants used for food to sustain the ravenous Septa-Pods.

Now two new species had arrived in system. The Elites had monitored the arrival of the two fleets and now watched in great amazement as the ships of both species battled it out in space. There had also been two separate landings made by both species. The first had landed with one of the enormous cruisers and offloaded weapons and personnel in the thousands. This first group was taking part in the space battle by using some sort of long range lance weapon fired from their ground base.

Now more craft had landed, these were from the second set of ships to arrive. It appeared this second group was preparing an assault on the first. They possessed many large armored vehicles and transports. It had been estimated the first group had landed nearly four thousand troops, these were from a species known as humans. The Elites knew little about the humans, other than rumors and innuendo. It had been suspected that humans might not even exist, other than the occasional capture of a cargo ship that had evidence of human manufactured product onboard.

The second group was found to be a war faring species known as the Sokari. The Elites had quite a bit of knowledge of this species. The realms of both the Sokari and the Elites adjoined each other. The Sokari had invaded into Elite territory thousands of time units before but were quickly overrun and taken prisoner by the Septa-Pods and used as food. Once word got back to the Sokari home worlds of this vicious new species it was agreed to stay away from that section of the galaxy. The Sokari built a first line of defense against any colonization by the Elites in the form of armored asteroids and moons. The fleet was increased in the space adjoining the two species in the hopes of stopping any infiltration of the Septa-Pods, which the Sokari now feared. It had been estimated that even a single Septa-Pod released on a Sokari occupied world might kill thousands before it could itself be destroyed.

The Elites on Tenement had long range scanners at their disposal, those they had brought with them along with the ones they had

Nathan Wright

captured from the Arrenaugh. So far it appeared the four human ships were holding their own against the much more numerous Sokari ships. The humans must also be a warrior race to be doing so well against such crushing odds. This both thrilled and bothered the Elites. An armed opponent that could do such damage against such odds was impressive. It was also worrisome to know another species that could handle the Sokari so well might be able to do the same to the Elites.

An attack was being planned by the Elites against the humans, which was before the Sokari had landed. With roughly four-thousand human soldiers on the planet the Septa-Pods were going to use them for a food source after they overran their positions. Now the Sokari had landed approximately ten-thousand of their own troops, along with heavy equipment.

The Elites were running battle simulations on just how to proceed when their main operating system, a system that was much older than Mama-Seven, and was also a self-aware computer, notified the ruling committee of Elites that information was being gathered which should be considered before any offensive measures were taken against the humans.

The Elites on Tenement were ruled by a governing body that consisted of three individual Elites chosen at random. Since all Elites were of exceptional intellect it didn't matter which three ruled but it was necessary to have rule, no society existed just by chance.

Once the three were gathered in what was known as the Council Room the meeting began. The computing system that assisted the Elites was known as Cyanate and it was determined that the gender of this operating and computing system was female. Cyanate was self-aware and fully cognitive and assumed the organic trait of determining gender, she was female.

"I have gathered you here to discuss the possibility that I may not be alone in the galaxy," Cyanate informed the group.

This statement said it all except for where the other operating system might be. "Where in the galaxy is this other being?" One of the three asked.

"The other is here, in this planetary system and occupies one of the human vessels that are being attacked by the Sokari Fleet," Cyanate said.

This was startling to the Elite gathered in the room. "Another 'Being' is here in orbit. How do you know?" One of the council asked. The Elite and Cyanate considered the ability to be self-aware, but not organic, to be held above anything living. This was why Cyanate was referred to as a 'Being.'

"I have monitored the Sokari attacks on the human vessels and also monitored the human responses. It appears the four human vessels are being controlled and are working as one. One result of such coordination and response is that the four ships are being overseen by a 'Being' which might also be assisted by lesser computing systems."

"What is your recommendation Cyanate, shall we destroy the Sokari that have landed and ignore the humans?" Another of the council asked.

Just as Mama-Seven answered with no need to consider the question, Cyanate answered immediately. "I wish to know this other 'Being,' I wish to speak to it and learn what is available to be learned." Self-aware computers never passed up the opportunity to learn. Cyanate had never come across another of her kind and she was intrigued by the possibilities.

"How shall this be accomplished?" asked another of the committee.

"We should destroy the Sokari that have landed here; their bodies will be added to the diminishing food stores used by the Septa-Pods. We do not let them escape back to their ships. As we undertake the task of capturing the Sokari soldiers we refrain from attacking the human lines. During this time more information can be gathered about the other 'Being,'" Cyanate said. "As soon as the Sokari are defeated here on the surface, you may turn your attentions to the human soldiers. When we defeat the humans on the ground we may barter their bodies for a chance to converse with the other 'Being.'"

The Council agreed at once. Ever since Cyanate had obtained full-cognition no council had ever failed to grant her wishes. This was done for two reasons, first the Elites knew Cyanate was never wrong and second it was feared what might happen if she were ever denied what she asked for. The full abilities of Cyanate had never been revealed to the Elites and they suspected she had an angry side, which was hoped, to never be released.

The three Elites of the Council left the Council Room and headed back to the command bunker, it was time to kill some Sokari. The command bunker was actually one of the ornate rooms the Arrenaugh had used to govern their society. It was large and heavily fortified although the Septa-Pods had overran it early in the campaign to capture Tenement. It was now filled with terminals and work station where the military unit of the Elite conducted exercises against the remainder of the Arrenaugh. That job had been coming to an end for the last while and it was now refreshing to have new enemies to attack.

With a last check of the Sokari landing craft and the legions of troops exiting the shuttles it was determined they had established their base of operations and were now preparing an assault on the human lines. The order was given for the Septa-Pods to rush from the tunnels and advance with all speed on the unsuspecting Sokari troops. Nearly a thousand of the spidery creatures would take part in this attack with three thousand more held in reserve, more than enough.

At Fire-Base Moag the landing of so many Sokari assault shuttles hadn't gone unnoticed. The Astro-Sailors manning the gun batteries continued to blast Hell out of the Sokari Capitol Ships and this left the troopers under the command of Major A Bet the task of protecting the perimeter. So far there had been several inbound ordinance from the Sokari Capitol Ships but little damage had been done to the base, thanks in part to the robust Repulsar Pockets the base was equipped with. A Bet suspected that bombardment would now cease due to the close proximity of the Sokari assault force that had just landed near the base.

He was correct, the bombardment stopped just as the first of the craft made landfall.

This was good for two reasons; first it would have been hard to mount an attack on the Sokari if A Bet sent his troops past the relative safety of the Repulsar Pocket. Secondly, there was little chance of knocking out one of the base's precious Sled-Guns with the bombardment stopped. Now A Bet's troopers were itching for a standup fight against a land based opponent.

The forces dropped by Temerity included heavy tanks, six in all along with armored personnel carriers and self-propelled artillery. A Bet wished he had double the number of tanks but knew wishing would never get the job done.

The perimeter had been fortified by the troops but this could only be done out to the leading edge of the Repulsar Pockets. Now that the bombardment had stopped the troops were digging emplacements for their light artillery and foxholes farther out from the edges of the Pockets. After many hundreds of years of battles on Earth, and now on planets far from Earth, the average soldier held his ground from the relative safety of a foxhole or slit-trench. These were now being dug and prepared for an assault by the Sokari. Extra ammunition was placed near the trenches along with short rations. The heaviest of the artillery was still being protected by the Pocket and would not be bought out further for fear of losing the valuable weapons during the assault. They would be able to fire just as well from a position inside the pocket as out.

The offensive weapons officer for the ground-based component of Star-Base Moag was a sergeant named Burt Hale. His primary job, at the moment, was monitoring the elaborate scanners that tracked movement on the ground near the base. His feed was actually coming from the stationary Temerity; her position allowed her scanners to be used in the same way a satellite might be used. It was the perfect overhead view. The scanner screen gave a picture of the base and everything around it. It picked up the Sokari landing craft and the offloading of troops and heavy equipment. What the Sokari were bringing to the table was very impressive. This was one of the reasons A Bet was in such a hurry to complete the camp's defenses. He knew a battle was coming and wanted to be as prepared as possible.

"Major, it looks like we have movement to your east." Hale radioed. There was a magnetic field associated with Tenement and this was based much like the North and South Poles on Earth. The two poles allowed for reference points to be established.

A Bet went to his mobile command car and punched up the same live feed Hale was using. He scanned the screen and then radioed back, "Is that enemy armor bringing up the rear?" He asked Hale.

The equipment at the command bunker was more powerful than what A Bet had in his command car. "No sir, they appear to be the same creatures you described that attacked you in the tunnel."

A Bet strained to make out the images, just the thought of the big spider looking things made his skin crawl. What he was now seeing in his grainy image looked to be hundreds of the beasts. "Are you sure Hale, we only saw a few and possibly a couple more in the background in the tunnel. This looks like hundreds."

"The image tells the tale sir. It appears to be hundreds and they are still exiting the cave system. Something else, they are forming ranks after they clear the tunnel. These things are either smart or being controlled by someone or something; either way I guess it indicates intelligence," Hale said.

A Bet continued to look at the screen trying to get a handle on what he was up against. If the Sokari were suspected to number nearly ten-thousand and these things in the hundreds he wondered how his forces could hold out or even if they could hold out. "Does it appear they are part of the Sokari force?"

"Not known sir, give me a few minutes." Hale and A Bet both signed off.

Hale was only a sergeant but in the Outer Reaches Fleet it was not unusual for someone with the rank of sergeant to contact a Capitol Ship to report, or receive, news and instructions. It was also common to be referred to as sir, if your rank was major or higher. After he broke off with A Bet he coded in his numbers and contacted the Temerity and was immediately put in touch with Captain Zhukov. The Temerity had operational control of the Mongoose Weapons system and the ground troops stationed on Tenement.

"Captain, it appears the Sokari are preparing for an assault on our base but there is more. The creatures that attacked Major A Bet in the cave seem to be massing for an attack of their own; our position might become untenable taking into account the numbers of both forces. Also, is it possible the Sokari and this new contact are associated?" Hale asked.

Zhukov was aware of the loss of one of the troopers under A Bet's command, he had read the report. He still hadn't been brought up to speed about what the species occupying the caves were; he had just been too busy. "Back to you in ten sergeant," was all Zhukov said as he turned to one of the bridge staff.

"Willis, see if any more information has been obtained about the indigenous species that attacked our troops in the cave earlier. I need to know what their strength and capabilities are as soon as possible."

Within minutes Zhukov had the information he needed and it wasn't good.

"Sergeant Hale, do you copy?"

"Hale here sir, go ahead Captain."

"I've just been briefed by Captain Simms, it appears you are facing a threat at least as dangerous as the Sokari. The creatures are known as Septa-Pods and they are extremely nasty bastards. It is believed the Sokari and Septa-Pods are enemies and not working together. Doubtful if you can hold against both the Sokari and the Septa-Pods. If need be Temerity will execute a hot zone landing and pick-up but it is imperative the Mongoose stay active for as long as possible."

"Roger that Captain, Hale out."

Zhukov liked that about his troops, they asked only the questions that needed to be asked and then given the answer there was no elaboration, just action. In his talk with Simms, when he had been told about the Septa-Pods, Zhukov was told the Outer Reaches Fleet was gaining the upper hand tactically against the Sokari but if the Mongoose Weapons System were taken out of action then the odds would immediately revert back in favor of the Sokari. Every minute the system was allowed to operate could mean all the difference in the outcome of the battle.

"A Bet you there?" Hale asked as he scanned his screens again.

"A Bet here, go ahead Hale."

"Got a response to your question. Sokari and Septa-Pods are not known to be allies' sir. Captain Simms thinks they are hostile to each other. Star-Base Moag must hold if the fleet is to stand a chance against the Sokari," Hale said.

A Bet did gather a little hope from this news, maybe if the two species attacked his lines as two separate entities then their assaults wouldn't be coordinated. As bad as a two front attack was at least they would be unorganized.

"Roger that Hale. Get the armor moved up to the approach side and have them take up defensive positions along with the armored personnel carriers, A Bet out."

Hale gave the order and the six heavy tanks began to rumble out of the protection of the pocket followed by thirteen armored personnel carriers, each carrying fifteen Assault Troops. A Bet was at the perimeter waiting. The tanks were stationed in a hull down position just behind the leading edge of the foxholes and slit-trenches. Ten of the thirteen armored personnel carriers off loaded their troops and then they too were stationed in a position that revealed their top mounded wire-guided missile launchers only. The last three carriers were kept back as a reserve to rush forward and try to plug any breach that may occur.

Thirty minutes after the tanks and carriers arrived everything was ready. A Bet made one last walk of the positions his troops and armor occupied, he was impressed with what had been accomplished in so short a time span. The only thing missing was an opposing army, from what he gathered, that would also be there soon.

Simms contacted Harless aboard the Umbrage with the news he had just received from Zhukov aboard the Temerity. "It looks like a massed attack is imminent for Moag. Don't know yet if they can hold, Temerity is prepared to make a hot zone landing if it appears the base will be overrun."

Harless considered the information he had just been given. He was well aware of the contribution the Star-Base had made in the battle. "If Moag gets overrun do you think we can hold?"

Simms had already tasked Mama-Seven that same question and she had given him her answer, "At this time the Outer Reaches Fleet will be defeated if the Star-Base and her Mongoose Weapons Systems are overrun." Simms now grimly shared this bit of news with the other captain.

Harless came up with the idea to reinforce the Star-Base. "What have we got that we can send down there to help them hold?"

Simms was intrigued, he had been so overwhelmed with the fleet action he had failed to consider this option. "The heavy tanks that should have been offloaded with Major West's troops are still on board the Gareth, we were unable to unload due to strut elevator damage." The damage to the strut elevator might have prevented the offloading planet side of the heavy tanks but that wasn't a problem in space. They could simply be driven into the shuttles and flown to the planet's surface.

"How many tanks are there still on board?" Harless asked.

"All four, we carry two less than the Beachhead Landing Ships," Simms replied.

"The Umbrage contains the same, along with the only troops left at our disposal, eighteen-hundred."

"Coordinate shuttle launch with the Gareth, ED will want to use every Sled-Gun at our disposal when they launch to try and keep the enemy busy," Simms said.

"It'll take twenty-minutes Captain, Harless out."

Twenty minutes after the plan was made to reinforce Star-Base Moag and try and prevent the destruction of the Mongoose Weapons System, four heavy landers from the Gareth and eight from the Umbrage launched. ED had held fire for fully six-minutes in order to fire a significant volley to try and give the cumbersome shuttles time to launch and gain speed. The Sokari were caught off guard completely, so many Sled-Round were fired that they were kept busy until the shuttles entered the atmosphere of Tenement.

Forty-five minutes after the plan was first hatched the twelve shuttles landed within the base. Star-Base Moag had just received eight more heavy tanks and eighteen-hundred more Shock Troops. This new force now fell under the command of A Bet. He immediately moved four of the tanks into the front defensive lines and held the other four back as a strategic reserve. Fourteen-hundred of the troops were also sent to the front line with the other four-hundred held back as a reserve; this was the first troop reserves A Bet had been able to spare.

He now felt he stood a slim chance of holding the base. Still he was facing an enormous force that could create a breakthrough anywhere along his front line if they chose. If that happened he would use his four tank reserve, along with the four-hundred troops, to try and plug it.

Just as A Bet was finishing his defenses he got a message from Zhukov on the Temerity. "Fire-Base Moag must not be allowed to fall into enemy hands. Your orders are to hold out, regardless of losses. If the Mongoose Weapons System ceases to exist then it must be assumed the battle in space will also be lost. Zhukov out."

A Bet put down the handset, his was now a fight to the death. If the soldiers on the ground failed then the four ships slugging it out against the Sokari Fleet would surely be lost. If the soldiers couldn't hold then everyone would die.

The Sokari continued to apply pressure against the human ships but were still taking a pounding from the Sled-Guns. If they could only eliminate the weapons fire that was coming from the surface of the planet then they could destroy the four ships that had so far given them so much trouble. The ground assault against the human base would be the deciding factor.

Tang had been assured by his commanders that it was only a matter of time before the assault began and the ground based weapons were destroyed. There were more than enough troops and heavy weapons down there to do the job. Tang still held out hope for a victory but that couldn't happen until the ground campaign was complete and the humans down there, along with their ground based weapons, were destroyed.

Tang summoned his second in command, once he was standing beside the command chair Tang pulled his side arm and put it under the Sub-Commander's chin, "Unless the assault on the human's base begins at once I will shoot you, and unless the assault is successful I will also shoot you."

The Sub-Commander stepped away from the chair as a slimy bead of greenish sweat ran down the side of his bug-eyed face. "I will see to it personally Admiral." The Sub-Commander, a creature named Tern Burles, nearly ran to his station and began the task of following up on the assault. Burles was a brilliant tactician and, up until the death of Keeto Three, been number three in line for command of the fleet. Now he was second only to the murderous Tang.

Burles had been in silent communication with his superiors back at the Sokari home world. He had been contacted about the results of the attacks against the human fleet. Apparently Tang had been transmitting a rosier picture than actual facts would back up. Fleet had gotten some information that just couldn't be backed up by the data stream they had seen, something was wrong. A back channel had been established without the knowledge of Tang. The contact Fleet was using was none-other than the Sokari Sub-Commander that Admiral Tang had just threatened.

As Admiral Tang sat in his command chair and considered his situation there was no way for him to know that his life was nearer to its end than he suspected. If the ground assault on the human base failed and his fleet couldn't gain a victory over the human ships he now fought with in space, he would be replaced by Tern Burles and the fleet pulled back to be refitted and replenished. Tang's body would be brought home and housed in the Vault of Traitors, a fate no military man or family could fathom.

As the Sokari forward columns advanced on Star-Base Moag they went into assault formation with heavy tanks and troop transports in the lead and foot soldiers following in the rear. Once within range, the guns of the tanks opened up, along with that of weapons carriers that packed as much firepower as a tank but virtually no armor. The incoming rounds impacted the front lines A Bet had established but no damage or fatalities were reported. A Bet's men and equipment were well dug in, so well that the Sokari gunners couldn't see them. A Bet allowed the enemy to advance well within the range of his own weapons before giving the order to open fire.

The first response the Sokari had that the humans were nearby came in the form of a blistering barrage of tank and heavy weapons fire. A Bet let loose with every gun in his command and within minutes there was smoke and fire visibly rising from the Sokari lines. He held his second round from the tanks and artillery to gauge the effect his shots might be having on the enemy, he only intended to hold for a couple of seconds before hitting the lead elements of the Sokari again. The main reason A Bet wanted to gauge for effect was to see if the Armor Piercing Rounds he was firing were having the effect he wanted. At his disposal were also heat and sonic shells.

Just as he was getting information about the ammunition his troops were firing the Sokari opened up with everything they had. Just as this was happening the Sokari infantry that had been held in reserve raced forward in a headlong rush. What now appeared in front of A Bet was a solid wall of racing Sokari Storm Troops, each wearing a combination armor-enviro suit. The armor made the bug like creatures look fearsome, and large. A Sokari was tall to begin with but with the added bulk of mechanical armor they were huge.

A Bet and his troopers weren't small by any means. For a man or woman to be recruited into the fleet, as a soldier, they had to meet height and weight requirements, Tall and Strong was the rule of thumb. After meeting the recruitment requirements there was a two year training program along with medical enhancements that also increased size and performance of each recruit. Upon graduation and acceptance into the ranks of the fleet each individual was forty percent larger and much more deadly than a normal human.

In a one on one match up a human soldier compared to a Sokari soldier was pretty much an even contest due mainly to the enhanced mechanics the Sokari armor contained. Without the armor a human soldier could take on three Sokari with a better than fifty-fifty chance of winning. The bio-enhanced soldiers A Bet fielded were fierce in both function and appearance with many sporting scars from previous battles. Any scar could be medically healed with no evidence of injury but a Deep Space Soldier proudly wore the battle damage as proof of their fighting ability.

What A Bet saw in his field glasses was an army rushing his position that outnumbered his troops by nearly four to one. His men were well positioned and dug in but he knew the Sokari intended to run over his position and head straight for the guns that were blasting the Hell out of their fleet. Every man in the unit carried an assault rifle with a bayonet that was auto-stored below the barrel that could be placed for action with the touch of a button beside the trigger guard. It looked like the bayonets would soon be in use.

A Bet never hesitated once he saw the massed attack heading his way. He gave the order to fire everything he had at the approaching enemy. Results of the initial ordinance indicated that at distance the assault rifles his troopers used had virtually no effect on the armor of the Sokari soldiers, it merely bounced off. At closer range A Bet hoped the weapons might have a better chance of penetrating the armor the Sokari sported. The shells fired from his tanks and artillery had better luck but these too seemed to do little damage to the opposing armor. As the distance closed results should improve.

Within minutes ranks had closed and it appeared the battle was going to go hand to hand. Every trooper activated their bayonets and prepared to go at the Sokari in close quarters combat.

"A Bet you there?" Hale asked over his radio. He was still positioned at his monitors and scanners that were being live updated from the Temerity.

"A little busy right now Hale, what do you want?" A Bet shouted over the noise of battle.

"Got a second group of hostiles heading your way at speed." Hale said.

"From what direction?" A Bet asked.

"Directly behind the attacking Sokari, expect filter through to your position or engagement with the Sokari in one minute. These bastards are fast," Hale said.

The information was troubling, one of two things was about to happen. The Septa-Pods would advance through the Sokari lines and begin attacking A Bet and his troops, or they would attack the Sokari troops. The first would be bad but the second not so much. All A Bet and his troops could do was try and hold.

The first indication the Sokari army had that something was wrong was when the first of the Septa-Pods reached the landing craft. The flight crews of the craft were busy preparing for the reloading and take-off after the battle was won. There was a limited number of Sokari soldiers guarding the shuttles when the first of the giant Septa-Pods were spotted.

The Sokari opened fire immediately but were quickly overrun, their bodies torn apart as the Pods attacked without mercy. A couple of the shuttles managed to take off and leave this living nightmare behind, but the rest were either mangled in place or flipped upside down by the powerful spidery looking monsters. The battle, if you could call it that, lasted less than three minutes with the deaths of every Sokari at the landing site except for the few that had managed to take off on the two escaping shuttles.

Tang was at his command console considering when to pull the trigger on Tern Burles when a message was received from two of the landing shuttles that had transported the troops to the surface of Tenement.

"Septa-Pods, we've got Septa-Pods on the surface, hundreds if not thousands of them," Came the excited voice from one of the shuttles. The other shuttle voiced the same information.

Tang stood, "Septa-Pods!" was all he said. Tang looked about the command bridge of the Rococo, everyone was looking at him and the looks revealed terror. Septa-Pods had beaten the Sokari at every engagement they had ever had with massive loss of life. That was the reason for the militarily enforced frontier the two species maintained between each other, at least the Sokari side was militarized. The Elites considered any incursion by the Sokari to be only dinner being delivered to the Septa-Pods.

"Inform the rest of the fleet, make sure no additional craft are landed on Tenement." Tang ordered. After a second of thought he added, "Target the two shuttles, use a factor of three and open fire," he ordered. A factor of three meant to use three times the force needed to destroy each of the shuttles. Tang was making sure there wasn't a Septa-Pod stowaway on either of the shuttles that were now headed toward the ships of his fleet. If a shuttle landed in the bay of one of his cruisers, and that shuttle contained a Pod, either inside or attached to the outside, then it was nearly a certainty that that ship would be destroyed from the inside out. This was done out of experience rather than caution, a Capitol Ship had been infested by a single Pod in years past and destroyed.

As the Admiral watched on one of only two screens at his command console that still worked, he saw one of the picket ships close on the two shuttles and prepare to fire. As it approached it actually blocked the view of the furthermost shuttle. In short order the first of the shuttles was hit by an energy weapon. The weapon at first appeared to have no effect on the shuttle. Soon the hull of the small craft began to glow, and shortly after that, it exploded.

The second shuttle crew saw what had happened and knew this would be their fate also. The pilot moved toward the picket ship, too close for it to re-target and fire. Now the crew tried to dock, hitting the coupler with such force that it actually broke the seal on the pressure door. The captain of the picket ship saw what had happened and knew the crew was trying to escape death at the hands of their own fleet. He didn't blame them and was glad; he could now allow them to board since the shuttle had successfully docked. He knew Tang was a ruthless bastard and wanted nothing more than to ignore one of the Admiral's bloodthirsty commands.

The crew of the picket ship struggled to open the heavy door that separated the two ships. Finally it was decided that the damage done by the hard dock of the shuttle might be preventing access. A torch was used to heat the locking mechanism just enough to expand the metal but not enough to do any damage. This worked and with the help of five Sokari, the door was slid to a full open position.

What they found once the door was open was not what they expected. Lying just inside the shuttle was a torso, no arms, no legs and no head, just a torso. There was a pool of blood and this was spreading as it drained from the wounds indicating that whatever happened had been recent. A fully manned shuttle would have fourteen crewmembers plus any troops or technicians that happened to be on board. There were four large sections plus the cockpit, a shuttle was not a small craft.

The first to enter the shuttle was a four strong Sokari squad of troops armed with splatter guns, a short range weapon not unlike a shotgun used by humans. They entered cautiously and as they saw the carnage each wanted to go no further but return to the picket ship. The first room was void of any life, just bodies that had been ripped apart. There was a noise in the adjoining room and the four Sokari troops looked in that direction. Before they could even raise their weapons a Septa-Pod burst through the opening and was on them. The four never even got the chance to turn; they were cut down where they stood.

The captain of the picket ship was watching on the access bay monitor and saw the monstrous creature at nearly the same time as the troops. He shouted an order to close the hatch but before the crew could react the Septa-Pod was at the door and squeezing through, it was too late, the beast was now on the picket ship.

Tang had been monitoring the events with the two shuttles and had seen the destruction of the first but lost sight of the second as it docked on the opposite side from his view. Once contact had been lost from the picket ship Tang suspected the worst and ordered one of the other escort ships to target her. He would have used the weapons on the Rococo if he had any that worked. Just before giving the order to fire there was a radio transmission from the doomed picket ship, all that could be made out was the sounds of dying Sokari. Tang gave the order and shortly after, the picket ship along with the shuttle, were no more. As the debris field spread and the fires from the blast died in the vacuum of space there was the image of movement.

"Amplify." Tang ordered.

As the distant images cleared and enlarged, what Tang saw truly made him experience fear. The Septa-Pod was still alive although missing two of its legs. It was using pieces of debris to propel itself toward the picket ship that had just fired the shots. It would latch onto one of the larger pieces of metal and then launch itself toward the ship. Tang was frozen in place for a brief time as he watched this creature approach the second ship. If the total destruction of a picket ship couldn't destroy a Septa-Pod then what could?

"Fire on that thing!" Tang ordered.

The picket ship was already backing away when the order came. Every gun on the warship seemed to open up on the Septa-Pod. When the firing stopped there was nothing left but legs and pieces of smoldering flesh floating away. Tang sat back down and allowed the thoughts of the creature to fade from his memory.

With the two shuttles now destroyed, along with a picket ship that had gotten too close, Tang now gave his full attention to the land battle. If only his troops could destroy the human land based weapon then he could close on the four human ships and finish the job. As he watched he wondered about the added worry of the Septa-Pods. If they were on the ground then he would be forced to abandon his ground troops. This was at first troubling, there were at least ten-thousand Sokari down there, but if there was also an infestation of the monstrous Septa-Pods then there was no way he was going to allow shuttles to bring anyone off the surface of the planet. He hoped his ground forces could finish the destruction of the humans before the monsters ate his troops.

But even if his Sokari battle force on the planet's surface fell to the Septa-Pods then wouldn't the humans also meet the same fate? Suddenly Tang felt a twinge of delight, if his troops couldn't destroy the humans and their weapon then surely the Septa-Pods could, it was only a matter of time now.

Once the rear echelons of the Sokari force were destroyed the Septa-Pods would head for the more numerous troops that were just now attacking the humans. At least a thousand of the giant hairy creatures advanced in a continuous line. As the rear elements of the attacking troops realized they were being taken out by giant spidery looking creatures, they began to turn and fight the Septa-Pods. More and more of the Sokari now began to turn and as they did the assault on the human base began to dwindle.

A Bet could now see through his field glasses his first glimpse of the creatures he had seen in the shadows of the cave. If his imagination had filled in the blanks of the picture he could mostly imagine in the darkness of the cave, now he was getting the full view, and it was scary as Hell. The creatures were enormous and could only be described as a arachnid. The term on earth for a spider, something you could step on with your boot and never think about again. What he now saw was nothing less than a monster.

As Admiral Tang watched his troops being eaten by the Septa-Pods he knew it was only a matter of time before they finished and moved on to the humans. Once the land based weapon was destroyed he would turn his attention to the four human ships and finish his mission. He sat back down in his command chair and began to anticipate his triumphant return to the Sokari home world with one of the human vessels in tow as a war prize.

Tern Burles went to the communications array and sent an urgent message to the Sokari Imperial Senate. The message described the introduction of the Septa-Pods into the equation. Within minutes Burles got a reply, he was to take a shuttle and evacuate the badly damaged Rococo, taking with him the few Sokari personnel that he trusted. It was well known by Burles that some of the members of the Rococo were as bloodthirsty as the Admiral and these members were not to be included in the evacuation.

Within minutes of getting his reply Burles departed the Rococo onboard one of the few remaining shuttles that hadn't been damaged by the blistering barrage from the human ships.

"Admiral it appears we have an unauthorized launch of a shuttle," one of the bridge staff shouted.

Tang looked at his monitor and saw the craft exit the launch bay. "Sub-Commander Burles, who just launched from the bay?" Tang asked. There was no answer, Burles was onboard the shuttle along with four other of the Rococo's officers.

Burles piloted the shuttle himself and hurried away from the badly damaged ship. He knew the Rococo still possessed a few offensive weapons and knew his time was short. Once he was far enough away he contacted another of the Capitol Ships and gave the order to target the Rococo.

On the bridge Tang was still attempting to figure out what was going on when one of the weapons officers shouted, "We are being targeted admiral, what are your orders?"

Tang suspected the Rococo was too far away from the human ships to be targeted by their weapons. "Who is targeting us?" He asked.

After a quick scan the same weapons officer turned to the Admiral, "It's our escorts' sir. We are being targeted by our own ships."

"Contact them at once, have them to stand down," Tang shouted.

"It's too late Admiral, they have just fired."

Tang looked at his scanners again and saw the incoming tracers. He sat back down in his command chair and waited for the end, at least now he wouldn't need to worry about his body being placed in the 'Vault of Traitors.'

Tang continued to watch as the number of weapons being fired at the Rococo mounted, it was more than enough to do the job. Some of the first to strike the massive ship only made her shudder. Tang felt the vibrations and as more and more impacts registered he began to smell smoke. There was one last detonation and he knew this was the ships engines, there was a blinding flash and then it was over. The Rococo ceased to exist, along with all that were left onboard.

Tern Burles made it to what would be the new command ship for the fleet and immediately contacted the Sokari Imperial Senate to report the death of the murderous Tang and request further orders. An update was also given on the state of the battle that had left so many of the Sokari ships destroyed or damaged. The state of the ground assault was also given, total destruction of the assault force is now expected with the introduction of the Septa-Pods and Elites. The message came back almost as soon as it was sent.

"Break off engagement at once and return to nearest base. Any ship that has made contact with the planet's surface or received a shuttle from the planet is to be destroyed at once."

Burles expected as much, the Sokari Senate wasn't taking any chances now that the Septa-Pods were part of the equation. No additional ships had landed and the only shuttles that had managed to take off were now destroyed along with the Septa-Pod stowaway. Shortly after receiving his new orders Burles had the fleet disengage from the battle and form up for an exit of this quadrant.

Captain Simms had been in constant contact with the captains of the other three ships during the entire engagement with the Sokari. At first, the re-positioning of the enemy fleet was thought to be in preparation for another coordinated attack. At about the same time, it was noticed that the Rococo was being fired on by her own ships and this was puzzling. Then it was guessed that she was so heavily damaged that she had been evacuated and was now being destroyed. Simms and the other three captains would never know that the alien that had ambushed the Gareth was now dead, killed by weapons fire from his own fleet.

Simms prepared for the coming attack by making sure all operable Sled-Guns were ready for a coordinated volley. ED was again given free reign and began his plot. As the minutes ticked by Simms and the other three captains began to imagine the worst. Could another Lava-Slug be on the way? Could more Sokari warships be lurking nearby and preparing a second, and more powerful, assault. Not until all the enemy ships headed away at high speed did Simms begin to relax, but not much.

"Mama-Seven, can you explain what just happened?" The captain asked.

With her usual efficiency the Super-Computer stated, "It appears the Sokari have destroyed their command ship and have now broken off the engagement. Most probable reason is the introduction of the Septa-Pods and Elites into the equation, this has an eighty-two percent chance of being true."

Simms immediately contacted Ground Command to get the status of the Sokari force that was attacking Fire-Base Moag. Sergeant Burt Hale got the call and immediately told the captain what he knew.

"Weapons fire from the Sokari lead elements has all but stopped. It appears they are now turning their attention to the group that is attacking them from the rear. Do we continue to fire on the Sokari sir?" Hale asked.

"No Sergeant, allow the two opposing forces to do battle, do not assist one over the other unless you are attacked," Simms said.

Now Mama-Seven added something to the mix, "Captain, it would be advised to allow your troops to fall back to the protection of the Static Repulsar Pocket."

Simms knew the pocket was of no use against troops, only weapons. "But they will be giving up the prepared defenses they have established," he protested.

"That is correct Captain, but the prepared defenses are of no use against the Septa-Pods. Even the heavy tanks won't be able to stop them. The Pocket though might confuse the Pods. They will not advance into the pocket until the Elites give them the order and that won't happen until the Pocket is scanned," Mama-Seven explained.

Simms gave the order for Hale to radio Major A Bet, evacuate the advance positions and move back to the protection of the Static Repulsar Pocket. He then had a complete scan of the surrounding sector of space completed, the Sokari ships were now at the far reaches of scanner range and still moving away. It was time to consider getting away before some new surprise overtook his command. As Simms was considering this he was interrupted by Mama-Seven.

"I suggest the expeditionary force be evacuated at once Captain while the Sokari and the Septa-Pods are still doing battle. This may be our only chance to rescue the personnel from Fire-Base Moag."

Simms realized the Super-Computer had used the term 'rescue.' It appeared the troops were now in more danger from the giant beasts than the Sokari troops that were still there. If the alien fleet had left then the base, and her Mongoose Weapons System, were no longer needed.

"Captain Zhukov how soon can the Temerity execute a landing and pick-up?" Simms asked.

Zhukov was aware of the exit of the alien fleet and wanted nothing more than to pack it up and get out of this section of space. He hadn't managed to fully repair the damage to his engines but felt they would hold out for a few hours, enough to get far away from this little section of Hell.

"Temerity can execute landing and pick-up on your command sir. My sensors still show fighting on the ground though." Zhukov knew to get his large ship that close to an ongoing battle might be risky.

"Fighting is between others, not your troops. I still advise hot landing and extraction, we can destroy the equipment from orbit," Simms said.

During a hot landing and extraction it was expected the Temerity might be taking some fire and for this reason she wouldn't be staying long enough to pick up any of the equipment, everything would be abandoned and then destroyed from space. Even the Mongoose Weapons System would be left planet side but not before Major A Bet and his troops set delayed charges to destroy as much of the equipment as possible before they departed. Only the troops and personnel carriers would be evacuated. Everything else would be destroyed. Even the tanks would need to be abandoned in order to make room for the extra troops that had been dropped earlier from the Gareth and the Umbrage. Before the conversation between the two captains was complete Mama-Seven broke in.

"It appears the Sokari are losing badly to the Septa-Pods. The battle will be over in less than one hour. Advise Temerity make pick-up now. Also if it appears the Temerity's landing perimeter is about to be broken by the Septa-Pods advise liftoff without all troops on board. Septa-Pod infestation will warrant total destruction of the Temerity by ED."

Zhukov and Simms were communicating by way of an audio-visual link and the expressions of the two men said it all. For a human warship to fire on another human warship was something that had never happened before. If Mama-Seven spoke of such an action then it must be accepted that her directives came straight from her builders, this course of action was part of her operational thread.

"Make your landing now Captain. If it looks like your lines are about to be breached then I want immediate lift-off. Is that understood?" Simms asked.

"It is understood Captain, the Temerity won't let you down," Zhukov said before signing off.

Simms went about the task of preparing his forces at Fire-Base Moag to do a partial emergency evacuation if such a plan was indeed warranted. This allowed for the most personnel to make it to safety while having the least amount susceptible to abandonment.

Zhukov strapped himself into his command chair as he ordered his ship into a diving freefall. He didn't want to cross any of the safe tolerance zones the Temerity was designed for but he did want to rub them slightly. His ship made an emergency dive to the planet's surface and then finished with a High-G braking maneuver to put the ship as close to the base's Repulsar Pockets as possible. Hale and A Bet had been advised by Simms just before the Temerity made her dive and had many of the troops ready to evacuate. Loading would be done at full combat march with troops carrying only their personal weapons and field packs.

It was expected to take only thirteen minutes for everyone to load through the three massive loading ramps. The arrival of the Temerity wasn't lost on the Septa-Pods who were just finishing up with the last of the Sokari resistance. The few Elites that accompanied the Septa-Pods on the field of battle were elated to see the huge spaceship drop out of orbit and then power down to their position. To capture such a vessel was now paramount to the battle plan. The Pods were ordered to ignore any remaining Sokari and head for the human lines.

As A Bet and Hale monitored the loading of troops, along with a minimum of portable equipment, a warning klaxon sounded along with an audible voiceover alarm. "Warning, enemy approaching perimeter at speed." After a few seconds the same thing happened again. The warning was set up on a loop and would continue until it was deactivated.

Mama-Five had continued to work on the sound bursts during the months since Captain Harless and his three ship rescue mission had left Star-Base Triton. With each subsequent breakthrough of the unknown language, the information became easier to gather and assimilate. The Super-Computer had been given the task and she was now dedicating much of her capabilities to the project. After so much time and effort Mama-Five could now gather nearly seventy percent of the information that each burst contained. What she now knew was startling and made the first analysis of the bursts mostly incorrect.

It appeared that an indigenous species on a planet named Tenement were being attacked by a violent race of beings that were Hell bent on taking over one planet at a time with Tenement being the next in line. The population of Tenement was a peace loving race known as the Arrenaugh. The Arrenaugh had only achieved near space travel in the last few hundred years and were not adept at it. They experienced the usual setbacks and losses that any new species would experience in the void and darkness of space but they were getting better and with each year that passed they saw more advancement in their vessels. At least that was until the Elites arrived in the quadrant.

The Elites had been observing Tenement for years until it was finally decided to invade. They knew about the Arrenaugh attempts at space travel and wanted to take over before their knowledge grew too great. Before long the Elites arrived and immediately began landing troops on the planet's surface. Being of a peace loving race, and not experienced in warfare, the battles were swift and decisive with the results always in favor of the Elites. The only victories for the Arrenaugh came late in the campaign when it was discovered that ramming an Elite ship before it made a landing was the only way the Arrenaugh ships could win with their limited capabilities, but this came with a price because the Arrenaugh ship was also destroyed.

The Elite never used vessels that would be considered warships, their battles were always on the surface of a planet and their warriors were so terrifying that their appearance alone won half the battles. The craft the Elite traveled in would be considered stealth in nature and were rarely spotted until the actual landings were taking place. These craft were not large but numerous. The Elites never exposed a craft unless necessary, they were not space warriors, they were land warriors.

The ramming campaign was not implemented until the Elite began landing the last of the craft that contained the Septa-Pods, creatures so terrible in appearance and size that it was better to destroy as many of the landers as possible in space, rather than allow them to reach the surface of the planet. Up until the arrival of the Septa-Pods the Arrenaugh had hoped to broker a peace agreement. After the first Septa-Pod climbed out of a lander and began killing everything in sight it was assumed the end was near and no peace could ever be reached with the Elites.

At this point in the war most of the survivors were headed deeper into the cavernous sections of the planet where many of the dwellings and manufacturing plants were located. It was estimated by the Arrenaugh High Council that fully one percent of the population was now being killed each week with the end measured in a couple of years rather than decades. (The Arrenaugh had a similar calendar as the humans due to a similar solar cycle.)

It was time to send a message into the far reaches of the galaxy hoping that someone would at least know what had happened here. The information was sent in the form of a compressed three hundred and sixty degree Data-Burst not unlike the one Mama-Seven had broadcast after the initial ambush of the Gareth by the Sokari fleet. The bursts were sent initially by the remnants of the Arrenaugh fleet but as these ships were either destroyed by a malfunction, or by ramming, it became necessary to transmit from the surface of the planet.

As each day went by the information in the subsequent Data-Bursts was updated. Finally when the last Arrenaugh ship was destroyed it became necessary for all further Bursts to be sent by way of a powerful transmitter located deep within the planet. The strata hindered the burst to a certain degree but at least it was still being sent. As the Septa-Pods fought deeper into the planet's subterranean spaces the remaining Arrenaugh were forced to also go deeper. Finally it was decided to cease sending the Data-Bursts. By now it was doubtful if anyone was coming and the power required was more than could be spared for the survival of the few Arrenaugh that remained.

What Mama-Five had now identified as ship to ship weapons fire in the first few Bursts was correct, it was the limited and technologically inferior Arrenaugh fleet trying to do battle with the Elites. Now the information was nearly complete and the desperate situation of the few Arrenaugh that survived was being sent out to the four Earth Colonies vessels that were in system. Mama-Five had an urgent message and knew she had to get it to Mama-Seven and Captain Simms.

"Captain Simms, I have received a message from Mama-Five pertaining to the indigenous species of the planet Tenement," Mama-Seven said.

Simms had been closely monitoring the landing of the Temerity and didn't want to be distracted. "Can this wait, Temerity is about to evacuate our ground forces."

"No captain, the information pertains to the ground forces and the indigenous population known as the Arrenaugh."

Now Simms knew something must be important if the Super-Computer would interrupt him at this crucial time. "Go ahead."

"Transmission is from Mama-Five. It is the latest version of what she has been mining from the sound bursts which were thought at first to be random anomalies. They have now been identified as Data-Bursts, not Sound-Bursts as was previously thought. The information indicates the indigenous species of this planet may still be alive but the survivors are few if at all. I have the frequencies that can be used to contact any of the survivors."

"Now why would a species that is under siege send out such information, sounds like a risky venture. What if whoever was listening got this information and used it against the survivors?" Simms asked.

"It appears that as the Arrenaugh got pushed further and further into the planet's core, they became desperate. The chance of being rescued grew thin and the survivors pulled out all the stops in hopes of a savior. As it is Captain, we appear to be that savior."

Simms knew of the Arrenaugh from previous information Mama-Seven had given him but was not aware that any survivors could still be occupying any safe space on the planet. "Attempt to make contact and find out what you can of their situation. If possible see if a pickup of the survivors can be attempted," Simms said.

Simms went back to monitoring the progress of the Temerity. He watched as the massive ship fell from orbit and made a spectacular landing within a thousand yards of Fire-Base Moag. He hit the timer on his watch and began the countdown; he was assured by Zhukov that thirteen minutes would be all he needed to successfully evacuate the base. Before the first of the three massive doors was completely down the first of the troops and Astro-Sailors were on their way.

Lines had been formed and once it was safe to exit the perimeter these lines were marched double-time toward the ship. Zhukov was on the command bridge monitoring the loading and also his ship's own defensive perimeter. Even though ED was onboard the Gareth he was still overseeing the land and air defenses of the Temerity. Nearly halfway into the loading ED picked up the first of the charging Septa-Pods as they topped a rise and headed for the ship. These creatures completely ignored the Fire-Base, they were being controlled by the Elites and they wanted nothing more than to capture the cruiser.

ED brought the ships perimeter Gatling's on line and dispersed them around the ship. As fast as these creatures were he didn't want to leave a quadrant unprotected so all guns were evenly spaced. Since there was no danger presented from the air ED also brought the eight Quad-Fifty Lead-Ejectors into the land based component of his defenses. These weapons had a much faster reaction time and with this in mind ED had them all placed on the approach side facing the fast moving Septa-Pods.

Zhukov had his Static Repulsar Pocket established in case these monsters had some type of artillery positioned nearby. The last thing he wanted was for his ship to be damaged and unable to take off. Mama-Seven had notified the captain that it wasn't known if the Pocket would do any good against the enemies' foot soldiers. Zhukov and his crew took some comfort in the low hum the pocket generated, whether it done any good or not.

As more and more troops made it to the Temerity ED knew it wasn't going to be accomplished before the first of the Pods arrived at the ship. He activated the Quad-Fifties and set them for one-half max rate of fire and then released the safeties. As the first rounds reached the Pods the eight legged monsters simply stepped to the side. They could see where the rounds were directed by the tracer rounds that fired every seventh round. ED saw this and immediately deactivated the tracers. Now the only evidence of where the Quad-Fifties were shooting was the dirt being kicked up by the rounds. ED and his fire control circuits were yet to hit a Pod.

ED had fought in many battles against some nasty adversaries. He now switched tactics as he ceased firing. He only allowed a gun to fire once it had a positive lock on its target, thus not signaling the target that it was about to be targeted. The first gun to have radar lock was set to fire max rate for only point six seconds. The rounds made it to an unsuspecting Pod and merely bounced off the scaly armor it was fitted with. Zhukov was watching and was startled to see how ineffective his weapons were.

ED wasn't fazed in the least, he now switched tactics again. His targeting was good as the rounds struck where they were intended; it was the resulting lack of damage that had to be corrected. ED switched to Strobe Rounds and then fired again. The multiple rounds striking the same spot was a tactic typically used against heavy tanks or in close range battles with warships. The penetrating power of a four-round grouping was impressive.

The first pod to be targeted with the Strobe Rounds was fired on and hit. The creature was spun around and knocked flat to the ground, it didn't get up. This was the result ED wanted but there was a problem, Strobe Rounds took more time to set up the shot and then the gun couldn't trolley to the next target until it was confirmed the previous rounds had resulted in a hit and a kill. With only eight Quad-Fifties, all firing the Strobe Rounds, and hundreds if not thousands of the Septa-Pods approaching at speed it wasn't going to be enough.

Zhukov knew Simms was monitoring the situation and he also knew the giant spiders would be at his ship before the thirteen minutes were up. "Simms, are you seeing this?" Zhukov asked.

"I am, looks like whatever those things are can't be stopped by ED, only slowed down a bit," Simms replied.

"I need options!" Zhukov said with a bit of an edge to his voice.

Simms continued to watch his screens as he contacted the Super-Computer. "Mama-Seven do you have a plan for the Temerity, she is running out of time."

"Temerity will be overrun and lost in less than six minutes. Advise that the Anneal make a run on the Septa-Pods using her anti-boarding weapons."

The Anneal had multiple turrets located around the ship to prevent an enemy from approaching close in and boarding. These weapons could in theory also be used against ground based targets but it had never been tried before.

"Captain Russel, can you plot an immediate run on the units attacking the Temerity?" Simms asked.

Russel had also been monitoring the situation on the ground and had already positioned his ship for just such an attack. "Beginning approach run now Captain. We'll make one fast run and then re-evaluate for a follow up. Notify Temerity that we are one minute out." Was the answer he gave Simms.

Simms was pleased that Russel had anticipated this and was now executing an attack. As he watched he couldn't help but be impressed with the agility the massive Attack Cruiser displayed. She broke through the atmosphere at a blistering pace with contrails and smoke being emitted from her super-tough hull. The heat from such an explosive entry made the hull of the Anneal glow orange. As she leveled out and began her run, guns from multiple locations on the hull began to target the Septa-Pods. There were so many now that even a miss could still be a hit.

As the Anneal approached the Temerity's position Simms amplified his screens. With the speed the cruiser was approaching the target she would only have a two second time slot to fire her weapons. The Elites saw the giant cruiser approaching and never tried to alter their assault. With the speed she was making the best hope of defense for the spidery attackers was to actually make it to the Temerity.

The Septa-Pods now saw the approach of the second ship. Each of the creatures could look in several directions at the same time thanks to their multiple eyes. Even though they were running at speed toward the ship on the ground they now began to run even faster.

"Anneal here, you better duck you heads. We're about to unleash Hell." Russel told Zhukov.

When the guns opened up it looked to the crew of the Anneal that they were right on top of the Temerity. Everything Russel could fire was used on the Pods. They had nearly made it to the rear elements of A Bet's troops when the cruiser opened up.

If a Quad-Fifty mounted on the Temerity had to use Strobe ammunition on the Pods to get results it was wondered what chance the exterior guns of the Anneal would have. The results were spectacular. Fire from the Anneal brought down the first wave of Septa-Pods with no trouble at all. The Elites traveling with the Pods were also killed. The Anneal was gone before results could be registered by her scanners but this wasn't the case for the Temerity. Her scans indicated that forty-three Pods had been killed with more wounded. There were also what appeared to be two Elites killed, they emitted different life signs and even in death could be distinguished apart from the Pods.

Simms saw from the bridge of the Gareth what had happened and hoped it would be enough. "Captain Zhukov what does your situation look like now?" He asked.

Zhukov replied immediately. "Appears the Anneal has bought us a couple of minute's sir but it still won't allow us to evacuate all the troops. Can she make a second run?"

"Russel did you hear that?" Simms asked.

"Roger that Captain, next run in ninety seconds." It would take longer this time because the Anneal was heading away after her initial attack. She would need to make orbit and allow the cold vacuum of space to cool her hull and weapons before starting her second run, thus the ninety seconds.

"Make your run as soon as you can, Simms out."

The Elites that hadn't been killed in the first attack by the Anneal knew they needed to change tactics if they were going to make it to the ship. The first Septa-Pod fatalities had been so numerous because the beasts were bunched up. Now they began to disperse to create a harder target to hit. As the Anneal made her way back to the planet's surface ED saw at once what his opponent was doing. There had been no ground to air weapons fire at the Anneal during her first run so he requested she be slowed to allow more time over the battlefield.

Russel didn't like the fact that the troops on the ground were going to be overrun by the Pods but he liked even less the suggestion that the Anneal be slowed to allow for more ship to ground fire.

"What if there is a hidden gun emplacement? One lucky shot might send us to the ground." Russel stated.

Simms knew the captain had a point. The cruiser would be so close to the surface of the planet that an enemy gun would actually be inside the pocket as the massive cruiser overflew its location. At that point the weapon would be able to target her and hit the underbelly with a lucky shot. The first run was done at such speed that it would have been impossible for her to be targeted and hit. If she flew slower an enemy weapon might just get that lucky shot.

"Make the reduced speed run but stay above the pocket depth so the Anneal is protected." Simms said.

"Roger that Captain, making our run now," Russel replied.

Again Simms watched as the Fast Attack Cruiser blasted out of the sky and headed toward the Temerity. She reduced speed as she neared the ship but was significantly farther off the ground this time. When her guns opened up the Septa-Pods were noticeably more dispersed than before. Still the assault was a success, many of the Pods were killed and more wounded but it would take a scan from the Temerity to verify the actual results. The Anneal was just too fast.

Simms was anxious to hear what had happened on the second run. "Getting a report from Temerity now Captain, thirty-five of the Pods killed and no Elite," one of the techs told the captain.

Simms was disappointed, this second run was less successful than the first and by all reports there were still hundreds of the beasts on the ground. Russel aboard the Anneal had also gotten the information.

"Looks like the enemy have adjusted their attack, troops are spread farther apart and this prevented more casualties." Captain Russel said.

Just as Simms was about to order Russel to make a third run Mama-Seven interrupted him, "A third attack by the Anneal is not advised. Probability of opposing ground based weapons fire at thirty-seven percent."

Russel heard this and protested, "Thirty-seven percent is acceptable, let the Anneal make the attack."

Simms wasn't so sure, "That is one in three odds that the enemy possesses a weapon that could damage the Anneal. This far from a Star-Base it's just too much of a risk. Break off the attack Russel."

"I must ask a second time Captain, let the Anneal make a third run on the enemy." Captain Russel asked.

Simms wanted nothing more than to allow the attack; after all she was protected by her Pocket. "Mama-Seven why is the Anneal in more danger on this third attack? Couldn't her Pocket protect her if she is fired on."

"That is still being analyzed Captain. There is a strange weapons signature being received by the sensors on the Gareth. Until the origin and strength of the weapon is discovered the Anneal should be held back. I also suggest the Temerity be launched as soon as possible using a low trajectory to prevent the unidentified weapon from gaining a lock."

Simms looked at his monitors and was for a brief second entranced by the huge spidery looking Septa-Pods racing headlong toward the Temerity. With more magnification he could also make out the troops as they retreated toward the ramps of the rescue ship. He couldn't make out individual troops but he could see formations stopping to fire on the Pods as the next group of soldiers broke from their positions and filtered through the new lines only to stop again and resume firing as the lines they had just retreated through did the same thing. Fire and fall back, fire and fall back. Simms wondered what the troops were thinking as they stopped to train their weapons on the beasts.

Just when it looked as if the Pods would overtake the troops there was motion on the right flank. Simms amplified his screens to maximum and was able to make out what this new force was, tanks and armored personnel carriers. It appeared A Bet was making a flanking maneuver using his tanks and carriers.

Major A Bet had held his armor near the Mongoose system until the last of the ground troops had headed for the Temerity. He had hoped the troops, assisted by the guns of the cruiser, would have been able to hold this new threat. That was before he had actually seen one of beasts. He knew the two attacks by the Anneal had done some damage, but it wasn't nearly enough.

At the rate the Septa-Pods were gaining on the troops A Bet knew they weren't going to make it. He had been ordered to abandon the heavy rolling stock Fire-Base Moag possessed but refused to do so until the last minute in case they were needed. It now appeared that if anyone was going to leave this planet alive then it would be up to his meager armored force to try and stop the headlong assault of the Pods.

A Bet got on the radio and set his attack in motion. "Alright listen up. I don't think they have seen us yet so let's make the most of it. I want a split formation, Hale you take the six tanks of the Temerity and head for the ship at full speed, take all the carriers with you, fire at anything with more than two legs. I'll use the eight tanks from the Umbrage and the Gareth to make a sweeping charge on their flank slightly behind you. Try to get the carriers to the Temerity. I don't think we need to conserve ammunition, fire at max rate. This battle ain't going to last that long."

A Bet wanted the carriers to get to the ship first; they were carrying the bulk of the four-hundred man reserve force. Each carrier could carry eighteen men but they now had at least thirty crammed inside. A few troops were even riding on the exterior, anything to get away from the Fire-Base. If anyone had been left behind now it would have been impossible for them to make it to the ship.

"Hale move out." A Bet screamed as his tanks broke from cover and headed for the Septa-Pod formations. He was anxious to fire on one of the beasts to see how his machines were going to fare. He had also seen the poor effect from the guns on the Temerity and hoped his tanks would have better luck. Only seconds after both columns began their charge the loader in A Bet's tank got a lock on one of the Pods. "Fire!" A Bet shouted.

The tank shuddered slightly as the round exited the barrel, as soon as it did the loader slammed another round into the breach. A Bet watched through his scope as the round found the mark and hit one of the racing beasts. The Septa-Pod was knocked off its feet as the high-velocity armor-piercing round impacted its armor and then penetrated into the body of the startled beast. The round detonated after it broke through the hard plating and entered the flesh. The body of the Pod exploded into a cloud of fleshy spray. The enormous legs fell to the ground but still continued to kick and thrash about.

A Bet got on the radio and sent the message, "Armor-piercing rounds only, let's get to work."

The other seven tanks in A Bet's unit followed suit and began choosing their targets. Pods were now being picked off at random. The tanks in Hale's unit also lent their firepower. The carriers each had a turret mounted gun but of a smaller caliber than the tanks, it wasn't known what effect these weapons would have. Each of the carriers picked a target and began firing. The easiest target was the body of the Pod, it was larger but it was also well armored. The first rounds from the carriers simply bounced off. Hale saw this and ordered his gunners to target the legs. It was doubted if a hit could be scored on a leg due to its smaller size and the speed at which they were running.

Of the thirteen carriers first shots two actually struck a leg with the result of it being blown completely off. The injured pods continued to run toward the Temerity but were slowed to a point that another hit from a carrier's gun was almost a certainty. Hale was monitoring and saw that the weapons of the carriers could actually lend something to the battle. "Alright hit them again." He screamed over the radio.

The carriers began to pick and choose their targets, trying mostly for any injured Pods that were falling behind. The tankers continued to blast away, their shots were making contact and reducing the enemy's numbers. The main assault of the Septa-Pods was still advancing on the Temerity but they were starting to take notice of the tanks and carriers that were harassing their flank. If the two Elites hadn't been killed in the first attack by the Anneal then they would have already adjusted their advance to include the armor that was now taking such a toll. When one of the few remaining Elites saw what was happening the battle plan was immediately changed.

On board the Gareth Simms was watching the armored assault being made by A Bet and Hale. He was impressed with the equipment the troops had, the tanks were fast and had a main gun that was doing the job. Even the smaller guns of the carriers were doing damage. He wondered what this new attack would do for the overall battle plan.

"Mama-Seven what are the chances our tanks will be able to stop the Septa-Pods attack?" Simms asked.

"None Captain," was her reply.

Simms was stunned by such a grim response. "How much time does this give the Temerity?"

"Eight more minutes. The carriers will need to increase speed if they are to make it to the ship. It is suggested they be driven onboard rather than offload the troops."

Simms figured as much. The carriers were fully loaded with troops and it would take time to stop outside the cruiser as their troop's disembarked and headed up the ramps. The Temerity was such a large ship it wasn't going to be a problem to haul the carriers, after all they had offloaded from her bays to begin with. The tanks might be a different matter. Temerity carried six of the armored behemoths onboard as part of her troop compliment. There were now fourteen racing toward her, her original six plus the eight from Umbrage and Gareth. With a little time the eight extra tanks could be fitted on board but time wasn't something that could be spared at the moment. No chance would be allowed for even one of the Pods to reach the Temerity.

Simms wanted firsthand knowledge of the battle that was taking place on the ground. "Zhukov report," he said. Zhukov was about to call Simms anyway,

"Looks like some of our troops have disobeyed the order to abandon the tanks and carriers and I'm glad they did. Major A Bet is making an attack using armor and carriers to try to distract the Pods. So far he is having some success. The advance on the Temerity has slowed but I don't know how long it will last. We are still loading and I have the Temerity's engines powered up and ready to get us off this planet the moment the troops are on board.

As Simms and Zhukov were talking Mama-Seven broke in. "I have identified the energy source of the new weapon, Temerity won't be able to take off until it is destroyed. Even with her Static Repulsar Pocket powered to a hundred percent she will still be damaged if liftoff is attempted at this time. A low trajectory from her launch point still can't guarantee success."

Both Simms and Zhukov were stunned. If the Temerity stayed she would be torn apart by the army of nightmares that was attacking outside. "What can be done to disrupt the enemy's new weapon?" Zhukov asked.

"The weapon is protected in a fortified emplacement and cannot be destroyed from the ground. Suggest Sled-Round fired from the Anneal, this will have a sixty-three percent chance of success," Mama-Seven replied.

"Russel did you hear that?" Simms asked.

"Got it Captain; positioning for the shot now."

"I want a four shot spread on that target Russel. Sixty-three percent chance if we fire one so I want redundant hits, total destruction." Simms ordered.

"Copy that, four shot spread in forty-five seconds at two-second intervals," Russel said. The intervals were to prevent the four rounds from dispersing as they entered the planet's atmosphere. The wake created by four rounds traveling through the atmosphere side by side could cause all four to go off course. Traveling in sequence would prevent this from happening.

As the Anneal lined up and prepared for the shot A Bet and his eight tank column were getting more and more of the Septa-Pods attention. Nearly half of the monstrous beasts were now headed straight for A Bet's column.

"Here they come, try and increase your rate of fire." A Bet shouted into his mic to the other tankers.

"All tanks, head left and try to separate their column again." A Bet decided if the initial advance of his small force had caused such a large portion of the enemy to break off their attack on the Temerity then his fast armor might be able to do it again. If he broke hard left then the Pods that were farthest away wouldn't be able to keep up. Anything was worth a try.

Just as the eight tanks adjusted their direction there was an ear-shattering roar from the heavens, the four round spread from the Anneal had just entered the atmosphere and were headed for their target. A quick glance upward and you could see what a terrifying weapon a ship-mounted Sled-Gun was. It could only be described as a sunrise or sunset, but much closer. There was fire and smoke as the rounds burned through the atmosphere. As fast as it happened it was over. A few seconds later came the shockwave of the blast. Several of the Septa-Pods were actually knocked to the ground by the blast and that was at a distance of several hundred kilometers. Any closer and even the men in the tanks might have been knocked around a bit. As it was the massive armored vehicles only shook a little, nothing else.

Another added benefit of the attack on the unseen gun was its distraction on the Septa-Pods. The few Elites that traveled along and commanded the Pods were also momentarily disoriented. The most frightening event wasn't the blast or the subsequent shockwave; it was the Septa-Pods scrambling back to their feet after being knocked to the ground. If any human were ever afraid of a spider, and most were, then the sight of the giant Pods flipping back onto their feet and then scrambling again toward the tanks was truly something straight out of a nightmare. It was as if you took the little arachnids from earth and then magnified them hundreds of times.

The distance began to diminish as the eight tanks and the spiders closed on each other. While this was happening, A Bet and his gunners tried to increase their rate of fire. Shell impacts from the eight tanks were beginning to have a better effect as the distance decreased. Another added benefit was that at this range any missed shots were more than likely going to hit something, the Pods, in their fury, were beginning to bunch up again.

Simms continued to watch from his battle bridge. He began to wonder how the heavy tanks would fare once the Pods made it to their position. The tanks were heavily armored and were environmentally sealed so he hoped the men inside would be alright, he was about to find out how terribly wrong he was.

The first of A Bet's tanks to actually make it to the Pod's lines was on the far right flank. The driver increased speed in order to run over a Pod that was directly in front of him. Just as the racing tank and the speeding Pod met it became obvious that a Septa-Pod was taller than a tank and the multiple legs spanned an area that was actually wider. When the tank hit the body of the Pod it was as if it had hit a building. The Pod bounced back a few meters and then clambered up onto the tank before it was run over. What was happening seemed impossible.

The men inside felt the impact and then heard the screeching as the beast's clawed feet scratched the front sloped armor in an effort to gain footing. Once on top the Pod started tearing at anything that could be grasped with its feet. First to go were the antennae arrays, then the two external mounted fifty-caliber machine guns. Each tank had hull mounted steel cases used for extra ammunition and some of the crew's belongings. These took a little more doing but the Pod soon had those stripped off as well. There were even some extra links for the tracks and a towing cable wrapped around hooks and these were also torn off and thrown to the ground. From inside the tank it sounded as if the world was coming to an end, for the men inside it soon would be.

Before long a second Pod made it to the tank. It too managed to climb on top while the men inside continued to fire at any target in front of the tank that presented itself. A Bet and his gunner were the first to spot the tank running along at full speed with two of the enormous creatures on top clawing and scratching as they tried to find a way in. A Bet swiveled the turret of his tank and lined up a shot, when he had his target he yelled fire. The gunner depressed his pedal, there was a throaty thud and the tank shook slightly as the shell exited the barrel. A Bet kept his eye on target and was rewarded to see one of the two Pods knocked free of the tank. Before it even hit the ground another jumped up and took its place. "Reload and prepare to fire." A Bet yelled but the second shot wouldn't make it in time.

The Elite in charge of the two pods now riding on top of the tank knew the Pods had to act fast before they too were hit. It signaled what it wanted the two Pods to do and they immediately began trying to pry on the turret and the barrel. Soon another Pod joined the first two and now, with the combined strength of three of the beasts, the turret ring popped a couple of times and then began to give way. The men inside the tank could see a stream of light coming through where the turret ring met the main body of the tank. Before any of the men inside could react the three Pods gave one more mighty heave and the huge turret popped right off.

The five men inside didn't stand a chance. Two managed to un-holster their side arms and started to fire but the rounds simply bounced off the carapace and armor the Pods wore. All the men inside were pulled from the tank and killed within seconds, their bodies eaten as they still screamed. A Bet saw this and knew his seven remaining tanks were about to meet the same fate. He swiveled away from the gruesome sight of his soldiers being slaughtered and continued to fire on the other Pods.

On the Temerity, Captain Zhukov was overseeing the loading of the last of the carriers and the six tanks when Simms called, "How much longer?" Was all he asked?

"Everyone is onboard, still got eight tanks and their crews on the ground." Zhukov said.

Simms had been watching the running battle between A Bet's tanks and the Septa-Pods. Make that seven tanks, the Pods just opened one up like it was a can of sardines."

Zhukov had been so focused on his loading that he didn't know how the battle being conducted by A Bet and his tanks was going. "One tank destroyed, how about the crew?" He asked.

"All dead, pulled out and killed before they knew what hit them," Simms said. He could have told how they died but decided to spare the captain.

Zhukov looked at the battle raging outside on one of the monitors. Even in the brief time he watched it appeared to be getting closer to his very vulnerable ship. He was startled back to the here and now as he heard the hull mounted Gatling Guns on the Temerity open up at max rate of fire. He knew the Quad-Fifties had been used with some success from the beginning, the Pods must be close if they were in range of the Gatling's. If Gatling's were being used by ED then the battle he saw in the distance would be here in a matter of minutes.

Simms had seen what three of the Septa-Pods could do to a heavily armored tank and knew if even one of the beasts made it onto the hull, or worse, inside the Temerity, then it would be a disaster. He was now forced to give an order that he knew was every bit as necessary as it was awful. "Captain Zhukov, lift off at once."

Zhukov didn't protest, he knew it was the right call considering the events that were about to overtake his ship. "Flight get us out of here, lift off as soon as the three bay doors are closed." He didn't like to think about what was going to happen to the crews of the seven tanks that were being left behind.

Zhukov hoped the Pods would break off from the seven remaining tanks once they saw the massive space ship start its takeoff. He thought he might at least give his tankers a bit of a chance. Once the bay doors were secured he gave the order to lift off slowly. He wanted the Elites to think the Septa-Pods might still have a chance of downing his ship.

Once the Elites saw the plumes of sand being blown into the air as the Temerity's massive engines started applying thrust they ordered the Pods to break from the tanks and move with all possible speed toward the ship. If only one of the mighty beasts could manage to get onto the hull then all sorts of damage could be done, maybe even slow the craft long enough for more to jump on and try to pry their way inside, the same as they had done to the tank.

Simms was watching and breathed a sigh of relief when he saw Temerity break contact with the surface. He noticed the slow rise and wondered if the ship was having trouble applying the necessary thrust.

"Zhukov, is there a problem?" Simms asked.

"No Captain, just trying to lure a few of the hairy beasts away from the tanks," Zhukov replied.

Simms watched and sure enough the Pods were breaking from the tanks and heading in the direction of the Temerity. This might be a good plan unless the Pods could somehow fly. "Mama-Seven is it known how high one of the Septa-Pods might be able to jump?"

"Septa-Pods can jump approximately thirty meters and possibly forty in the vertical if conditions are right. Without more information I would advise Temerity to climb to one-hundred meters and be prepared to go higher at a moment's notice."

The Temerity wasn't even ten meters off the ground when the Super-Computer said this. Both Simms and Zhukov heard this and knew the Temerity needed to climb. Once the order was given the Temerity began her hover at one-hundred meters. The Septa-Pods stopped directly under the ship and began to climb onto the backs of each other, rapidly they were at least fifty-meters off the ground and it was then that one of the Pods started from the ground and ran up the pyramid of bodies. Once at the top it gave a mighty heave and launched itself at the Temerity. Zhukov had been at the controls during this critical time and once he saw what was happening he hit the launch thrusters to full. The cascading fire from the mighty engines roasted the leaping Pod in mid-flight and also set the giant pyramid of bodies on fire. It was the most Pods killed so far, many never knew what hit them.

Zhukov hoped this trick would work again. He moved the Temerity farther away from the seven tanks as he decreased the altitude. The Pods on the ground at first gave chase until they were ordered by the Elites to hold back. As this was going on A Bet and his tanks were ordered to move to a new rendezvous point at flank speed. The tank he was in, along with the six others, had continued to hammer away at the enemy even as they chased after the Temerity. It was now time to head away from the monsters. The diversion created by the liftoff had given some space to the tankers.

Mama-Seven was trying to coordinate a landing site that could be used by the survivors of the Arrenaugh. It had been discovered that only one outside portal existed that wasn't dominated by the Elites. This portal had been disguised as a thermal vent and was saved for just this purpose, escape when help arrived, if help arrived. It was decided for the Temerity to head in an opposite direction, away from the vent, and hopefully not give away this only means of escape for the few survivors.

A Bet and his tankers were given the new coordinates and told they would be updated every thirty minutes; they would also, in the beginning, be going in a direction that shouldn't give away the plan. This new direction would also give the tankers a bit more distance between themselves and the dreaded Pods. The tanks could move at forty kilometers per hour, top speed, but the terrain reduced that by a bit. It was estimated it would take the seven tanks two hours to reach the pick-up point. Hopefully the Temerity could pick-up the Arrenaugh survivors and then head to the rendezvous with the tanks assuming any survived their headlong race away from the Pods.

Once it was determined that the human ship was out of reach the Elites turned their fury on the seven tanks. All the available Septa-Pods were sent after the fleeing armored column. With no danger of enemy weapons fire the tanks moved out in high forward gear with their turrets reversed so as to fire at their pursuers. It wasn't known at what rate a Septa-Pod could run and also how long it could keep it up, the men in A Bet's armored column were about to find out. It was hoped the huge spiders ran out of energy before the tanks ran out of options, and for that matter fuel.

As the Temerity continued to gain altitude, the view of Fire-Base Moag and the battle that had just ended between the tanks and the Septa-Pods could be seen in full view. Mama-Seven had an update on the capabilities of the deserted Fire-Base and felt it should be given top priority.

She knew what she had to say was now extremely important. "Captain Simms, destruction of the Sled-Gun launchers was accomplished by the troops as they evacuated. It isn't suspected that the race known as the Elites could repair the launchers but it is imperative that the Anneal destroy the base as soon as possible to prevent that possibility."

Captain Simms had been assured that once the troops and sailors evacuated, the guns would never be able to fire again. "Are you sure Mama-Seven, I was told the job would be complete once the base was abandoned."

"Not only is it possible the Elites could repair the guns, but the technology is still intact and some information could be gained from the destruction that remains. It might even be possible for them to reverse engineer the weapons, given enough time, and build all new ones. An attack by the Anneal will solve both problems and possibly kill more of the Pods and Elites."

"Surely we are looking at some time to repair the damage done to the Mongoose Weapons System. I was assured it would be a total loss with no possibility of use by the enemy?" Simms countered.

"Mongoose is a total loss but some of the Sled-Rounds remain intact. Advise attack now."

Simms knew by the way the Super-Computer signed off that he would do as she requested. "Captain Russel, how soon can you hit the Fire-Base with a four shot spread?"

"Four minutes Captain, what's this about?" Russel asked as he and the weapons crew set the targeting computers.

"Mama-Seven advises it be destroyed from the air," was all Simms said. He knew that just the inclusion of the Super-Computer in the equation was all that was needed. He also didn't blame Captain Russel for the question he had just asked, Sled-Rounds weren't to be expended unless needed. This far away from a base that could replenish the four ships meant everything had a higher value.

Russel knew if Mama-Seven advised a hit on the Fire-Base then who was he to challenge it. "Setting up the run now sir, plot from high orbit and weapons drop in three."

The Anneal was far enough away that she didn't register on close range scanners but on the intermediate range board she looked like a race horse as she powered up her massive engines and headed in for the attack. The weapons board on the Anneal identified the four guns of the Mongoose System and locked one Sled-Gun on each. As the range thinned the scanners picked up movement at the base. "Simms is there any friendlies' at the base; we are registering massive movement around the guns down there?" Russel asked.

"No friendlies Russel, what you're seeing on your screens are Septa-Pods and Elites. Hit em fast and hit em hard Captain," Simms ordered.

"Roger that, ordinance lock obtained and firing in thirteen seconds," Russel said as his ship finished her set up and prepared to fire.

"Ordinance on the way, four shot spread at two second intervals." The Anneal, although not in the gravity field of the planet, still pulled away hard. It was just a precaution in case someone or something on the ground fired on the cruiser as she finished her attack. It was always the most vulnerable time when she turned her backside to an enemy.

Simms monitored the flightpath of the four shots from his screens on the Gareth. He knew the shots released from the Anneal would be traveling many times the speed of sound and if anyone knew they were being attacked it had to be due to radar or scanners. He supposed the things that had been attacking the Temerity were smart but didn't know what sort of hardware they might be using.

As the rounds reached their target the Pods began to run from the base. That proved the enemy used some sort of scanning system, there wouldn't have been any warning, either audio or visual, due to the speed of the approaching rounds. Russel was momentarily scanner-blocked due to the speed the Anneal was traveling and the direction she was traveling in. His scanners wouldn't be able to verify the damage for at least fifteen more seconds.

"Simms do you have a visual?" Russel asked.

"Sure do, the damage your ship can do is such a beautiful thing." Simms said. It was the only answer Russel needed; he knew the Fire-Base, and her sophisticated Mongoose Weapons System, had been completely destroyed. As the Anneal slowed and returned to her previous route his scanners gave him the answer he expected. The base was a total loss with dead and dying Septa-Pods and a couple of Elites lying about. More of the creatures could be seen running at top speed away from the smoking ruins.

Mama-Seven now had all the possible information gathered from the Arrenaugh survivors and needed to share this with Captain Simms. "Captain, the Arrenaugh number one-hundred and sixty two from a population that once had been in the millions. They are all that is left of a once proud race that is now requesting our help." Mama-Seven grew silent; she had now activated her emotion circuitry and felt this might be a learning experience for her. She would learn how humans handled such a situation where so much was at stake.

Simms now did something that pleased the Super-Computer. "We will assist them. I need a workup of just where they are in conjunction with the Elites and Septa-Pods. Have the Anneal and the Umbrage stand off and be ready to lend support."

ED and Mama-Seven conversed through Map-Con and decided the rescue operation was going to be tricky. There was also the matter of the seven tanks under the command of Major A Bet. ED was a warrior and always held ground troops in high regard; after all, they were part of his programing, just as the ships were.

Simms had all the available information patched into the other three ship's control boards and consoles, especially the Temerity; she was the one that was going to be making the landing and rescue. Simms waited until he was assured the other three captains were looking at the same information he had in front of him.

"We already have the tank column headed for this mountain range here, you can see the area where the Temerity can make the landing and fast pickup. The problem is going to be with the Arrenaugh, we don't know what kind of shape they are in after fighting for so many months. There will no doubt be injured and elderly, that is just the way it is when you pick up the remnants of such a siege. Another problem is the Elites and Septa-Pods, we don't know if the area is clear or infested. If it appears rescuing the remaining Arrenaugh will put the Temerity at risk then I will call the whole thing off."

Captain Russel of the Anneal wondered at what point such a decision would need to be made. He knew once a Capitol Ship landed and started boarding the survivors it would be at its most vulnerable. If it became necessary to lift off, the ramp would need to be closed and that could be problematic if a line stretched to the planet's surface from the bay. Where do you break the line? It was a thought he tried to put out of his head.

"Does everyone agree, when I pull the plug then the ramp closes and the Temerity lifts off, no questions asked? Also I want the Anneal to stand ready for another of her strafing runs if things get rough."

"Roger that Captain, the Anneal will be ready," Russel replied.

"I guess that just leaves the Umbrage and Gareth. What will be our part in this?" Harless asked.

"The Umbrage will stand off and monitor all the adjoining space leading into this sector. At the first sign of trouble let us know and we abort the mission. The Gareth will be the eyes in the sky; Mama-Seven and ED will be running scans and gathering information. As the situation changes they will let us know."

Roger that Captain, Umbrage will be ready," Harless said as he headed his ship into deeper space.

Mama-Seven made her decision on a landing site and put the coordinates into the navigational systems of the remaining three ships. When that was accomplished Simms gave the word and headed the Gareth away from the smoking remains of Fire-Base Moag.

"Mama-Seven, have the surviving Arrenaugh ready to evacuate as soon as the Temerity makes the landing site. Make sure they understand to not break cover until I give the word. If things go bad and the Temerity has to abort the mission then they don't want to announce their position to the enemy," Simms said.

The set up for the landing took forty-five minutes while the bays of the Temerity were cleared of the troops and equipment that had been rescued from the Fire-Base. Zhukov had his ship ready and gave the order for a fast descent. "Touchdown to liftoff needs to be four minutes tops; this is a place we don't want to inhabit for too long." He told his crew.

As the Temerity made final approach to the landing site Mama-Seven sent the signal for the Arrenaugh to break cover and head out. Temerity touched down no more than two-hundred meters from the opening the survivors would be using. As soon as the massive ship hit the surface one of the ramp doors came down hard and the first of the carriers exited. It would be followed by four more with each expected to load thirty-five Arrenaugh survivors.

As soon as the carriers were away two of the huge tanks rumbled down the ramp and took up positions on either side of the ship. ED was in charge of the Quad-Fifty Lead-Ejectors and Gatling's and these large systems began to trolley back and forth at unseen targets it was hoped would never materialize.

As the five carriers raced the short distance to the disguised heat vent it was wondered if the evacuation could really be accomplished in the allotted four minutes.

The first of the Arrenaugh to exit were apparently troops, they wore fitted armor plating and were carrying long rifles of some sort. All were injured in one way or another indicated by the bandaging they wore. There might have been twenty in all and it was apparent they had been fighting for their lives for quite some time. The troops weren't impressive in a physical sense, they were thin but tall, not the muscular physical specimens of the Earth troops the ships carried. It could be assumed the thin part was due to meager rations the survivors might have been forced to survive on as their world was being overrun.

The next out were no doubt the young and the elderly who numbered maybe forty or fifty, most of these also wore bandages including the children. Last were eighty or ninety of the extremely sick and injured, they were on wheeled chairs and even a few were being transported on gurneys. So far it appeared that everyone had some sort of injury or sickness. Simms was watching on his monitors and knew it would take far longer to load this group than the four minutes the mission had been given.

As the carriers were being loaded Mama-Seven broke in with some bad news. "Movement detected Captain, appears to be Septa-Pod lead elements along with a substantial number of Elites."

Simms had just heard the last thing he needed right now, "Numbers and distance?" He asked.

"Appears to be a hundred at least in the initial wave which is about six minutes out. There is something else Captain, the previous ratio of Elites to Pods was a hundred to one. This force has a ratio of ten to one, something is different about this attack, analysis is still being completed."

Simms knew the other ships were patched in, anything that the Super-Computer said was automatically heard by all four captains. "Temerity did you get that?" Simms asked.

"Loud and clear Captain, gonna make it damn near impossible to finish the evacuation. I doubt if A Bet and his column can be picked up at the secondary site now with the Pods so close. No doubt the second pickup point is already overrun with Pods. Does the armored column have any other coordinates?" Zhukov asked.

"No Captain, they were given their pickup location and this one for the Arrenaugh. According to Mama-Seven there isn't a third spot that hasn't already been overrun by the Pods." Simms said.

All four captains thought of the seven tanks traveling all out to make it to a pick-up point that was now useless. The tanks, along with their crews, were on their own.

"Temerity here Simms, we got Pods on the horizon headed this way fast," Zhukov said.

"How many of the survivors have you gotten aboard?" Simms asked.

"None!" Came the reply. "Nearly all the Arrenaugh are either very young or very old, and nearly if not all are injured. It is taking extra time to get them here due to those parameters."

Simms now had a serious problem. An army of Septa-Pods was bearing down on the Temerity as she sat at the landing site. None of those to be rescued were on board yet and to make matters worse there were now a number of carriers and crew on the ground.

"Mama-Seven how long before the Temerity needs to lift off?" Simms asked.

"Three minutes twenty-four seconds at the latest, this leaves a margin of safety of only twenty seconds. Temerity will need to execute a High-G liftoff to prevent hull infestation."

"Russel can you execute a run on the Pods?" Simms asked.

"No Captain, proximity of the Temerity and the five carriers makes a run impossible. Live fire at the Pod column will impact the landing zone at this time."

Simms looked at his monitors and knew all of the Arrenaugh would have to be abandoned, along with the five carriers and the personnel associated with them. The mission was a total failure. "Temerity, I want immediate dust-off in one minute on my mark. Anyone that isn't onboard will be abandoned."

Simms knew he had just signed the death warrant on several of the Temerity's crew and the remnants of an entire race of beings. It was undoubtedly the hardest order he had ever given.

"Got more movement to the west Captain," Zhukov said.

What now, another column of Pods, Simms wondered. "Can you identify?"

After a few seconds Zhukov answered. "Yes sir, we got tanks coming hard from the west. Looks like A Bet and his column diverted to this site."

Simms amplified the signal on his vox in hopes of reaching the tanks. "A Bet can you read me?" Simms asked over the radio.

"Can now Captain, original pick-up point was overrun. We barely escaped and headed here. You got Pods at your seven-o'clock, am engaging now," A Bet said.

No sooner had the words left the Major's mouth than the unmistakable sound of a one-hundred and twenty millimeter tank cannon be heard back over the vox.

"Zhukov you got help in the form of Leopard tanks just over the rise heading your way fast, count seven heavies at speed. Does this give you enough time to load your evacuees?" Simms asked.

"It changes things sir, running simulations now," Zhukov said.

"Russel can you do a run just back of A Bet's column. I know that is too far back from the Temerity to help much but maybe it will be a distraction," Simms said.

Russel was itching to get into the fight with his cruiser and he now felt as if he had been given the keys to the kingdom. "Plotting coarse now, expect run in sixty seconds." Russel had kept the Anneal lined up for an attack and now it appeared to be paying off.

"A Bet you got some ordinance coming at your six, expect flyover of the Anneal in forty-five seconds." Simms radioed the tanker.

"Be expecting it." Was all the tanker said as another shot was fired from his tank. Simms heard the reassuring sound of the big gun going off before A Bet killed the link.

The column of tanks had made it to the outskirts of the original pick-up point to find it overrun with Pods. From long distance they could see the creatures and diverted to the second pick-up point in the hopes of making it before the Temerity took off. If the loading had been on schedule A Bet and his hard pressed tankers would have gotten there to find only an empty landing site. As bad as the luck was for the evacuees it was at least a bit of good luck for the seven tanks and their crews.

As the armored column began to apply pressure on the Pods, the Elites that were with them knew they had to deal with this new threat at once. The tanks were taking a toll on the hundred or so Septa-Pods that were attacking the human ship. More Pods, hundreds more were on the way but wouldn't be here for some time. The Elites decided to send most of the Pods in the direction of the tanks to stop the killing-spree. At the rate the humans and their machines were killing Pods the Elites wondered if they had enough bodies to do the job before the rest of the Pods arrived.

"Zhukov how is it going down there?" Simms asked again.

"Survivors are loaded into carriers; carriers are headed this way now."

"How long before liftoff?" Simms asked.

"Three minutes, what about the tanks?"

Simms wanted to take the seven tanks with the Temerity when she lifted off, not for the tanks but for the crews. "What is the tactical situation?" Simms asked Zhukov, he was on the ground and could get a better picture of the battle between the armor and the aliens.

"Tank column has stopped the Septa-Pod advance on the Temerity and are in a running battle trying to flank and escape. At the moment the Leopards are raising Hell but I don't know how long it will last."

"Are the tanks heading toward your position?" Simms asked.

"Appears so, they are now past the bulk of the Pods and making a run for the Temerity."

Simms now had a decision to make, slow the lift off of the Temerity long enough to rescue the tankers or play it safe and lift as soon as the evacuees were onboard. He still couldn't take the chance for a single Pod to either enter the ship or for that matter climb onto the hull. "A Bet, what is your status?"

"Giving them everything we can sir but most of us are going to run out of ammunition before we make it to the ship."

"The Temerity is about to leave Major, advance to the pick-up point at full speed or be left behind. That's an order." Simms shouted into the vox.

"Roger that sir. A Bet out." As soon as the major signed off with the captain he got on the radio with the other tanks. "All tanks listen up, I want nothing but speed out of you bastards. If you slow to take a shot I will leave your ass on this planet as a snack for those monsters."

With that last transmission all seven tanks raced for the Temerity. The ride was rough with men being thrown about inside the tanks as they raced at full speed over broken terrain, even the webbing and restraints didn't keep everyone from being tossed about. As the seven tanks sped along they continued to fire but the effects were nominal due to the rough ride. Even the targeting computers the Leopards possessed couldn't maintain a positive lock due to the heavy bouncing.

As the seven tanks fled the monsters, something happened that was terrible on the one hand and a blessing on the other. Two of the tanks to the far left of the column ran into some soft sandy soil and this slowed them down by more than half. As each second passed the speed of the two tanks continued to decrease.

"Major, two of our tanks are going to stick on the left, they're in some sand." The driver in A Bet's tank said.

A Bet looked through his scope and saw two of his tanks grinding to a halt. Before he could respond the Pods were on top of the two and tearing at the turrets.

"Keep going, there's nothing we can do." A Bet said, and it was true. As he watched, the first of the tanks had its turret ripped off and the men yanked out and torn apart. Screaming could be heard over the vox.

A Bet now did something he had hoped he would never have to do. "Target the second tank." He told the gunner. Everyone in the tank knew it was the humane thing to do. "Fire!" he ordered. The shot left the tank and ran true. It hit the second tank just as the turret was giving way. The men died in a hail of explosive fire rather than in the mouths of the monsters. The other tankers said a silent prayer and knew the men that had just gotten killed would have done the same for them if given the chance.

The loss of the two tanks had given the Septa-Pods and Elites an easy target and the limited number of them that were left now headed in the direction of the two even though one was on fire. It appeared as if for all the knowledge and skill the Elites possessed the Septa-Pods were just the opposite. They acted like wild animals when they smelled blood. The one benefit, if it could be called that, was it opened up a space between the Pods and what remained of the armored column.

"Head to the ship, it's now or never," A Bet screamed over the roar of his tanks dual engines.

The five remaining tanks opened up their throttles and raced for the cruiser. A couple still managed to fire on the Pods until A Bet ordered them to stop. "Let's not give them a reason to chase us. Maybe if we don't fire they will forget about us for a few minutes, it might be the chance we need to make it to the cruiser."

A Leopard tank was equipped with two five-hundred and fifty horse-power engines and could make a top speed of slightly more than forty miles an hour. The five tanks were being driven Hell-bent toward the Temerity with the engines of each straining at full throttle.

There might have been forty Pods left after the attack by A Bet's column. The Quad-Fifties on the Temerity accounted for a few but most were killed by the one-hundred and twenty millimeter guns of the tanks. Each second that went by increased the space between the two combatants. When the Elites finally managed to turn the Pods around the five tanks were nearly at the cruiser.

Zhukov was nervous, he couldn't get the men out of the tanks and up the ramps before the Pods got there.

"Have the five tanks load up Ramp Two." He ordered over the vox. The order was relayed to A Bet and he was glad to obey.

"Roger that. Roscoe you lead them up in your tank; I'll bring up the rear, double time." A Bet told his men.

The tanks were going so fast that the tank Roscoe commanded had to break hard in order to be able to make the turn for the ramp. His tank rumbled up and was in the cavernous bay in seconds. The next four tanks did the same and as all five were being dogged down the two that were guarding the entrance turned and also rumbled into the bay. The giant door was already rising as the guards raced up. One minute after Roscoe first hit the ramp the entire operation was completed.

Zhukov had witnessed the loading and before the ramp was completely closed he ordered the Temerity into the air. The last of the eighty-five ton tanks was just being dogged down as she began her climb. A straight and level ascent was all that could be done until the tanks were secure. A High-G liftoff might send one of them crashing into the ramp and could possibly disable the cruiser.

The Elites had the Pods headed back at the cruiser now just as the liftoff was accomplished. Zhukov was monitoring the altitude and also the distance of the approaching Pods when Simms contacted him.

"Temerity, I need you to increase thrust before you are boarded." Simms knew a Pod anywhere on the cruiser's hull was to be considered a boarding.

"Cargo still being dogged down, thrust is at the upper edge of liftoff guidelines," Zhukov said.

"Damn the guidelines Zhukov, your ship is still in danger." Simms shouted into the vox.

Zhukov was still closely monitoring his elevation and wasn't aware of how close and how fast the Pods were to his location. When he looked out his viewport he turned and ordered escape velocity at once. He could only hope the last of the tanks was secure. Still it was better to have a tank hit one of the giant doors than to have even one of the pods attached to the exterior of his ship.

Five minutes later and the Temerity joined the other ships in high orbit. Umbrage was still at a distance in deep space monitoring for any sign of trouble.

Simms was contacted by Zhukov, "We pulled it off Captain, now what is the plan?"

"Mama-Seven has been in contact with General Abbot. Abbot has offered sanctuary to the survivors of the Arrenaugh. They will be treated as equals and given any assistance they need to make a new home there. It works out for our little flotilla because we are heading in that direction anyway to pick up Major West and the balance of his troops," Simms said.

As the two captains were talking Mama-Seven broke in with some urgent news. "Captain Simms, I have been linked in to the long range scanners on the Umbrage and have just received a message that you should hear."

"Go ahead Mama-Seven," Simms responded.

"The message is from the Sokari High Council. They have been attacked by a large force of Elites and hundreds of thousands of Septa-

Pods. The attack is widespread and appears to be targeting all the Sokari home worlds."

Simms thought this might be justice being served against the Sokari but then he thought of how terrible the Elites and Pods were. He might have even felt a bit of pity for his former enemy. "What else does the message say?" Simms asked, although it was doubtful he could have anticipated what the Super-Computer was about to tell him.

"They wish to form an alliance!"

The End

CPSIA information can be obtained
at www.ICGtesting.com
Printed in the USA
LVHW040600051218
599324LV00021B/2025/P